BL: 440

MVFOL

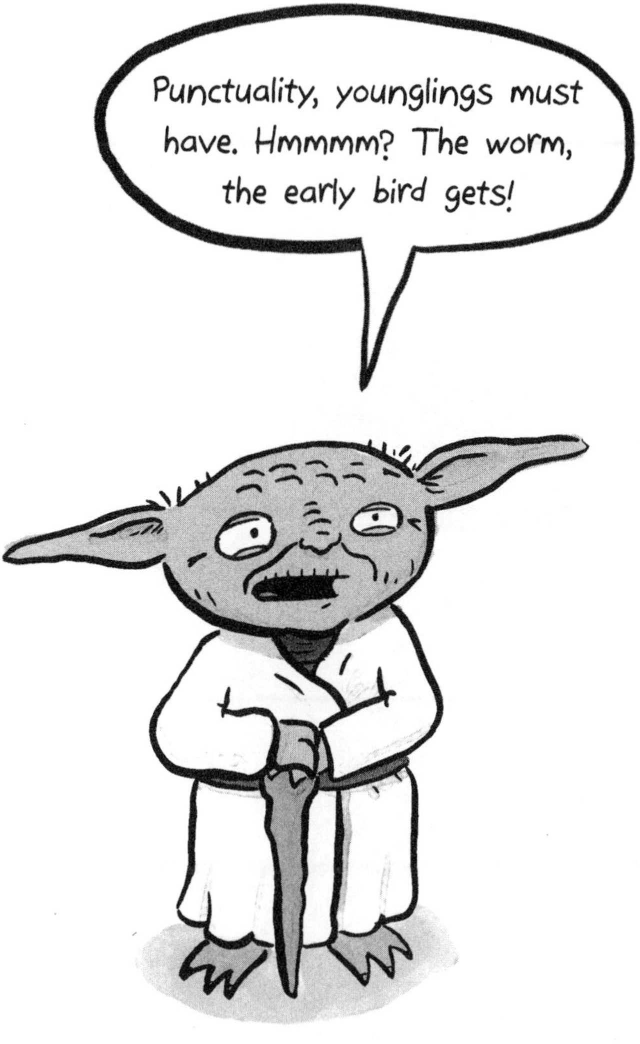
Punctuality, younglings must have. Hmmmm? The worm, the early bird gets!

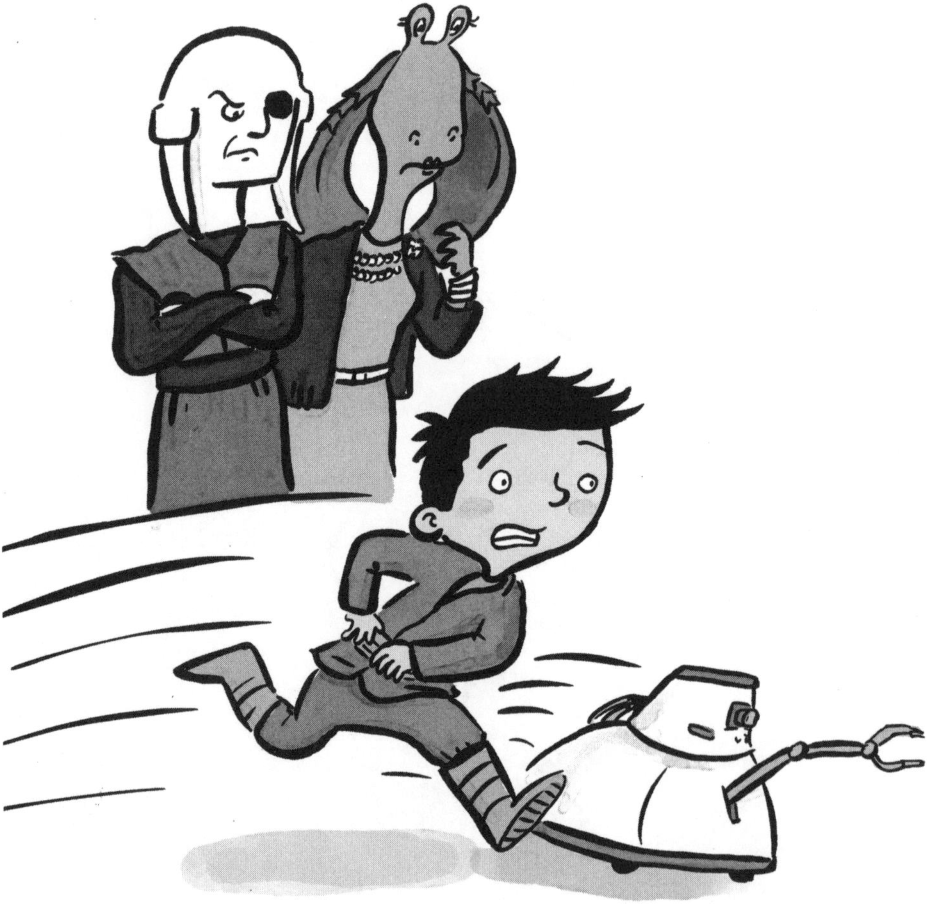

THE FORCE OVERSLEEPS

Jarrett J. Krosoczka

Scholastic Inc.

For Monte Belmonte and his theatrical Padawans—Atticus, Enzo, and Pax

This book wouldn't have happened if it weren't for the dedication by the following people: Thank you to Michael P., Rick, Sam, Debra, and the entire team at Scholastic for shepherding this along and entrusting me with the lightsaber. Much love to Michael S., Jennifer, and the entire team at Lucasfilm for allowing me the honor to play around in a galaxy far, far away. Thank you to Jeffrey Brown for originating this fantastic series. Big thanks goes to Joey Weiser for his invaluable help in shading this book. Thank you to Rebecca Sherman. And for their patience and love, Gina, Zoe, Lucy, and Xavier Krosoczka.

WWW.STARWARS.COM

WWW.SCHOLASTIC.COM

Published by Scholastic Inc., *Publishers since 1920.* SCHOLASTIC and associated logos are trademarks and/or registered trademarks of Scholastic Inc.

ISBN 978-0-545-87574-5

10 9 8 7 6 5 4 3 2 1   17 18 19 20 21

Printed in the U.S.A.   23
First printing 2017

Book design by Rick DeMonico

A long time ago in a galaxy far, far away....

Victor Starspeeder, Jedi Academy's most awesomest student, stood behind the closed curtain. This was his big moment—his debut as the star of the annual musical.

The curtains swung open, and the audience erupted with applause! Victor sang his heart out, hitting every note.

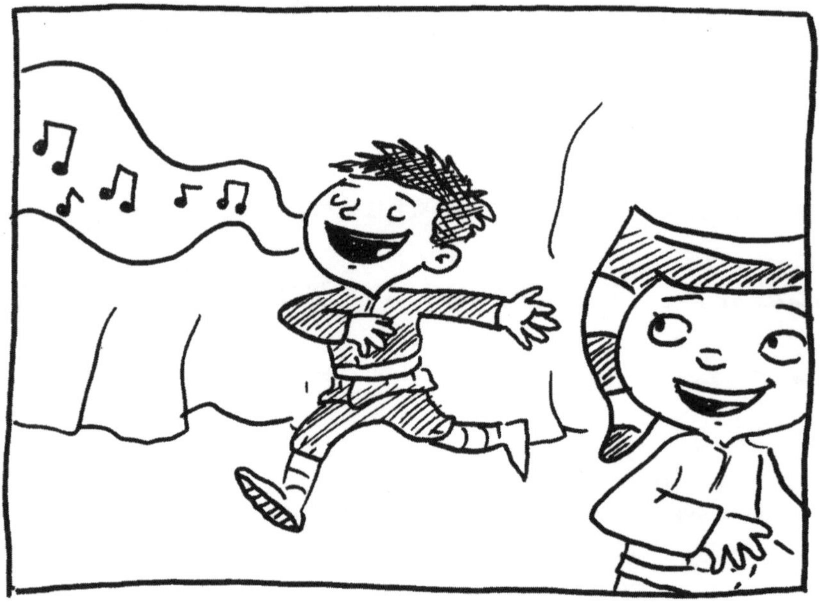

He delivered his lines with swagger, and then—the big moment. The kiss he would share with his costar, Maya.

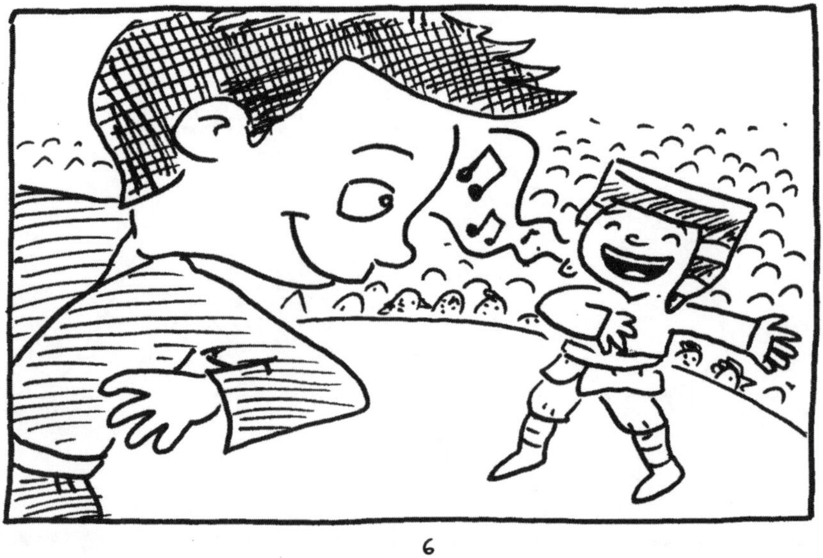

Victor leaned in, but then . . .

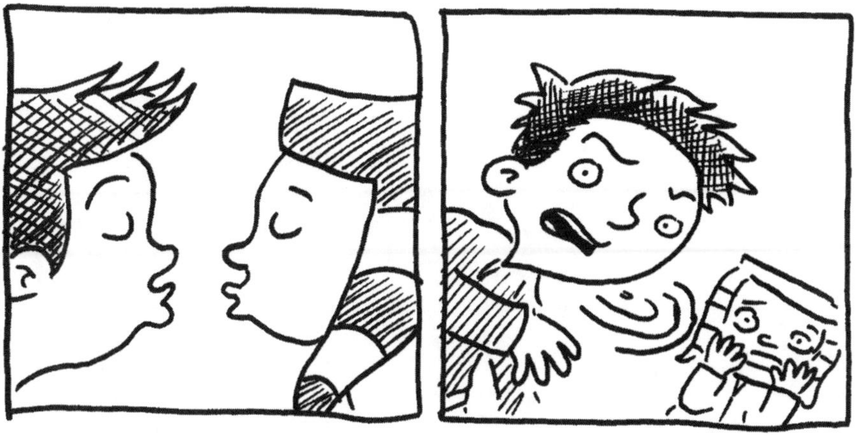

evil droids attacked!

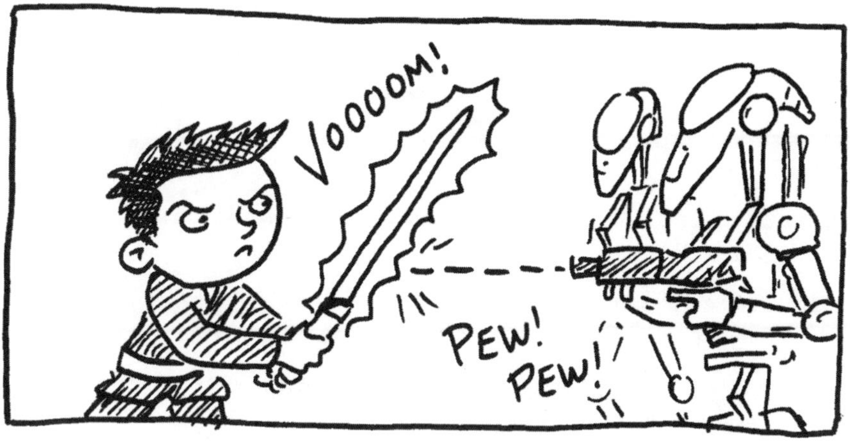
VOOOOM!
PEW!
PEW!

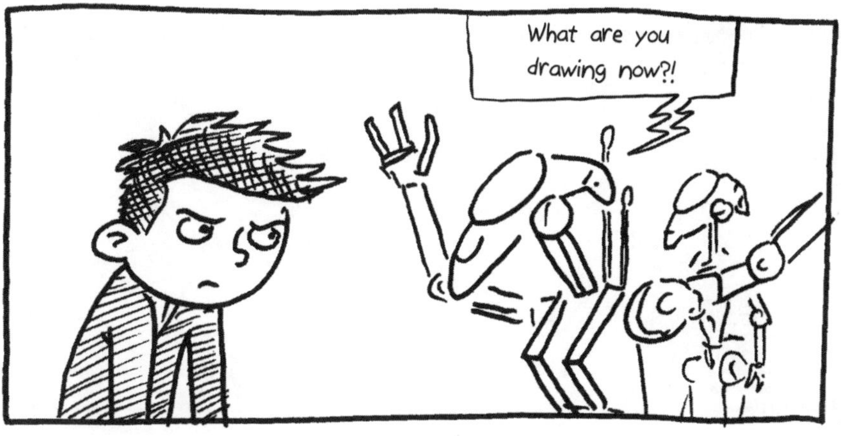
What are you drawing now?!

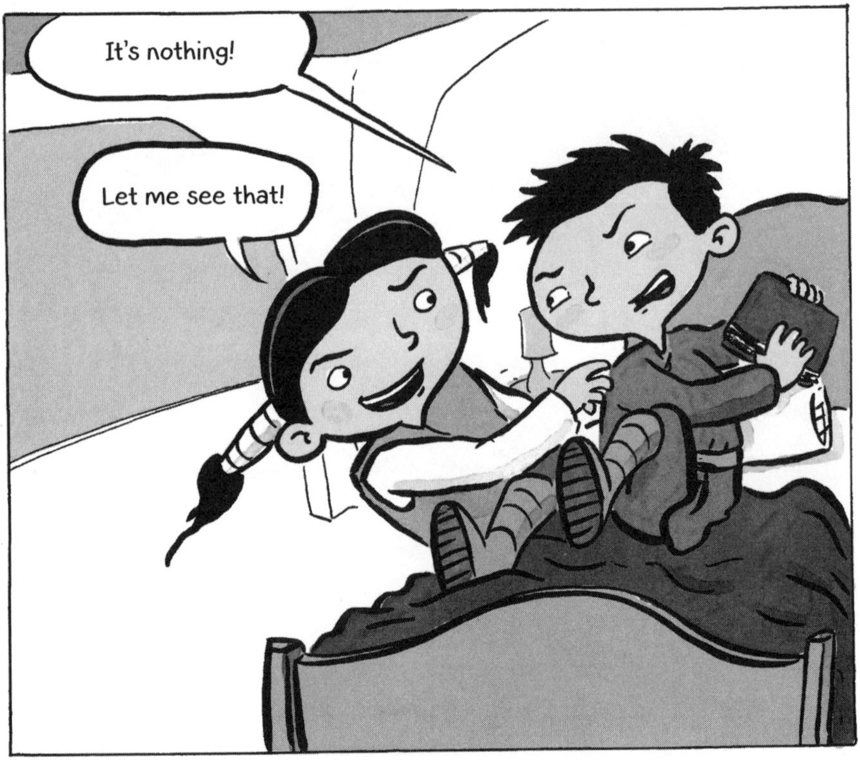
It's nothing!
Let me see that!

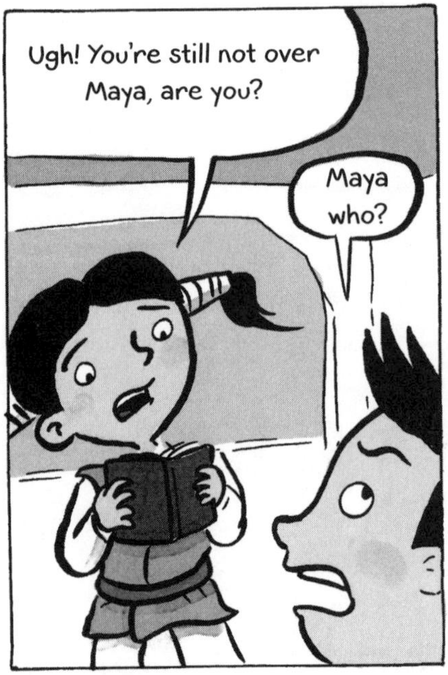
Ugh! You're still not over Maya, are you?
Maya who?

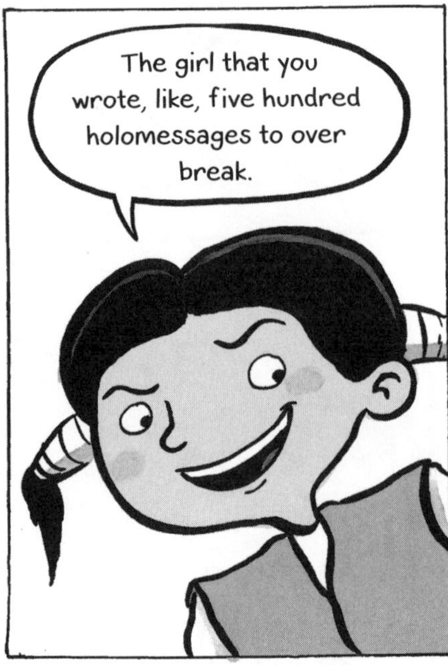
The girl that you wrote, like, five hundred holomessages to over break.

Hexaday

Sometimes I hate how my sister, Christina, knows me so well. But I didn't write Maya five hundred holomessages over break, it was more like one hundred. Maybe two hundred. But, when Maya didn't write me back, I thought maybe something was wrong. I mean, it couldn't be me. Who wouldn't want to be holopals with me? Maya must have been super busy because she barely even logged on to our holochats for book club.

I mean, okay, all right, I know she was super busy based on her Stargram posts. She seemed to be enjoying herself . . .

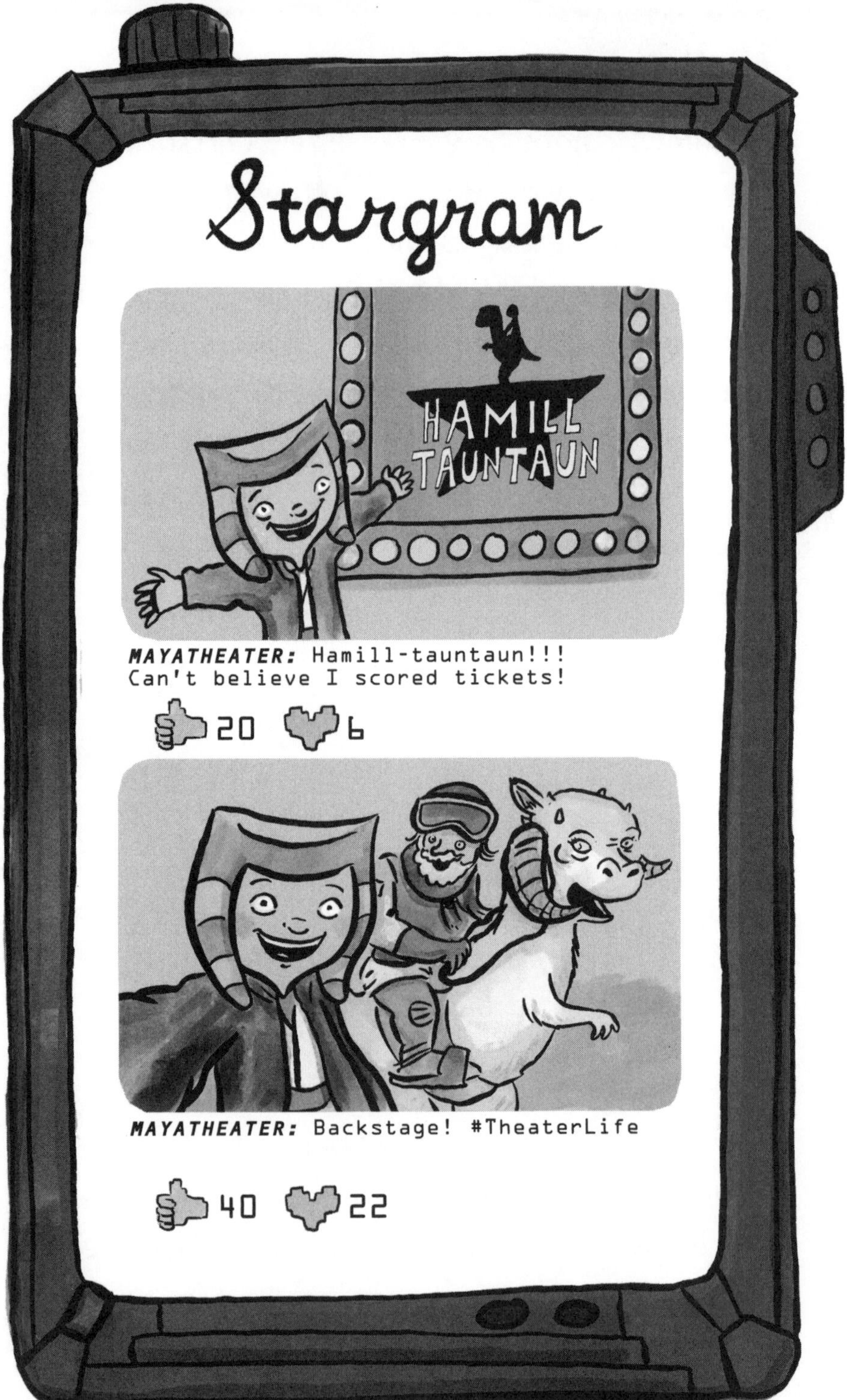
Stargram
HAMILL TAUNTAUN
MAYATHEATER: Hamill-tauntaun!!! Can't believe I scored tickets!
20 6
MAYATHEATER: Backstage! #TheaterLife
40 22

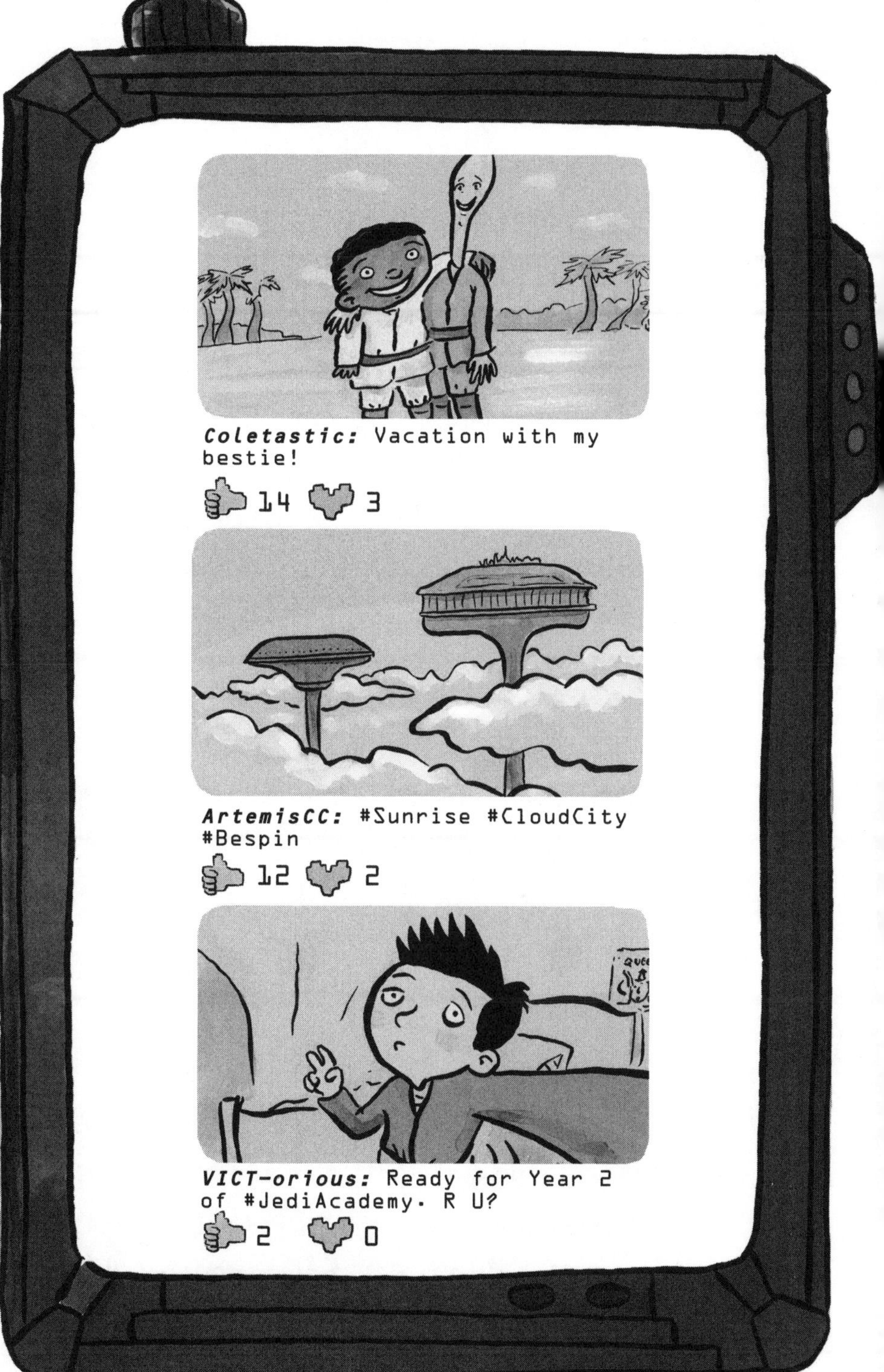
Coletastic: Vacation with my bestie!
14 3
ArtemisCC: #Sunrise #CloudCity #Bespin
12 2
VICT-orious: Ready for Year 2 of #JediAcademy. R U?
2 0

Heptaday

I'm so stoked for my second year at Jedi Academy. It'll be so much better than last year for a number of reasons. For one, I get to start at the beginning of the year. And for two, I know who my friends are. And I have some great ones. Coleman, Emmett, Maya, Artemis, and I have, like, the perfect group. I love it just the way that it is. Also—I am now a second-year student, so I can't wait to have kids that are younger than me around. They'll totally look up to me.

Then there's the annual musical. I remember thinking the drama club would be totally lame, but the theater thing is actually a ton of fun. And I'll be there early enough to audition for a part this year. I don't see how they wouldn't make me the star.

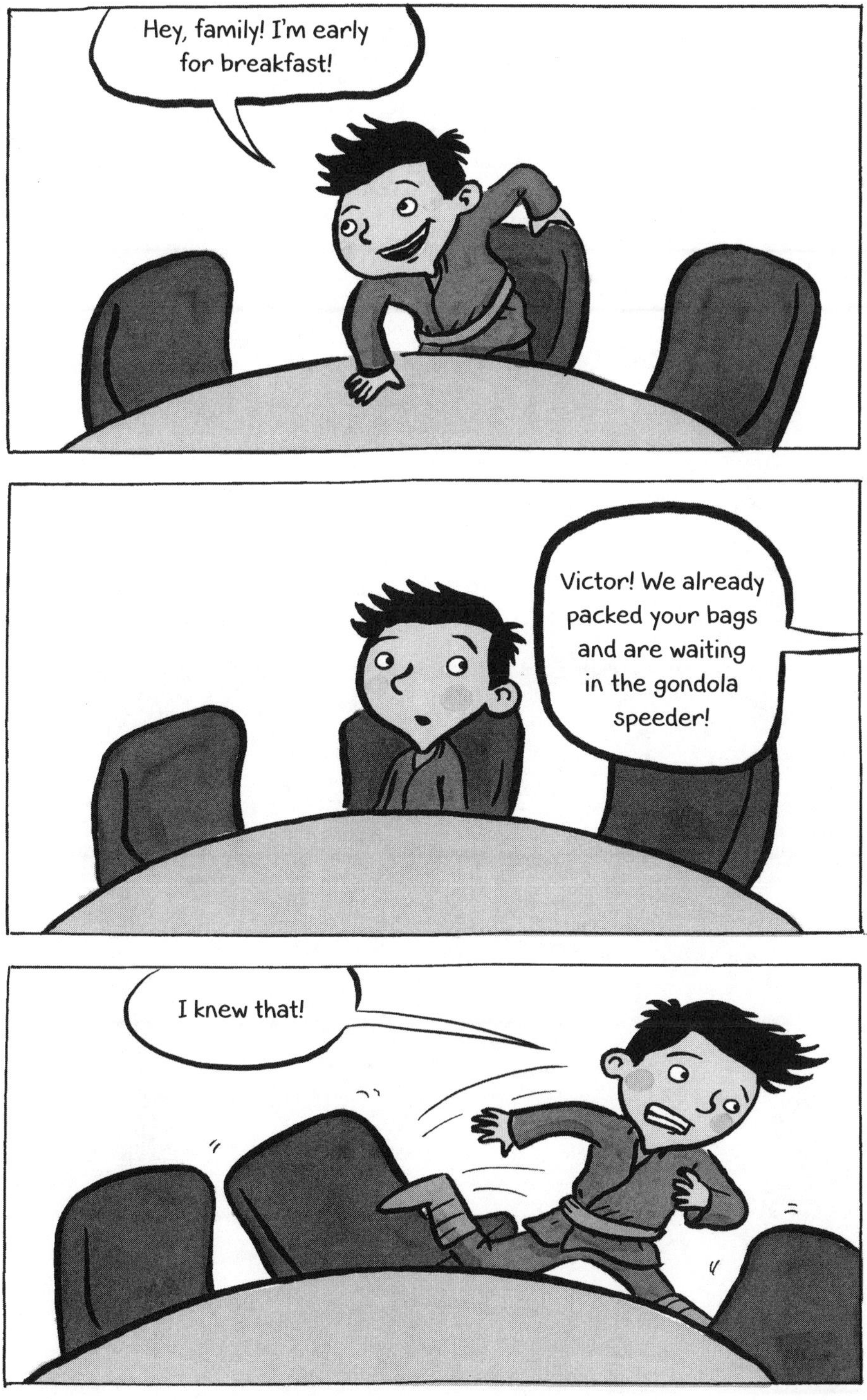
Hey, family! I'm early for breakfast!
Victor! We already packed your bags and are waiting in the gondola speeder!
I knew that!

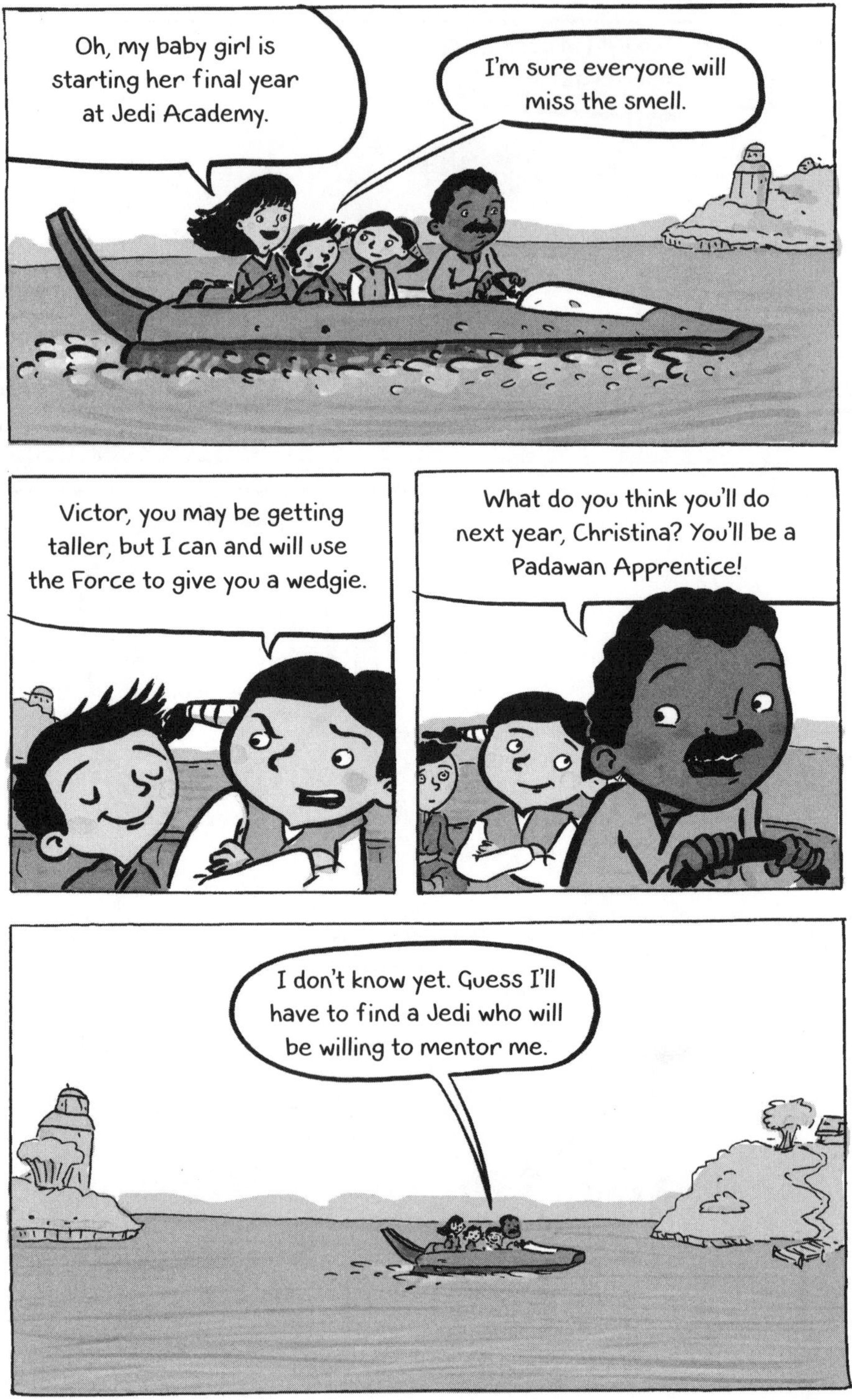
Oh, my baby girl is starting her final year at Jedi Academy.
I'm sure everyone will miss the smell.
Victor, you may be getting taller, but I can and will use the Force to give you a wedgie.
What do you think you'll do next year, Christina? You'll be a Padawan Apprentice!
I don't know yet. Guess I'll have to find a Jedi who will be willing to mentor me.

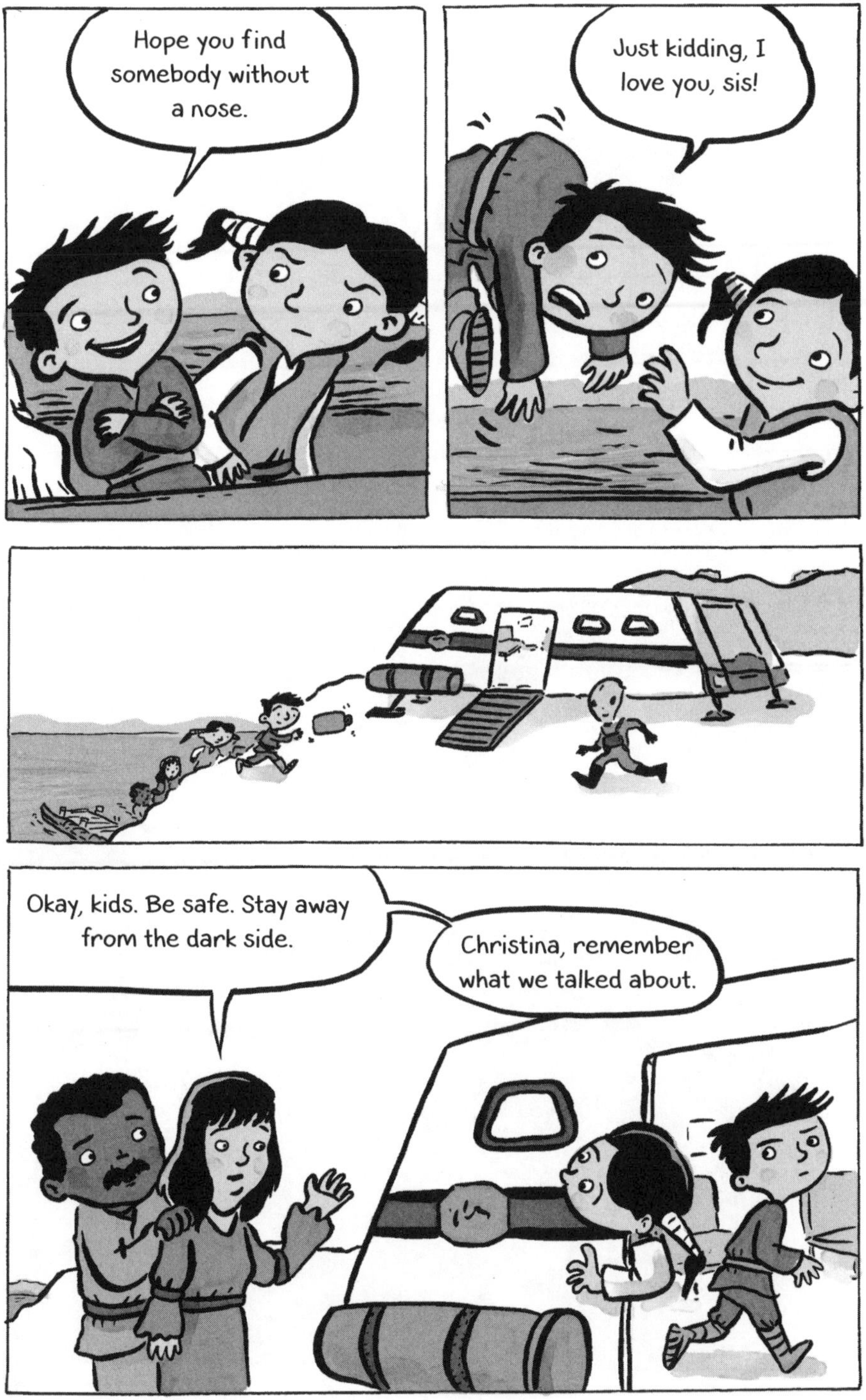
Hope you find somebody without a nose.
Just kidding, I love you, sis!
Okay, kids. Be safe. Stay away from the dark side.
Christina, remember what we talked about.

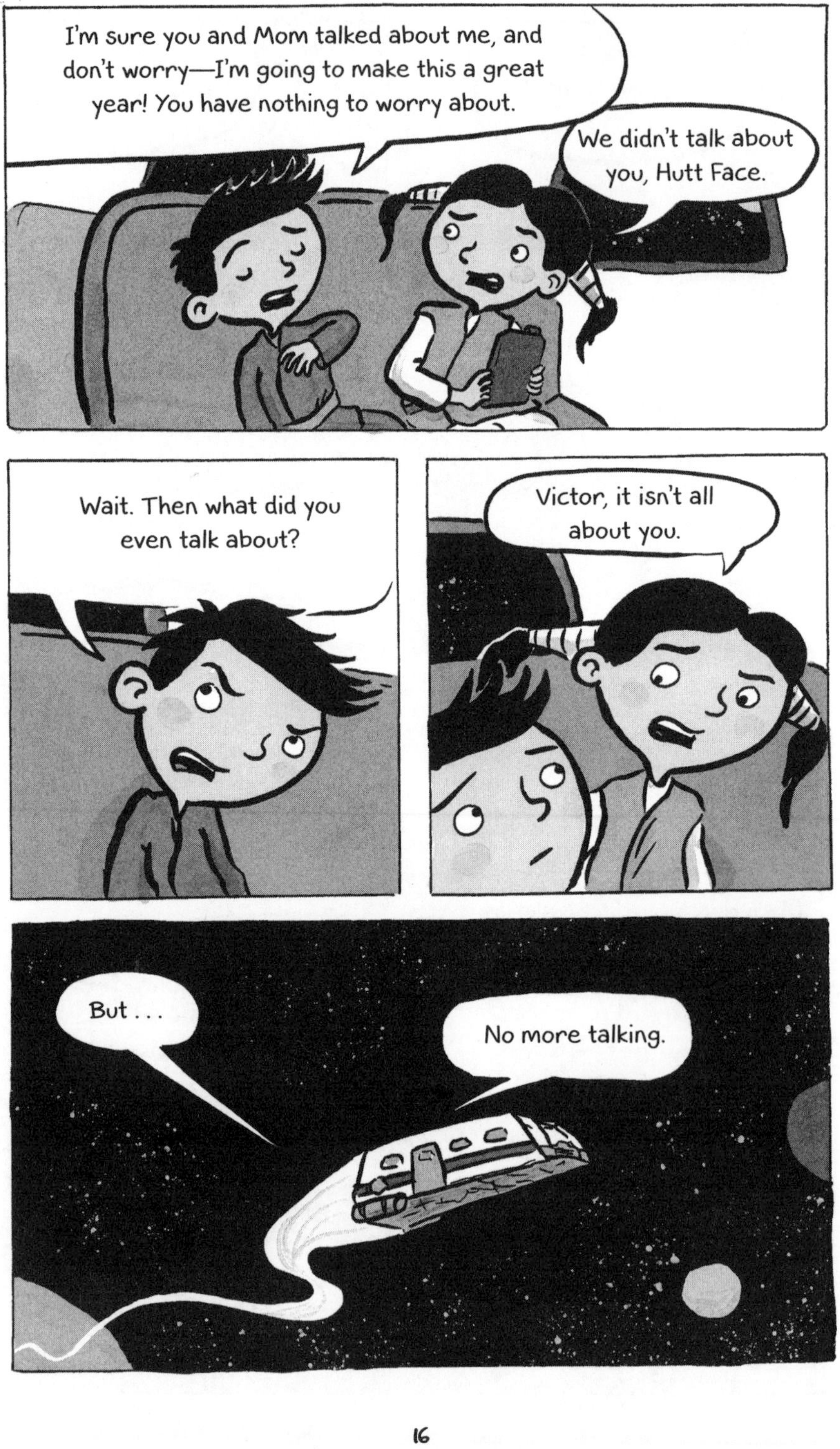
I'm sure you and Mom talked about me, and don't worry—I'm going to make this a great year! You have nothing to worry about.
We didn't talk about you, Hutt Face.
Wait. Then what did you even talk about?
Victor, it isn't all about you.
But . . .
No more talking.

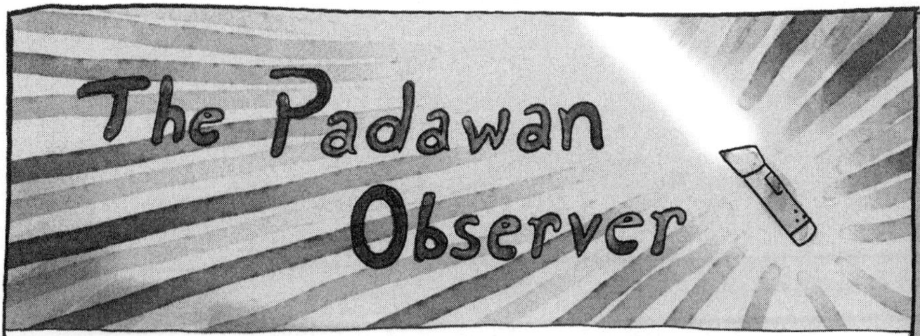
The Padawan Observer

EDITED BY THE STUDENTS OF JEDI ACADEMY Vol. MXVI #3

WELCOME BACK, YOUNGLINGS!

The faculty and staff at Jedi Academy eagerly await your return to Coruscant! Upon your arrival, please report immediately to your bunks. You will have so much catching up to do with your friends! We know that you will be tempted to venture out and explore the surrounding area, but we urge you all to stay on campus. While there have been rumors of Sith activity over the break, Principal Mar would like to assure everyone that they are just that—rumors. When asked for a further explanation, Master Yoda said, "Thieves and vandals roam Coruscant streets, not Sith. Hmmm. On the rise, crime may be. But no match for a Jedi a petty thief will be. All younglings have much work to do to become Jedi, yes? Your studies shall be prioritized. Stick to campus, you shall."

Please make sure that all forms are signed and handed in to your student advisor before the first day of classes.

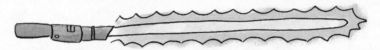

ASK MS. CATARA!

Dear Ms. Catara,

As excited as I am to see my friends again, I'm sort of nervous about the new school year. And not just because of these Sith rumors. What if my friends suddenly decide that they don't like me? Am I being silly?

Signed,
An Anxious Second Year

Dearza Anxious Second Year,

It's A-OK to have fears, but don't let them overwhelm you. Youza entering a new year, and that iz an exciting times! If your friends are youz friends, you'll have nothing to worries about. And glad to hear that the Sith rumors aren't a bothering you.

XO,
Ms. Catara

HUTTFIELD

TIME FOR MY MORNING EXCERCISES.

OR TIME FOR A SECOND BREAKFAST.

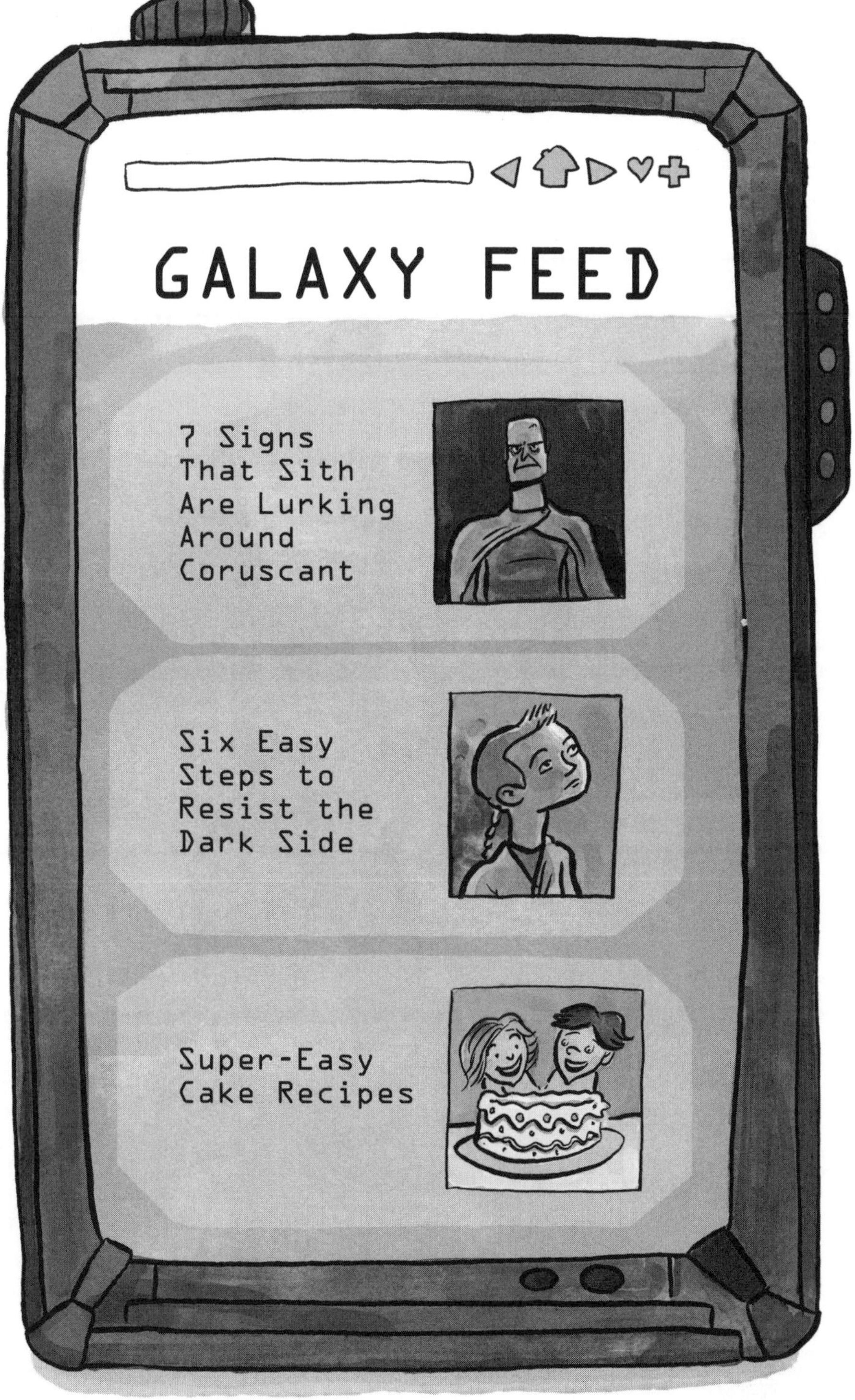
GALAXY FEED
7 Signs That Sith Are Lurking Around Coruscant
Six Easy Steps to Resist the Dark Side
Super-Easy Cake Recipes

Heptaday (continued)

Man, so weird that there is even talk about some dark side stuff happening anywhere near Jedi Academy. It's just insane to even think about. What dummy Sith would dare step anywhere near a school that is filled with so many powerful Jedi? I know that all of our teachers want us to think that there aren't Sith running around, but what if there are? What if they wanted to recruit new kids? I remember when I was a little kid, we'd be handed these flyers at our annual health checkup. They were super scary, but I never thought I'd ever need to worry about being anywhere near a dark side anything. Eh . . . I'm not worried. There's so much talent at Jedi Academy. And my crew and me? We wouldn't let them anywhere near us.

The dark side and YOU! Don't become a statistic.

Student Name: Victor Starspeeder
Level: Padawan
Semester: Three
Homeroom: Master Yoda

CLASS SCHEDULE

0730-0850: ADVANCED USING THE FORCE
Master Yoda will build on the lessons learned in Year One.

0900-0950: STARPILOT FLIGHT TRAINING PART 1
Mr. Zefyr will introduce students to the basic concepts of piloting a starship.

1000-1050: PHYSICAL EDUCATION
Kitmum will push students to compete in various sports games.

1100-1150: HYPERALGEBRA
Mrs. Pilton will enforce various math equations on the students, perhaps some will prove helpful.

1200-1300: LUNCH BREAK

1300-1350: HISTORY OF THE JEDI ORDER
If we don't understand the past, we are doomed to repeat it.

1400-1450: GALACTIC GEOGRAPHY
Principal Mar will lead an in-depth study on how the singular ecosystems of our galaxy relate to one another.

1500-1550: PERSUASIVE DISCOURSE
Whether arguing with your best friend or before the Galactic Senate, Jedi must be able to make their case.

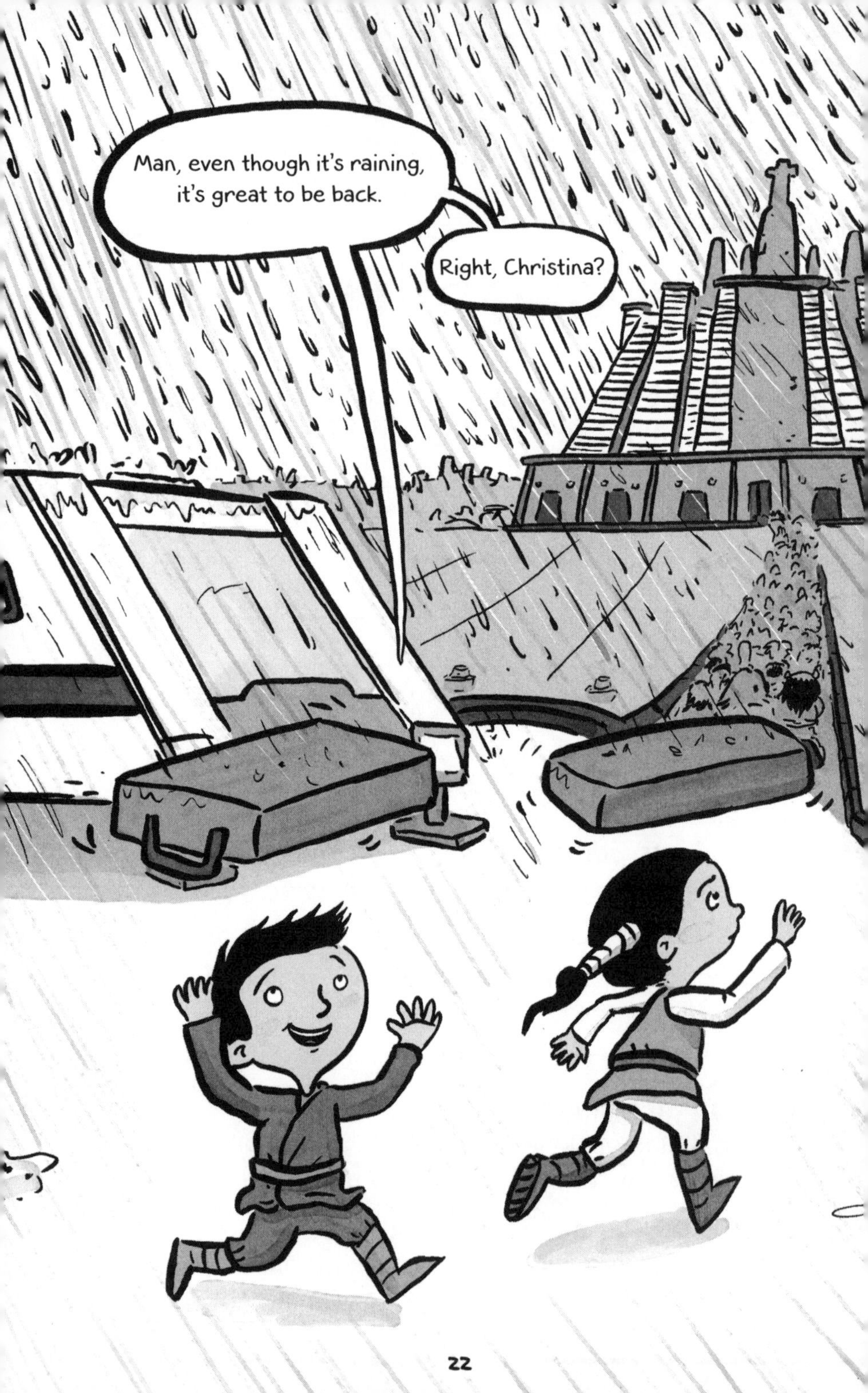
Man, even though it's raining, it's great to be back.
Right, Christina?

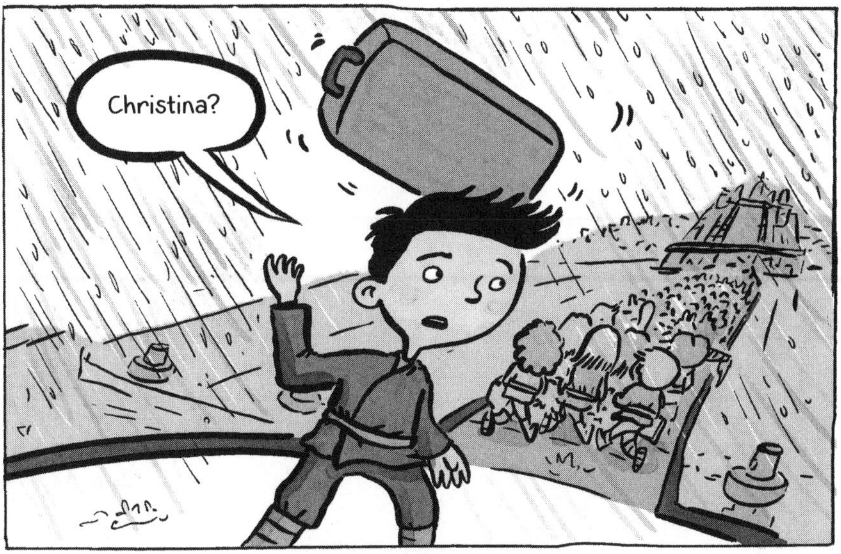
Christina?

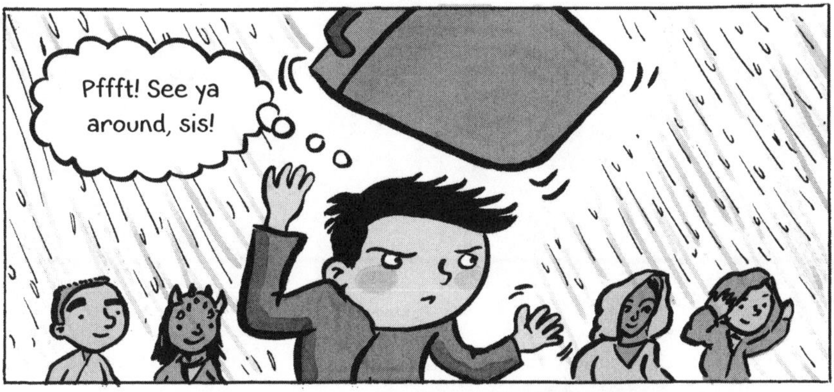
Pffft! See ya around, sis!

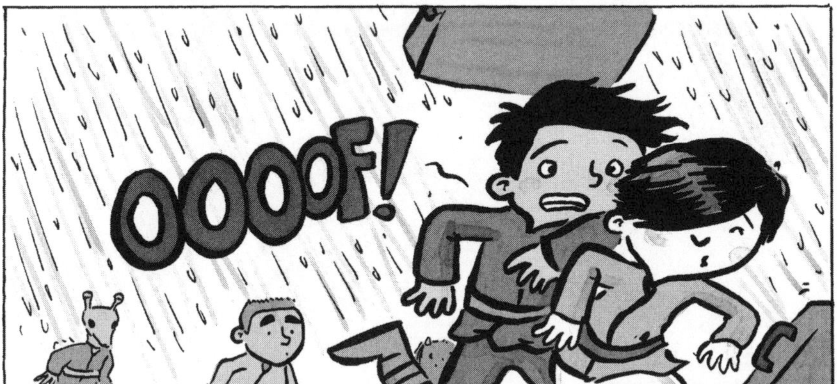
OOOOF!

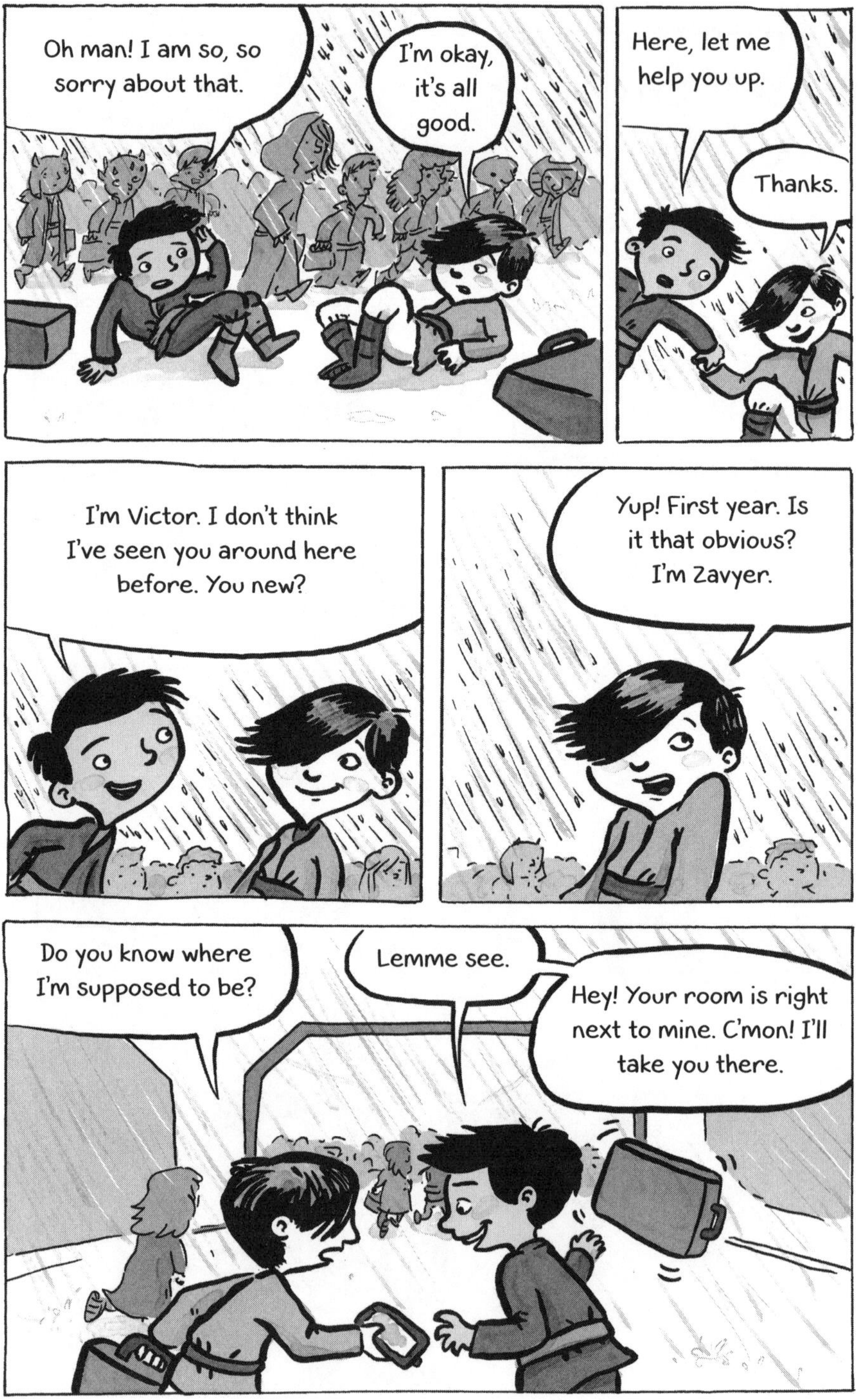
Oh man! I am so, so sorry about that.
I'm okay, it's all good.
Here, let me help you up.
Thanks.
I'm Victor. I don't think I've seen you around here before. You new?
Yup! First year. Is it that obvious? I'm Zavyer.
Do you know where I'm supposed to be?
Lemme see.
Hey! Your room is right next to mine. C'mon! I'll take you there.

Heptaday (continued)

I so remember being the new kid like it was just a few MONTHS ago. It isn't easy. You don't know where things are, you don't have any friends yet, and it's like everybody is ahead of you in your classes. I know that it was really, really nice of me, but I helped the new kid find his way around the school. That's just the kind of guy that I am. Zavyer seems like a cool kid. Plus, it'll be good for me to have somebody around that is even newer than I am. A good reminder to everyone that good ol' Vic isn't the newbie! I didn't mean to show off, but I carried both of our bags using the Force. He seemed pretty impressed.

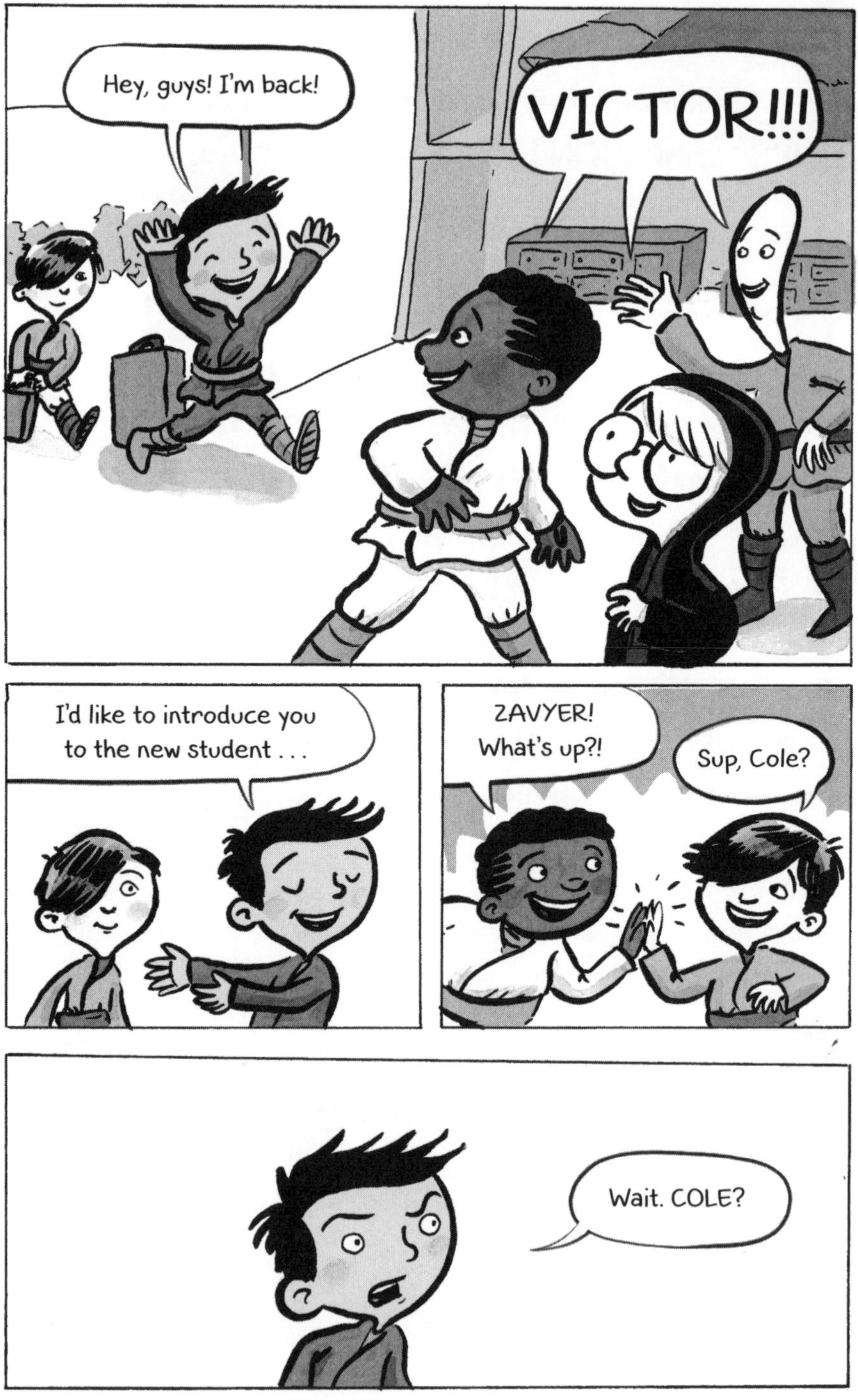
Hey, guys! I'm back!
VICTOR!!!
I'd like to introduce you to the new student . . .
ZAVYER! What's up?!
Sup, Cole?
Wait. COLE?

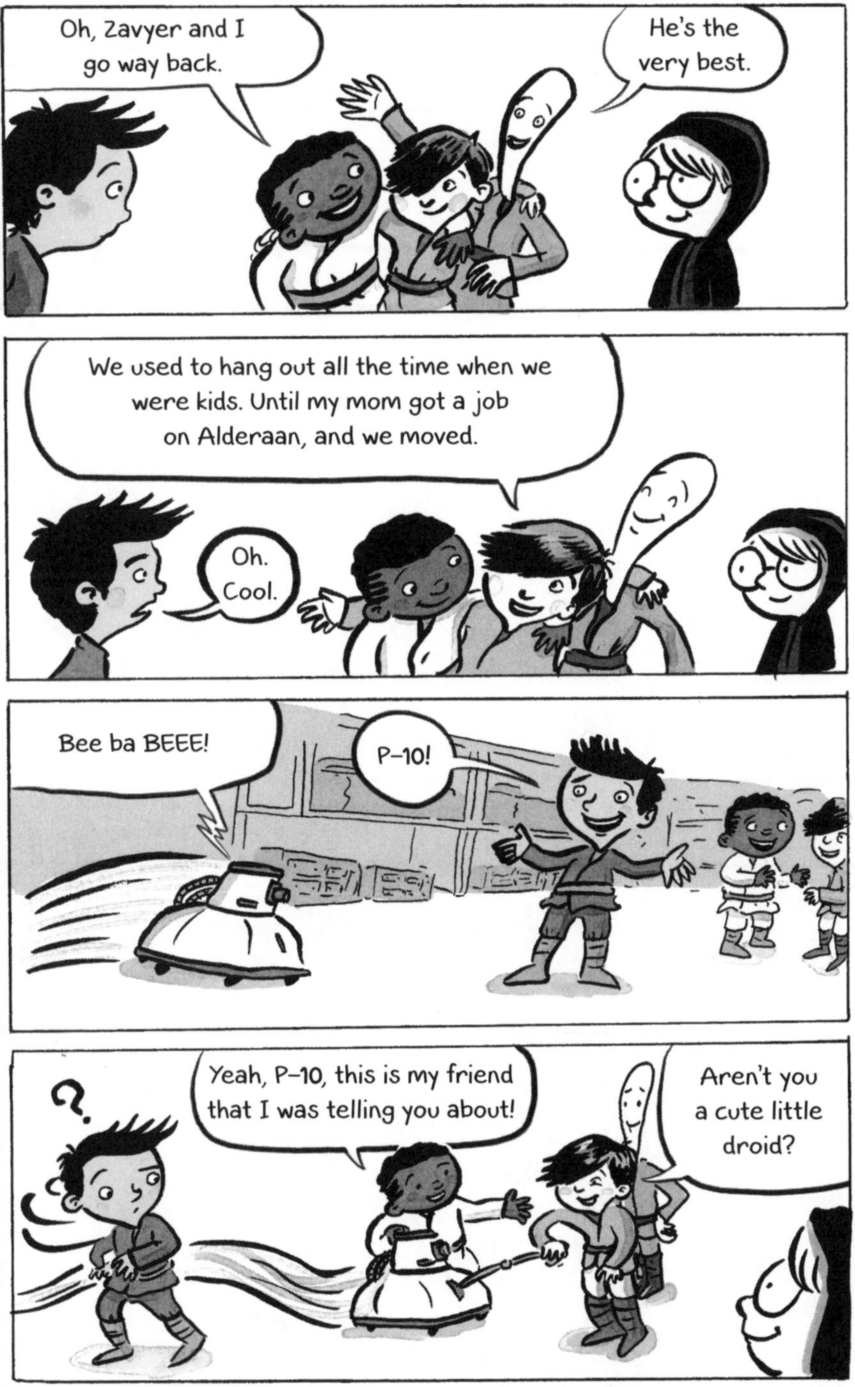
Oh, Zavyer and I go way back.
He's the very best.
We used to hang out all the time when we were kids. Until my mom got a job on Alderaan, and we moved.
Oh. Cool.
Bee ba BEEE!
P-10!
Yeah, P-10, this is my friend that I was telling you about!
Aren't you a cute little droid?

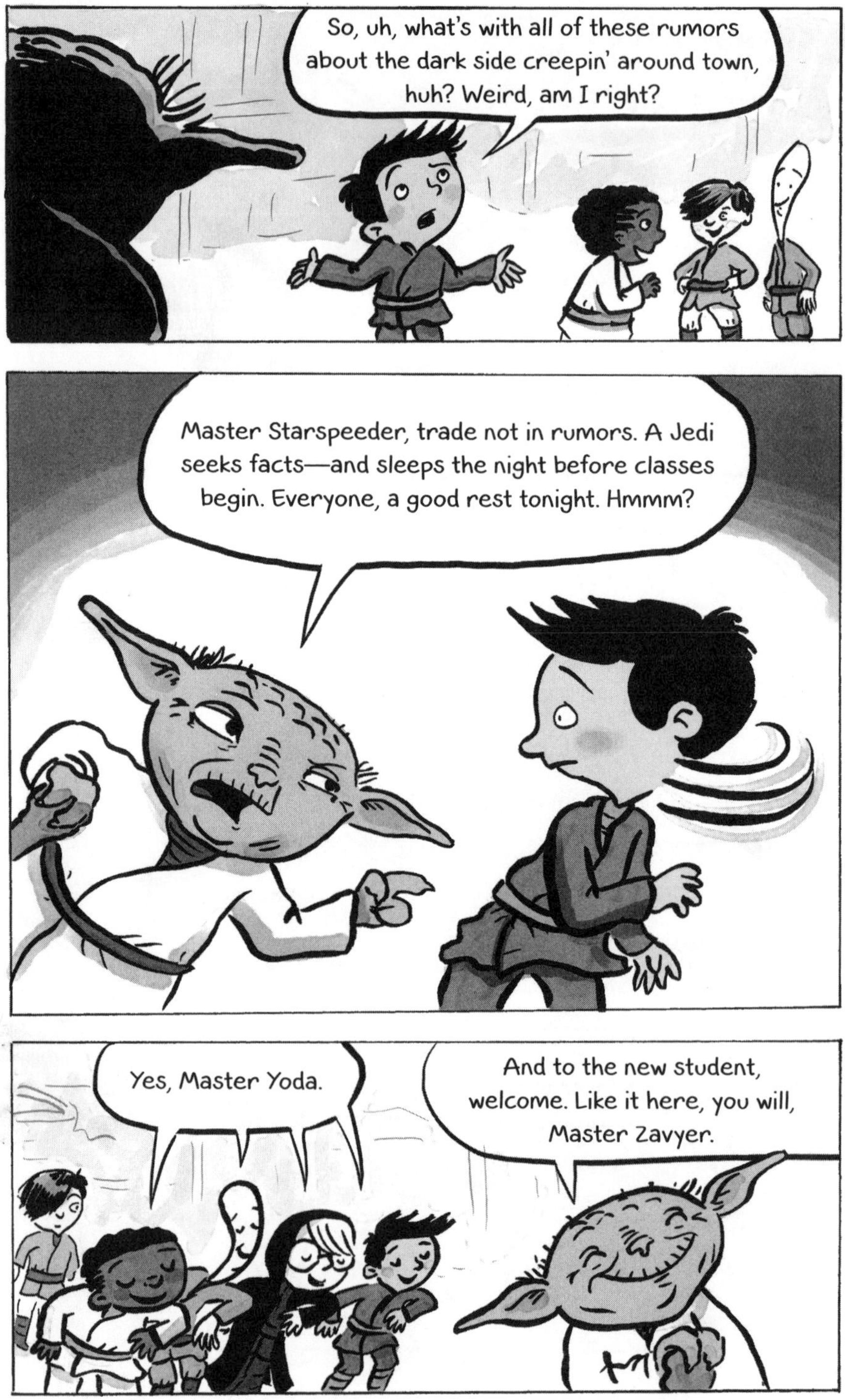
So, uh, what's with all of these rumors about the dark side creepin' around town, huh? Weird, am I right?
Master Starspeeder, trade not in rumors. A Jedi seeks facts—and sleeps the night before classes begin. Everyone, a good rest tonight. Hmmm?
Yes, Master Yoda.
And to the new student, welcome. Like it here, you will, Master Zavyer.

Monoday

I had every intention to put my best foot forward.
But it turns out that in order to do that, you need
to wake up on time and get to class when it starts.
I don't understand why my friends didn't wake me
up as they were headed out to class. And I can't
even believe that Zavyer kid that they all loved is in
my Force class. Apparently, this guy gets to skip a
whole bunch of courses because he is so ahead of
his peers. Then why, when I used the Force to carry
his bags, did he seem so amazed? Was he trying to
hide something?

The rest of my day wasn't so bad, I guess. It
was great to see Mr. Zefyr again. And by great to
see him, I mean he was as mean and as tough a
teacher as ever! But here's something exciting—we're
going to learn how to fly starships this semester!
Can't you picture it? I'm going to look so good in
that pilot's uniform. Mr. Zefyr insists that first
semester is all about learning the basics and that
there is no way that he would let us anywhere near
an actual cockpit, but still. A guy can dream, right?

I hadn't run into Maya yet. We don't have many
classes together. But I know that I'll see her at the
first Drama Club meeting. I have only one goal in
mind: Play. It. Cool.

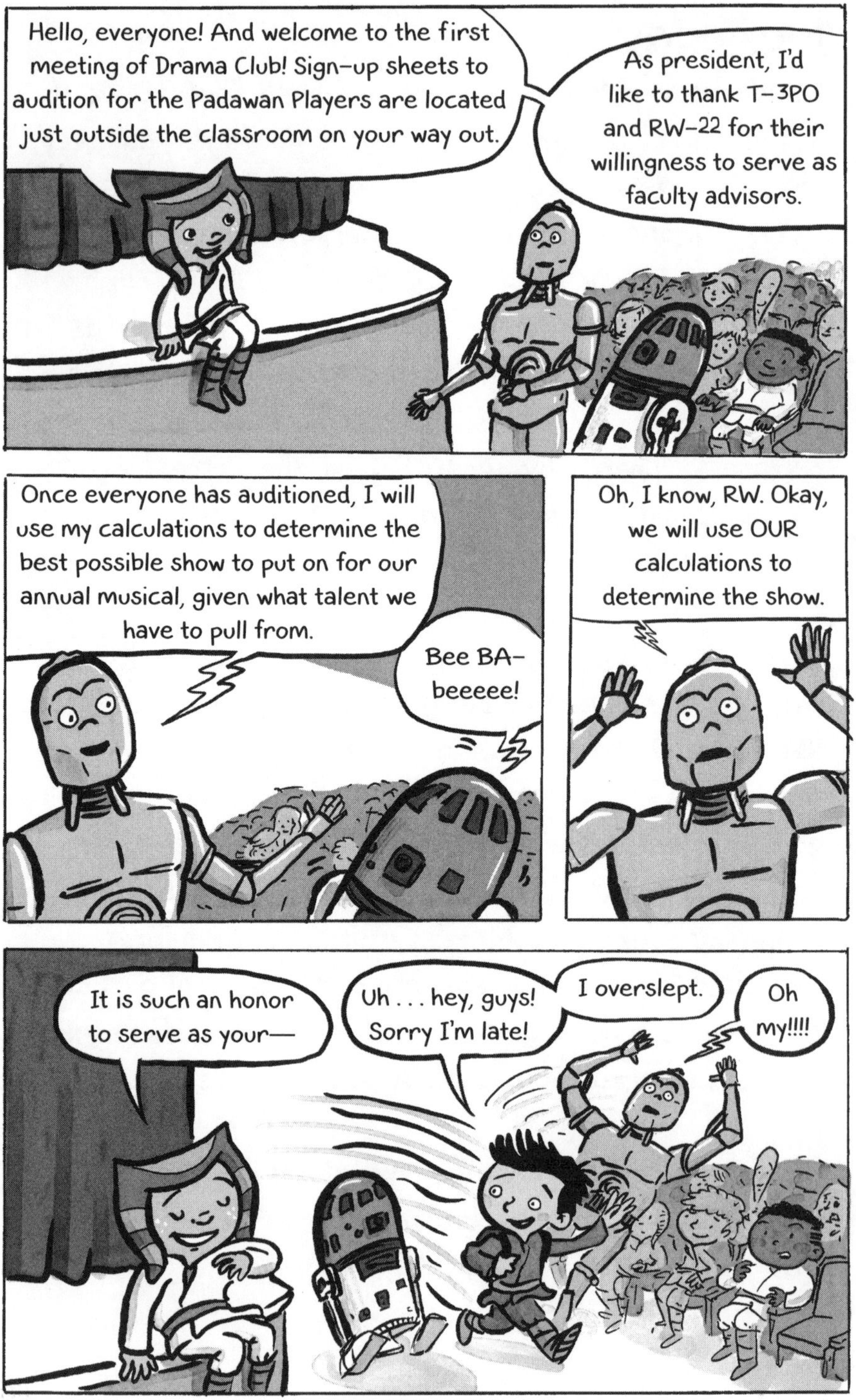
Hello, everyone! And welcome to the first meeting of Drama Club! Sign-up sheets to audition for the Padawan Players are located just outside the classroom on your way out.
As president, I'd like to thank T-3PO and RW-22 for their willingness to serve as faculty advisors.
Once everyone has auditioned, I will use my calculations to determine the best possible show to put on for our annual musical, given what talent we have to pull from.
Bee BA-beeeee!
Oh, I know, RW. Okay, we will use OUR calculations to determine the show.
It is such an honor to serve as your—
Uh . . . hey, guys! Sorry I'm late!
I overslept.
Oh my!!!!

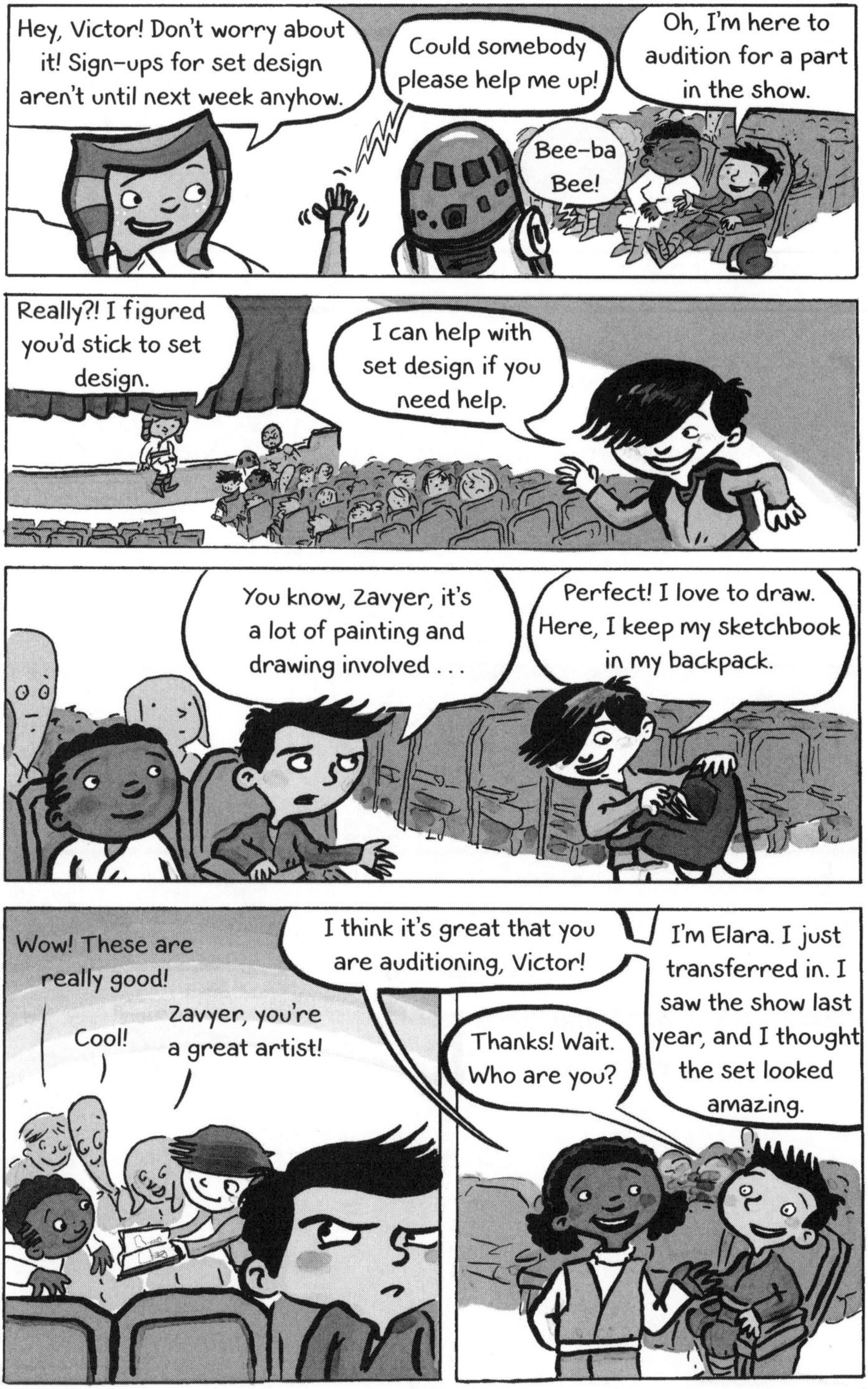
Hey, Victor! Don't worry about it! Sign-ups for set design aren't until next week anyhow.
Could somebody please help me up!
Oh, I'm here to audition for a part in the show.
Bee-ba Bee!
Really?! I figured you'd stick to set design.
I can help with set design if you need help.
You know, Zavyer, it's a lot of painting and drawing involved . . .
Perfect! I love to draw. Here, I keep my sketchbook in my backpack.
Wow! These are really good!
Cool!
Zavyer, you're a great artist!
I think it's great that you are auditioning, Victor!
Thanks! Wait. Who are you?
I'm Elara. I just transferred in. I saw the show last year, and I thought the set looked amazing.

Duoday

Why was Maya so surprised that I'd want to audition for a part? Does she not think I have what it takes? At least she was happy to see me. That was pretty cool. Ms. Catara tried telling me that it might be too much to both act in the play and design the sets.

Youza burdenin' youzeself. Yourza schoolwork will suffer!

But I can handle it. How hard can it be to memorize a few lines and pretend to be somebody else? Easy.

And it looks like I'll be spending a lot more time with Zavyer. T-3PO signed us both up as set designers. Which is great, because Xander is just the very best!*

*Ugh, okay. I am not so sure he is the very best. Does he really need to have drawing skills like me, too?

The Padawan Observer

EDITED BY THE STUDENTS OF JEDI ACADEMY Vol. MXVI #4

SEMESTER STARTS WITH STYLE!

The first semester is in full swing as new students adjust to life at Jedi Academy! By now, everyone should be familiar with how to navigate around the corridors. And remember, if you have any questions, ask a protocol droid. They're here to help! To all students new and returning, please remember to report any suspicious activity that you might see directly to Principal Mar.

FRIENDLY REMINDER

P-10 would like to remind everyone to put litter in its proper receptacles. While it is his primary function to keep the grounds in tip-top shape, it is not his primary function to pick up after you. Your parents' droid does not operate here.

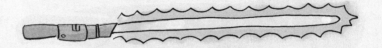

ASK MS. CATARA!

Dear Ms. Catara,

I have this new friend, and he's nice and all, but he's totally getting in my way. I mean, all of the things that I am good at and known for—he's really good at too. I'm nervous that all of my friends are going to like him better.

Signed,
I Was Here First

Dearza You Waz Heres First,

Well, first of allz, jealousy is an ugly emotion. For all youza knows, this friend of yours is jealous of you! And wouldn't that make you feel sad for them? Maybe they really look up to you, and you can't even seez that because you are blinded by your own emotions?

Thinks about its!
XO,
Ms. Catara

COMICS

WOOKIEE CIRCUS

SPOT THE DROIDRENCES!

"Rwooooar!"

HUTTFIELD

IT'S LIKE SHE DOESN'T EVEN KNOW I EXIST!

IT'S FUNNY BECAUSE IT'S TRUE.

YOUNGLINGS

I JUST CAN'T SEEM TO FIND THE RIGHT ASTROMECH DROID.

MAYBE THAT ISN'T THE KIND OF DROID YOU'RE LOOKING FOR, CHABA-DOWN.

OH, WOMP RATS!

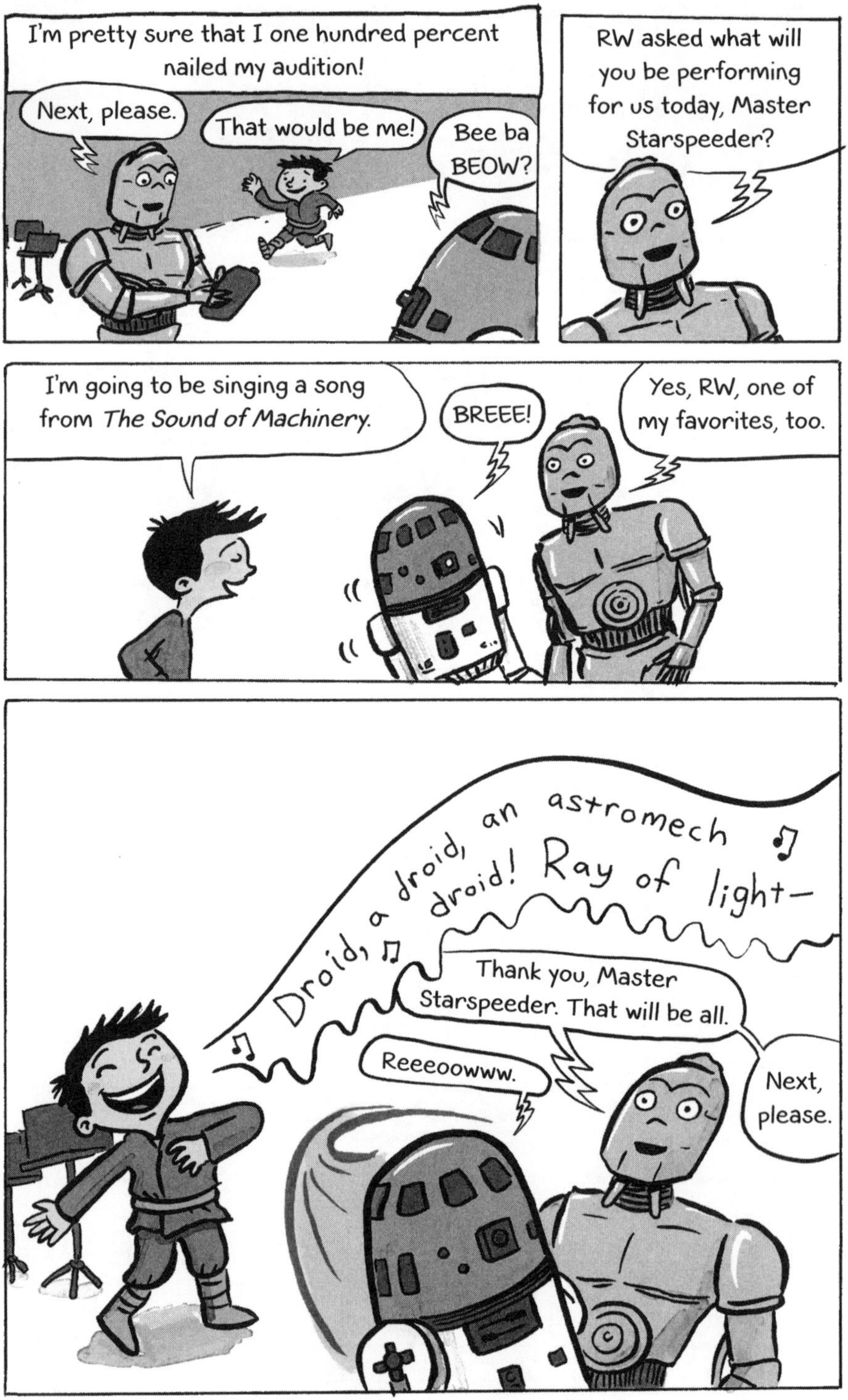
I'm pretty sure that I one hundred percent nailed my audition!
Next, please.
That would be me!
Bee ba BEOW?
RW asked what will you be performing for us today, Master Starspeeder?
I'm going to be singing a song from *The Sound of Machinery*.
BREEE!
Yes, RW, one of my favorites, too.
Droid, a droid, an astromech droid! Ray of light—
Thank you, Master Starspeeder. That will be all.
Reeeoowww.
Next, please.

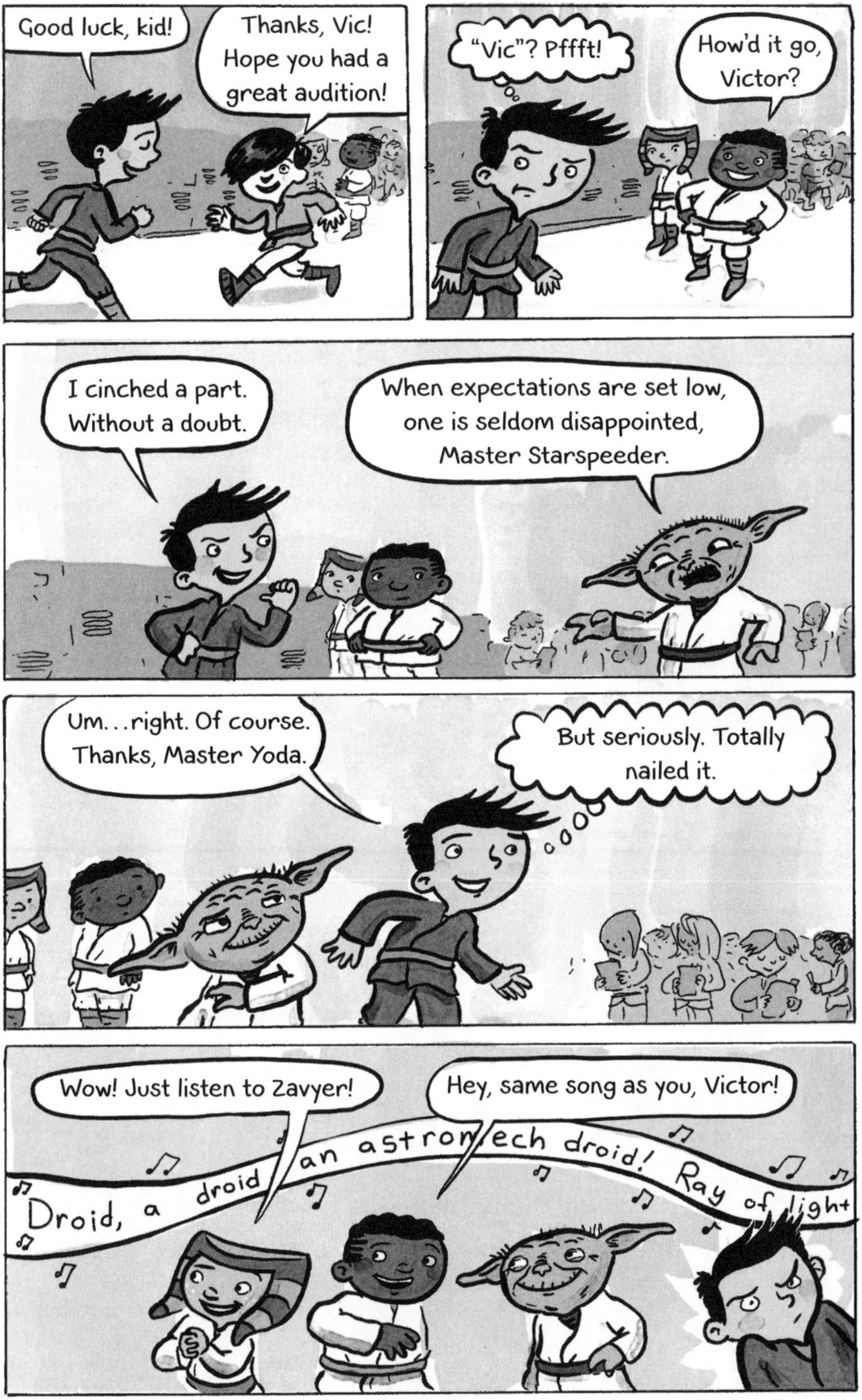
Good luck, kid!
Thanks, Vic! Hope you had a great audition!
"Vic"? Pffft!
How'd it go, Victor?
I cinched a part. Without a doubt.
When expectations are set low, one is seldom disappointed, Master Starspeeder.
Um. . .right. Of course. Thanks, Master Yoda.
But seriously. Totally nailed it.
Wow! Just listen to Zavyer!
Hey, same song as you, Victor!
Droid, a droid an astromech droid! Ray of light

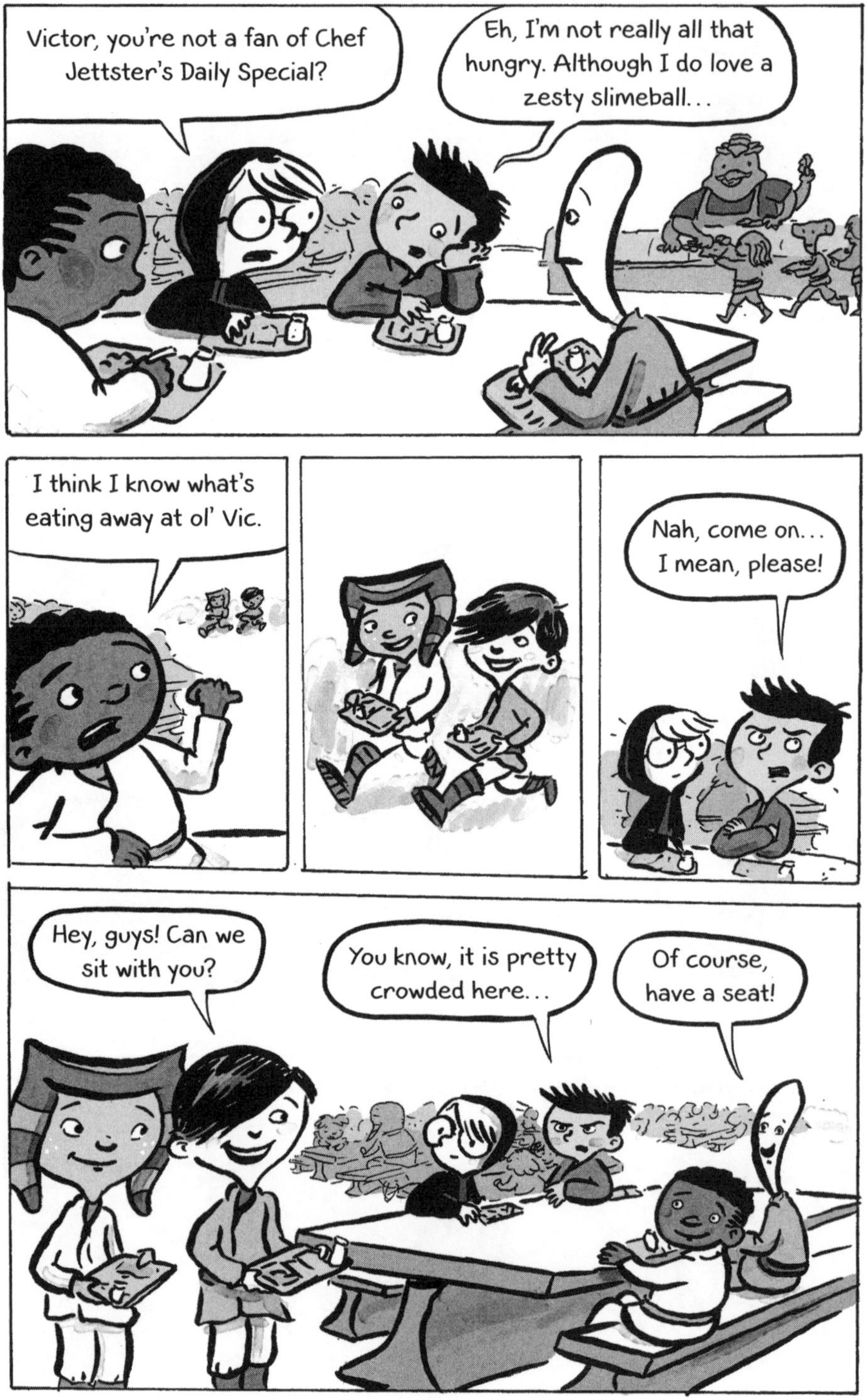

Victor, you're not a fan of Chef Jettster's Daily Special?
Eh, I'm not really all that hungry. Although I do love a zesty slimeball...
I think I know what's eating away at ol' Vic.
Nah, come on... I mean, please!
Hey, guys! Can we sit with you?
You know, it is pretty crowded here...
Of course, have a seat!

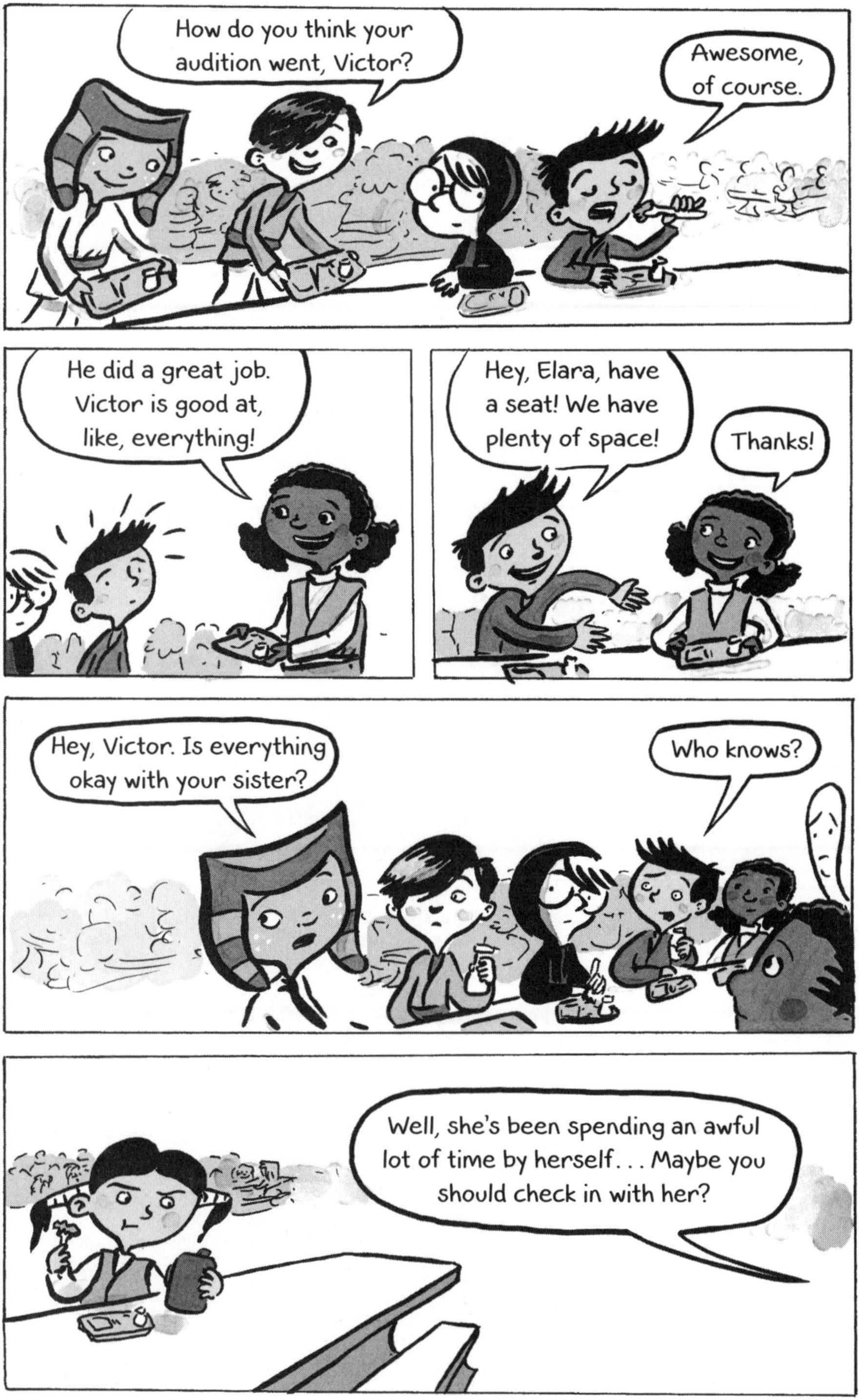
How do you think your audition went, Victor?
Awesome, of course.
He did a great job. Victor is good at, like, everything!
Hey, Elara, have a seat! We have plenty of space!
Thanks!
Hey, Victor. Is everything okay with your sister?
Who knows?
Well, she's been spending an awful lot of time by herself. . . Maybe you should check in with her?

Quadday

My sister can be a weirdo—most people probably think that about their siblings. But truth be told, I love Christina and I think she is super smart. Maya was right, though, it was odd to see her chilling by herself all the time. She usually doesn't want me around because I embarrass her in front of her friends. (It's way fun to egg her on.) But now that she isn't around her friends much at all, I can't figure out why she won't stop to talk with me in the halls.

Classes continue to get more intense. I like not being the youngest at the school, but, man, they just pile on the responsibilities as you get older! I feel like I spend all my waking hours working on homework for my classes. Or thinking about work for classes. Or worrying about getting into trouble for forgetting to do the work for classes. Which probably explains why I love getting to bed to sleep and turning my brain off for a little bit. Only problem is, my bed is so comfortable that I continue to oversleep. And as much as my bunkmates prod me to get up and out, I never seem to make it out of bed in time. But that Elara girl has been super helpful. Before she heads to class, she double-checks to see if I'm ready. And we like talking about the same things, so that's cool.

You're pretty great at everything, Victor.

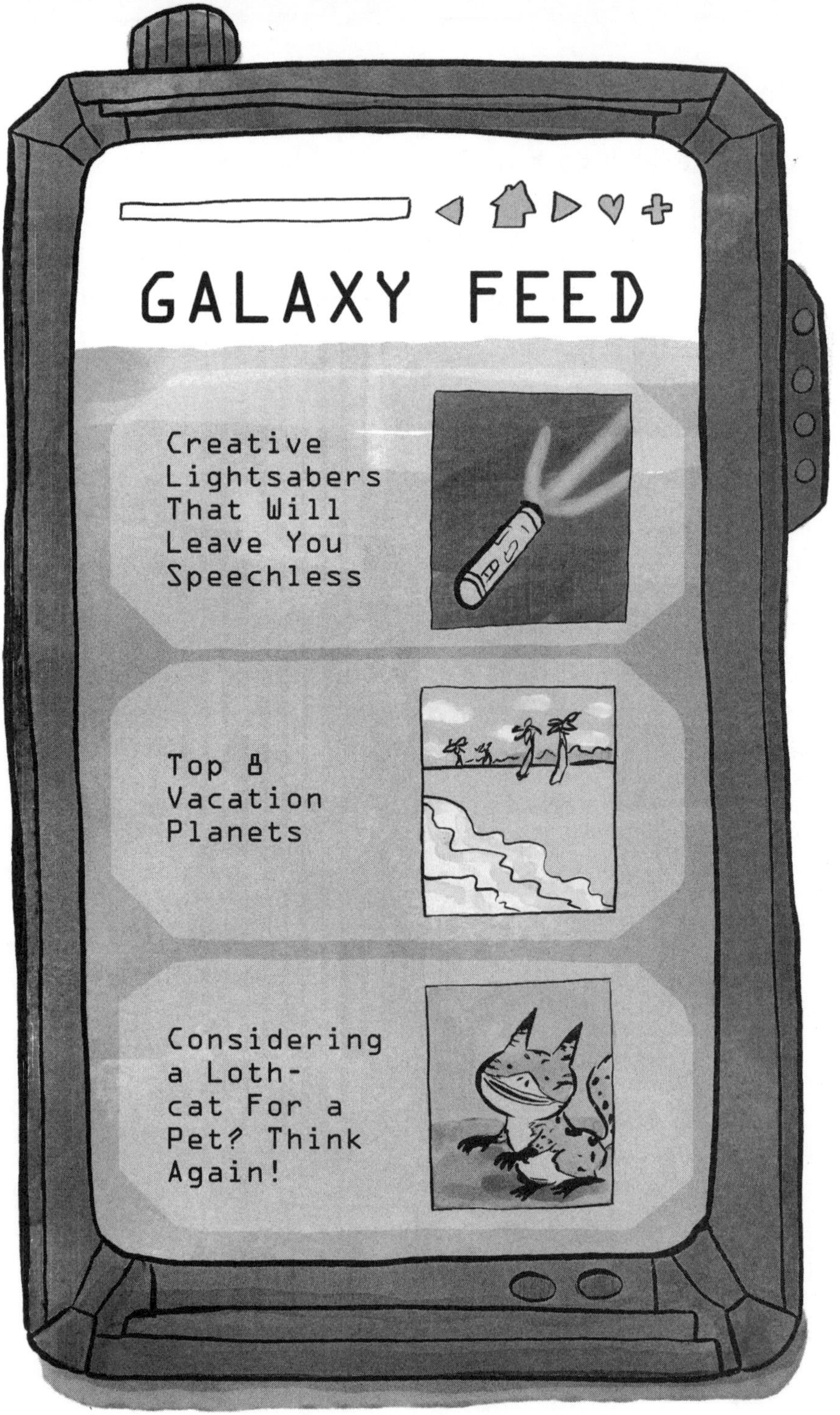
GALAXY FEED
Creative Lightsabers That Will Leave You Speechless
Top 8 Vacation Planets
Considering a Loth-cat For a Pet? Think Again!

Pentaday

T–3PO and RW–22 selected the annual musical. The Drama Club will be putting on a production of *Little Sarlacc of Horror.* And they posted the cast list. And who's playing the lead? You'd think I was, but no. I didn't even get a named part. I am Villager number two. Number TWO! That means that there is somebody a level ahead of me in the bit–part department. So who did get the lead you ask? Yup. You've guessed it . . . the new kid, Zavyer. I think that the entire galaxy is conspiring against me. I thought Coleman would be mad that he didn't get the lead again this year, but he was totally cool with it. He is going to voice the giant sarlacc puppet. Maya also got a major part, but there's no surprise there. She lives for this kind of stuff. She's also the president of Drama Club, so . . .

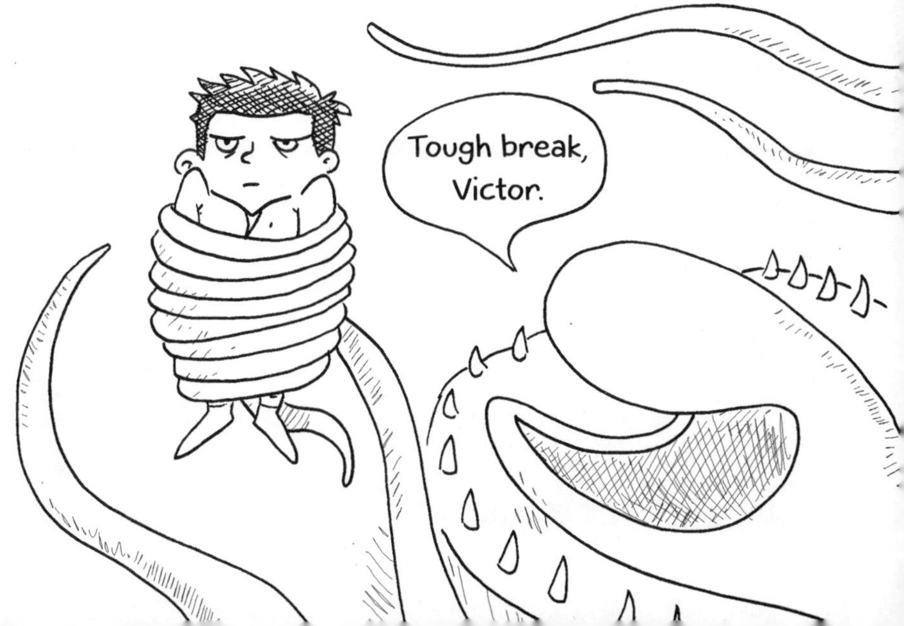
Tough break, Victor.

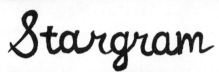

Stargram

Coletastic: Can't wait to fly one of these bad boys!

 5   6

MAYATHEATER:
#RehearsalAllDayEveryDay

 7   9

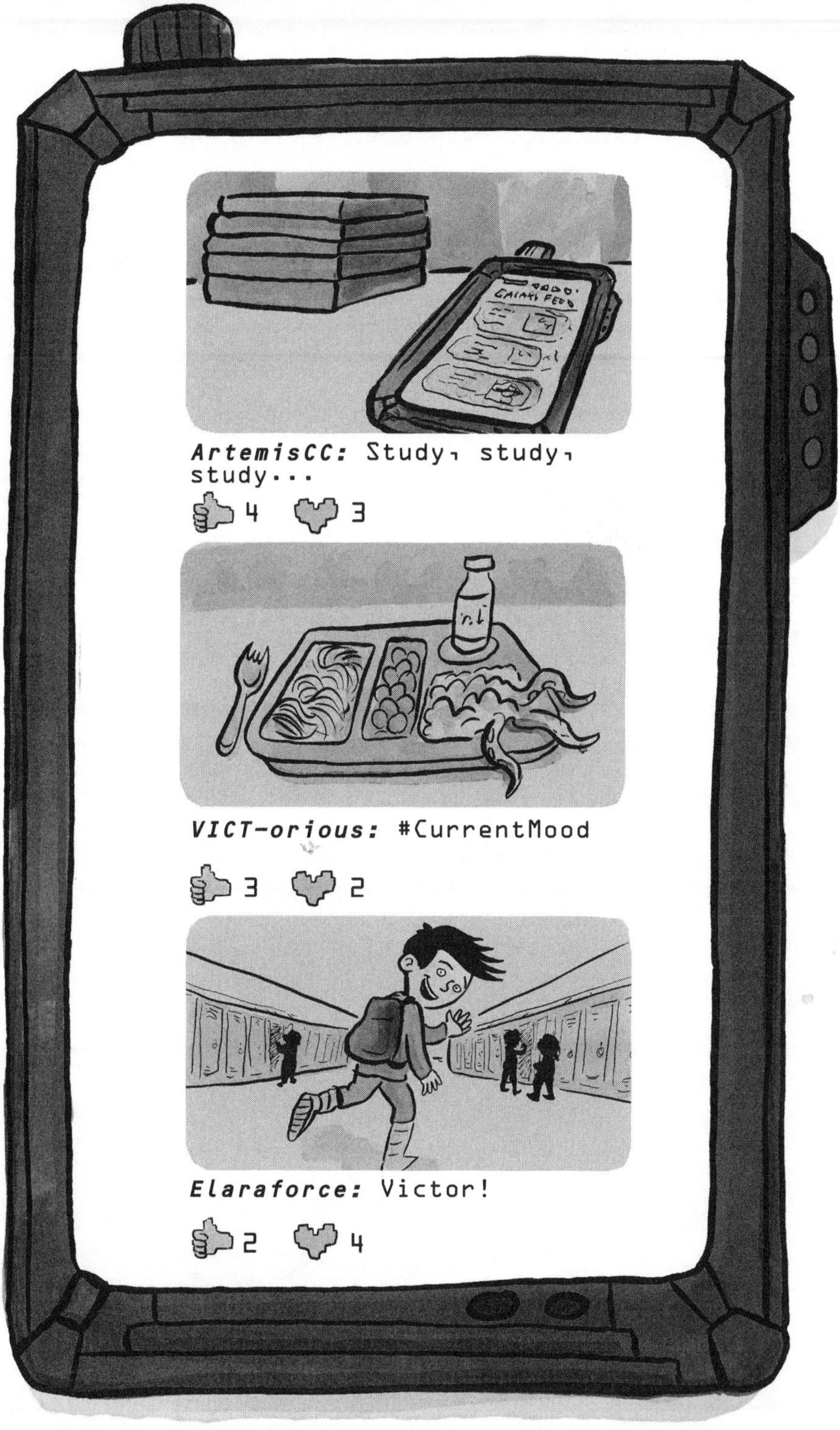
ArtemisCC: Study, study, study...
4 3
VICT-orious: #CurrentMood
3 2
Elaraforce: Victor!
2 4

Monoday

Today in class, Yoda presented our annual planet study. This year, our class will be focusing on Wutooine. Just about every important starship in the galaxy gets manufactured there. It's also home to the skyhopper tracks.

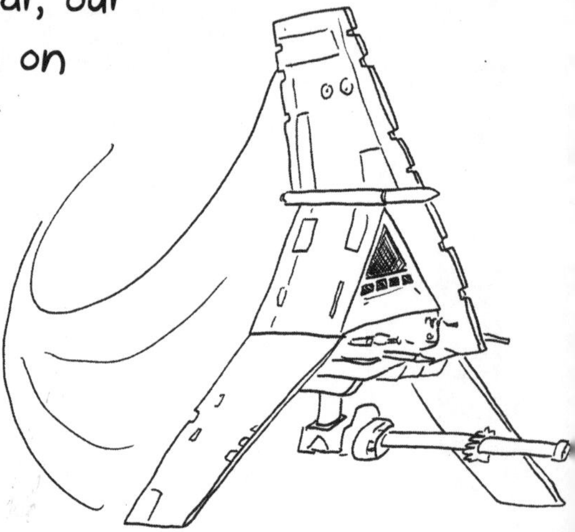

When we go on our field trip, I'm hoping we get to see some of the races. Yoda told us that since we are learning how to fly ships we ought to know how they are put together. Well, he actually said something along the lines of . . .

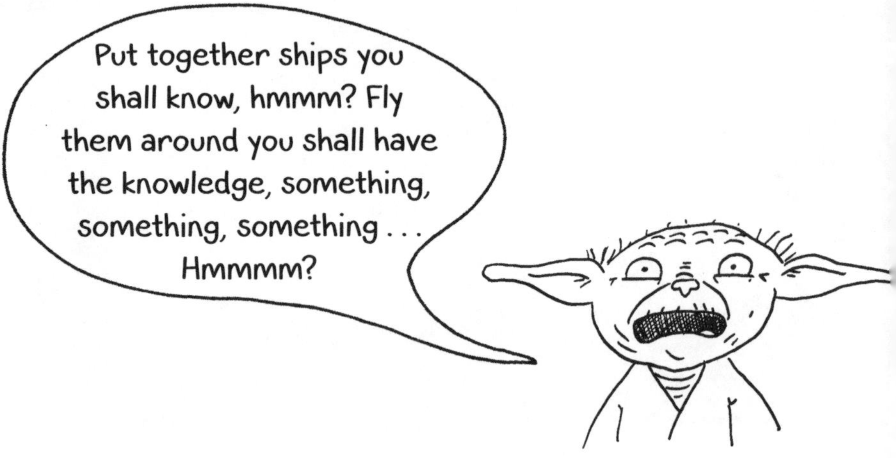
Put together ships you shall know, hmmm? Fly them around you shall have the knowledge, something, something, something . . . Hmmmm?

It's hard to remember anything Yoda says when you are so busy trying to decipher what he's saying!

My dad was really good at fixing up old ships. At least that's what Christina always said. Maybe someday I'll get a handle on how to do all of that technical stuff like my pops. Maybe I'll even get to design some new starships myself. It would be like designing sets for school plays, but way more complicated.

V-Wing fighter.
("V" for Victor!)

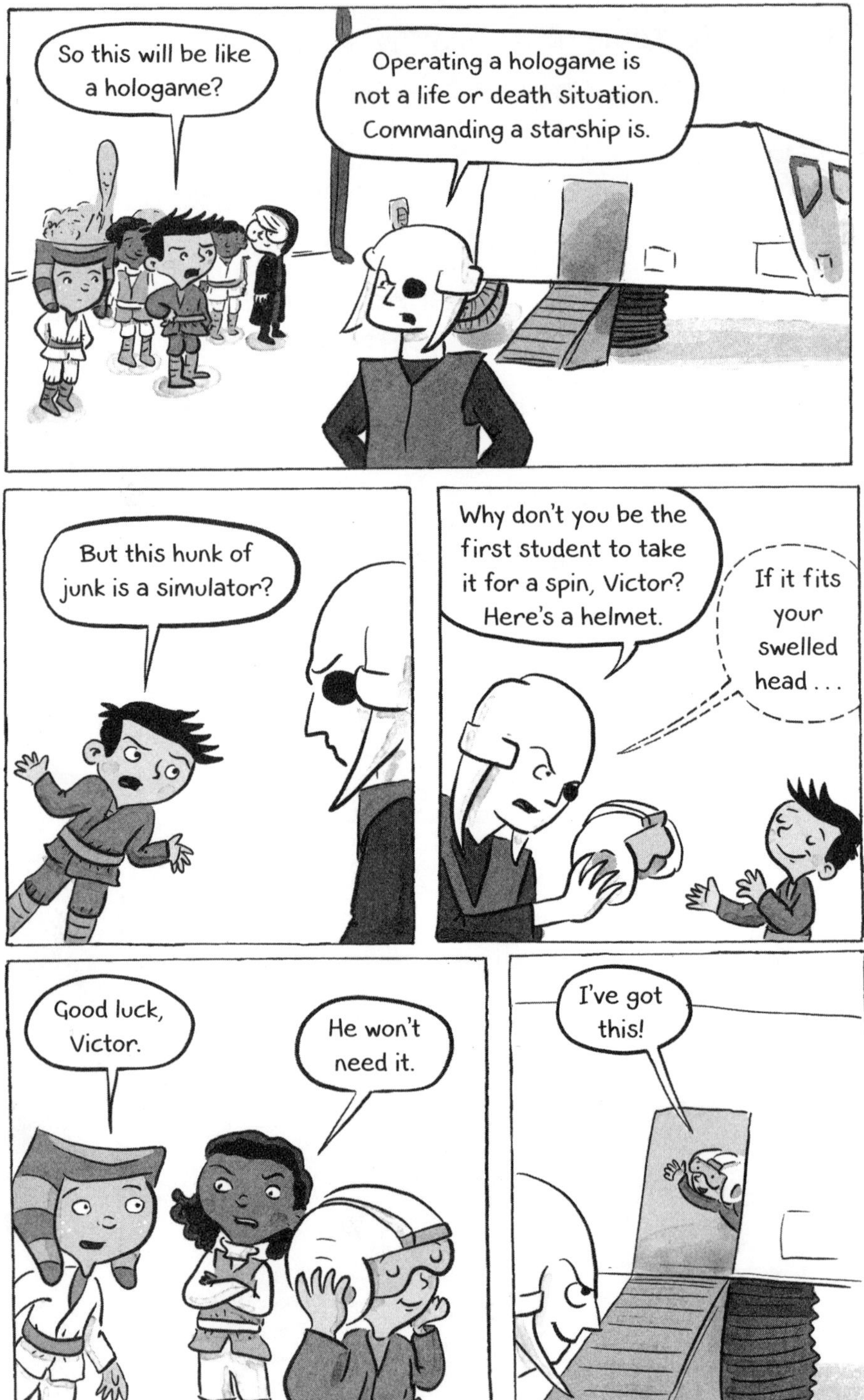
So this will be like a hologame?
Operating a hologame is not a life or death situation. Commanding a starship is.
But this hunk of junk is a simulator?
Why don't you be the first student to take it for a spin, Victor? Here's a helmet.
If it fits your swelled head . . .
Good luck, Victor.
He won't need it.
I've got this!

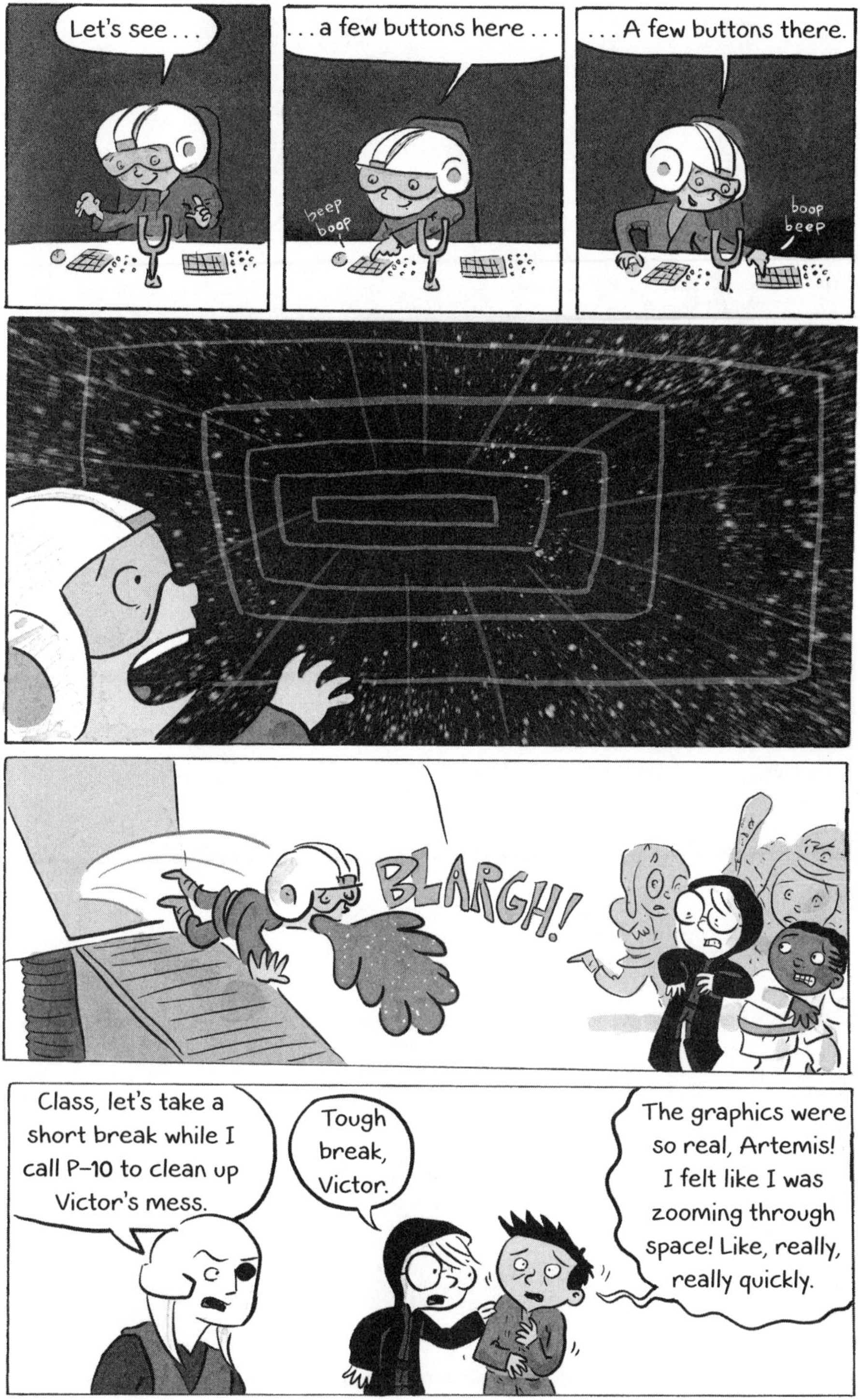

Let's see . . .
. . . a few buttons here . . .
. . . A few buttons there.
beep boop
boop beep
BLARGH!
Class, let's take a short break while I call P-10 to clean up Victor's mess.
Tough break, Victor.
The graphics were so real, Artemis! I felt like I was zooming through space! Like, really, really quickly.

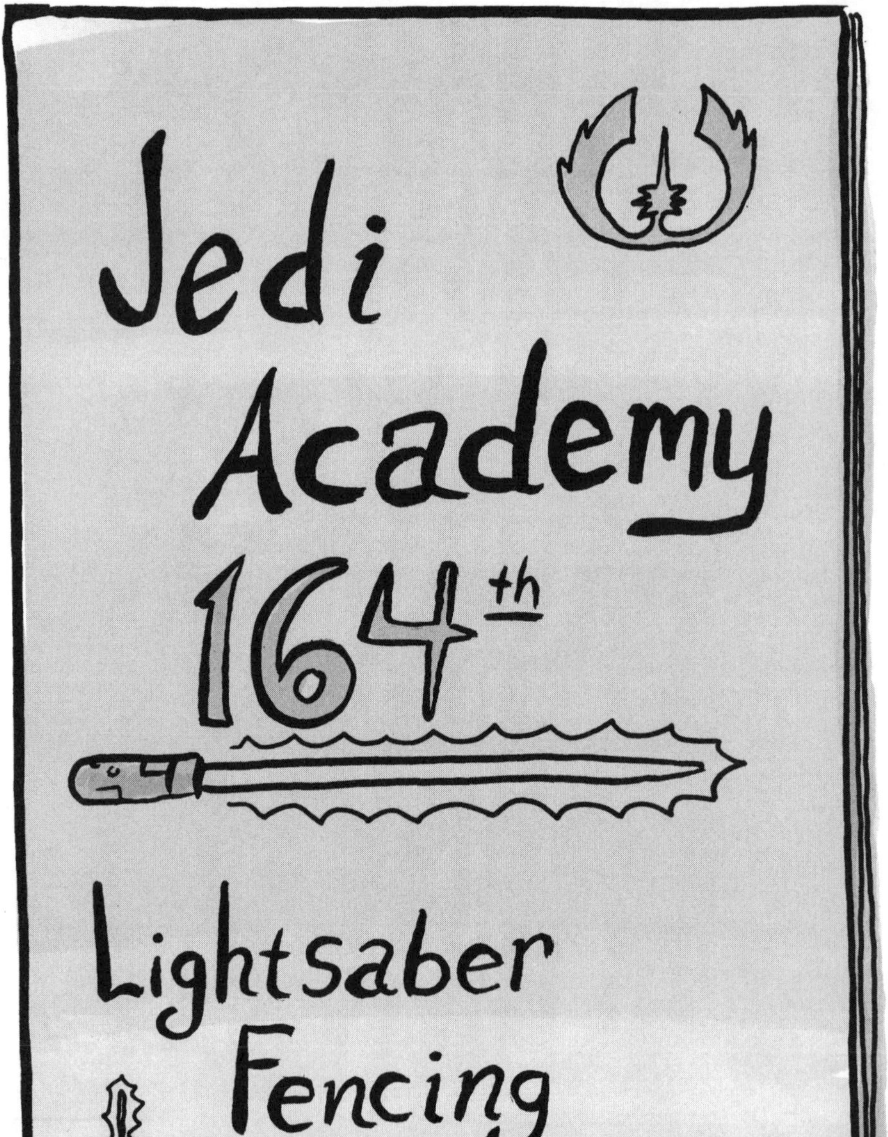
Jedi Academy
164th
Lightsaber Fencing Tournament
Per tradition, all will try out, top ten will compete!

Triday

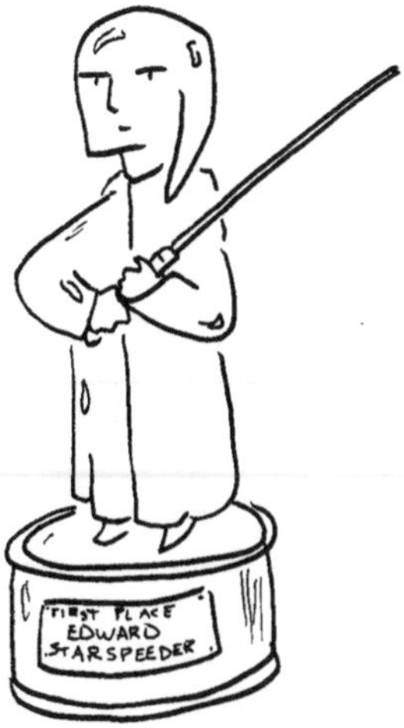
FIRST PLACE
EDWARD
STARSPEEDER

I've been stoked about the lightsaber tournament since I saw Dad's old trophy in the garage back on Naboo. Mom didn't much like keeping Dad's stuff around, but she told me that the trophy reminded her of happier times. He'd be so proud to know that I'm entering the lightsaber tournament and even prouder when I bring home the trophy for myself!

If only he could be here to share in the excitement. I know that he'd be one of those dads who came to every single school event, like Coleman's dad. Coleman thinks his dad is sort of annoying. But he has no idea how lucky he is to have that kind of enthusiasm around. Okay, maybe his dad could turn up with fewer corny posters . . .

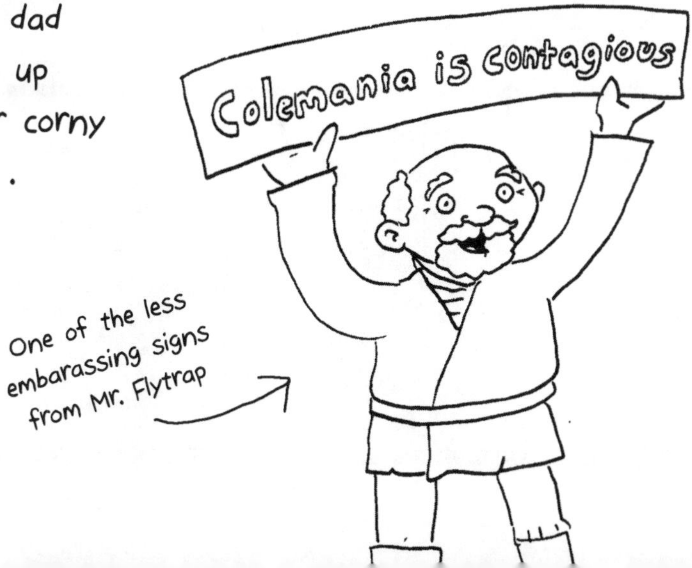
Colemania is contagious
One of the less embarassing signs from Mr. Flytrap

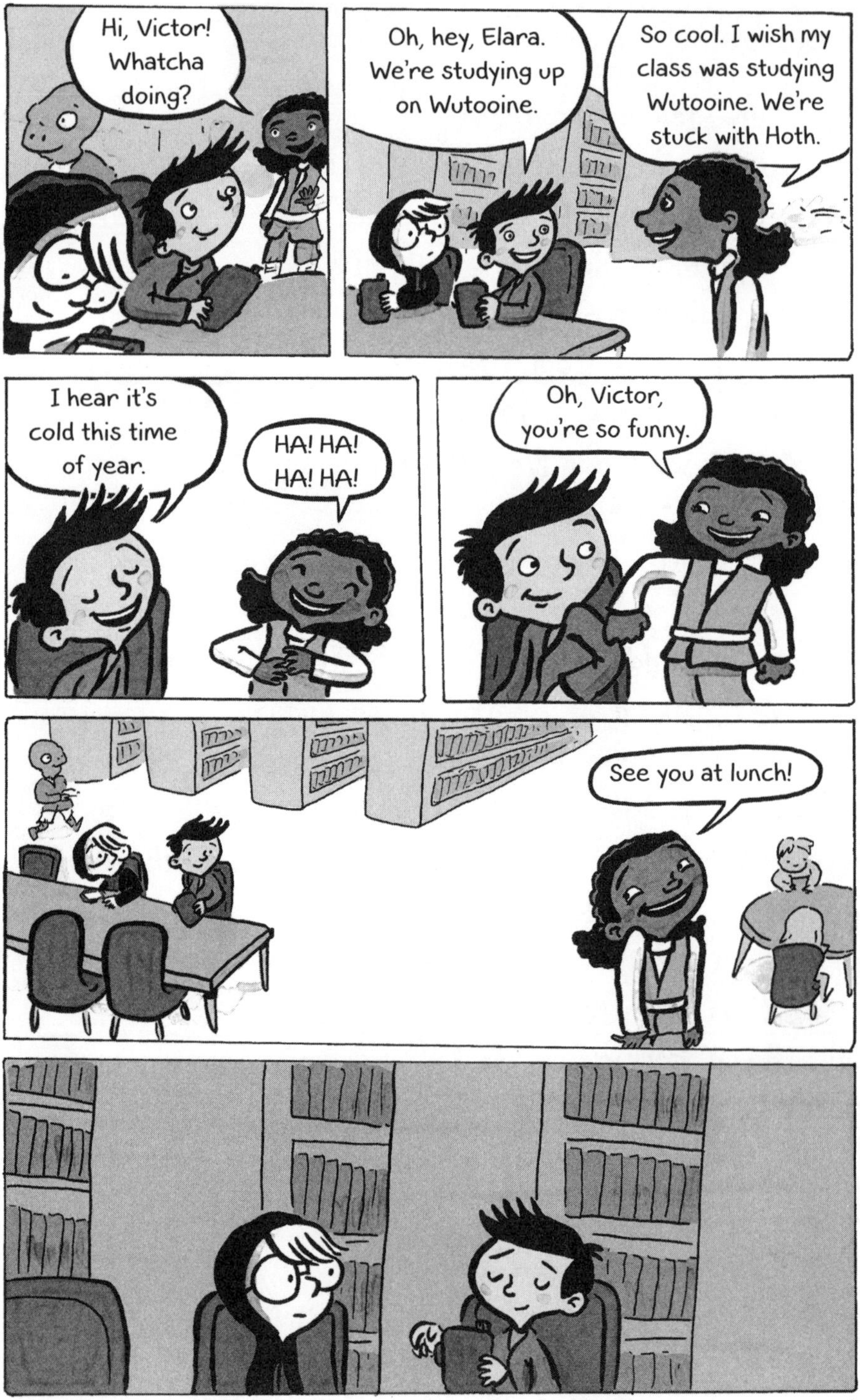
Hi, Victor! Whatcha doing?
Oh, hey, Elara. We're studying up on Wutooine.
So cool. I wish my class was studying Wutooine. We're stuck with Hoth.
I hear it's cold this time of year.
HA! HA! HA! HA!
Oh, Victor, you're so funny.
See you at lunch!

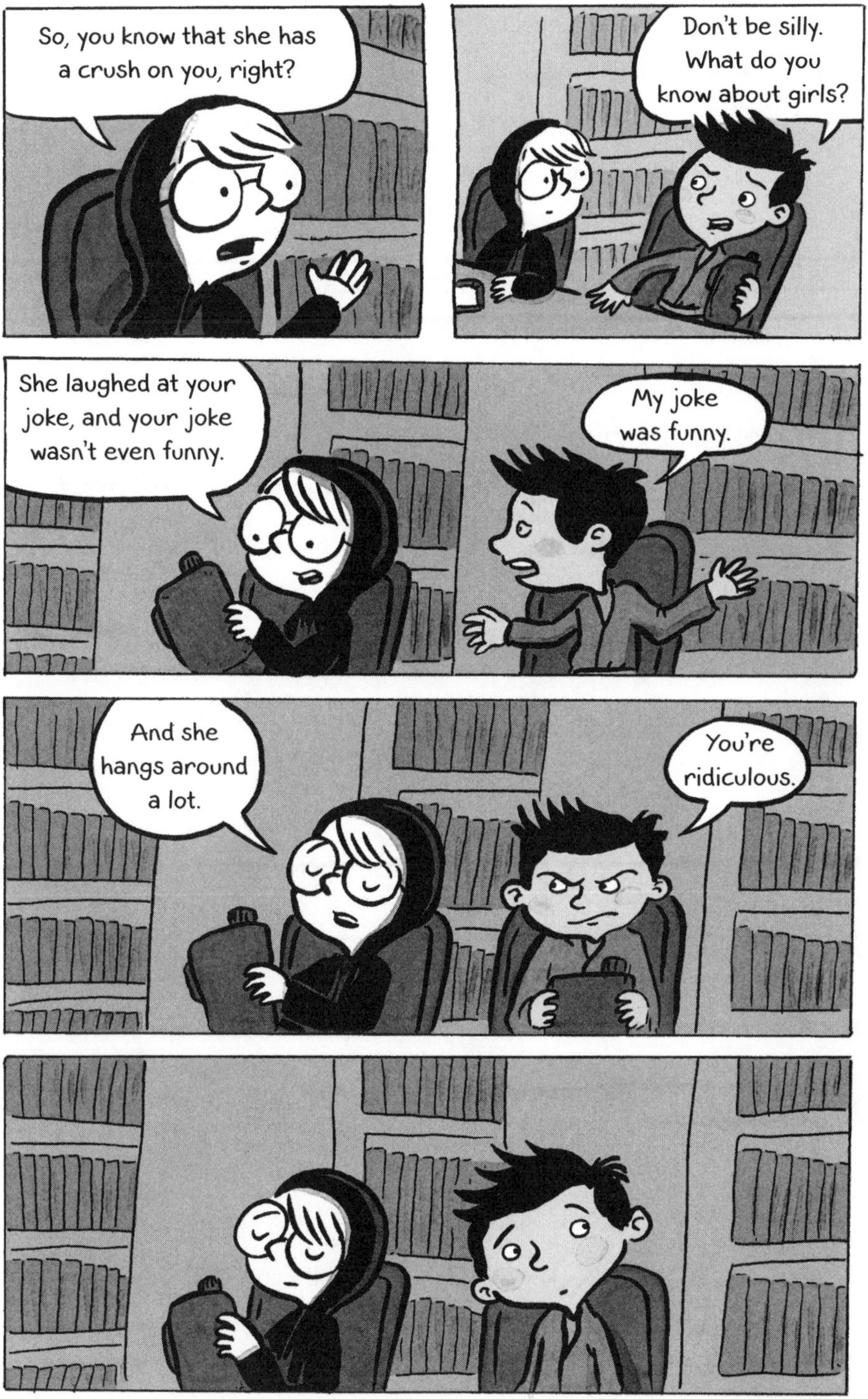
So, you know that she has a crush on you, right?
Don't be silly. What do you know about girls?
She laughed at your joke, and your joke wasn't even funny.
My joke was funny.
And she hangs around a lot.
You're ridiculous.

Hexaday

Coleman and Emmett can't seem to get enough of Zavyer. They invite him over to our room every night to play holochess. I'm not a big fan of holochess. I just don't see the point of it. Artemis says that's because I haven't taken the time to really learn the strategy. I watch my friends play, but I just can't catch on to it. Zavyer is really good at it and he offered to teach me how to play. He said he could bring his travel set for the flight to Wutooine.

I suppose I could try and let him teach me. But that would of course mean more time with Zavyer. But I guess we were going to be stuck on this field trip together anyhow.

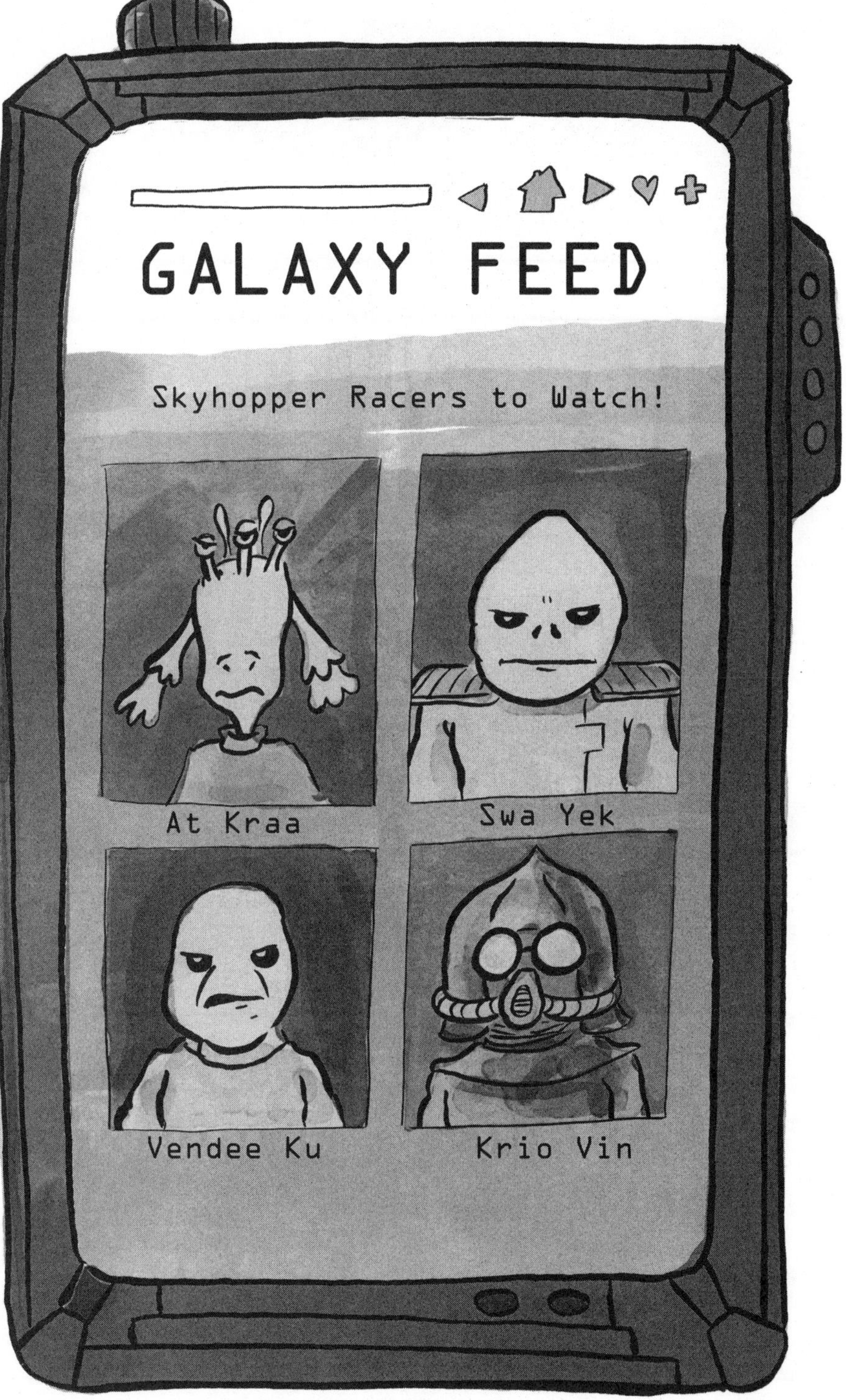
GALAXY FEED
Skyhopper Racers to Watch!
At Kraa
Swa Yek
Vendee Ku
Krio Vin

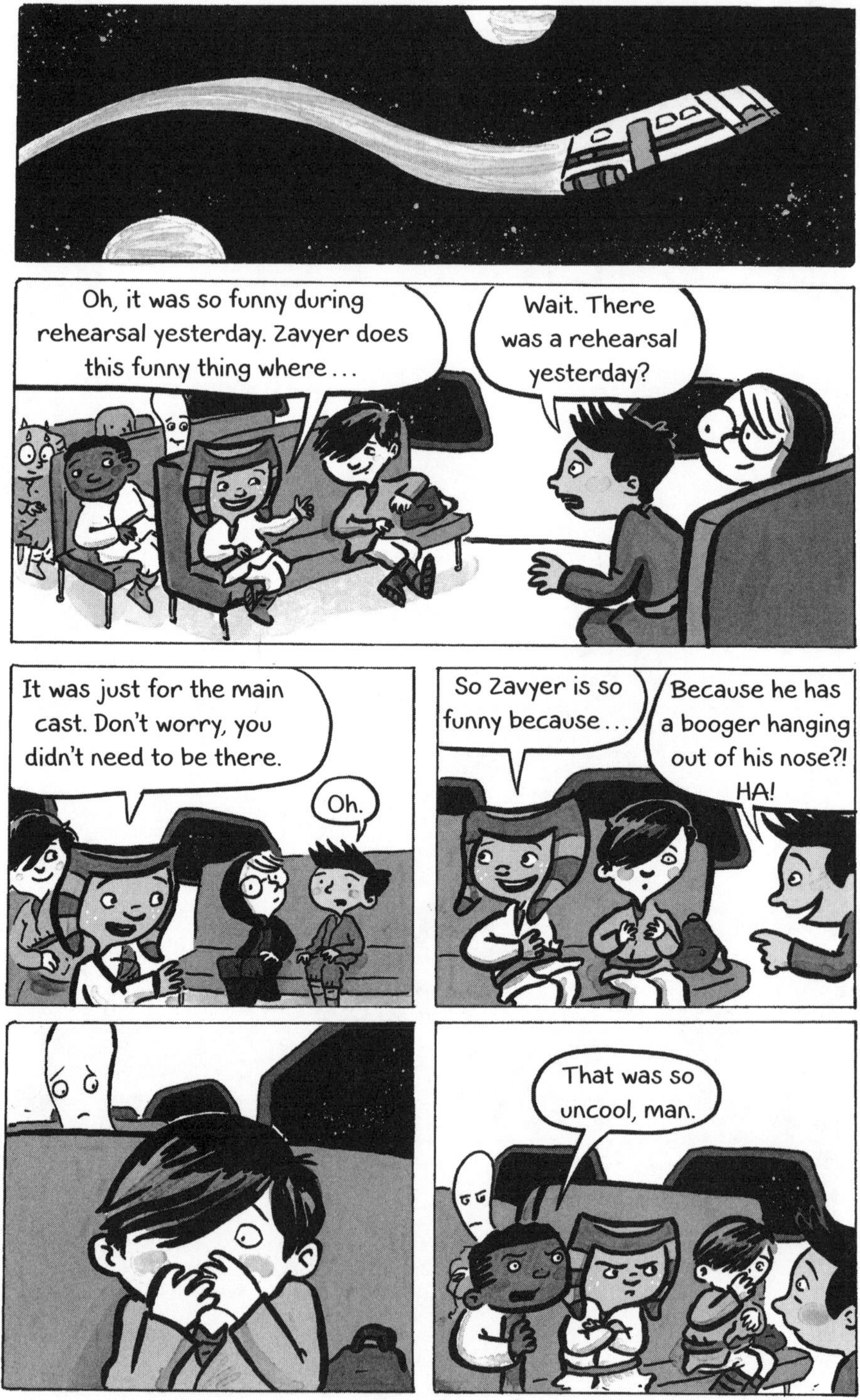
Oh, it was so funny during rehearsal yesterday. Zavyer does this funny thing where . . .
Wait. There was a rehearsal yesterday?
It was just for the main cast. Don't worry, you didn't need to be there.
Oh.
So Zavyer is so funny because . . .
Because he has a booger hanging out of his nose?! HA!
That was so uncool, man.

Duoday

It was a long trip to Wutooine. Understandably, nobody was very excited to talk to me after that dig I gave Zavyer. But you know who didn't hold a grudge? Zavyer. Man, that guy is even really good at being nice. He taught me a few of the basics of holo chess. I was grateful to finally see that we were making our initial approach to Wutooine. I was very much looking forward to stretching my legs and getting off that ship!

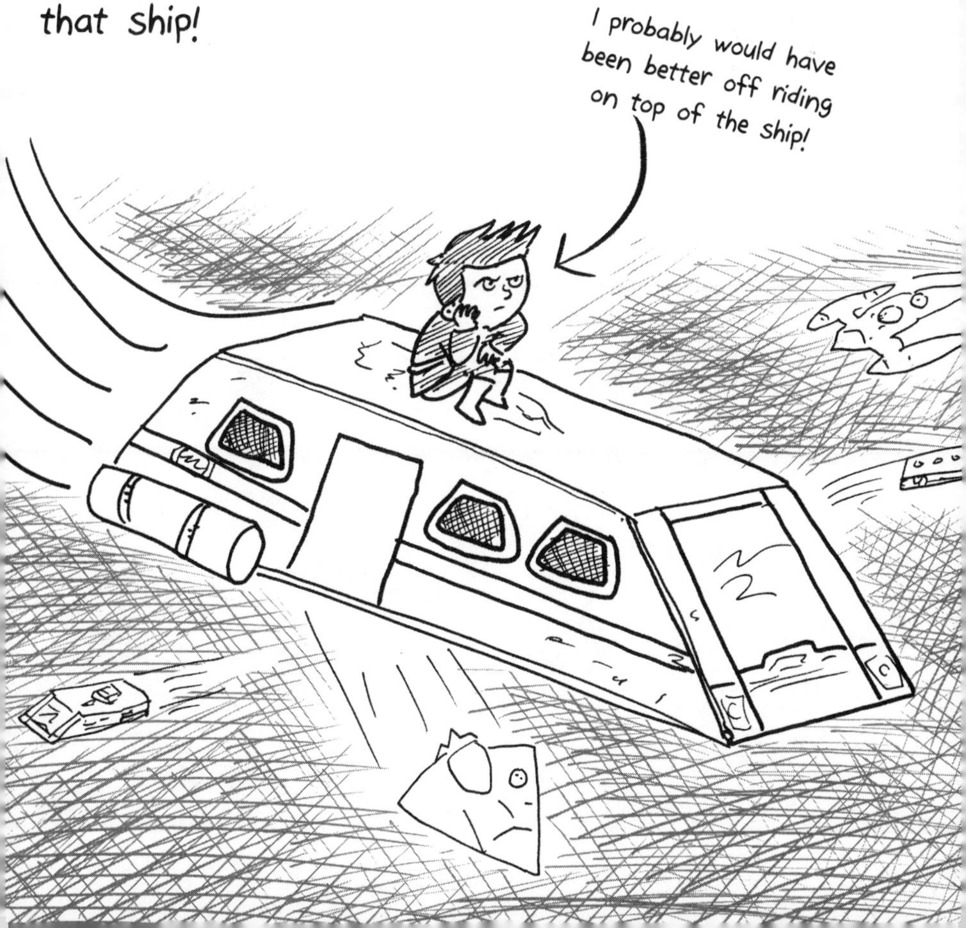
I probably would have been better off riding on top of the ship!

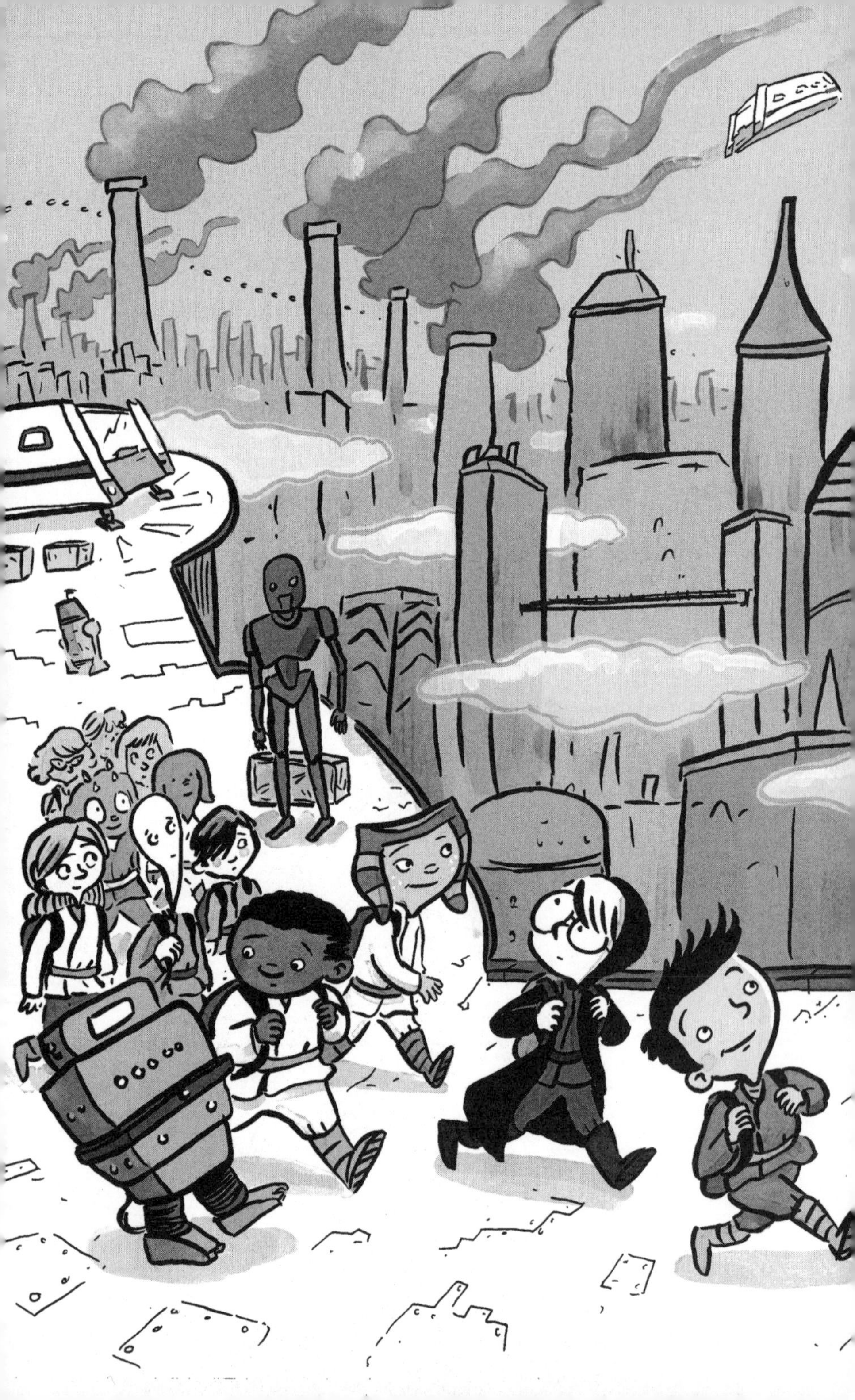

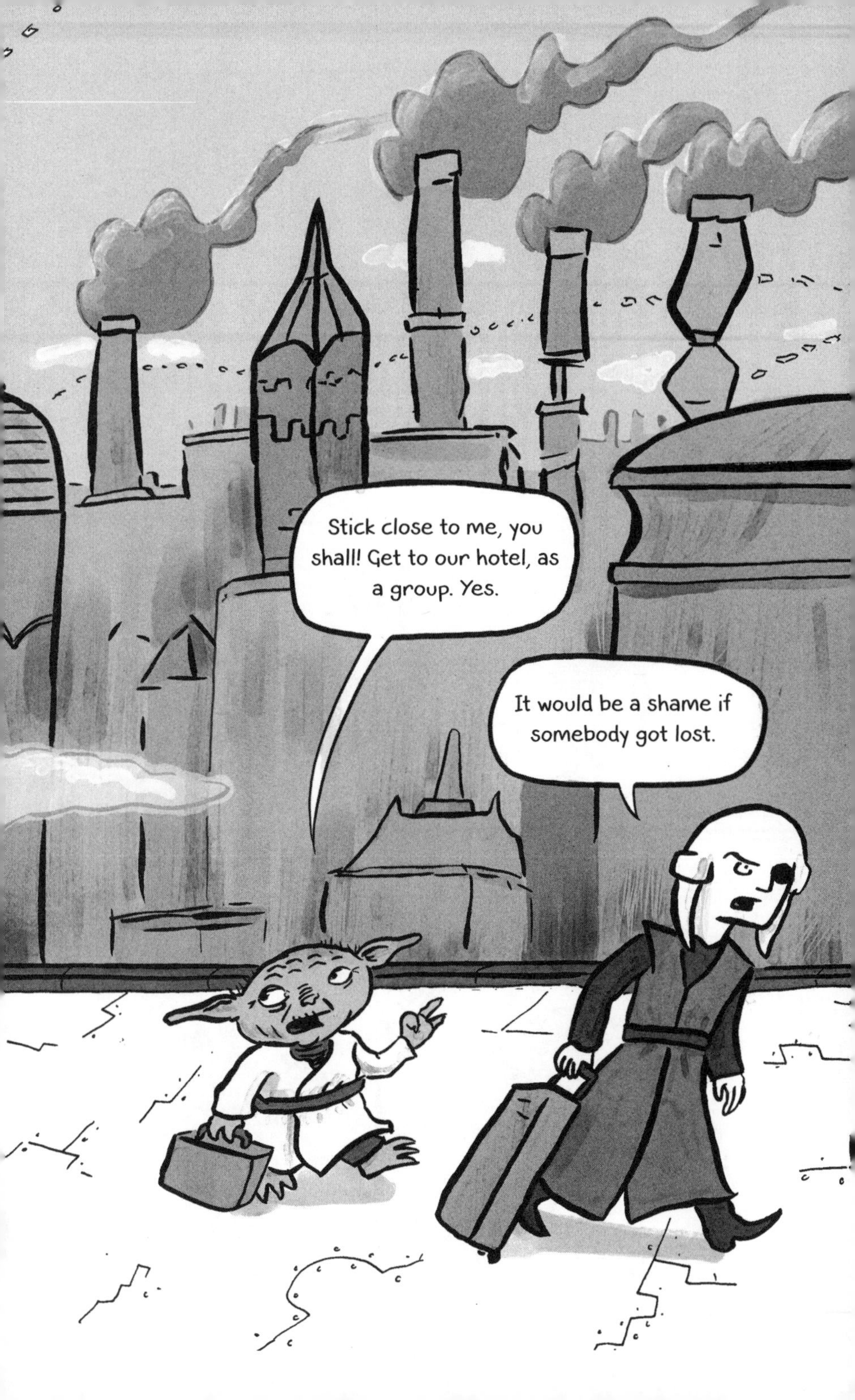
Stick close to me, you shall! Get to our hotel, as a group. Yes.
It would be a shame if somebody got lost.

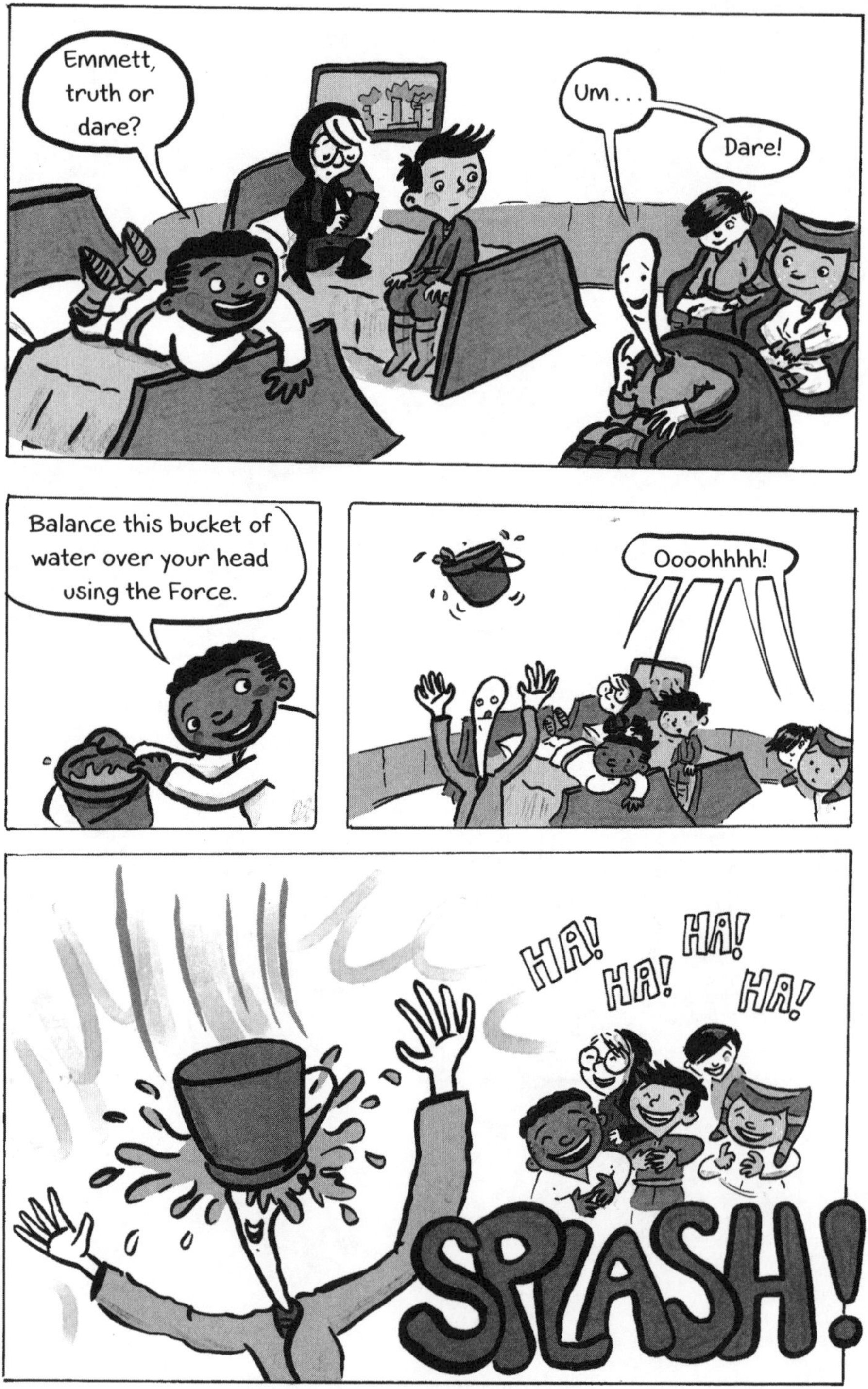
Emmett, truth or dare?
Um . . .
Dare!
Balance this bucket of water over your head using the Force.
Ooooohhhh!
HA!
HA!
HA!
HA!
SPLASH!

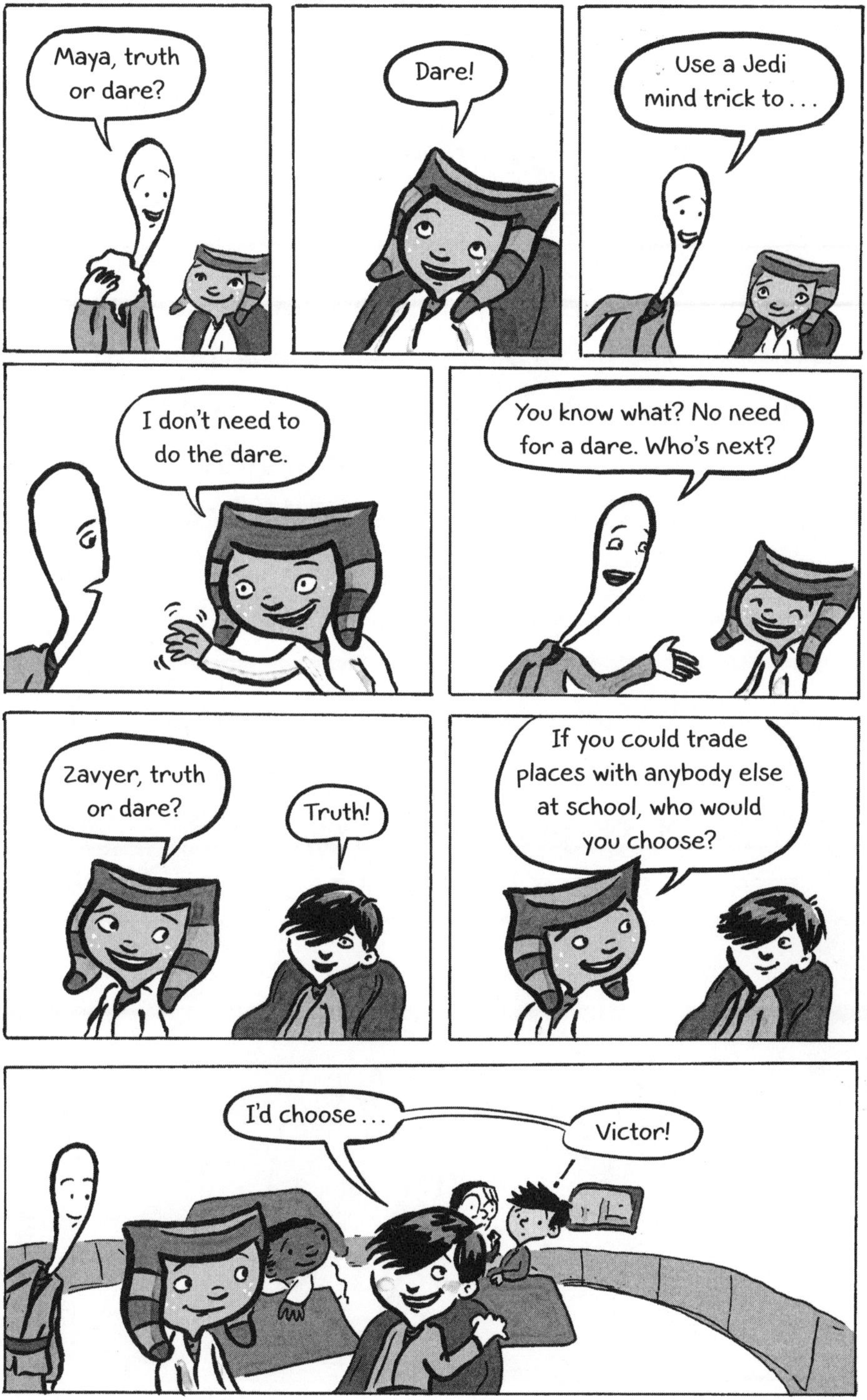

Maya, truth or dare?
Dare!
Use a Jedi mind trick to . . .
I don't need to do the dare.
You know what? No need for a dare. Who's next?
Zavyer, truth or dare?
Truth!
If you could trade places with anybody else at school, who would you choose?
I'd choose . . .
Victor!
!

Triday

Well, I guess Zavyer isn't half bad after all. I knew I liked that guy from the moment I first met him! We all stayed up well past lights out, talking about all sorts of things. Our lives back home, our families, and the upcoming semester break. Turns out Zavyer and I have more in common than I realized. His parents split a few years back, and he's only seen his dad a few times since. That can't be easy. I know Russell can get on my nerves sometimes, and he'll never replace my dad, but I am glad that he's around.

We were all really sleepy on the morning of the skyhopper race. As tired as I was, nothing could stop me for being totally amped for this. I've been drawing skyhoppers since I was a little kid.

I drew this when I was 4

by: Victor

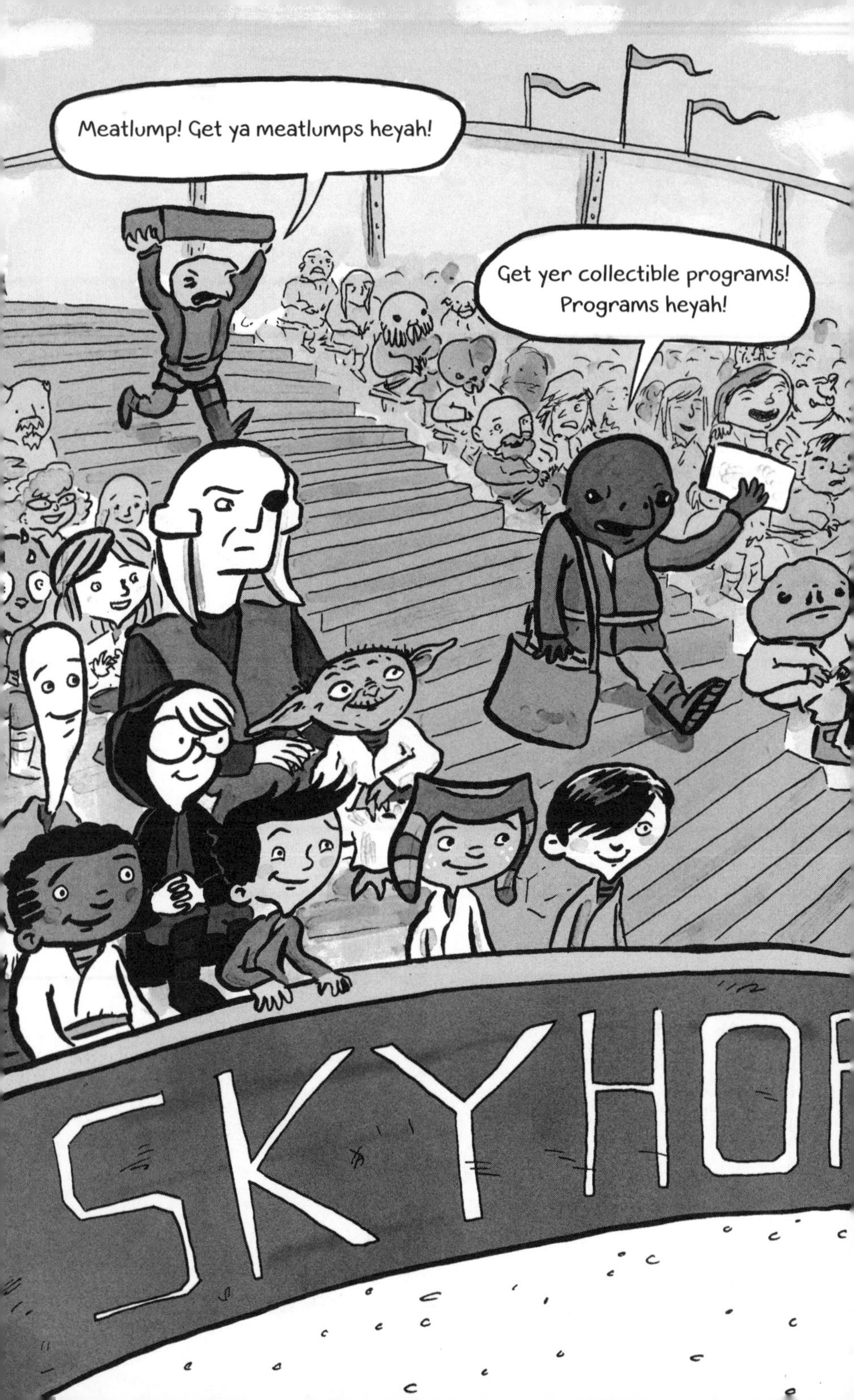
Meatlump! Get ya meatlumps heyah!
Get yer collectible programs! Programs heyah!
SKY HO

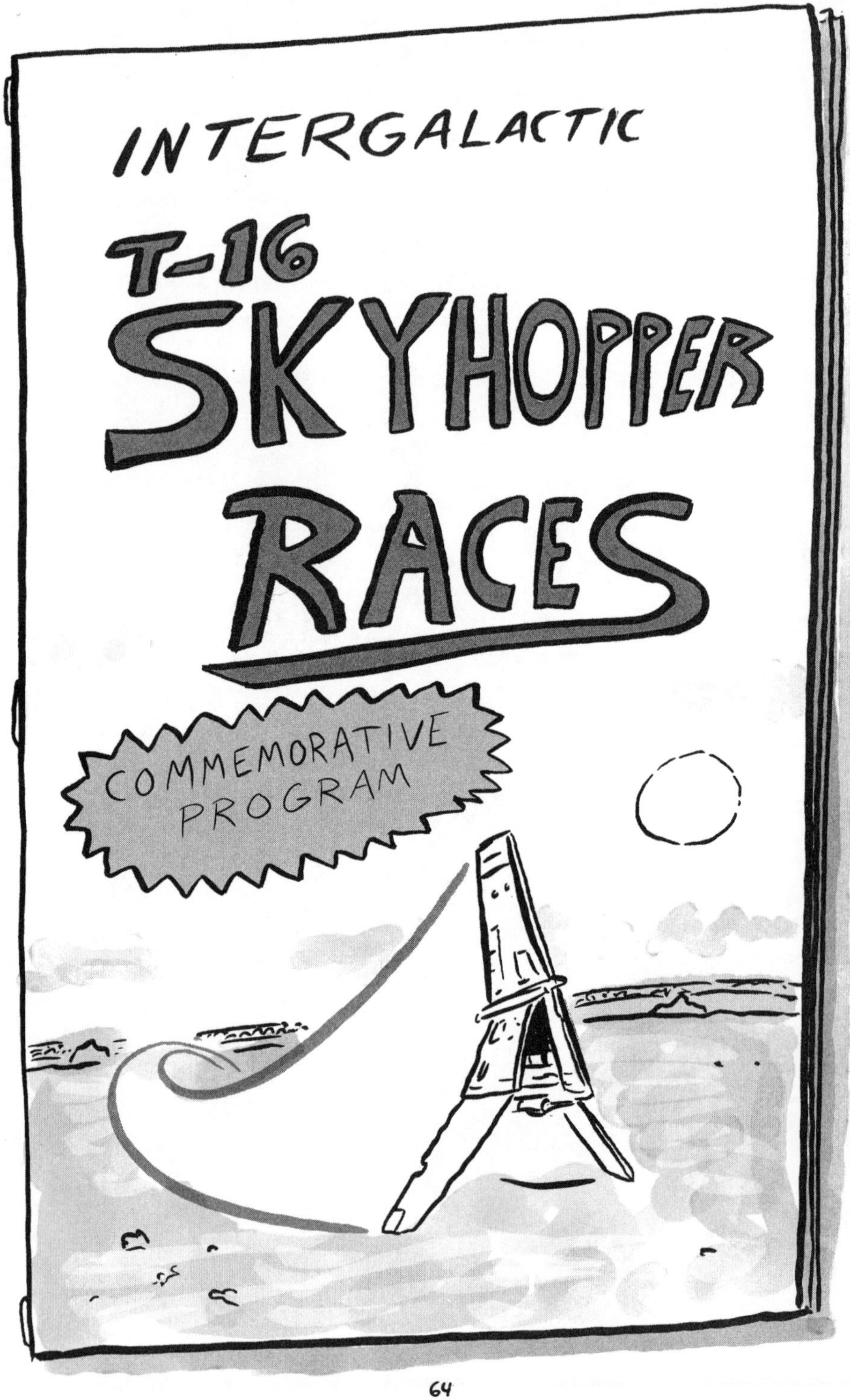
INTERGALACTIC
T-16
SKYHOPPER
RACES
COMMEMORATIVE PROGRAM

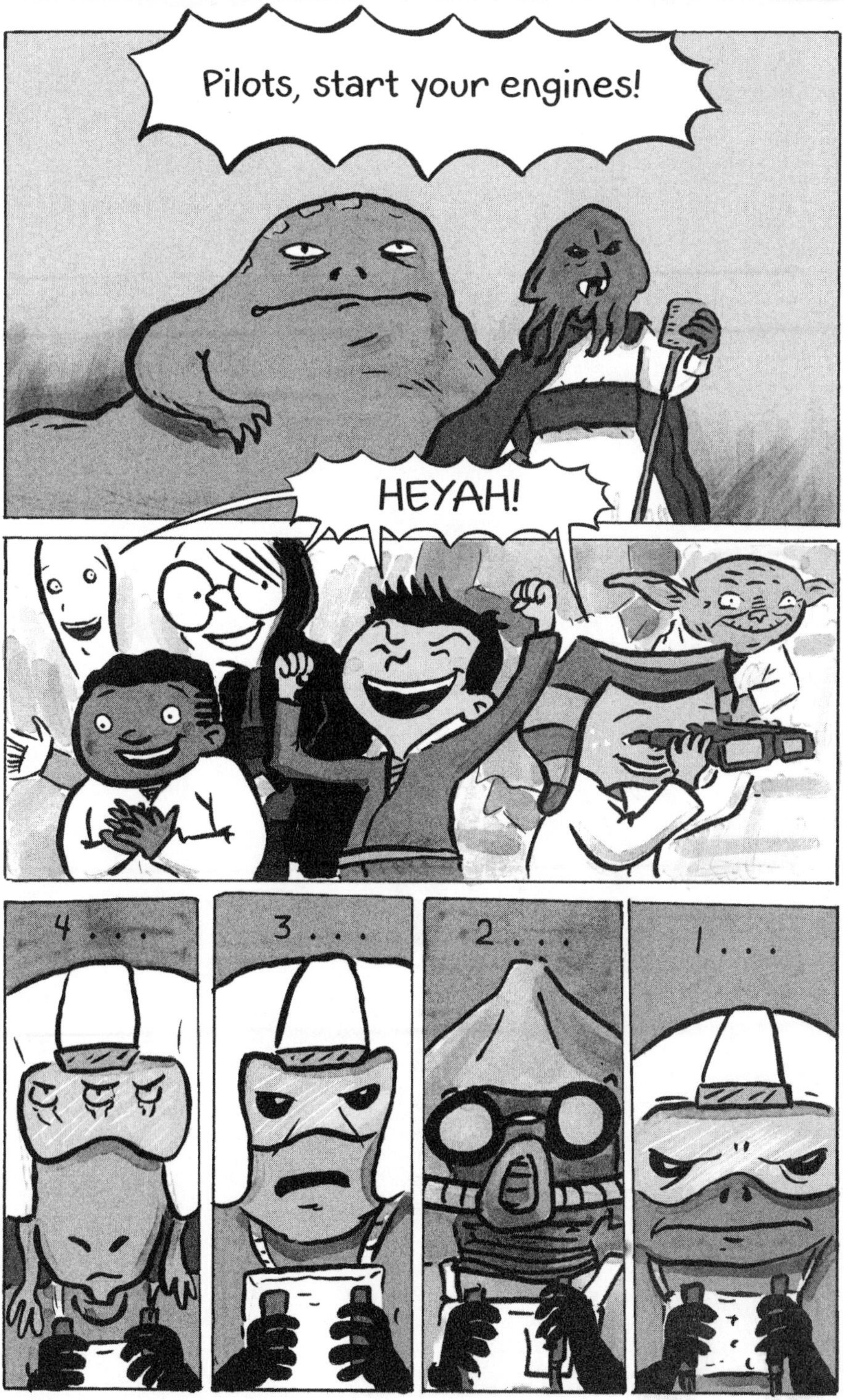
Pilots, start your engines!
HEYAH!
4 . . .
3 . . .
2 . . .
1 . . .

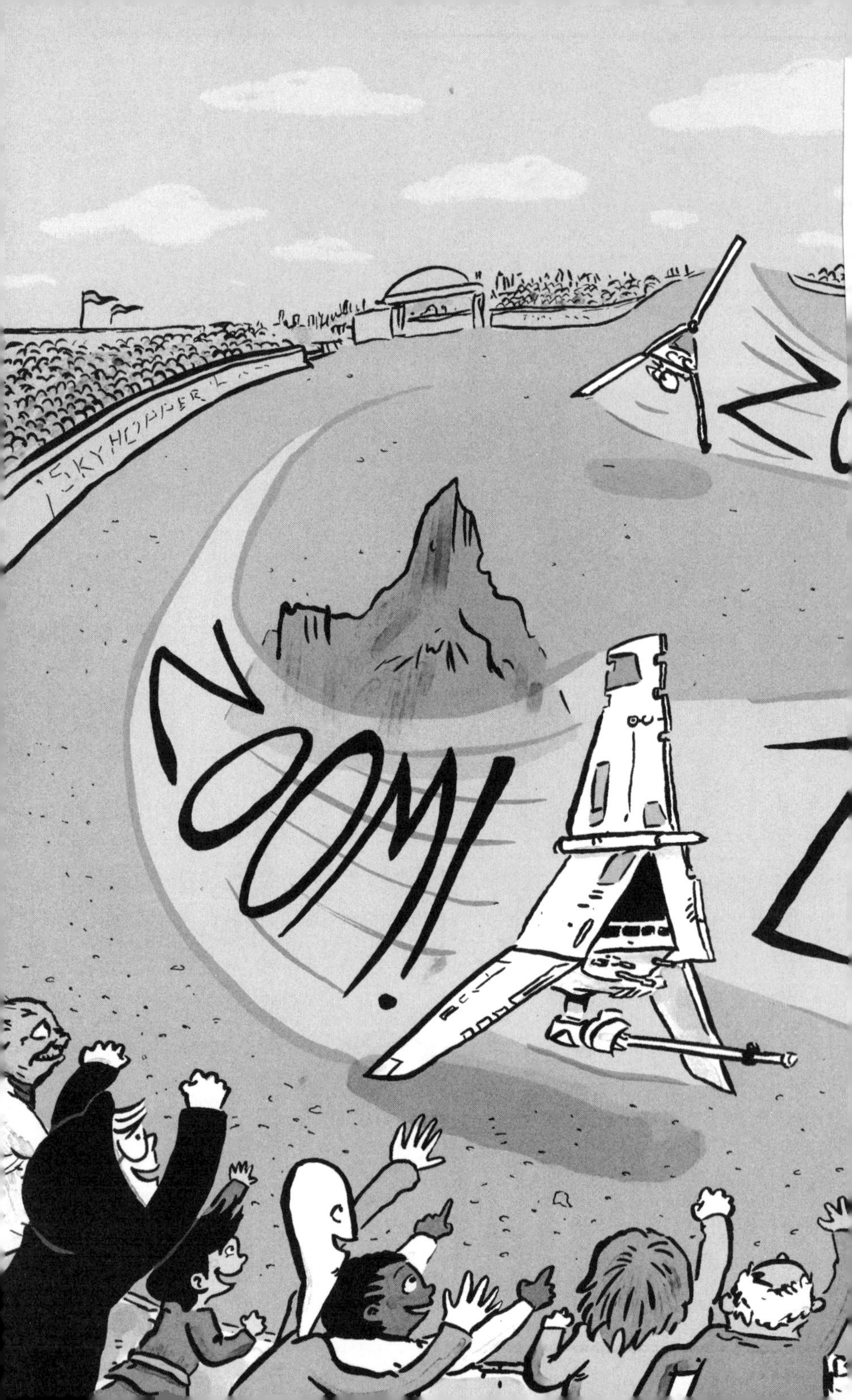
SKYHOPPER
ZOOM!

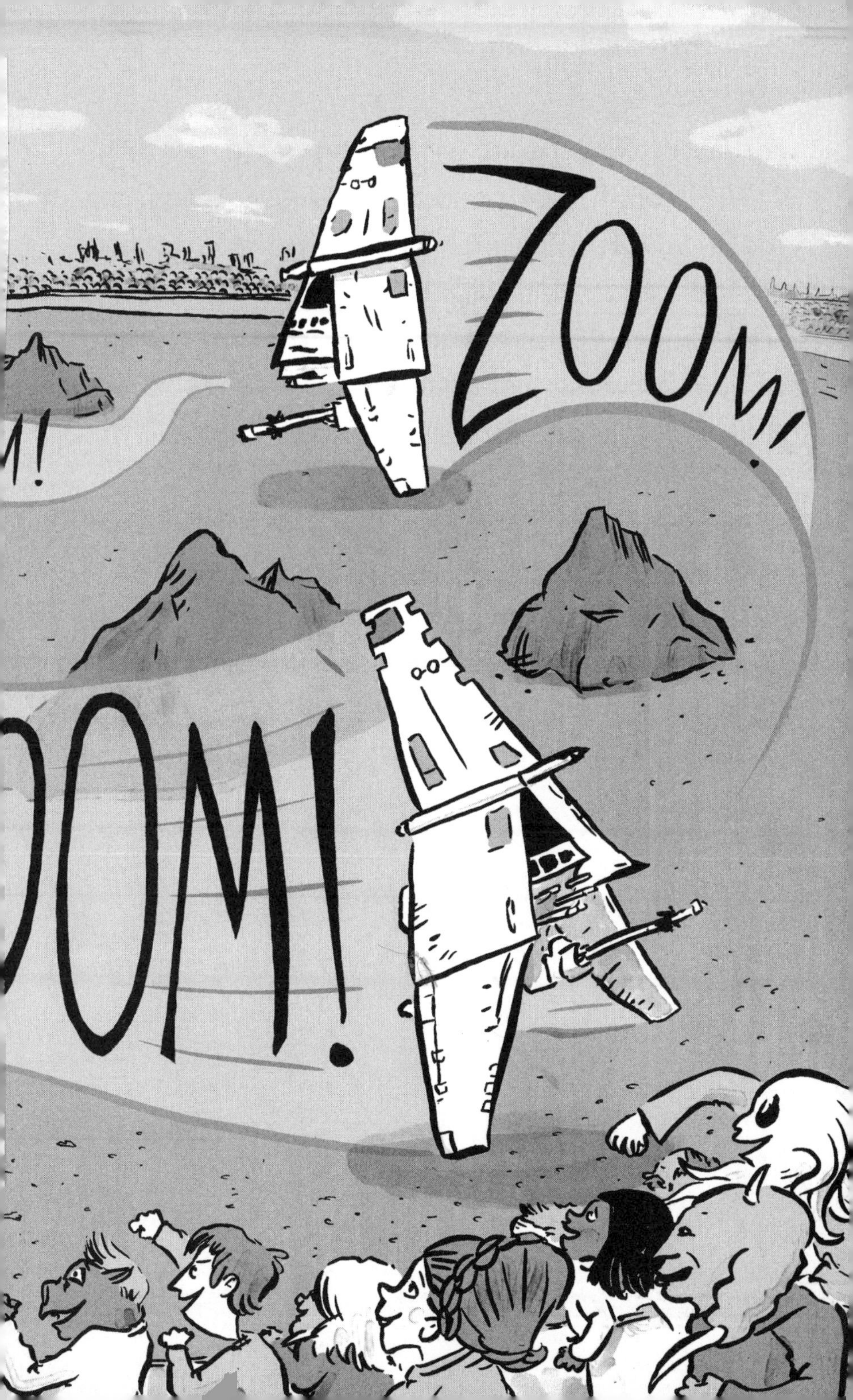
M!
ZOOM!
OOM!

Quadday

Ah, man! The races were even more exciting than I could have possibly dreamed. Holos can make you feel like you are right there, but nothing beats actually being there in real life. The smell of the exhaust, the roaring thunder of the crowds, the taste of meatlumps . . . it all added up to an unbelievable experience.

Afterward, we got to meet some of the racers and get their autographs. I'll post a few of them here in my journal. We went on to tour some of the factories that produced these incredible machines. I think over the upcoming semester break, I'm going to try my hand at making my own skyhopper model.

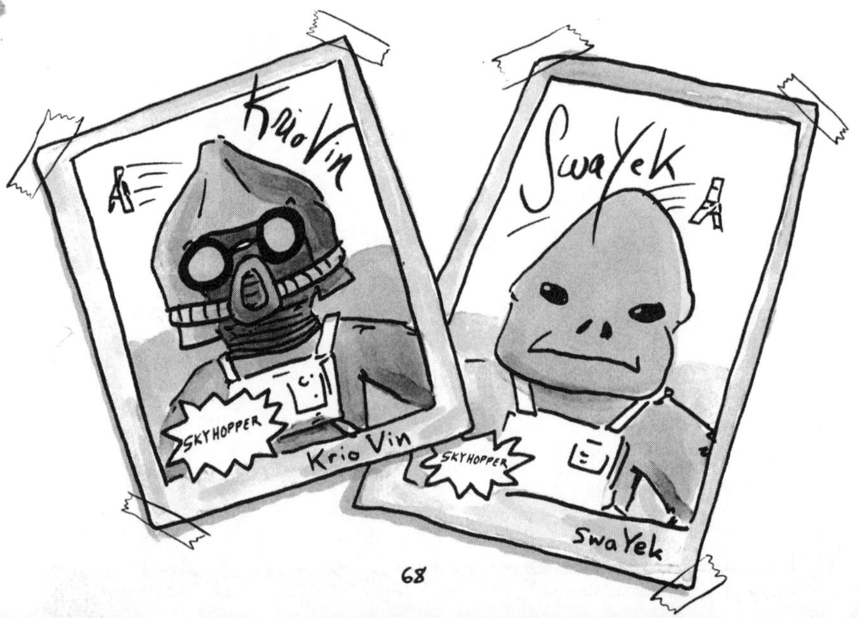
Krio Vin
SKYHOPPER
Krio Vin
Swa Yek
SKYHOPPER
Swa Yek

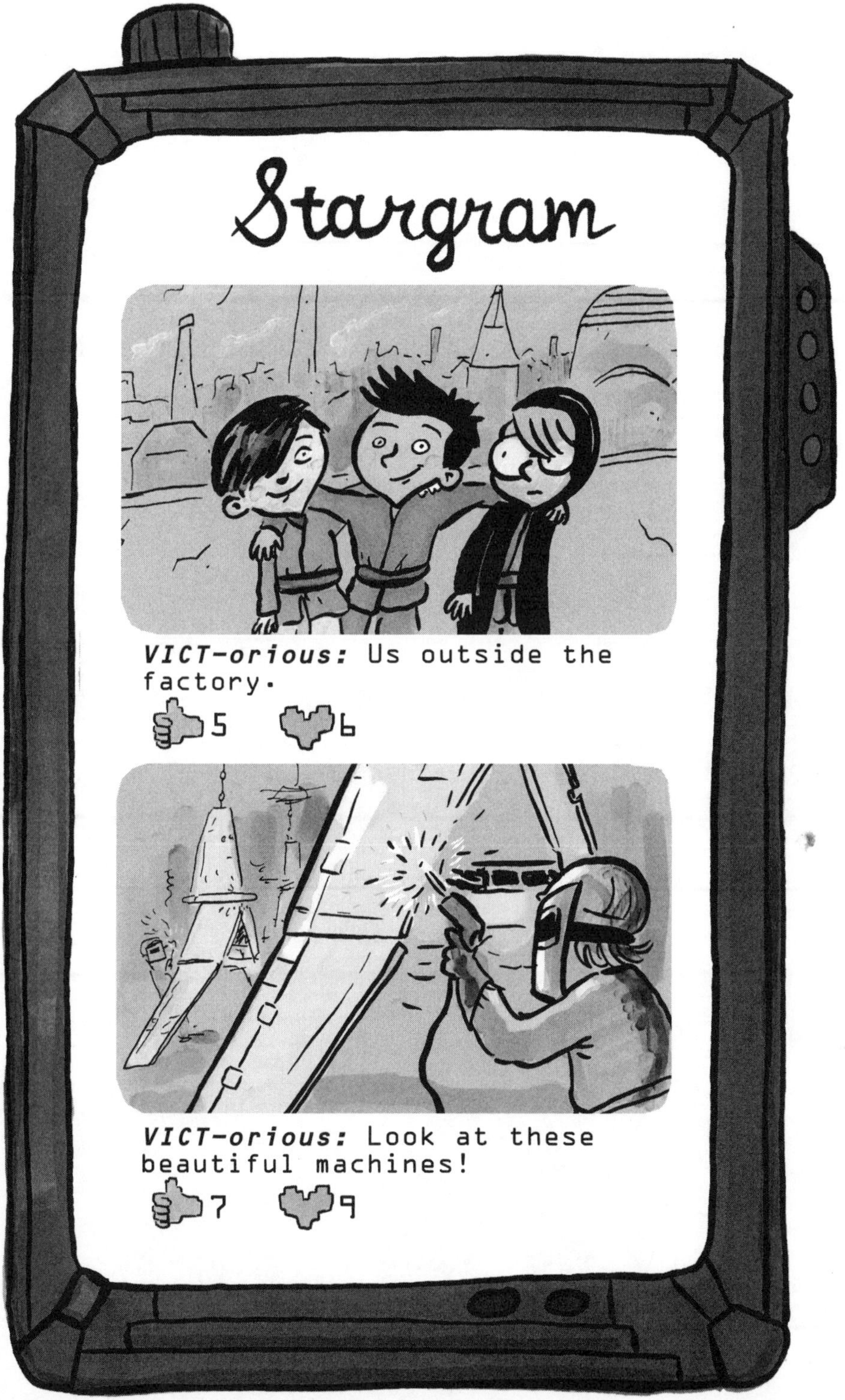
Stargram
VICT-orious: Us outside the factory.
5 6
VICT-orious: Look at these beautiful machines!
7 9

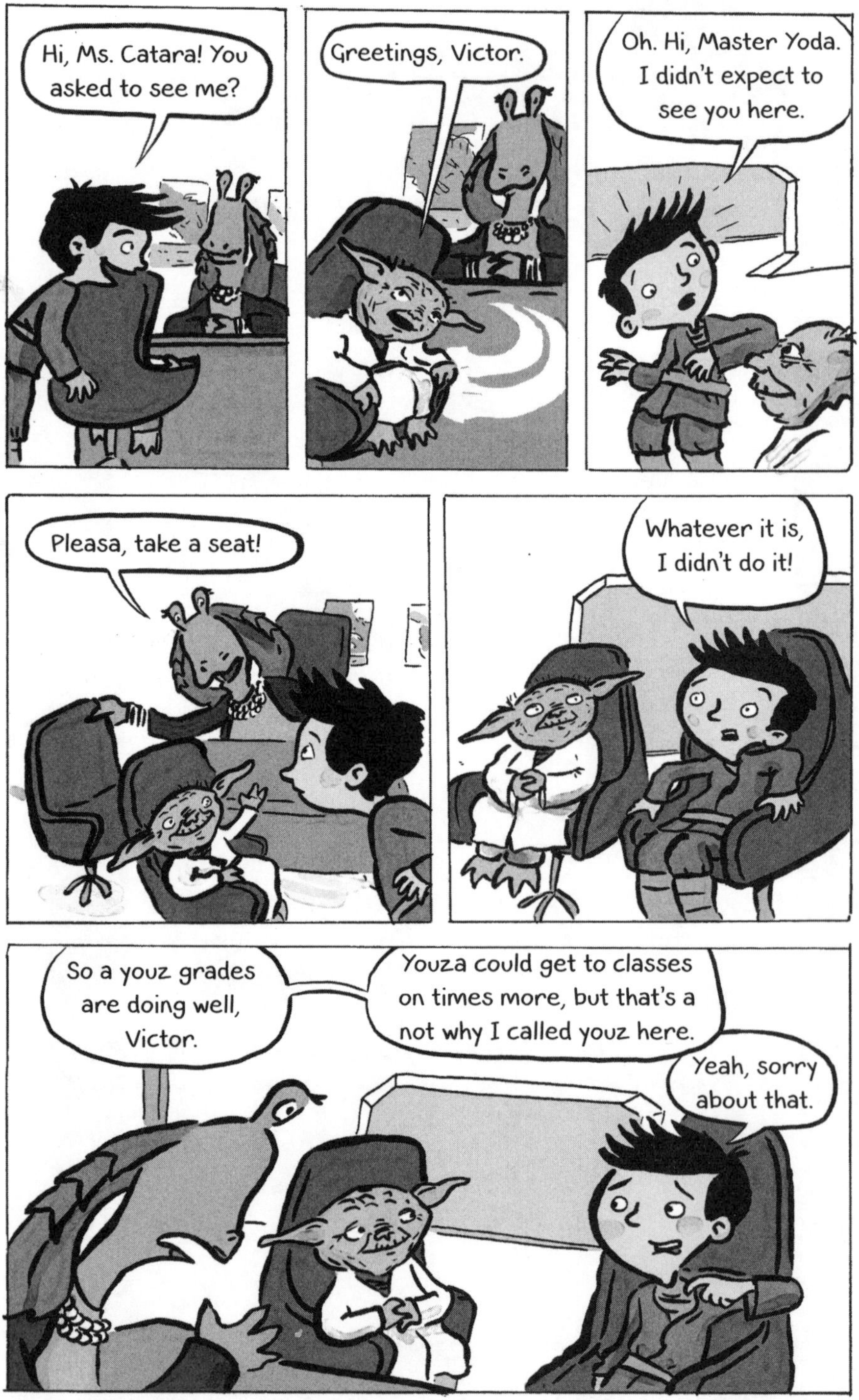
Hi, Ms. Catara! You asked to see me?
Greetings, Victor.
Oh. Hi, Master Yoda. I didn't expect to see you here.
Pleasa, take a seat!
Whatever it is, I didn't do it!
So a youz grades are doing well, Victor.
Youza could get to classes on times more, but that's a not why I called youz here.
Yeah, sorry about that.

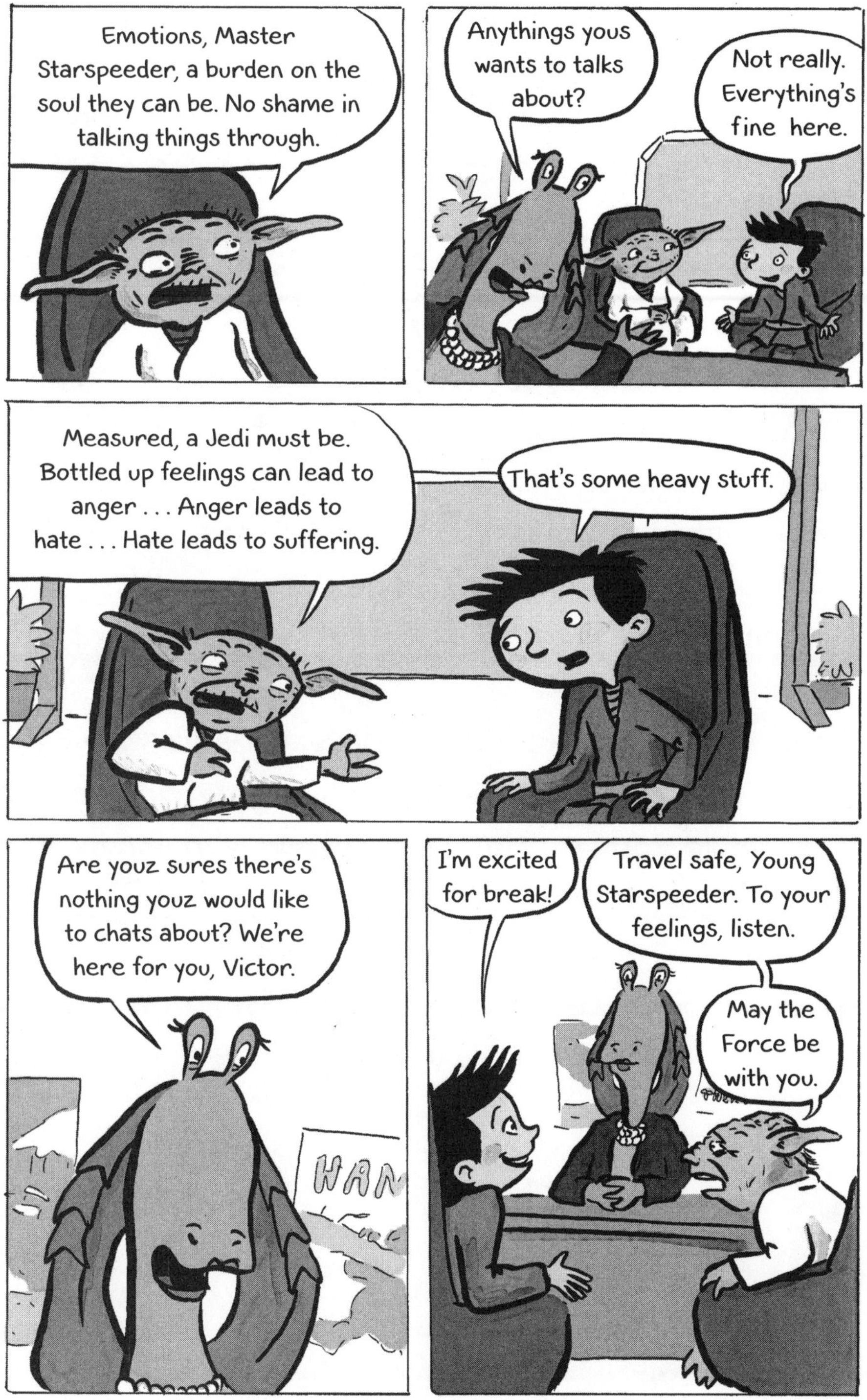
Emotions, Master Starspeeder, a burden on the soul they can be. No shame in talking things through.
Anythings yous wants to talks about?
Not really. Everything's fine here.
Measured, a Jedi must be. Bottled up feelings can lead to anger . . . Anger leads to hate . . . Hate leads to suffering.
That's some heavy stuff.
Are youz sures there's nothing youz would like to chats about? We're here for you, Victor.
I'm excited for break!
Travel safe, Young Starspeeder. To your feelings, listen.
May the Force be with you.

Hexaday

It was a long flight back to Naboo. Christina wasn't especially chatty, no surprise there. My datapad's battery ran out, so I read all of the school newspapers, which left me alone with my thoughts. Yoda was pretty confident that something was bothering me. And I guess he was right. Not that it was something that I didn't want to talk about, but more something that I didn't know that I needed to talk about. Those T-16 skyhoppers that I saw on Wutooine inspired me. They also totally made me think about my dad. He would think that it was so cool that I was having these experiences. If he was there to greet me when we got back home, he would totally help me build my own model, maybe we would even work on a real, full-scale version.

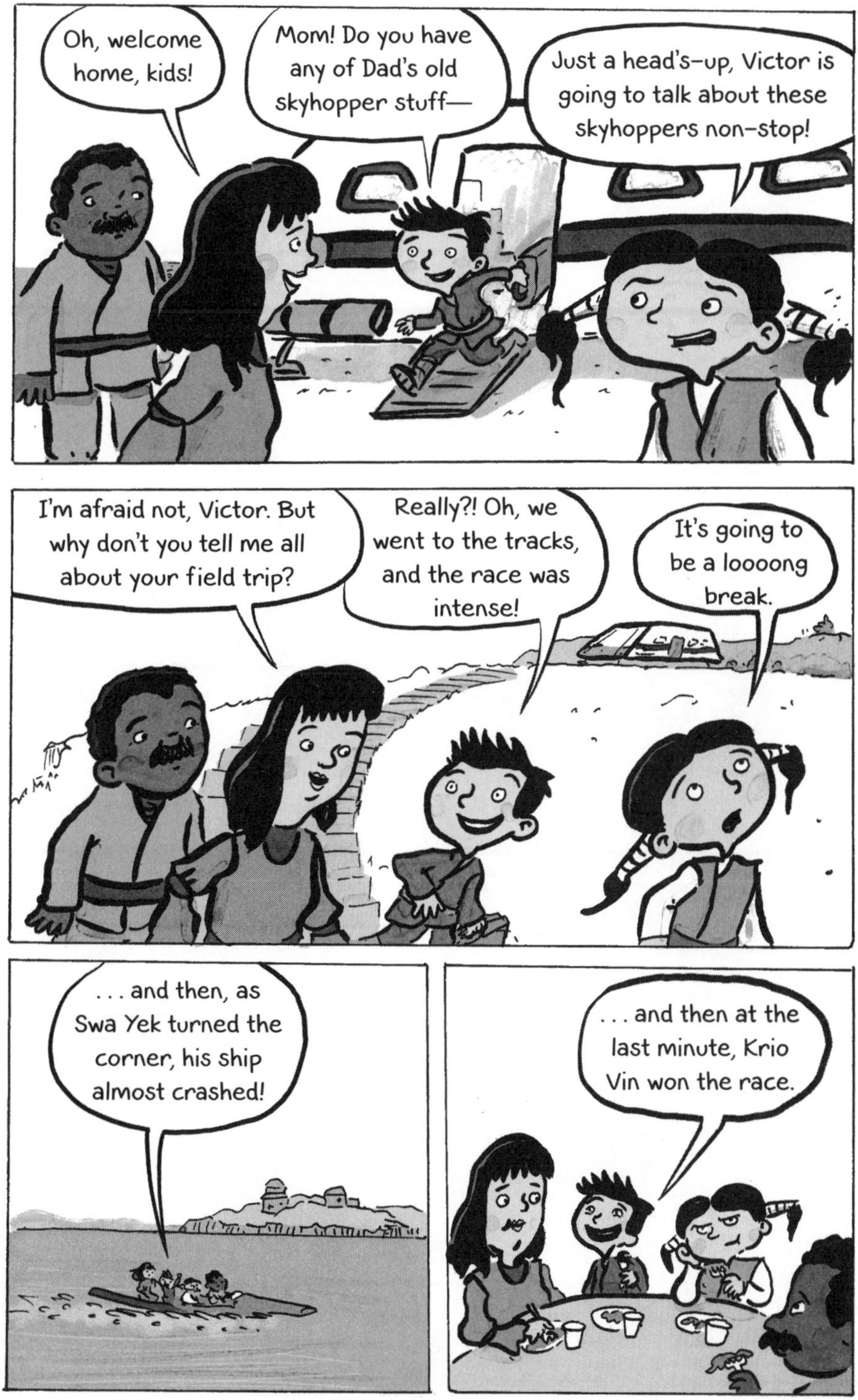
Oh, welcome home, kids!
Mom! Do you have any of Dad's old skyhopper stuff—
Just a head's-up, Victor is going to talk about these skyhoppers non-stop!
I'm afraid not, Victor. But why don't you tell me all about your field trip?
Really?! Oh, we went to the tracks, and the race was intense!
It's going to be a loooong break.
. . . and then, as Swa Yek turned the corner, his ship almost crashed!
. . . and then at the last minute, Krio Vin won the race.

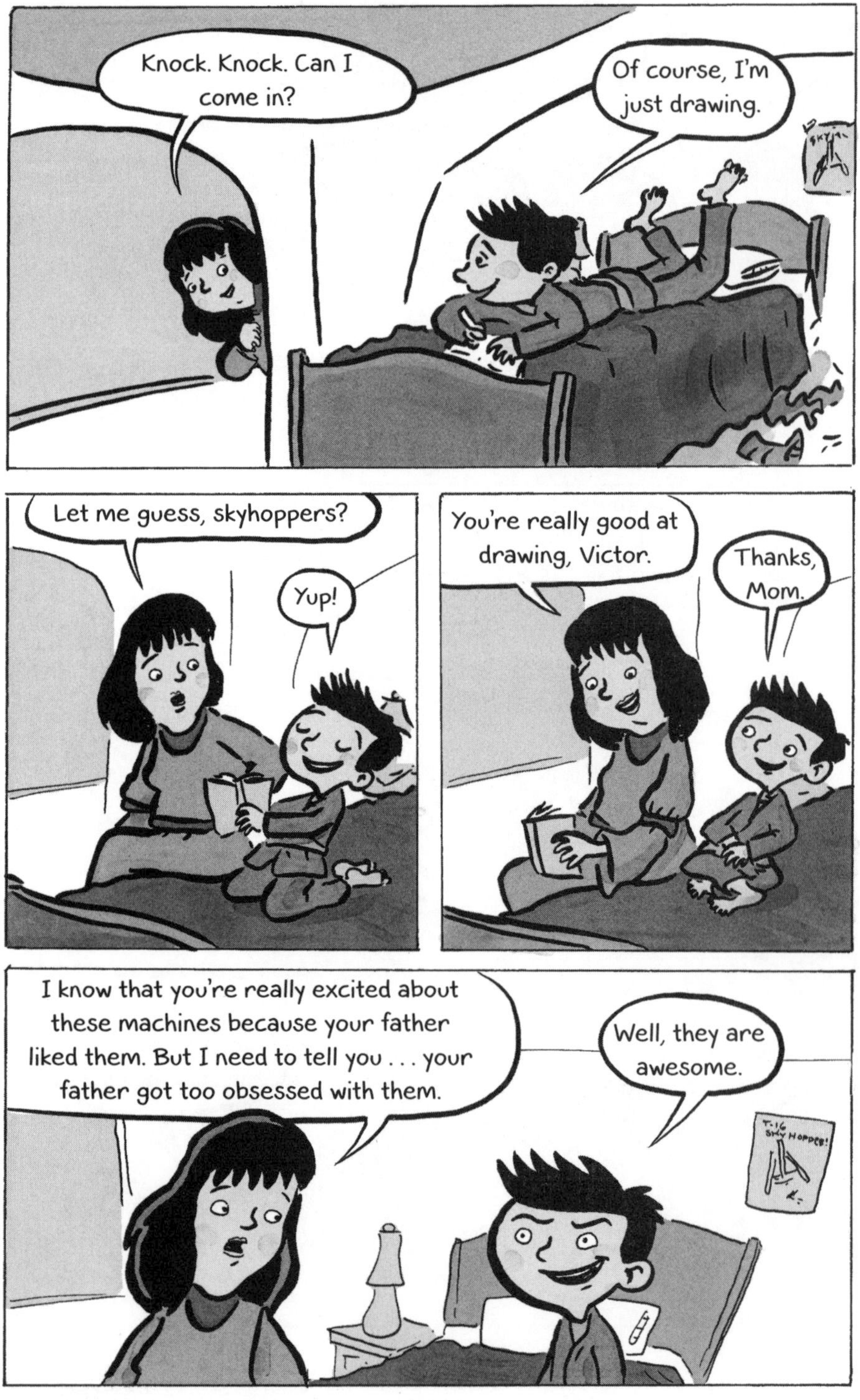
Knock. Knock. Can I come in?
Of course, I'm just drawing.
Let me guess, skyhoppers?
Yup!
You're really good at drawing, Victor.
Thanks, Mom.
I know that you're really excited about these machines because your father liked them. But I need to tell you . . . your father got too obsessed with them.
Well, they are awesome.

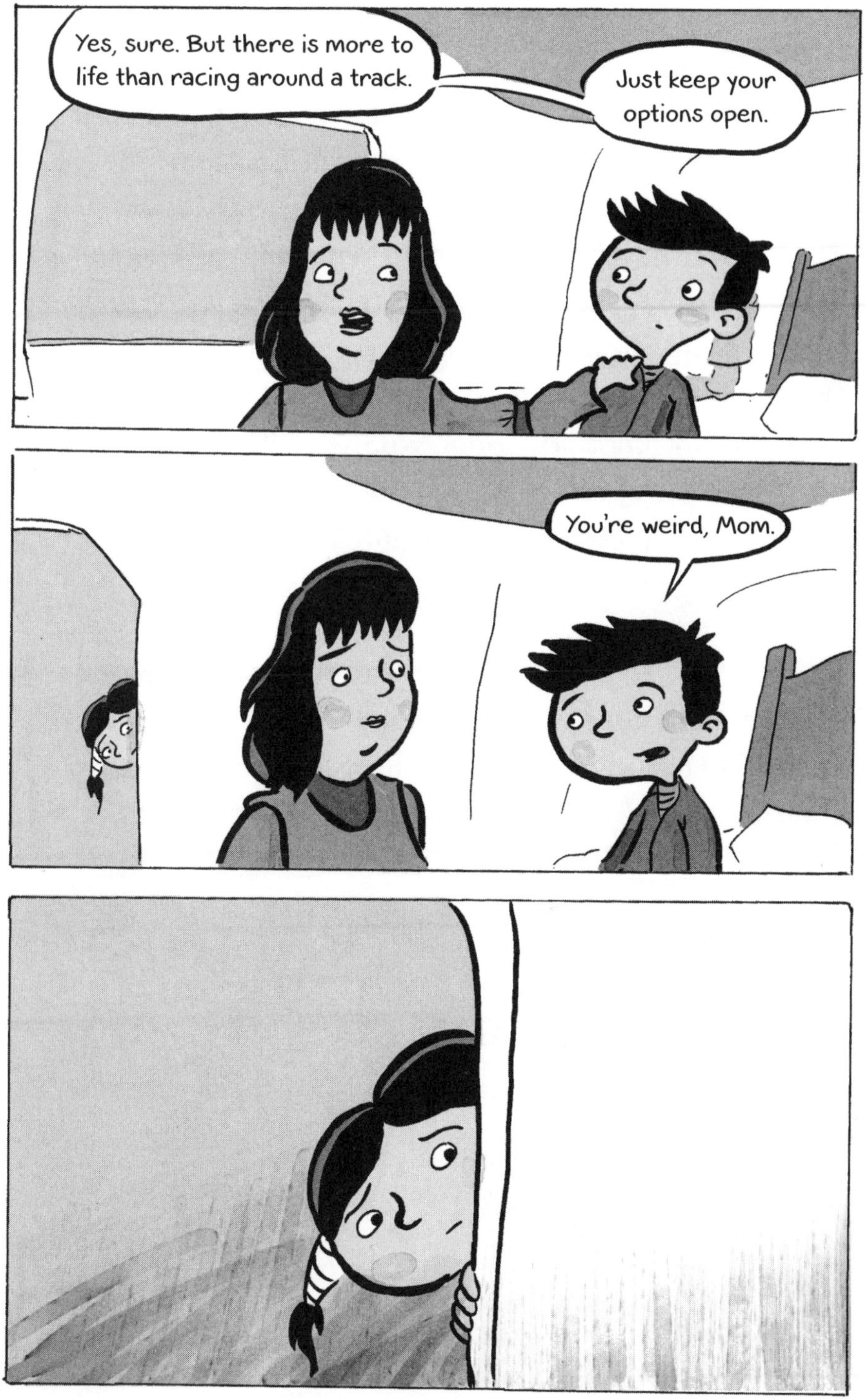
Yes, sure. But there is more to life than racing around a track.
Just keep your options open.
You're weird, Mom.

Heptaday

Vacation came and went, and it was time to travel back to Jedi Academy. Christina was so aloof the entire time we were home, even more than usual. She didn't even have any holochats with her girlfriends from school. Eavesdropping on those chats are usually my favorite things about being home with Christina. My sister's older friends are mysterious beings. Any time I asked Christina what was up, she just ignored me completely. Even here, on the flight back, she is keeping her lips sealed. I thought about what Yoda said, about needing to talk to somebody to get your feelings out. I wish I knew what she was bottling up. And I wish she would talk to me. And since she has made it abundantly clear that she's not interested in hearing about those T-16 skyhoppers, I opened up a program on my datapad that makes fart noises. If you can't help your sister, annoy her!

BWOP!

PFFFFT

The Padawan Observer

EDITED BY THE STUDENTS OF JEDI ACADEMY Vol. MXVI #5

EXCITING DAYS AHEAD!

Who is ready for a fresh start in the new semester? We here at *The Padawan Observer* are excited about a lot of fantastic events that are coming up at Jedi Academy. The annual alumni weekend is around the corner. So don't be surprised if some middle-aged Jedi are really excited to see their old dorms. As Yoda says, "Nostalgia is strong with these former students." If you haven't already signed up for the annual Lightsaber Tournament, be sure to see Mr. Zefyr before week's end.

What are you most looking forward to in the lightsaber tournament?

"The lightsabers."
-Victor, 2nd year

"Meeting the alumni."
-Nara, 3rd year

"Waaargh!"
-Kitmum, P.E.

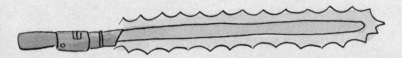

ASK MS. CATARA!

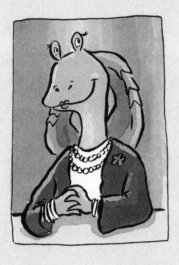

Dear Ms. Catara,

Longtime reader, first time writer. I consider myself pretty tough, but my spirits are down. My friends have been super mean to me. They don't include me in things, and I'm pretty sure that they are saying mean things behind my back. I can't even deal. But how do I deal?

Signed,
Perplexed Padawan

Dearza Perplexed Padawan,

My, my, my. It a sounds like youza gots yourself a tough situation. I says, it's a big school, and youza should find yourself new friends. It is not fair for anybody to be spreading lies about youza. Youza should report them to a teacher, or come see me in the guidance office.

I am a here to helps!
Xo,
Ms. Catara

HELP WANTED

LOOKING FOR EXTRA CASH? PART-TIME DISHWASHER NEEDED. GARY JETTSTER COULD USE A FEW EXTRA HANDS. PLEASE SEE HIM IN THE CAFETERIA IF INTERESTED.

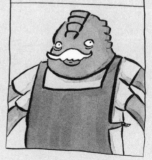

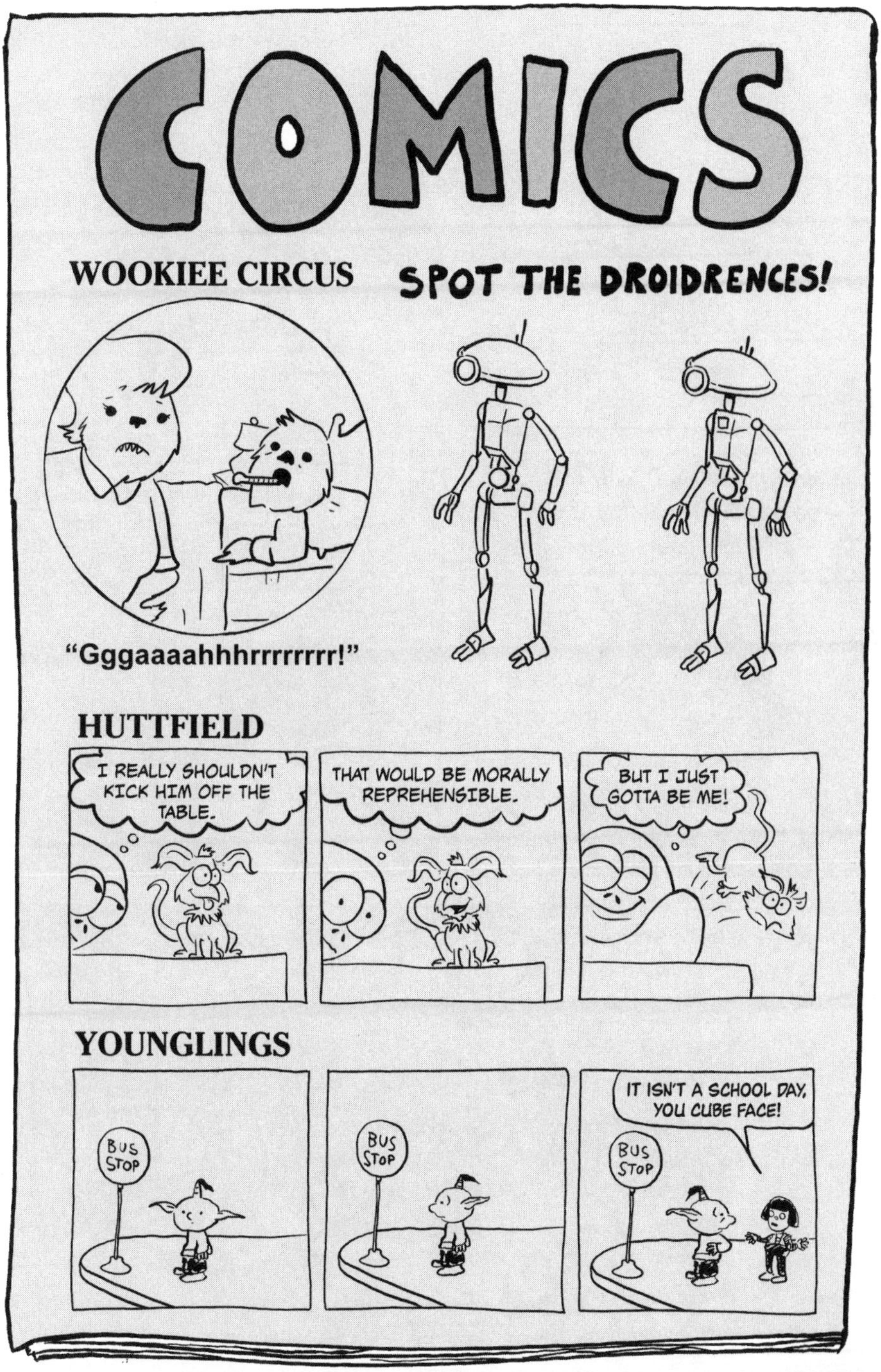

COMICS
WOOKIEE CIRCUS
"Gggaaaahhhrrrrrr!"
SPOT THE DROIDRENCES!
HUTTFIELD
I REALLY SHOULDN'T KICK HIM OFF THE TABLE.
THAT WOULD BE MORALLY REPREHENSIBLE.
BUT I JUST GOTTA BE ME!
YOUNGLINGS
BUS STOP
BUS STOP
BUS STOP
IT ISN'T A SCHOOL DAY, YOU CUBE FACE!

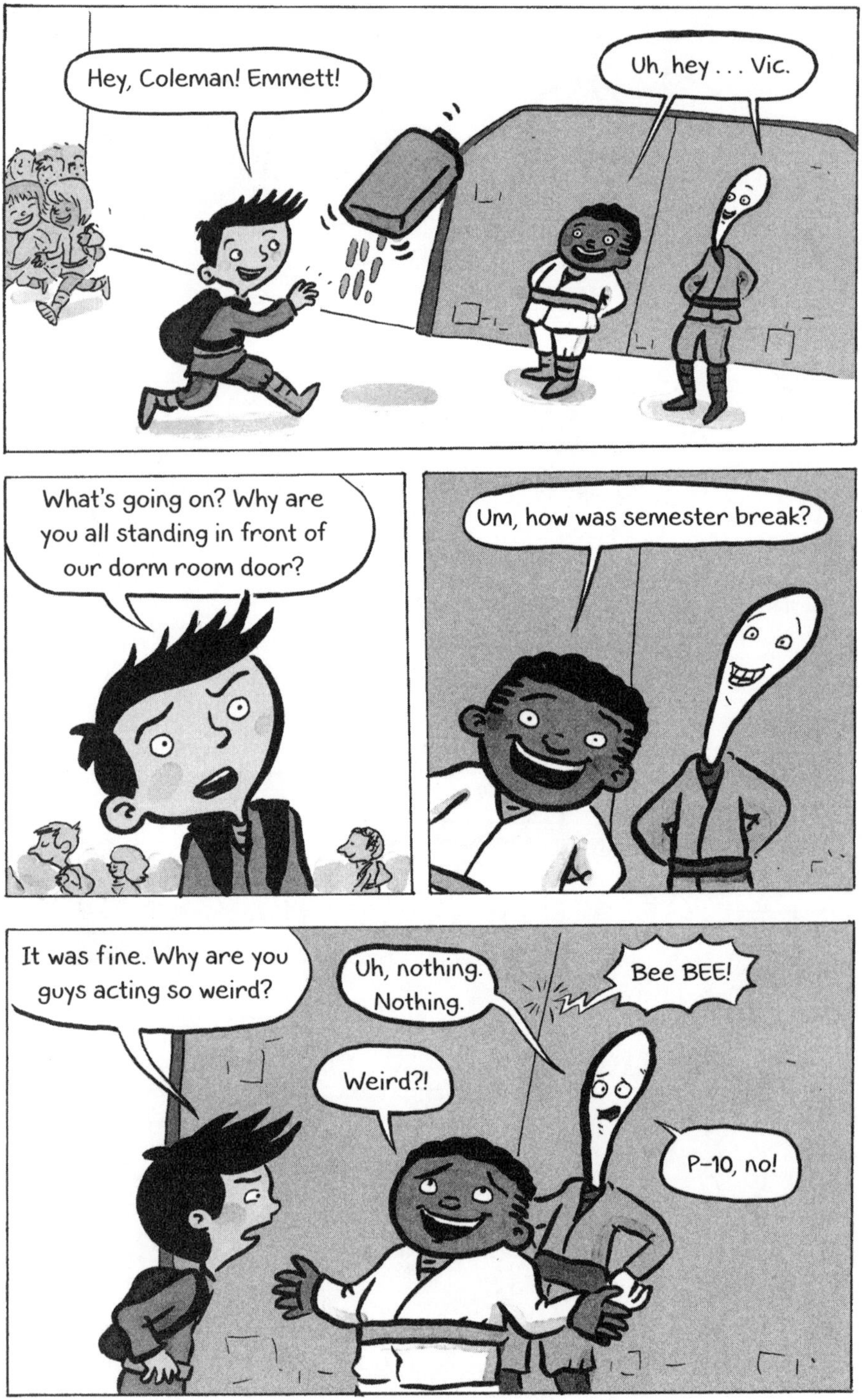
Hey, Coleman! Emmett!
Uh, hey . . . Vic.
What's going on? Why are you all standing in front of our dorm room door?
Um, how was semester break?
It was fine. Why are you guys acting so weird?
Uh, nothing. Nothing.
Bee BEE!
Weird?!
P-10, no!

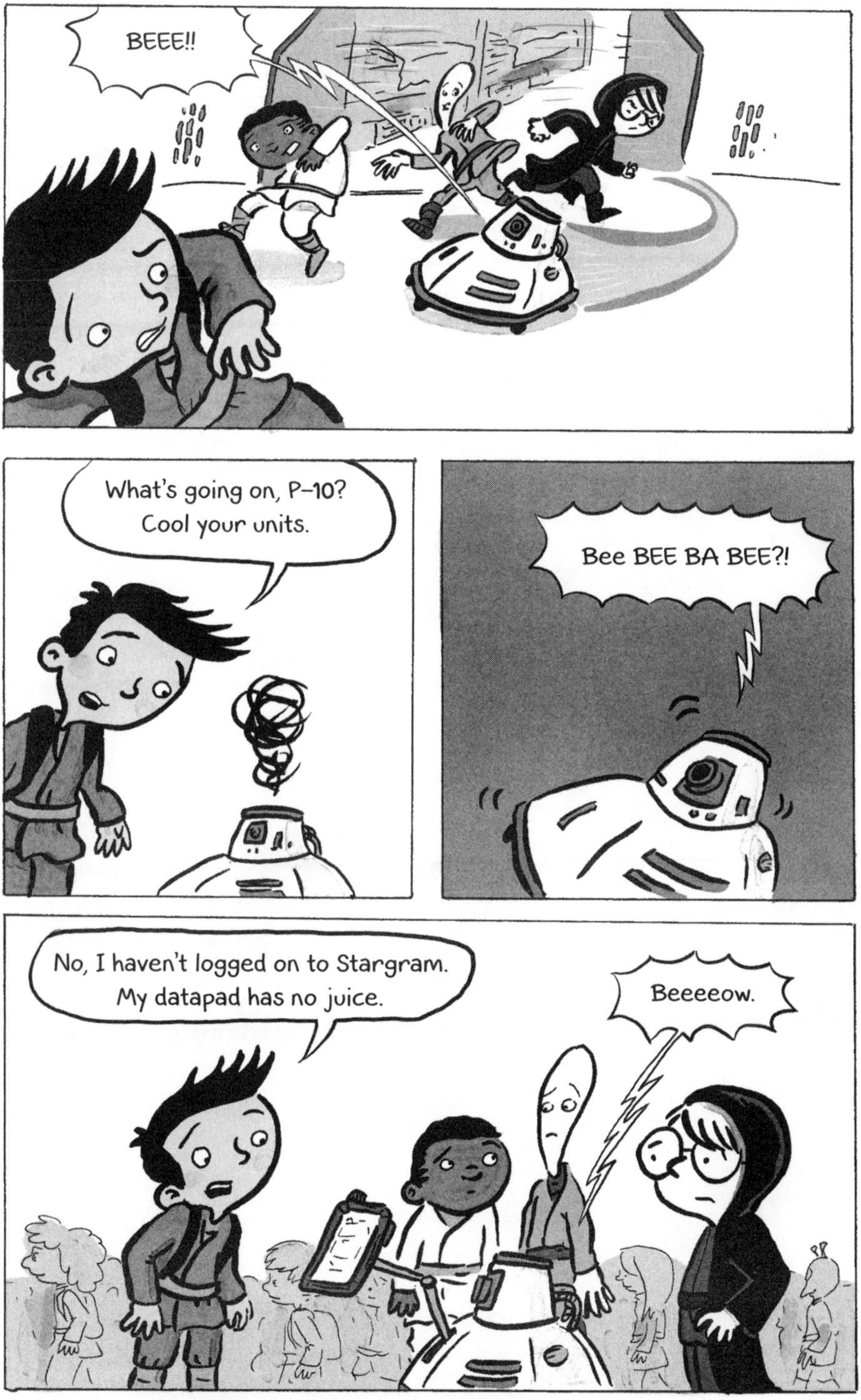
BEEE!!
What's going on, P-10? Cool your units.
Bee BEE BA BEE?!
No, I haven't logged on to Stargram. My datapad has no juice.
Beeeeow.

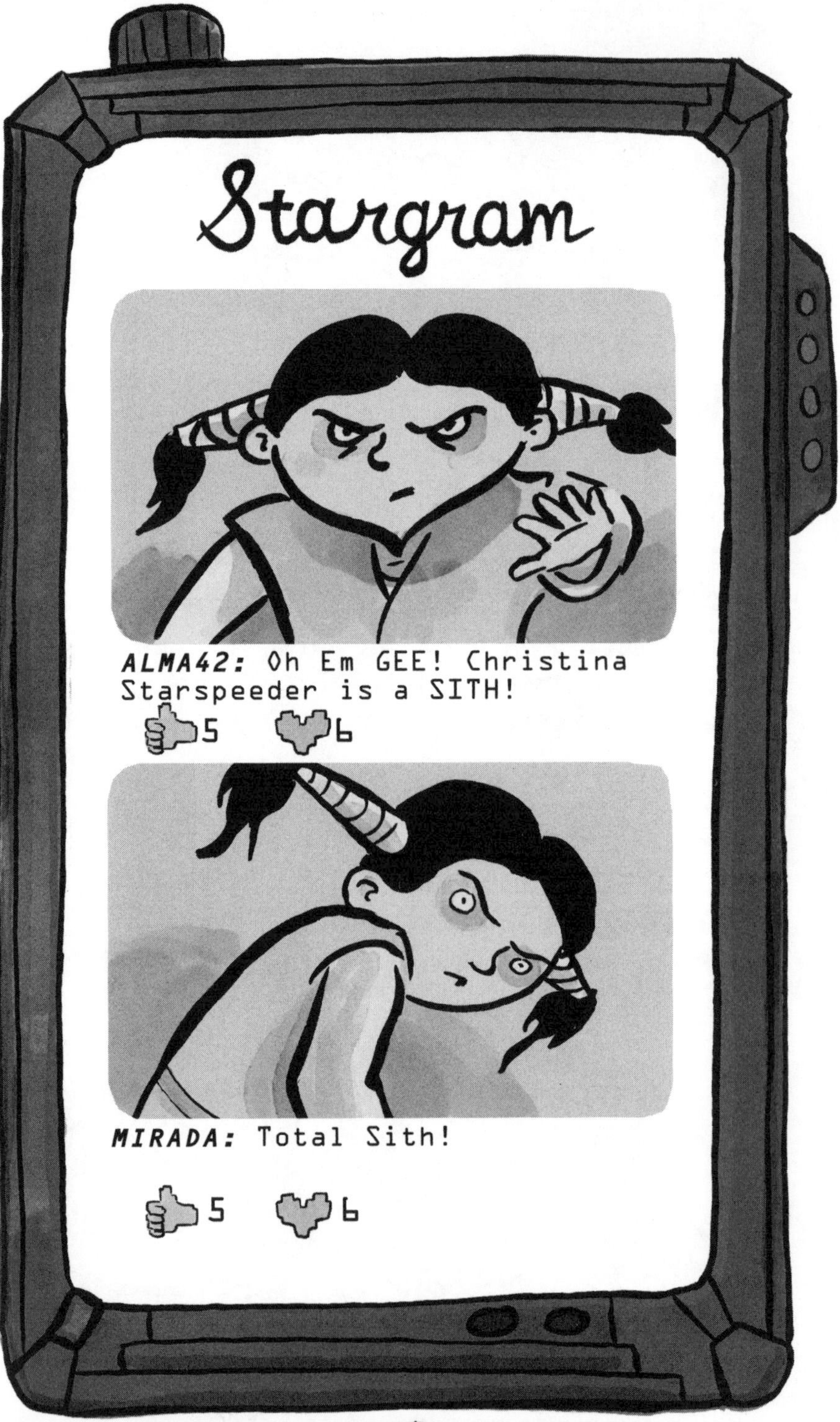
Stargram
ALMA42: Oh Em GEE! Christina Starspeeder is a SITH!
5
6
MIRADA: Total Sith!
5
6

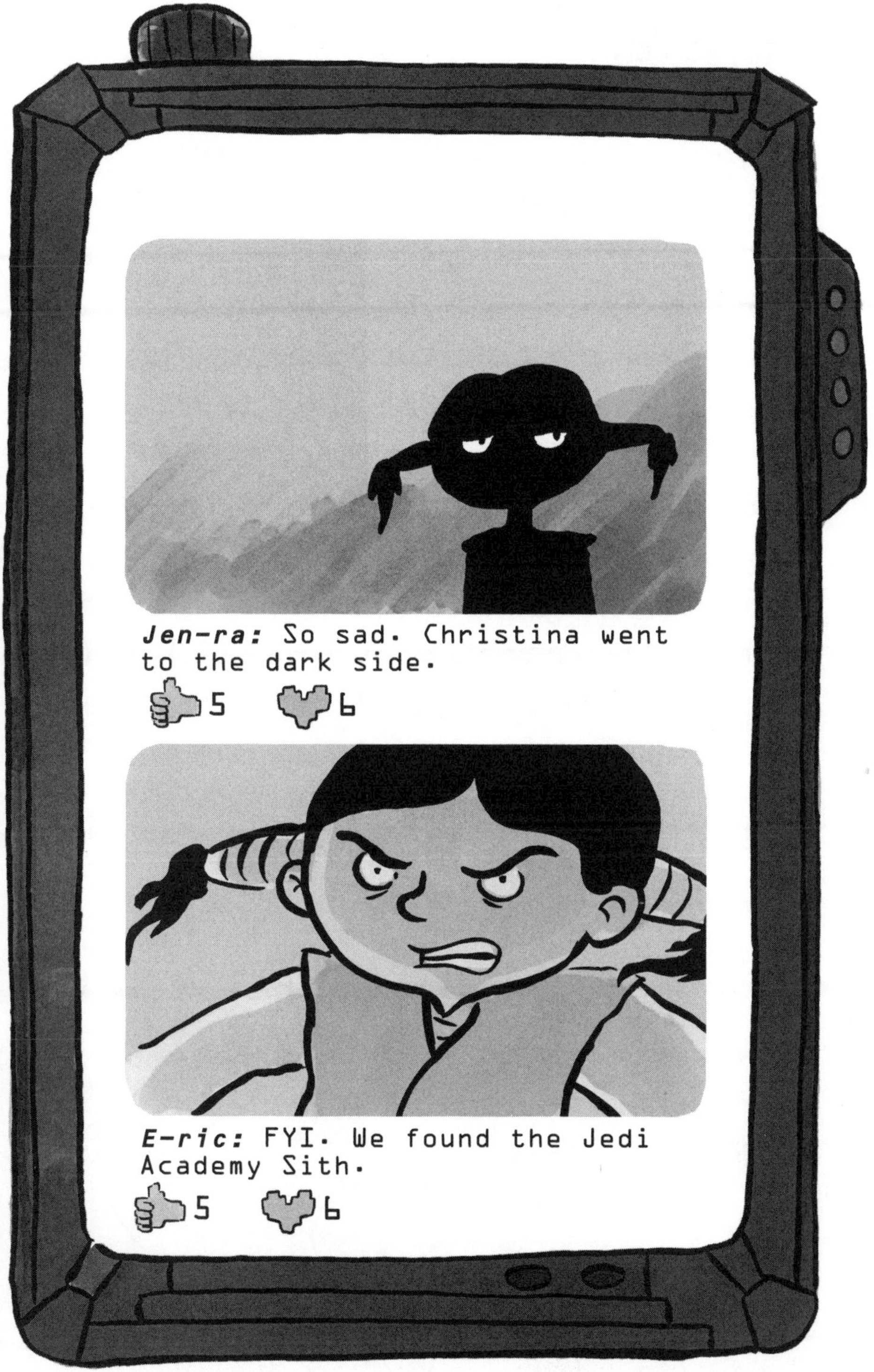
Jen-ra: So sad. Christina went to the dark side.
5 6
E-ric: FYI. We found the Jedi Academy Sith.
5 6

Monoday

I could not believe what P-10 showed me on Stargram. How could Christina's friends be so mean? What happened last semester to make her friendships fall apart like this? My sister is not a Sith! She can be tough on me, sure. I tease her about the Dork Side, yes. But she doesn't have a dark bone in her body. I can see why my friends were trying to protect me from these posts, but if my sister is being cyberbullied, I want to know about it! I was determined to get to the bottom of it. I headed down to her dorm room, even though P-10 tried to stop me. He thought it best I wait to calm down a bit. I ran to Christina's dorm with P-10 rolling behind me. Christina's so-called friends weren't around and neither was she. I closed my eyes and cleared my mind as best I could and searched my feelings. The gym. She was working off some steam, I was sure of it.

Force-sensitive siblings have a special connection.

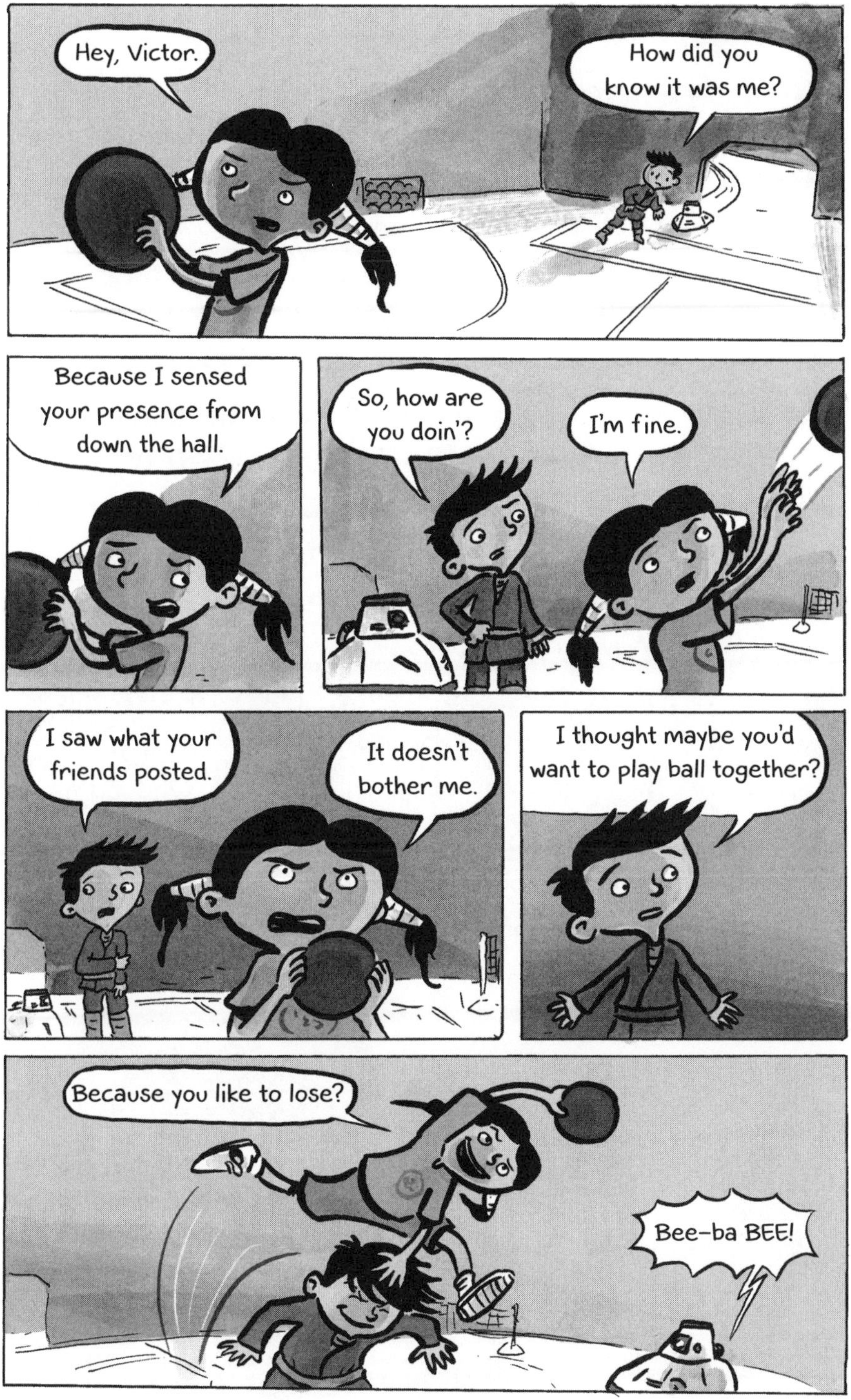
Hey, Victor.
How did you know it was me?
Because I sensed your presence from down the hall.
So, how are you doin'?
I'm fine.
I saw what your friends posted.
It doesn't bother me.
I thought maybe you'd want to play ball together?
Because you like to lose?
Bee-ba BEE!

Duoday

Artemis and I were on our way to Drama Club when I couldn't help but feel that people were looking at me differently in the hallway. They'd get all quiet when we walked by and then whisper when we passed. I'd hear things like, "Did you hear about his sister?" and "That's the Sith's younger brother." Those holos posted to Stargram were starting to go viral around school and people were falling for it! It made me think of how I treated Artemis at the beginning of last year. It was so unfair of me to make assumptions about him based on my perceptions. Now, I truly know how rotten it feels when people pass around rumors. When we arrived at Drama Club, everyone was chattering away, but fell silent at the sight of me. Then they avoided eye contact. That was awkward. Are my friends all falling for this garbage? The only person who came right up to me was Zavyer. He gave me a big high five and we looked over our sketches for the set design. We have to make a giant sarlacc puppet. It's going to be a challenge, but it will be a good distraction from all the messiness.

Yoda sent out holomail to every student at Jedi Academy. I guess those Stargrams made it to the faculty.

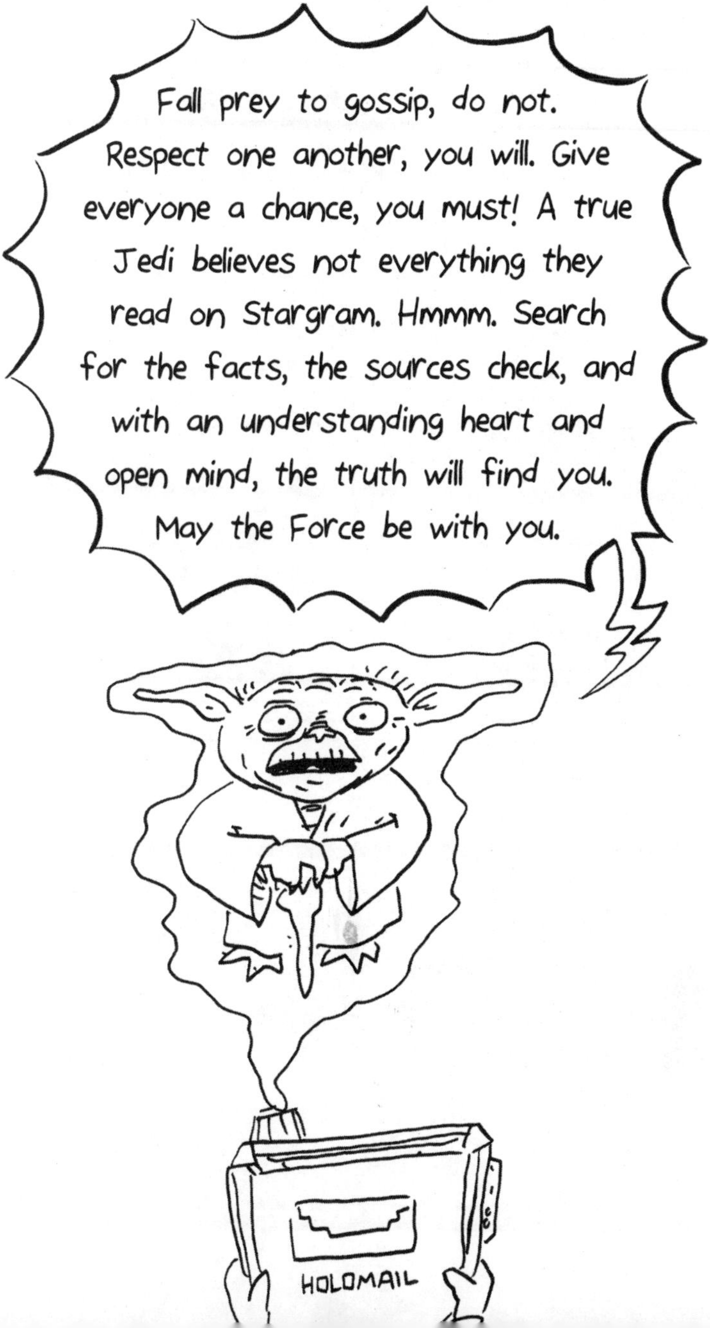
Fall prey to gossip, do not. Respect one another, you will. Give everyone a chance, you must! A true Jedi believes not everything they read on Stargram. Hmmm. Search for the facts, the sources check, and with an understanding heart and open mind, the truth will find you. May the Force be with you.
HOLOMAIL

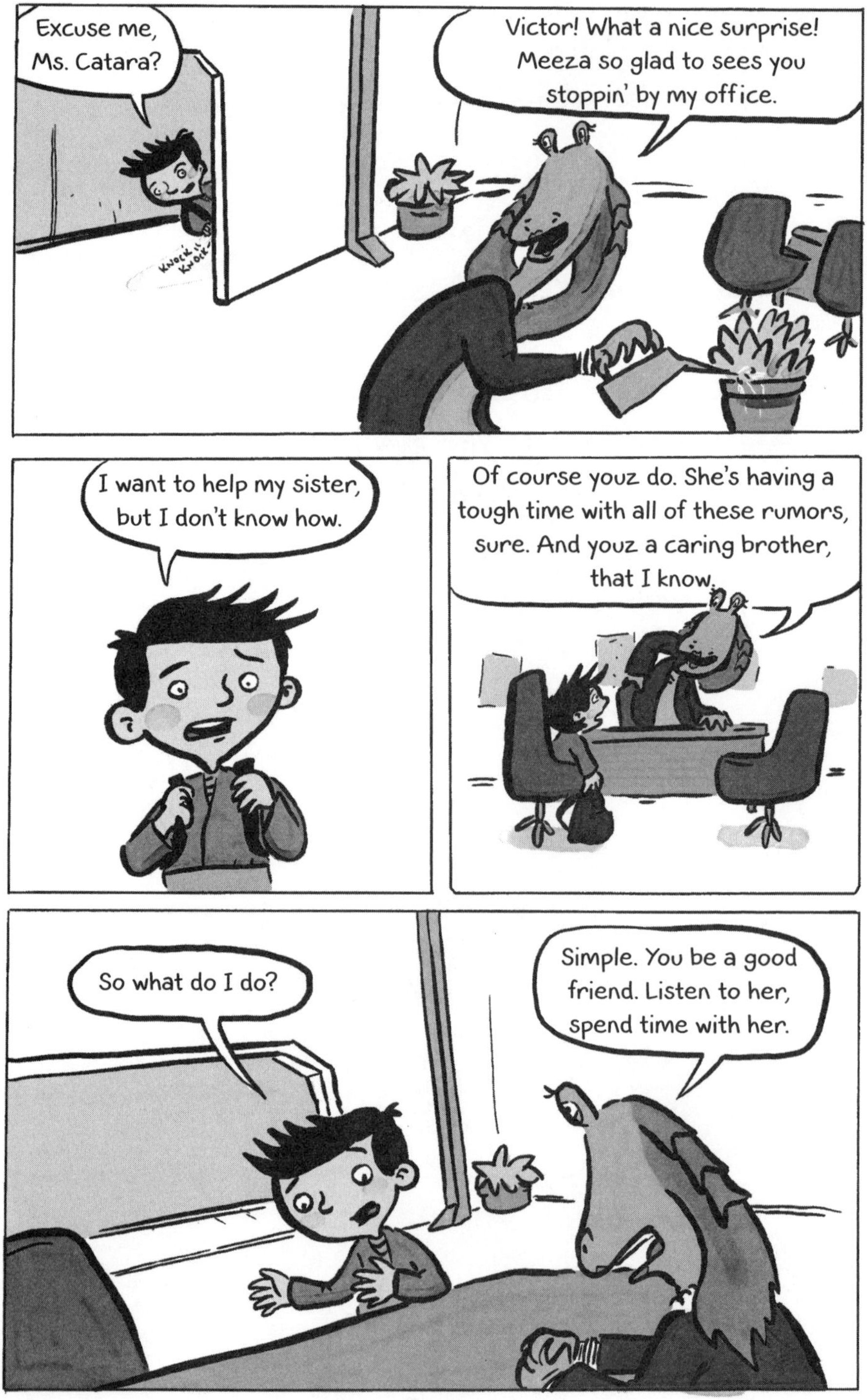
Excuse me, Ms. Catara?
KNOCK KNOCK
Victor! What a nice surprise! Meeza so glad to sees you stoppin' by my office.
I want to help my sister, but I don't know how.
Of course youz do. She's having a tough time with all of these rumors, sure. And youz a caring brother, that I know.
So what do I do?
Simple. You be a good friend. Listen to her, spend time with her.

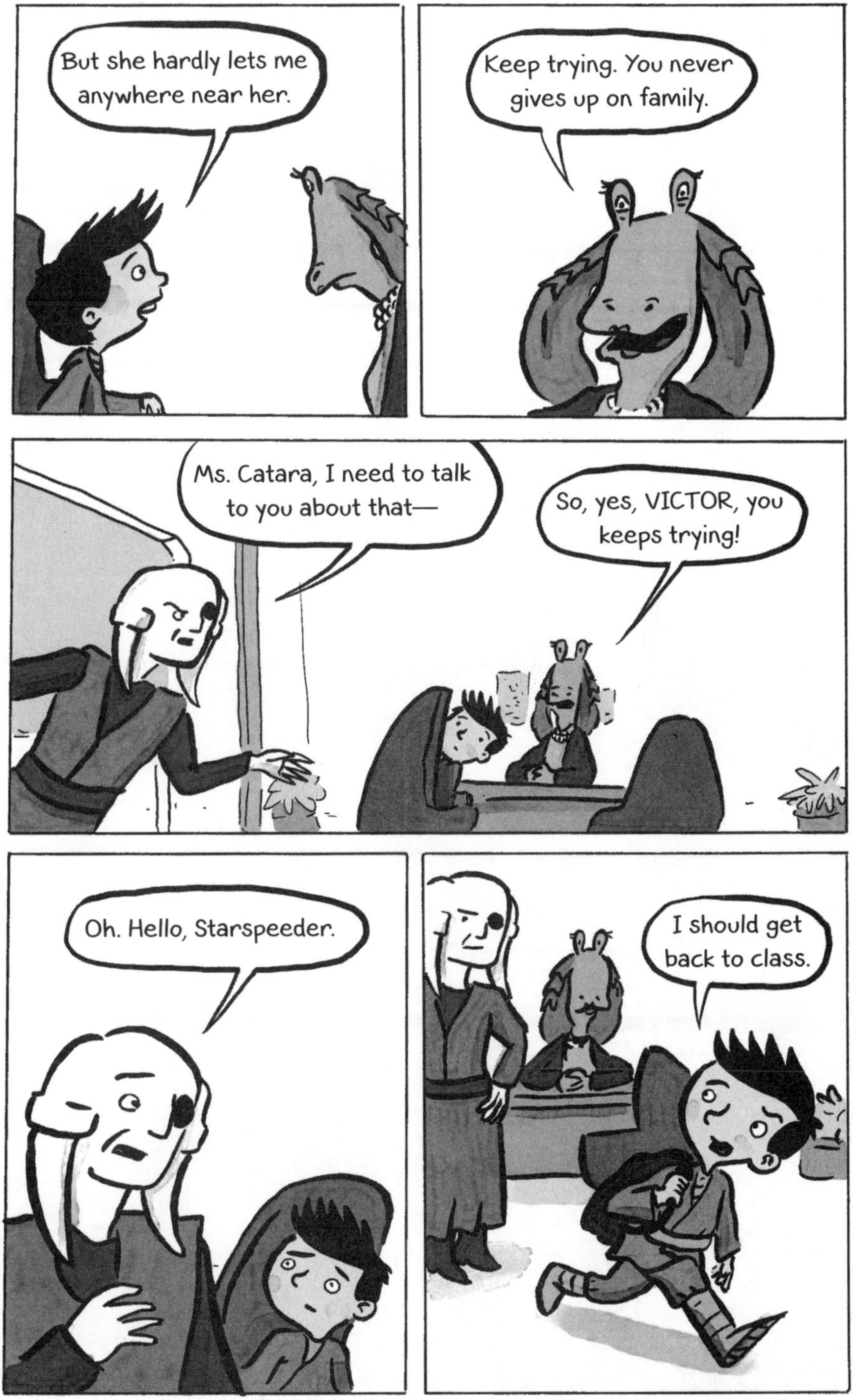
But she hardly lets me anywhere near her.
Keep trying. You never gives up on family.
Ms. Catara, I need to talk to you about that—
So, yes, VICTOR, you keeps trying!
Oh. Hello, Starspeeder.
I should get back to class.

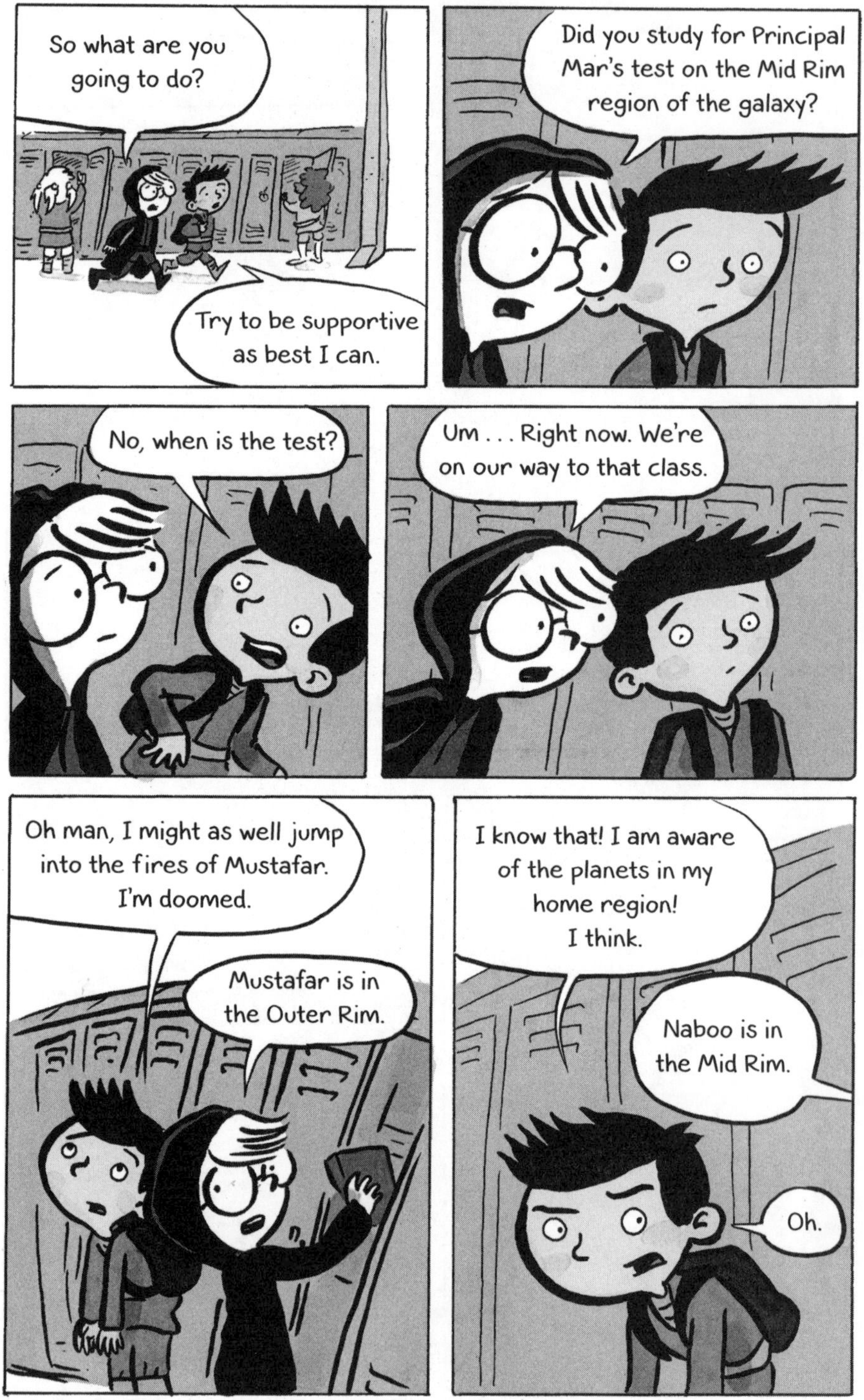
So what are you going to do?
Try to be supportive as best I can.
Did you study for Principal Mar's test on the Mid Rim region of the galaxy?
No, when is the test?
Um . . . Right now. We're on our way to that class.
Oh man, I might as well jump into the fires of Mustafar. I'm doomed.
Mustafar is in the Outer Rim.
I know that! I am aware of the planets in my home region! I think.
Naboo is in the Mid Rim.
Oh.

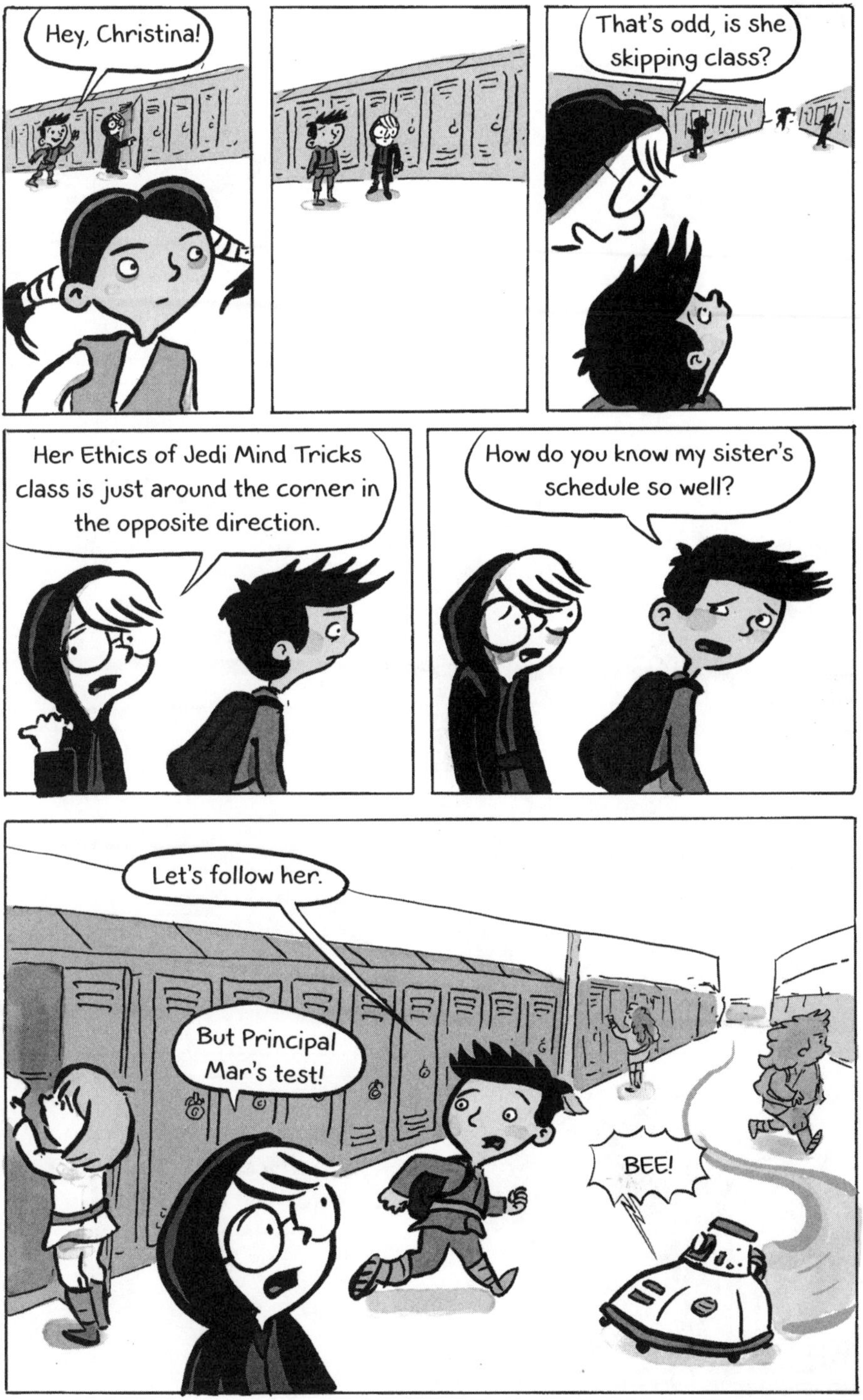
Hey, Christina!
That's odd, is she skipping class?
Her Ethics of Jedi Mind Tricks class is just around the corner in the opposite direction.
How do you know my sister's schedule so well?
Let's follow her.
But Principal Mar's test!
BEE!

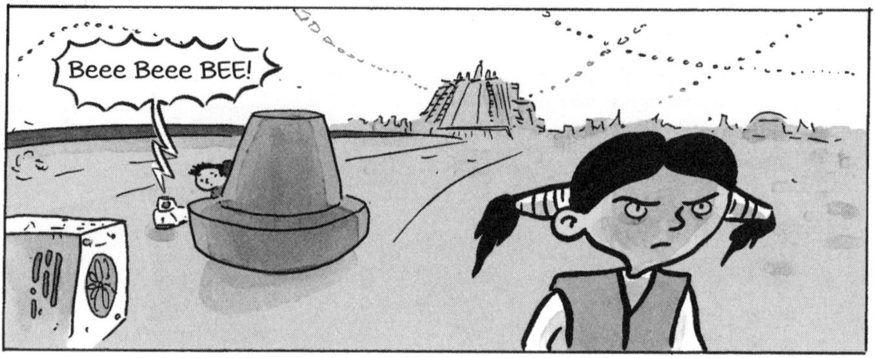
Beee Beee BEE!

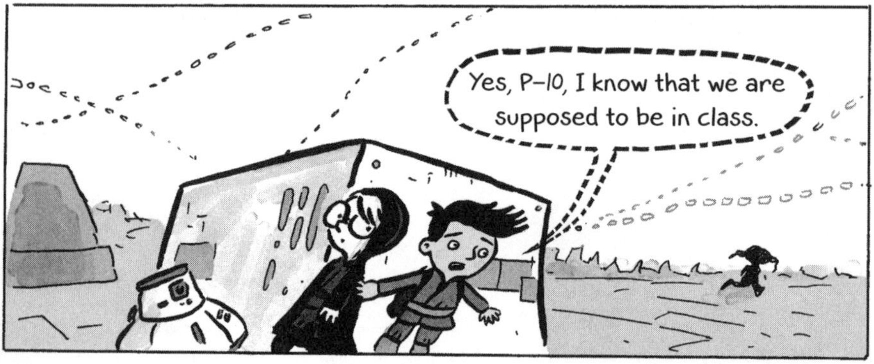
Yes, P-10, I know that we are supposed to be in class.

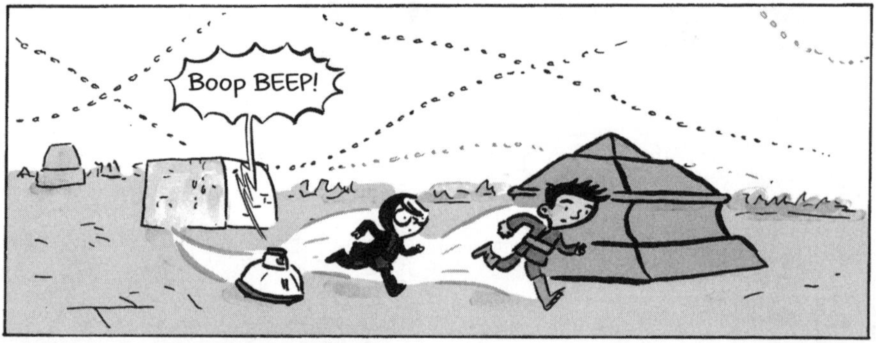
Boop BEEP!

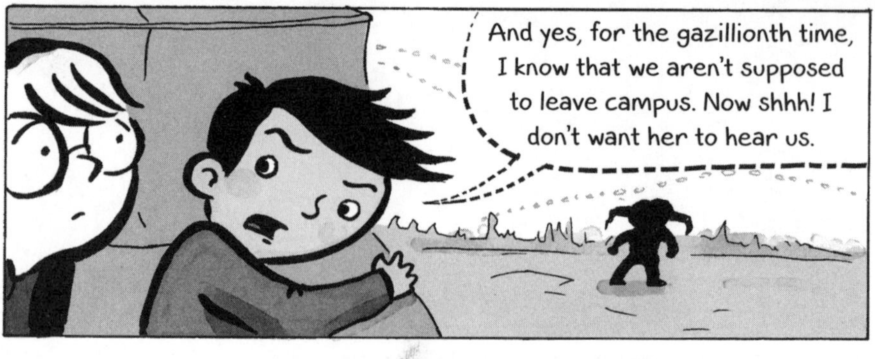
And yes, for the gazillionth time, I know that we aren't supposed to leave campus. Now shhh! I don't want her to hear us.

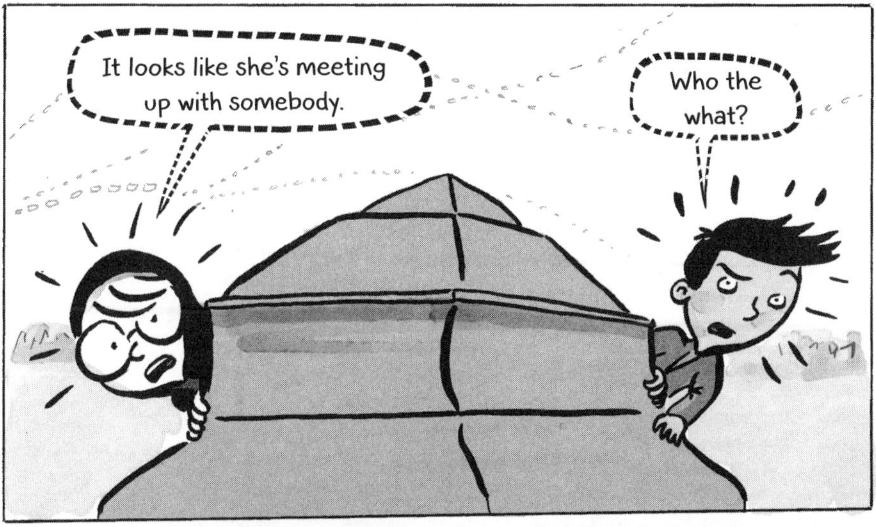
It looks like she's meeting up with somebody.
Who the what?

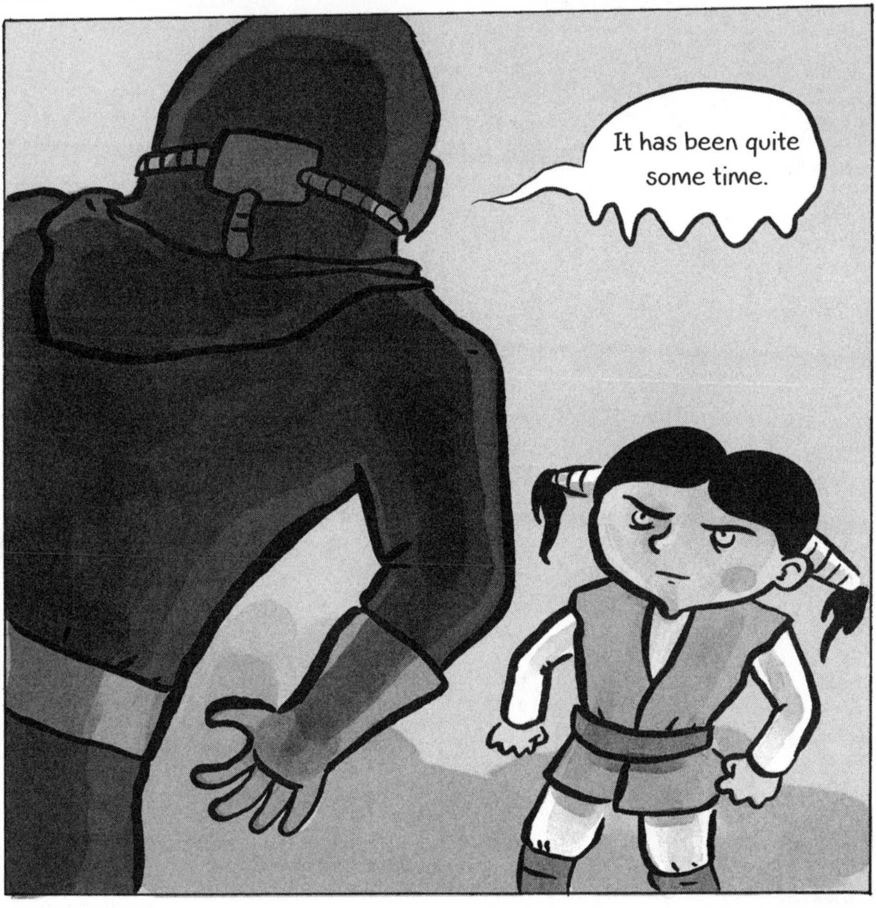
It has been quite some time.

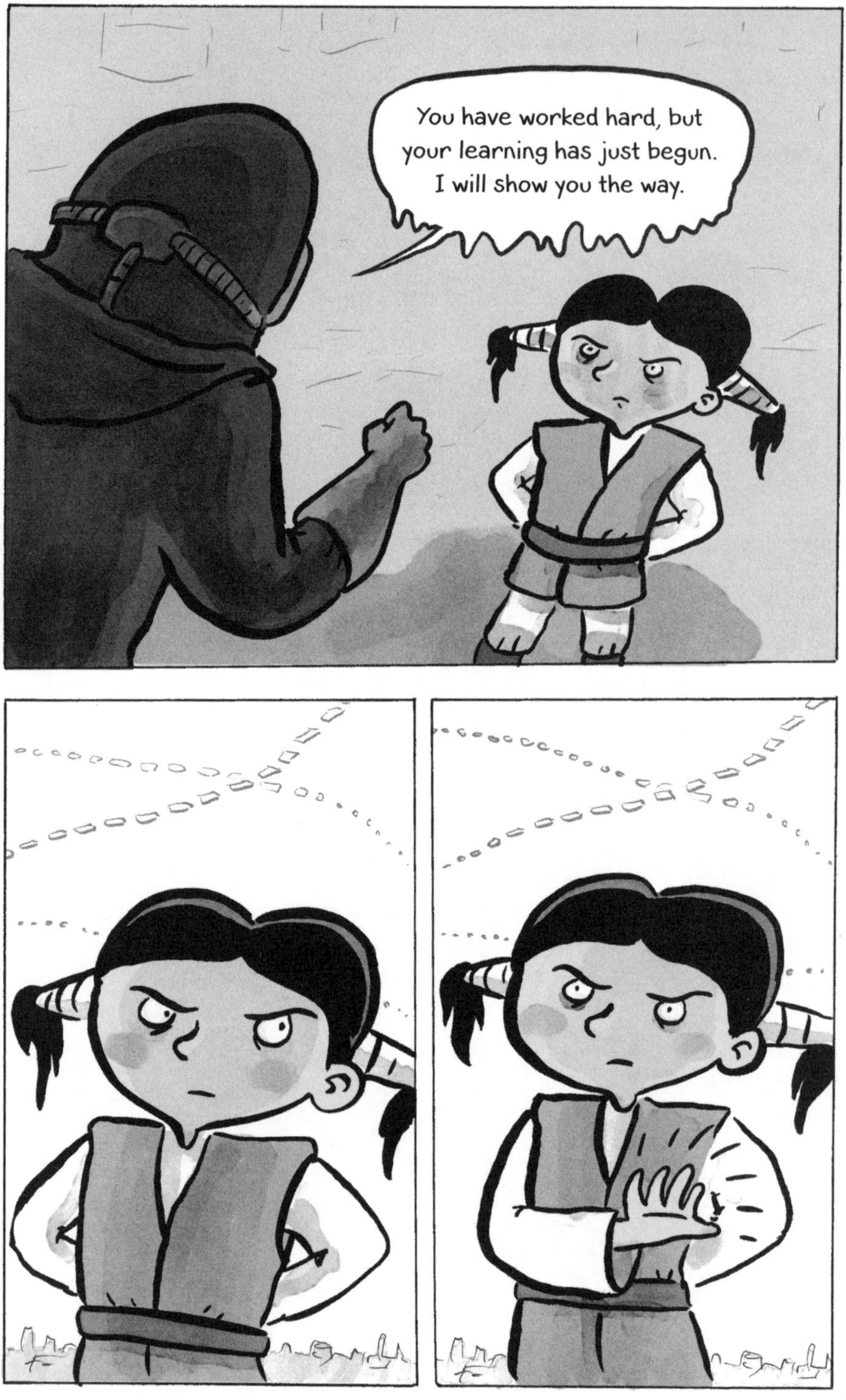
You have worked hard, but your learning has just begun. I will show you the way.

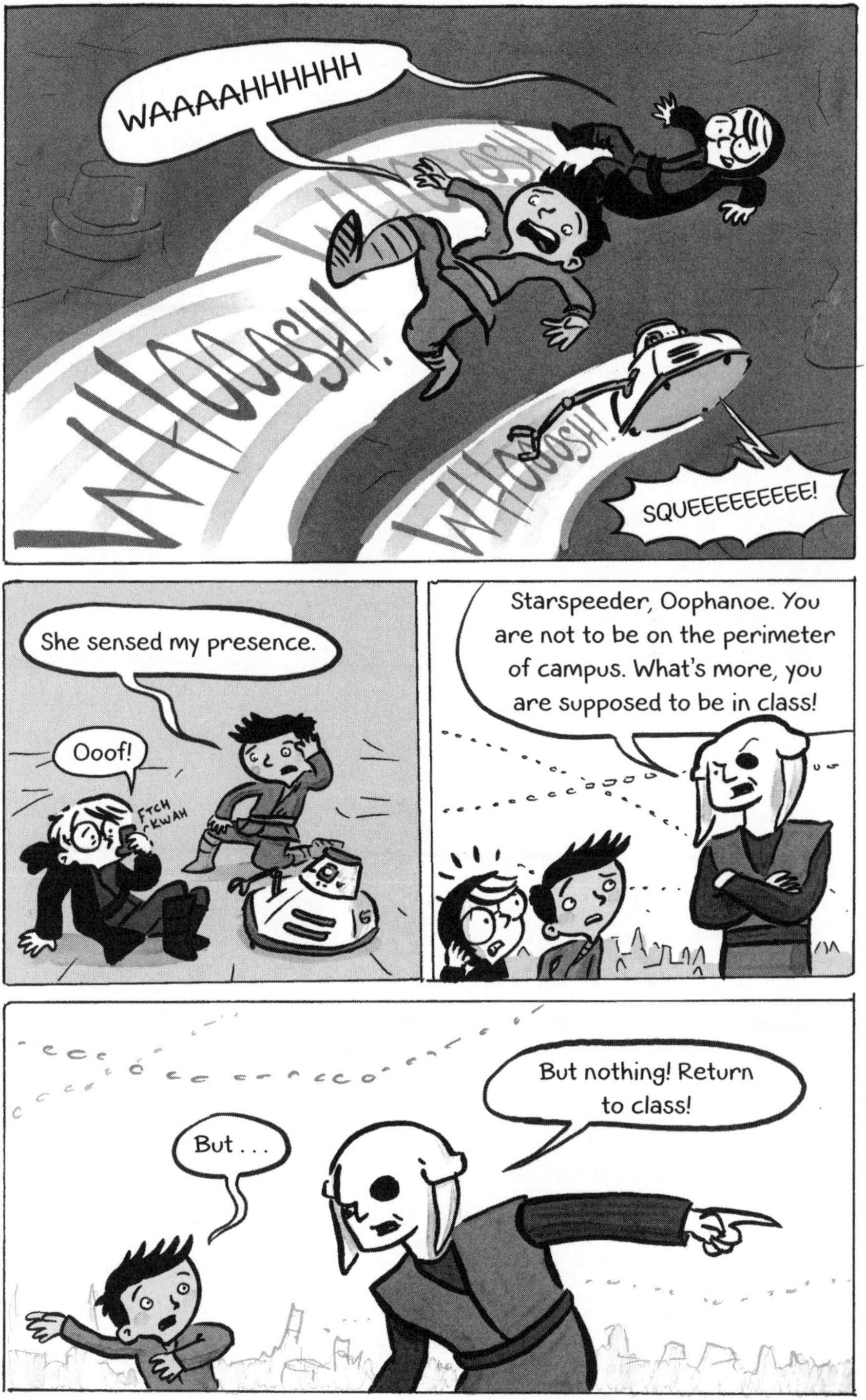
WAAAAHHHHH
WHOOSH!
WHOOSH!
SQUEEEEEEEEEE!
She sensed my presence.
Ooof!
FTCH
KWAH
Starspeeder, Oophanoe. You are not to be on the perimeter of campus. What's more, you are supposed to be in class!
But . . .
But nothing! Return to class!

Quadday

Mr. Zefyr said that he was going to be charitable with us and not punish us for wandering so far away. I think that he only did that because Artemis was with me. If it was just me, I'm sure Mr. Zefyr would have gladly given me detention for the rest of the year. As hard as I tried, I couldn't explain to Mr. Zefyr why we were there. He's always made it clear that he does not want to hear excuses, he wants to see action. But I'm so sad right now, journal. Because you know what? I think that my sister is collaborating with a legit Sith. I know that she sensed my presence and then used the Force to shoo Artemis and me away. She's gotten real STRONG. I mean, Artemis, me, AND P-10, that's a lot of weight to move, and to do so without even really looking?

I don't even know what to think anymore. It's like my world has been flipped upside down. Could all of those rumors be true? Christina Starspeeder—on the way to the dark side? I just can't even. And if she is walking down a dark path, how do I stop her?

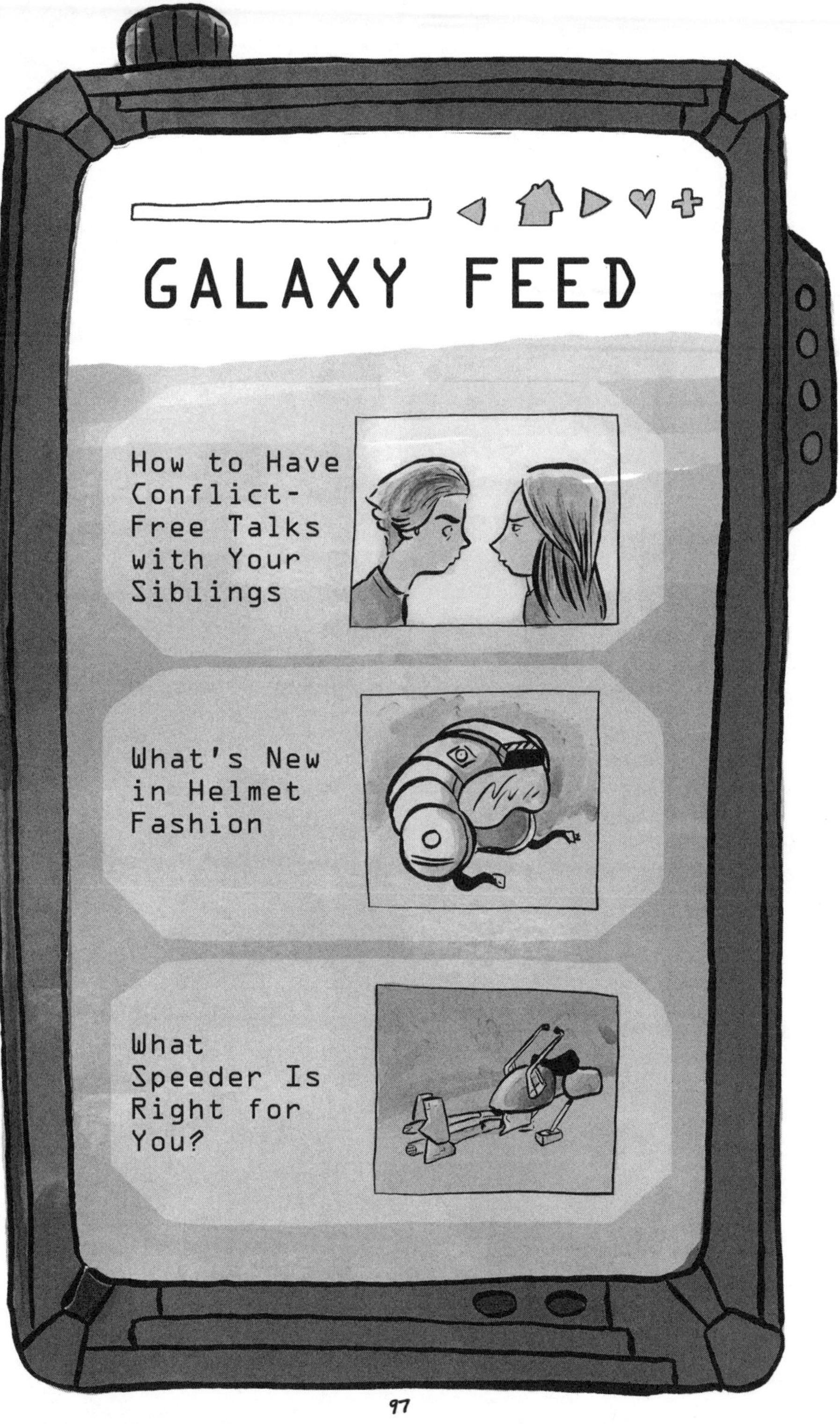
GALAXY FEED
How to Have Conflict-Free Talks with Your Siblings
What's New in Helmet Fashion
What Speeder Is Right for You?

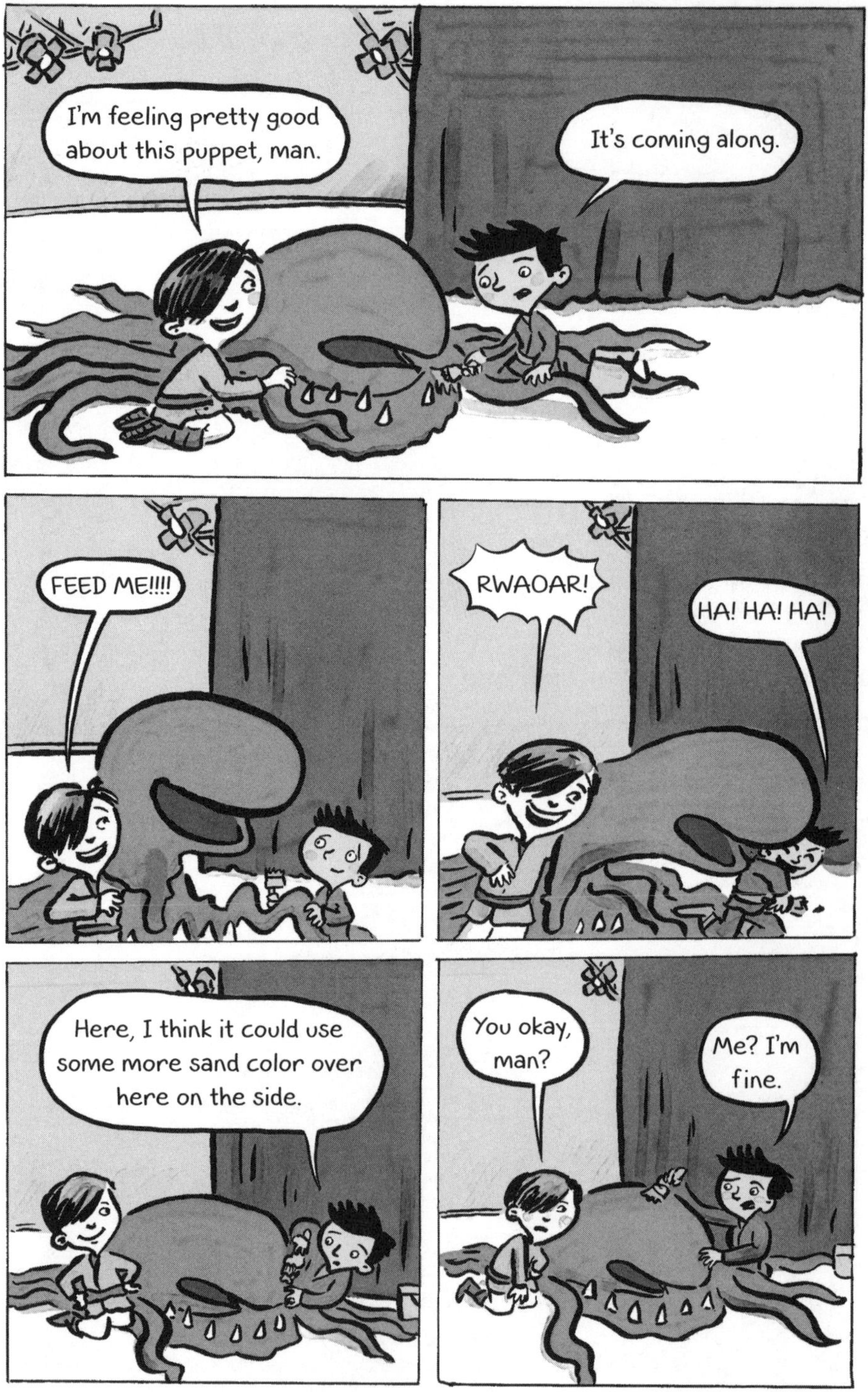
I'm feeling pretty good about this puppet, man.
It's coming along.
FEED ME!!!!
RWAOAR!
HA! HA! HA!
Here, I think it could use some more sand color over here on the side.
You okay, man?
Me? I'm fine.

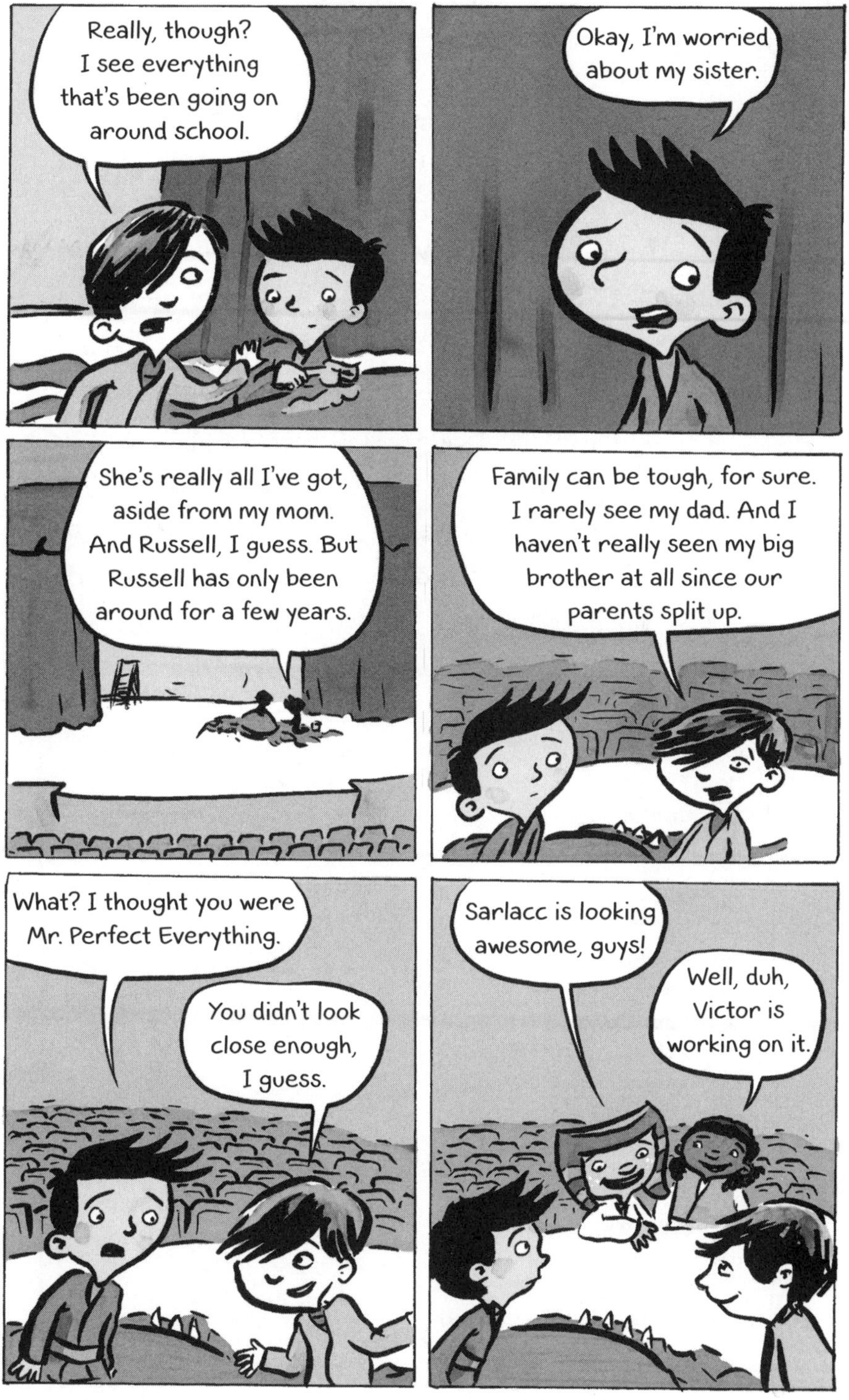
Really, though? I see everything that's been going on around school.
Okay, I'm worried about my sister.
She's really all I've got, aside from my mom. And Russell, I guess. But Russell has only been around for a few years.
Family can be tough, for sure. I rarely see my dad. And I haven't really seen my big brother at all since our parents split up.
What? I thought you were Mr. Perfect Everything.
You didn't look close enough, I guess.
Sarlacc is looking awesome, guys!
Well, duh, Victor is working on it.

Hexaday

I am running out of things to say to kids in the hallway who ask me about Christina. I continue to stick up for her, but it's hard to when I'm starting to believe that maybe they're right and I'm wrong. What happened? Was she angry that Dad was gone? Was she bored with her schoolwork? She's the smartest person I know. Ms. Catara told me that as much as I wanted to help, I also needed to focus on my studies. Principal Mar was not too pleased that I had skipped out on the test, yet he didn't even give me a detention. He did make me take the test that same day, so I still didn't get to study. Unless my guesses were spot-on, I probably flunked.

What species is indigenous to Kashyyyk?
A) Ewoks
B) Gungans
C) Wookiees
D) Hutts

This peaceful planet is known for its picturesque landscapes.
A) Trandosha
B) Ithor
C) Naboo
D) Bespin

This planet serves as a connector between the Outer and Inner Rims.
A) Ord Mantell
B) Glee Anslem
C) Iridonia
D) None of the Above

When in doubt, select C!

Mr. Zefyr pulled me aside in Lightsaber Dueling class and said that while he appreciated my enthusiasm, I needed to remain calm, especially in the midst of a lightsaber duel. Apparently, I freaked out Emmett, which I guess isn't saying much—he is startled easily. But Mr. Zefyr sensed the rage boiling within me. "Save that aggression for Kitmum's sports games," he grumbled. From watching holos about Jedi, I would assume that it was all about aggression, but Mr. Zefyr pointed to a quote from Yoda that he had hanging up on the wall of his classroom.

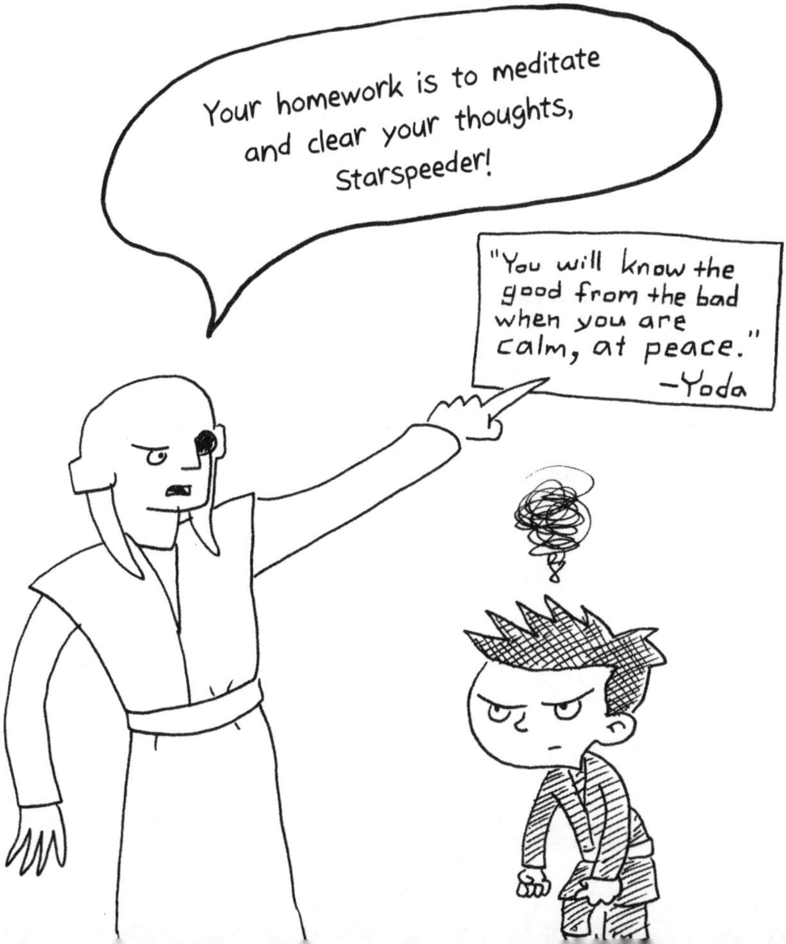
Your homework is to meditate and clear your thoughts, Starspeeder!
"You will know the good from the bad when you are calm, at peace." —Yoda

The Padawan Observer

EDITED BY THE STUDENTS OF JEDI ACADEMY Vol. MXVI #6

ALUMNI WEEKEND BRINGS YOU JEDITALKS!

It's that time of year again! Jedi Academy is so proud to welcome back cherished members of our alumni community. Whether you are celebrating your first reunion or your two hundredth, the students have so much to learn from you. Students, we encourage you to check out some of the wonderful lectures we have lined up for you. All JediTalks will happen in the auditorium unless otherwise noted in the schedule. Students participating in the lightsaber tourney, please see Mr. Zefyr to go over protocol.

WEEKEND HIGHLIGHTS:

-Tour the updates of our cafeteria!

-Meet up with old classmates at the Jedi mixer.

-Shop the Jedi Academy store for official Jedi Academy–branded robes!

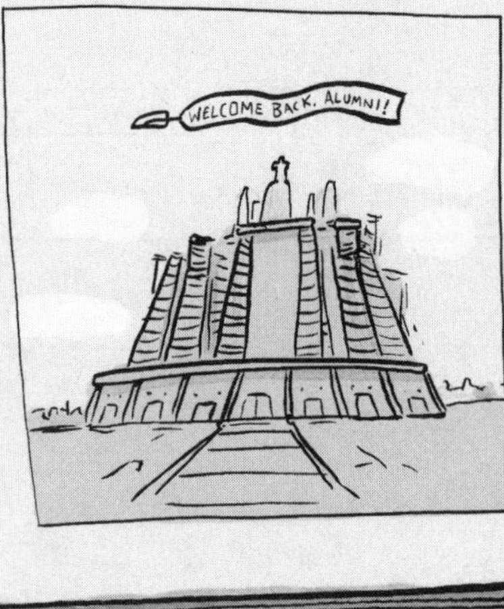
WELCOME BACK, ALUMNI!

JEDITALKS

Schedule

0730
"In My First 600 Years, Learned I Have"
Speaker: Yoda

0830
"Designing Your Destiny"
Speaker: Argo Chum Chum

0930
"Communication Without Lightsabers"
Speaker: Kinstar Badara

1030
"So You Want to Be a Jedi Knight?"
Speaker: Karly Panchoo

1130
"Sensing Beyond Your Senses"
Speaker: Lars Stranom

1230
"Using Jedi Mind Tricks to Affect Change"
Speaker: Okul

1330
"Robes Make Not a Jedi Great"
Speaker: Kwon Lee

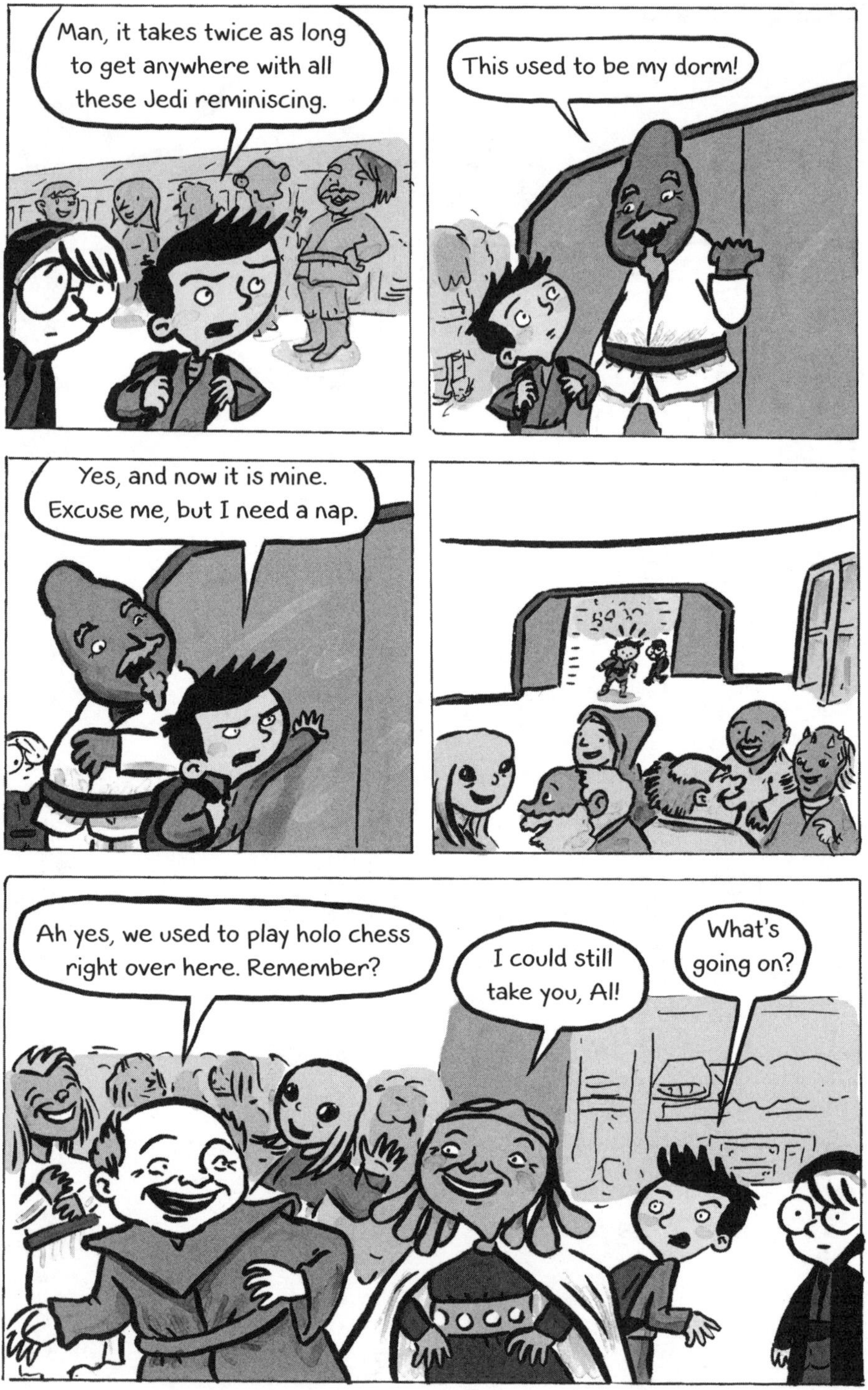
Man, it takes twice as long to get anywhere with all these Jedi reminiscing.
This used to be my dorm!
Yes, and now it is mine. Excuse me, but I need a nap.
Ah yes, we used to play holo chess right over here. Remember?
I could still take you, Al!
What's going on?

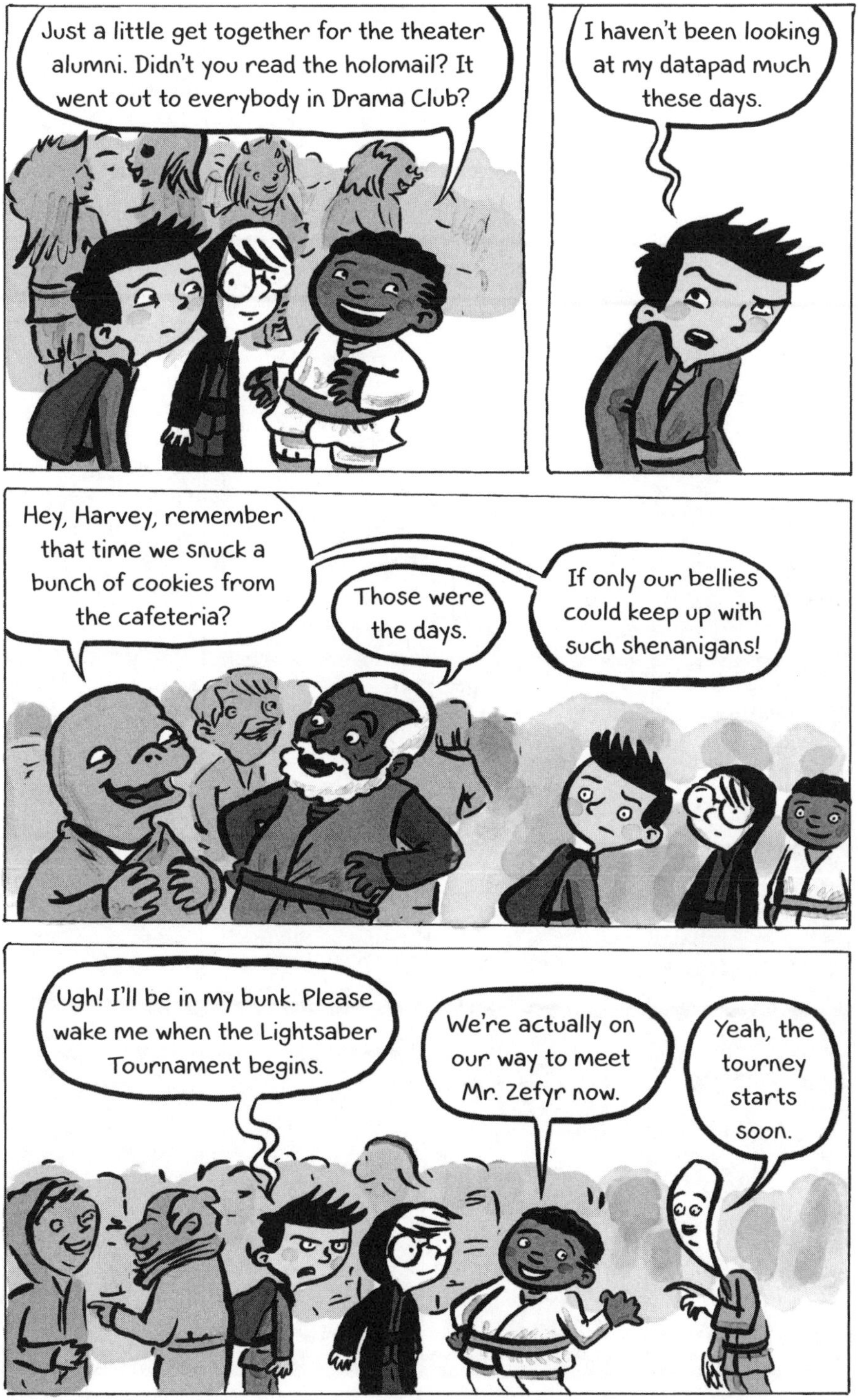
Just a little get together for the theater alumni. Didn't you read the holomail? It went out to everybody in Drama Club?
I haven't been looking at my datapad much these days.
Hey, Harvey, remember that time we snuck a bunch of cookies from the cafeteria?
Those were the days.
If only our bellies could keep up with such shenanigans!
Ugh! I'll be in my bunk. Please wake me when the Lightsaber Tournament begins.
We're actually on our way to meet Mr. Zefyr now.
Yeah, the tourney starts soon.

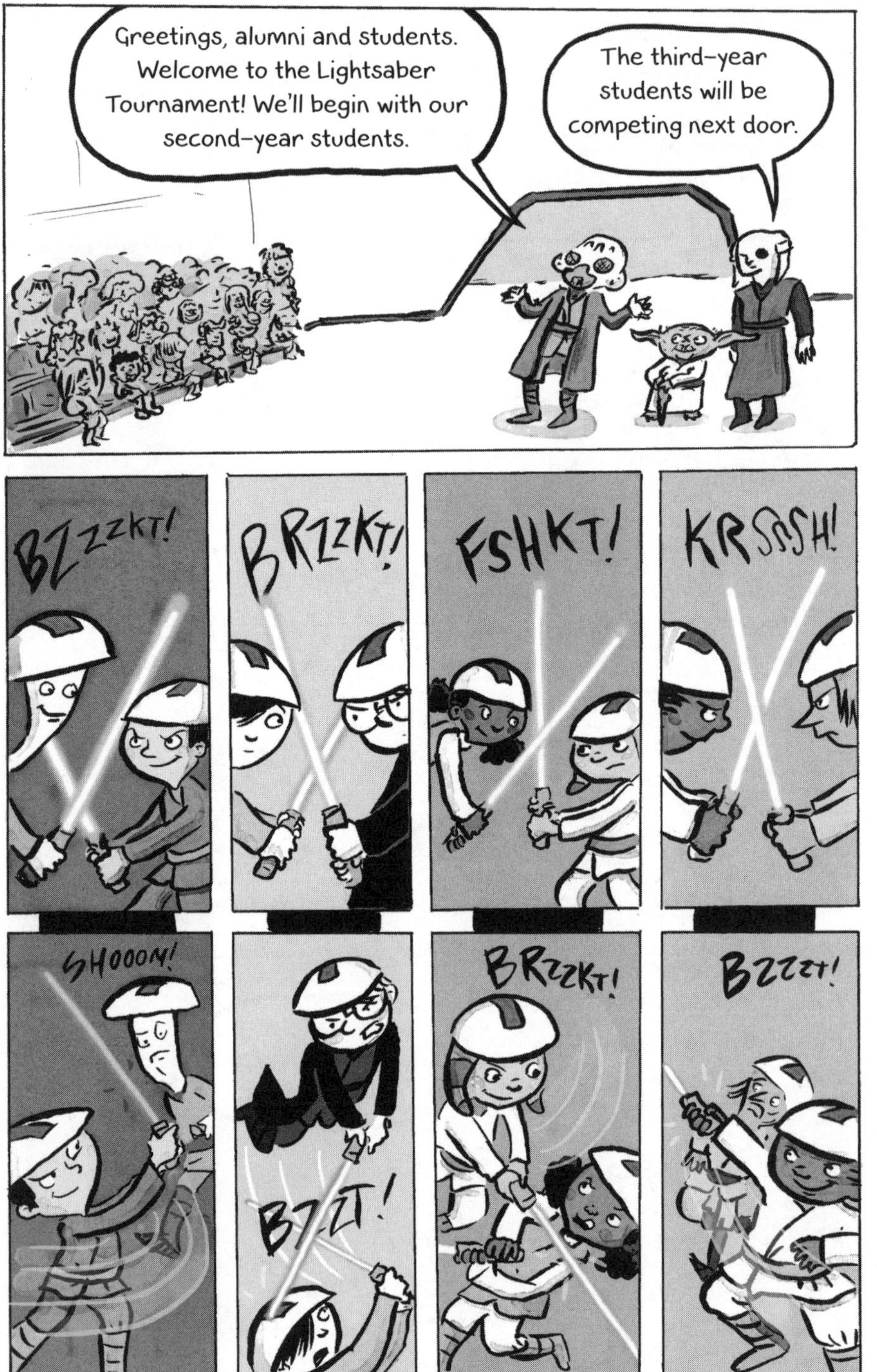
Greetings, alumni and students. Welcome to the Lightsaber Tournament! We'll begin with our second-year students.
The third-year students will be competing next door.
BZZZKT!
BRZZKT!
FSHKT!
KRSSSH!
SHOOOM!
BZZT!
BRZZKT!
BZZZT!

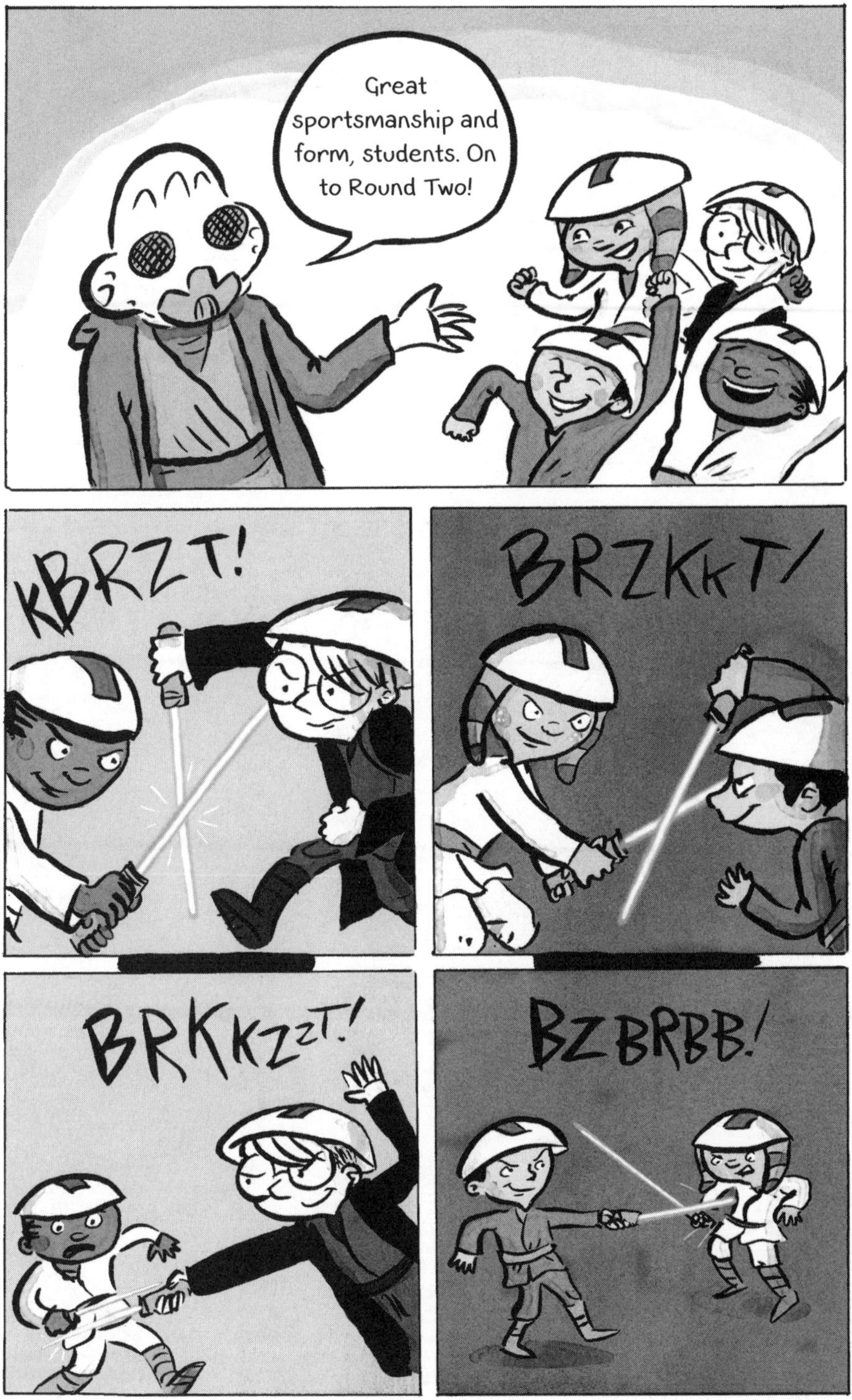

Great sportsmanship and form, students. On to Round Two!
KBRZT!
BRZKKT!
BRKKZzT!
BZBRBB!

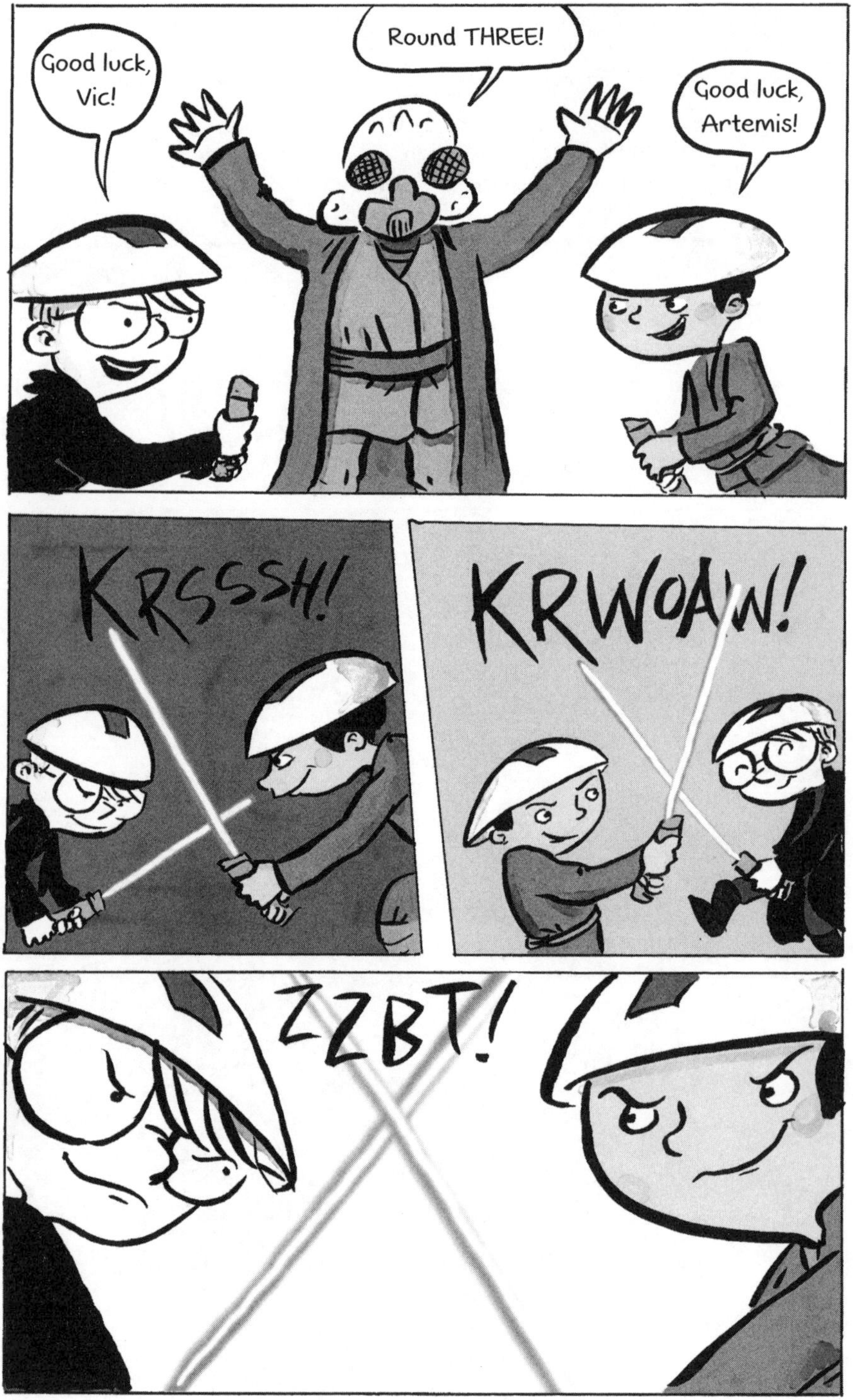
Good luck, Vic!
Round THREE!
Good luck, Artemis!
KRSSSH!
KRWOAW!
ZZBT!

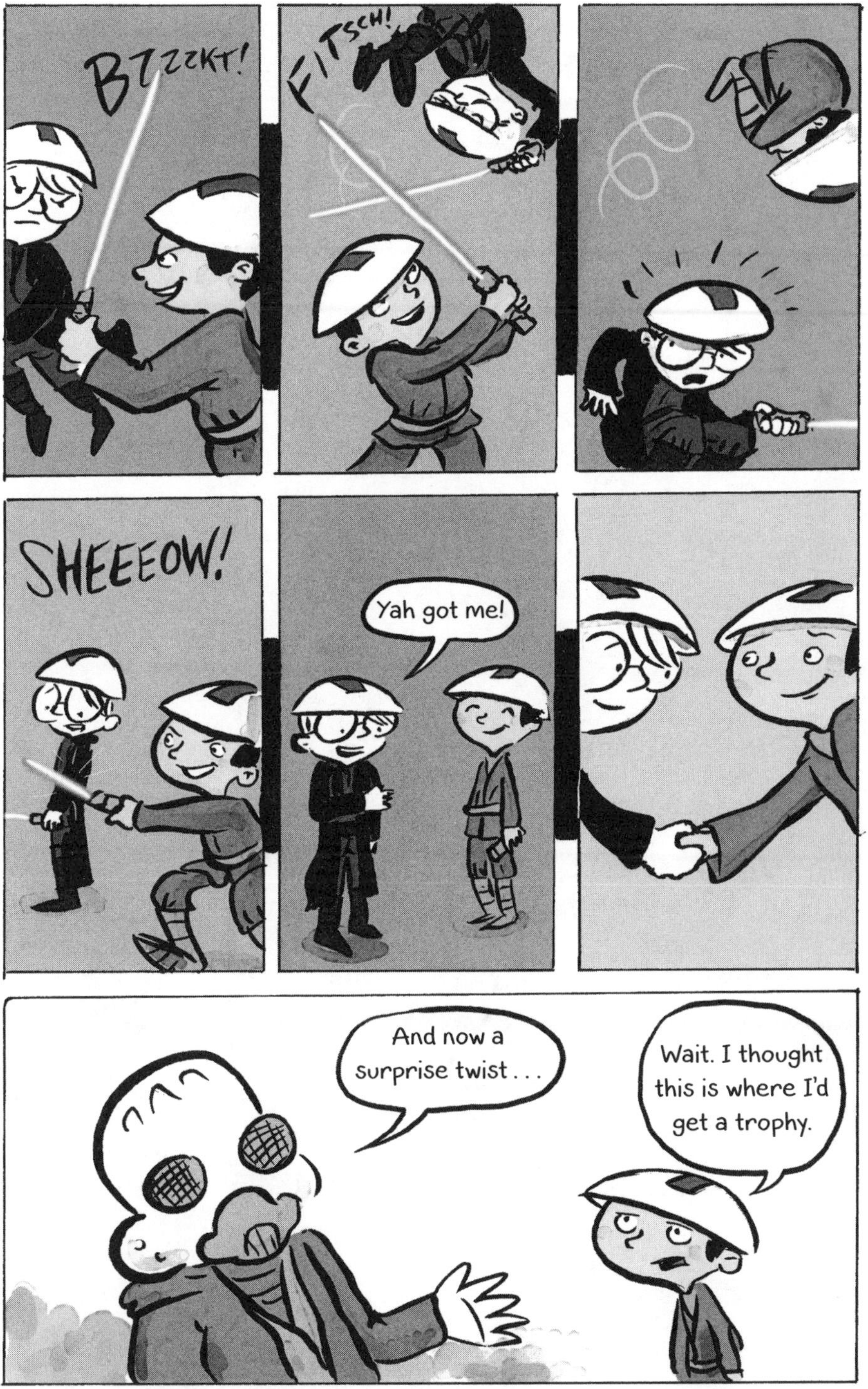
BZZZKT!
FITSCH!
SHEEEOW!
Yah got me!
And now a surprise twist . . .
Wait. I thought this is where I'd get a trophy.

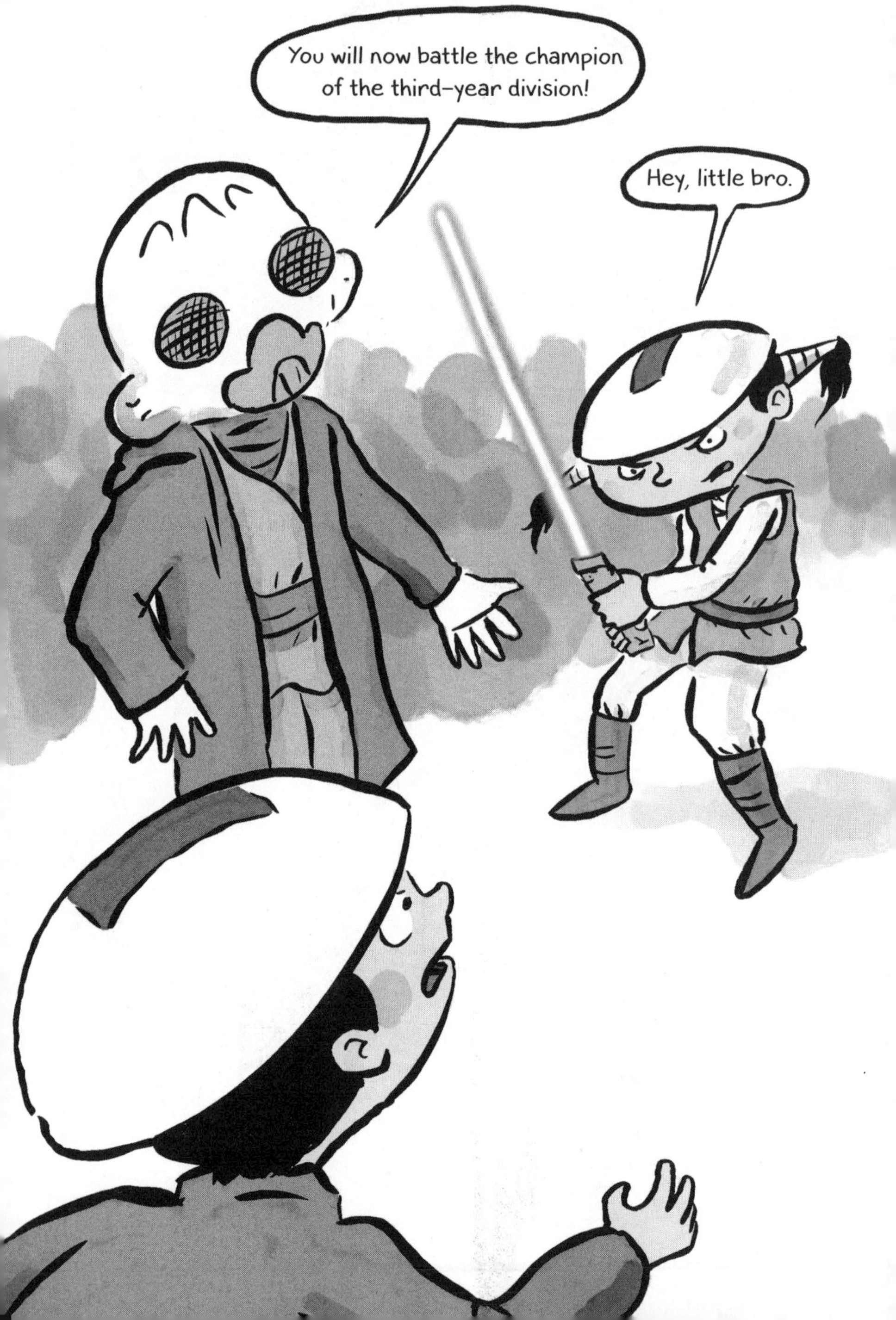
You will now battle the champion of the third-year division!
Hey, little bro.

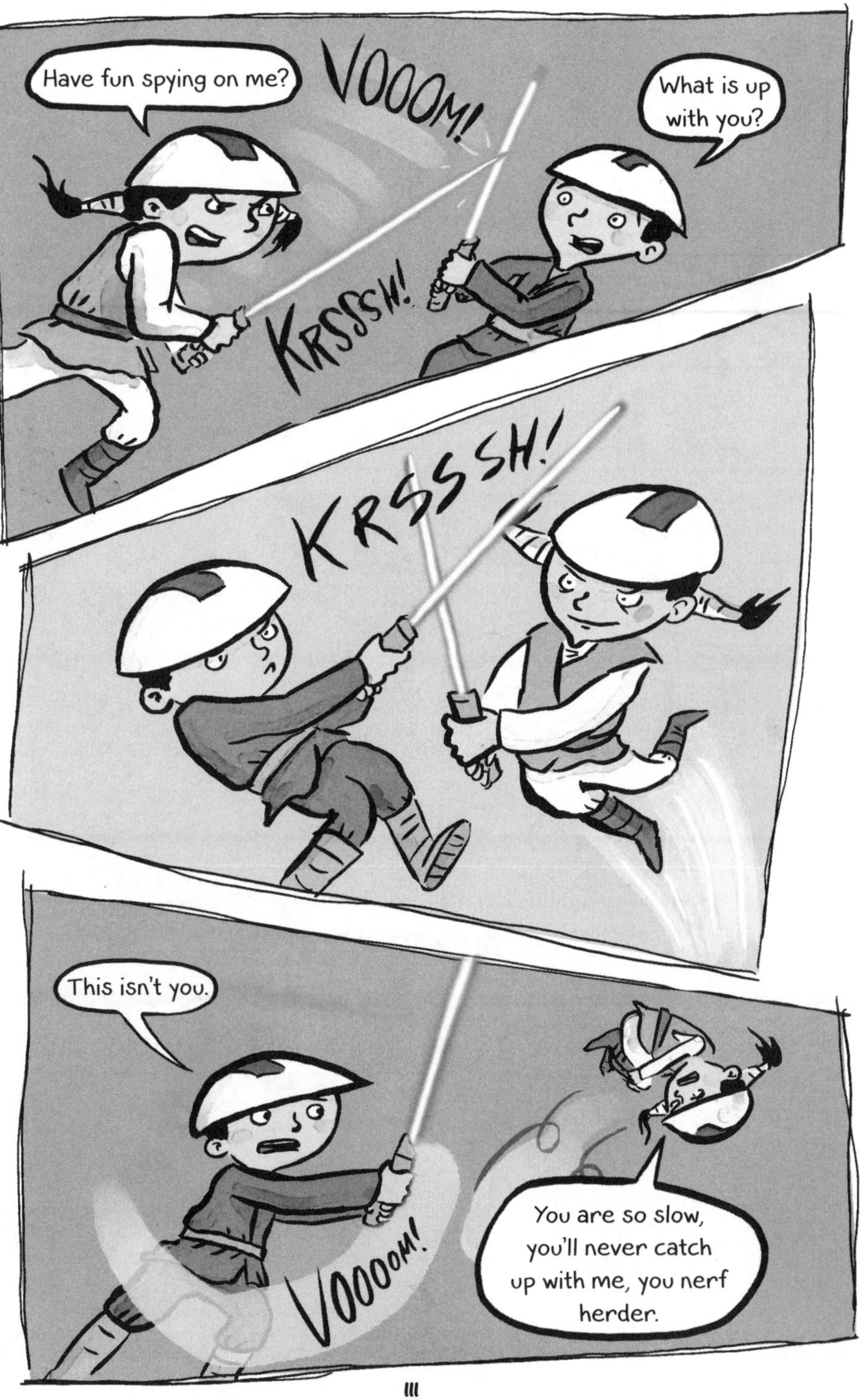
Have fun spying on me?
VOOOM!
What is up with you?
KRSSSH!
KRSSSH!
This isn't you.
VOOOOM!
You are so slow, you'll never catch up with me, you nerf herder.

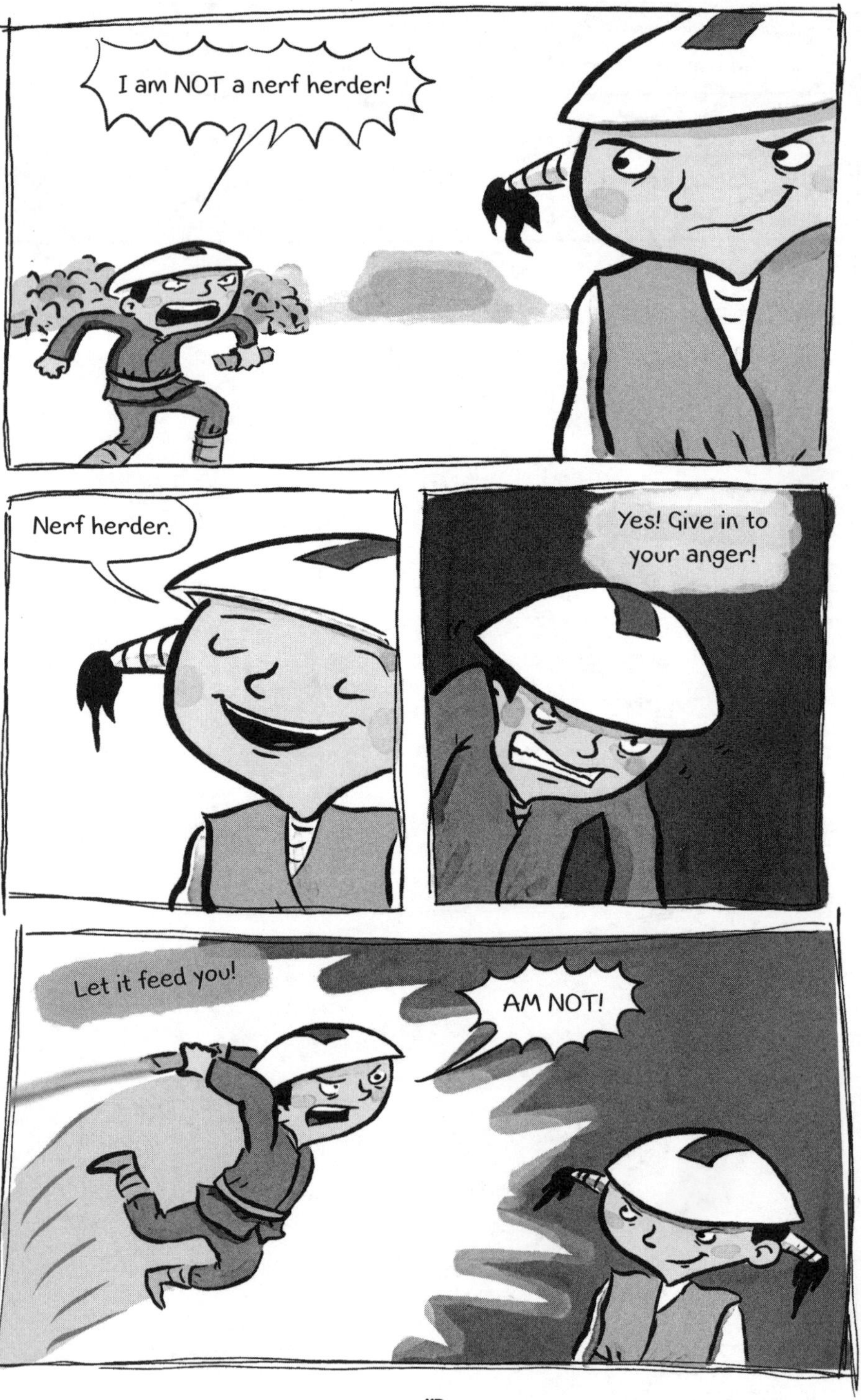
I am NOT a nerf herder!
Nerf herder.
Yes! Give in to your anger!
Let it feed you!
AM NOT!

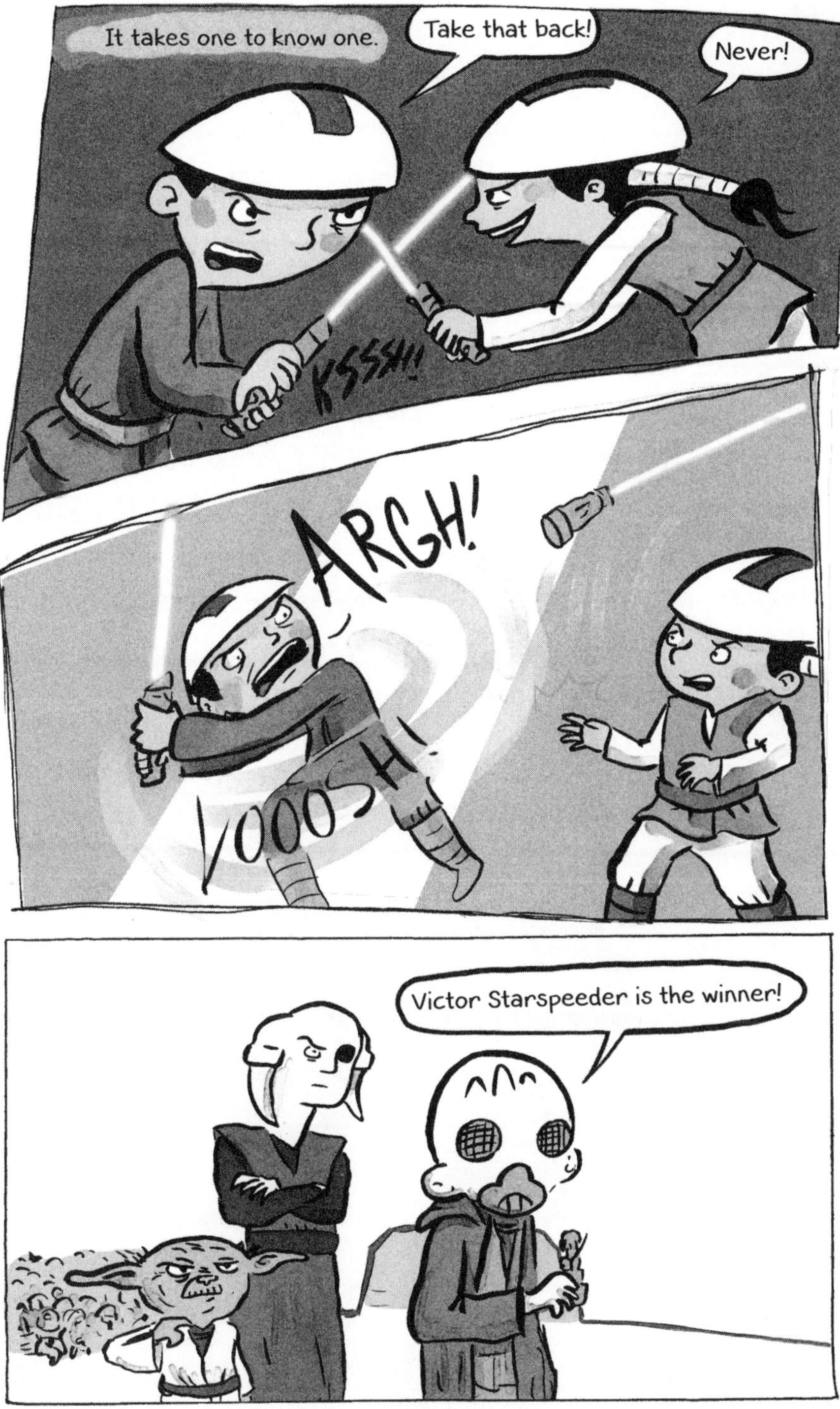
It takes one to know one.
Take that back!
Never!
KSSSH!!
ARGH!
VOOOSH!
Victor Starspeeder is the winner!

Pentaday

Christina knew just what she was doing when she called me a nerf herder. I didn't care about the Lightsaber Tournament trophy as much as I wanted her to take back the nerf herder crack. I really didn't expect to win. When I saw that I would have to face Christina, I figured she'd beat me. But there was, like, this voice in my head egging me on. I've never experienced that before. It was weird. "Clear your mind, a Jedi must," is something that Yoda says all the time. But I thought he meant things like thinking about ice cream and cake and things like that. I thought my obsessing over T-16 skyhoppers was the problem. Is it even possible to have thoughts in your brain that aren't yours? Ugh! Middle school is so confusing.

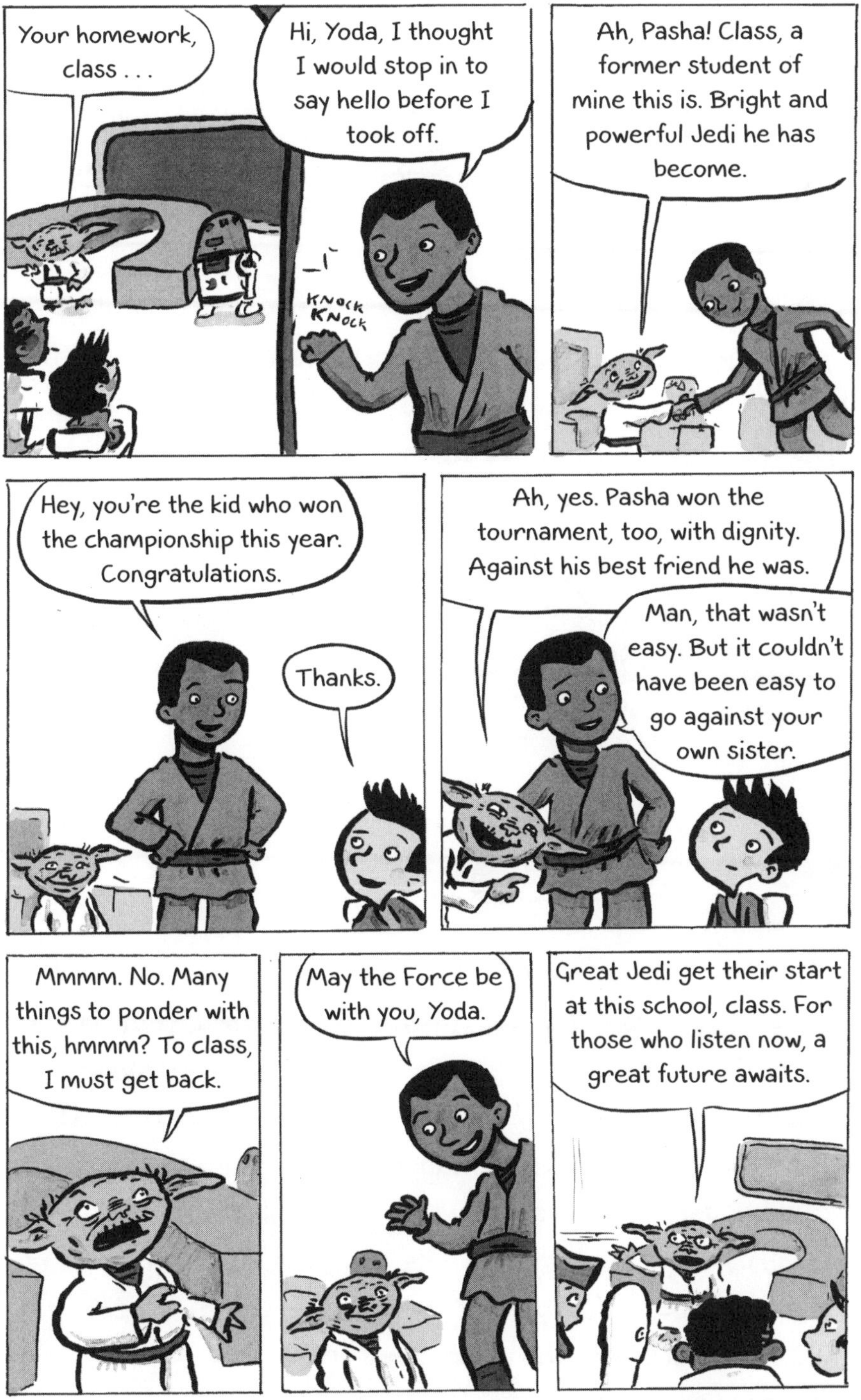
Your homework, class . . .
Hi, Yoda, I thought I would stop in to say hello before I took off.
KNOCK KNOCK
Ah, Pasha! Class, a former student of mine this is. Bright and powerful Jedi he has become.
Hey, you're the kid who won the championship this year. Congratulations.
Thanks.
Ah, yes. Pasha won the tournament, too, with dignity. Against his best friend he was.
Man, that wasn't easy. But it couldn't have been easy to go against your own sister.
Mmmm. No. Many things to ponder with this, hmmm? To class, I must get back.
May the Force be with you, Yoda.
Great Jedi get their start at this school, class. For those who listen now, a great future awaits.

Duoday

It's the end-of-year crunch. All my final exams are coming up and all my essays are due. Artemis kept reminding me that I should have started working on these a long, long time ago, but I've had a few things on my plate. But anyhow, how hard could it be to write a five-page essay on the ramifications of trade deals on local famers on Tatooine? That essay is just going to write itself.

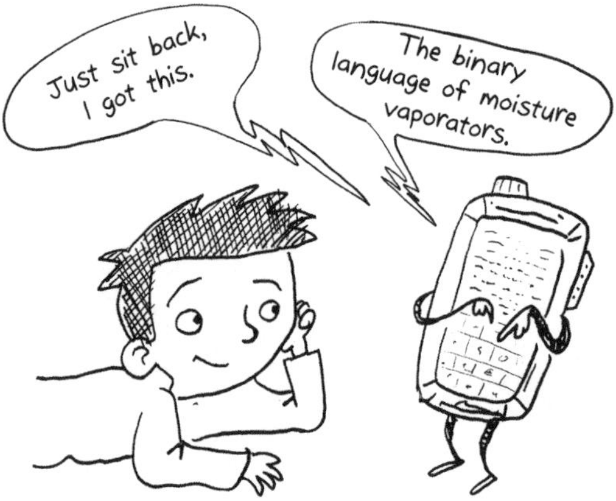
Just sit back, I got this.
The binary language of moisture vaporators.

Elara has been coming by to offer to be my study buddy. It's nice enough of her, but I find that every time I take out my datapad to read up on molecular biology in sentient beings, I end up scrolling over to news about what's happening in the world of skyhoppers. And really, what info will really help me in twenty years anyhow? The physical aspects of some species that I'll probably never encounter or the latest stats of who won what race and with what modifications made to their craft?

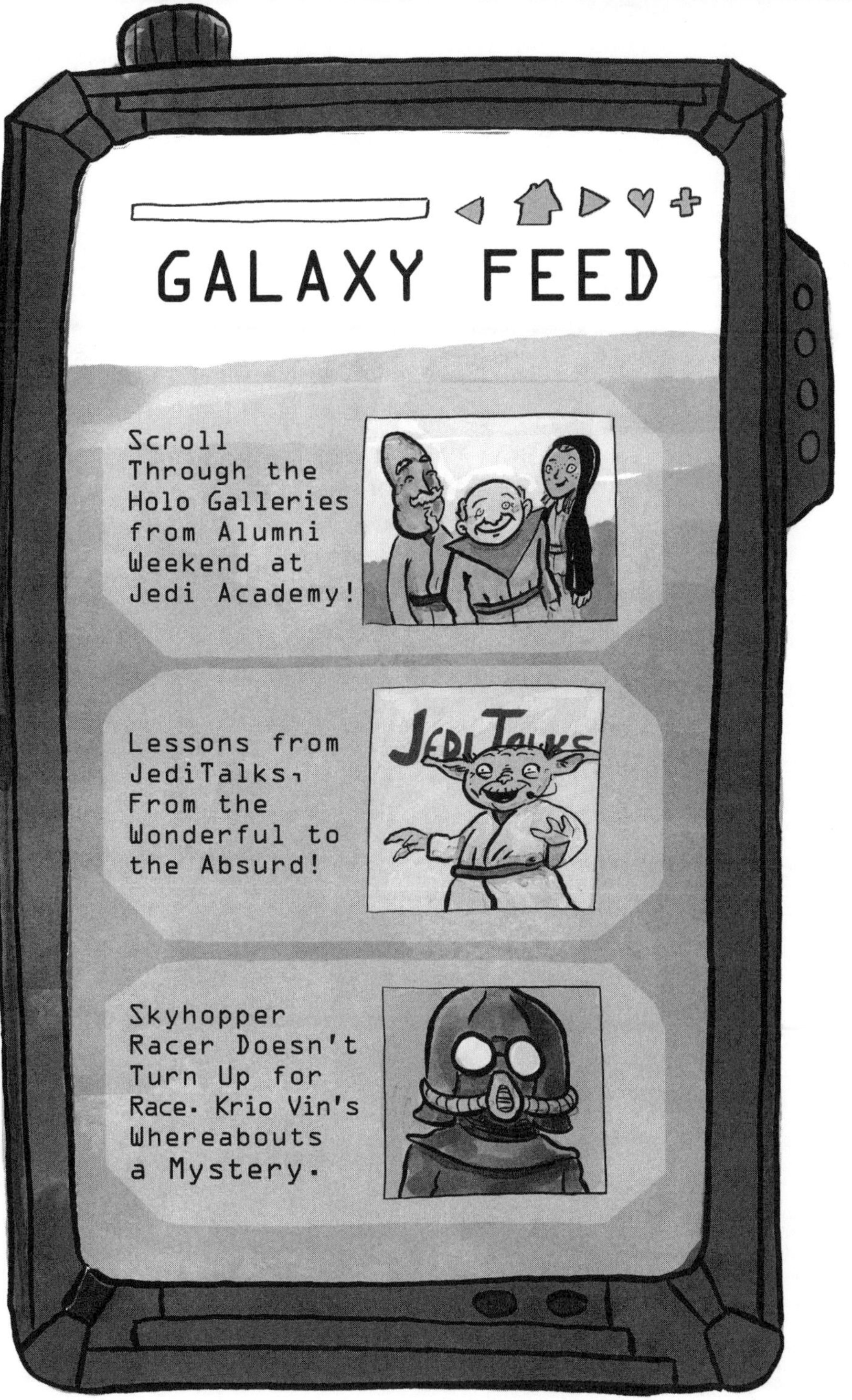
GALAXY FEED
Scroll Through the Holo Galleries from Alumni Weekend at Jedi Academy!
Lessons from JediTalks, From the Wonderful to the Absurd!
Skyhopper Racer Doesn't Turn Up for Race. Krio Vin's Whereabouts a Mystery.

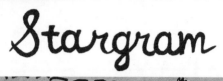

Stargram

MAYATHEATER: One of the last rehearsals before final exams!

 5 6

ArtemisCC: #StudyLife #ClassicJedi

 7 9

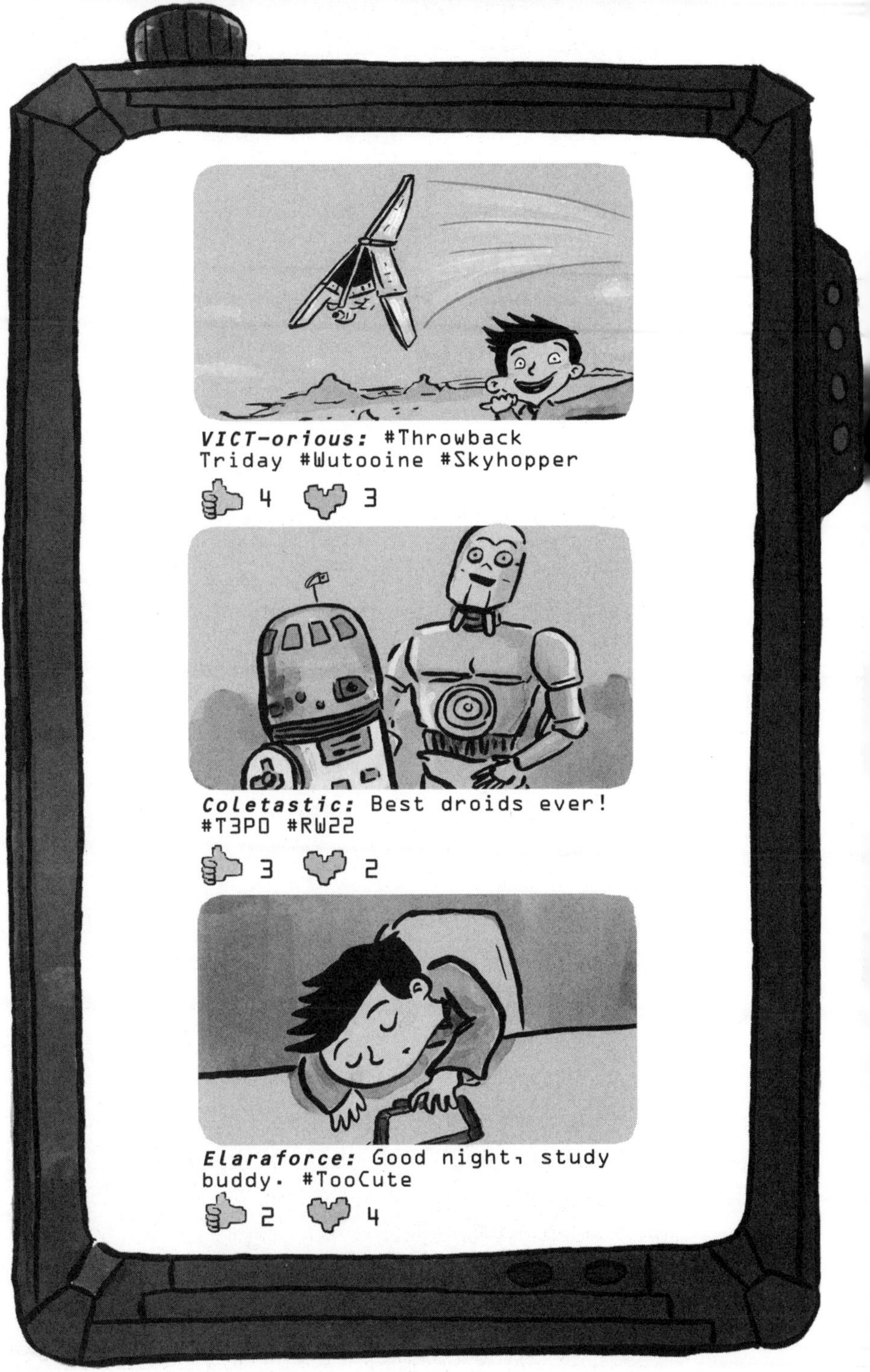
VICT-orious: #Throwback Triday #Wutooine #Skyhopper
4 3
Coletastic: Best droids ever! #T3PO #RW22
3 2
Elaraforce: Good night, study buddy. #TooCute
2 4

Quadday

T-3PO and RW-22 are short-circuiting—literally! Their motherboards can't handle the stress and pressure running on their motors with the musical's opening night approaching. The sarlacc puppet that Zavyer and I rigged up needs a little work. It's meant to fit over Coleman, who plays the part of the carnivorous creature. But it needs a few modifications . . . Coleman does need to be able to see out of the costume . . .

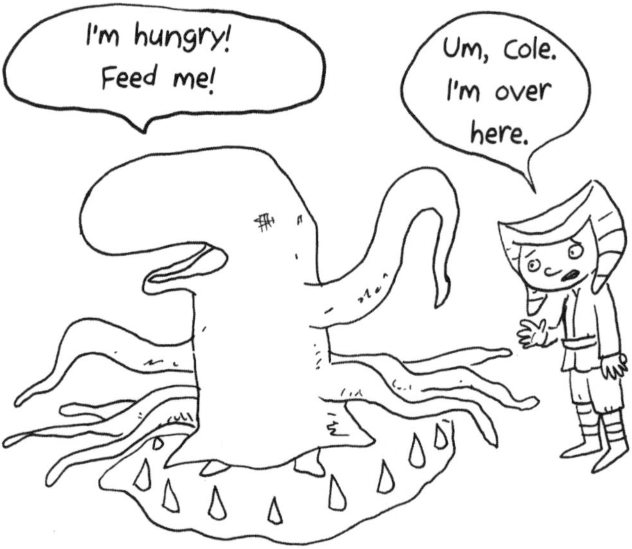
I'm hungry!
Feed me!
Um, Cole.
I'm over
here.

Apparently, sight is integral to theater work. I suggested Coleman just use the Force to find his way around stage, but T-3PO didn't agree.

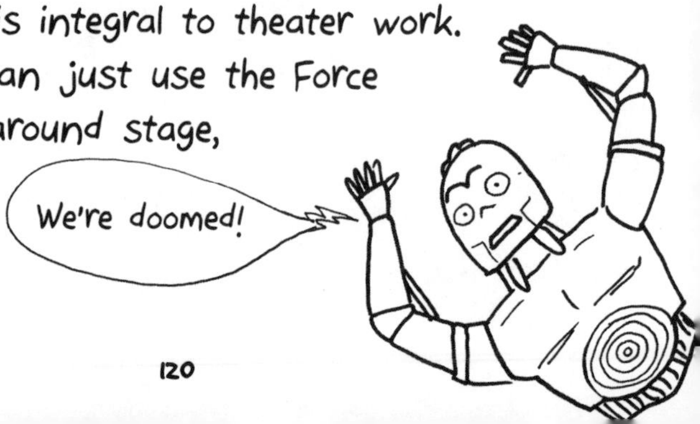
We're doomed!

Mr. Zefyr's final exam will be interesting. The good news is that I've managed to get through simulated flights without throwing up. It isn't as easy as you would think, but your body eventually gets used to all the motion and pressure. P-10 is certainly grateful that I'm keeping my food down—those simulators are hard to clean. (Never mind the helmets.) Also, they should never schedule that class after lunch.

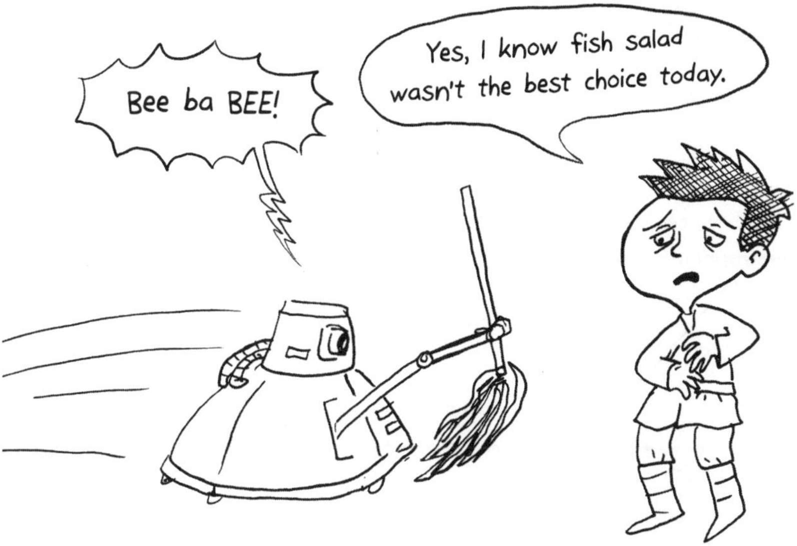
Bee ba BEE!
Yes, I know fish salad wasn't the best choice today.

Actually, out of all my exams, this is the one that I feel best about. I think that I am destined to work with these machines. They move fast and powerfully through the sky, which is pretty much me. Mr. Zefyr keeps saying that life isn't a skyhopper race, contemplation and quick thinking can mean all the difference between safe passage and obliteration. Mr. Zefyr can be so dramatic. You get used to it.

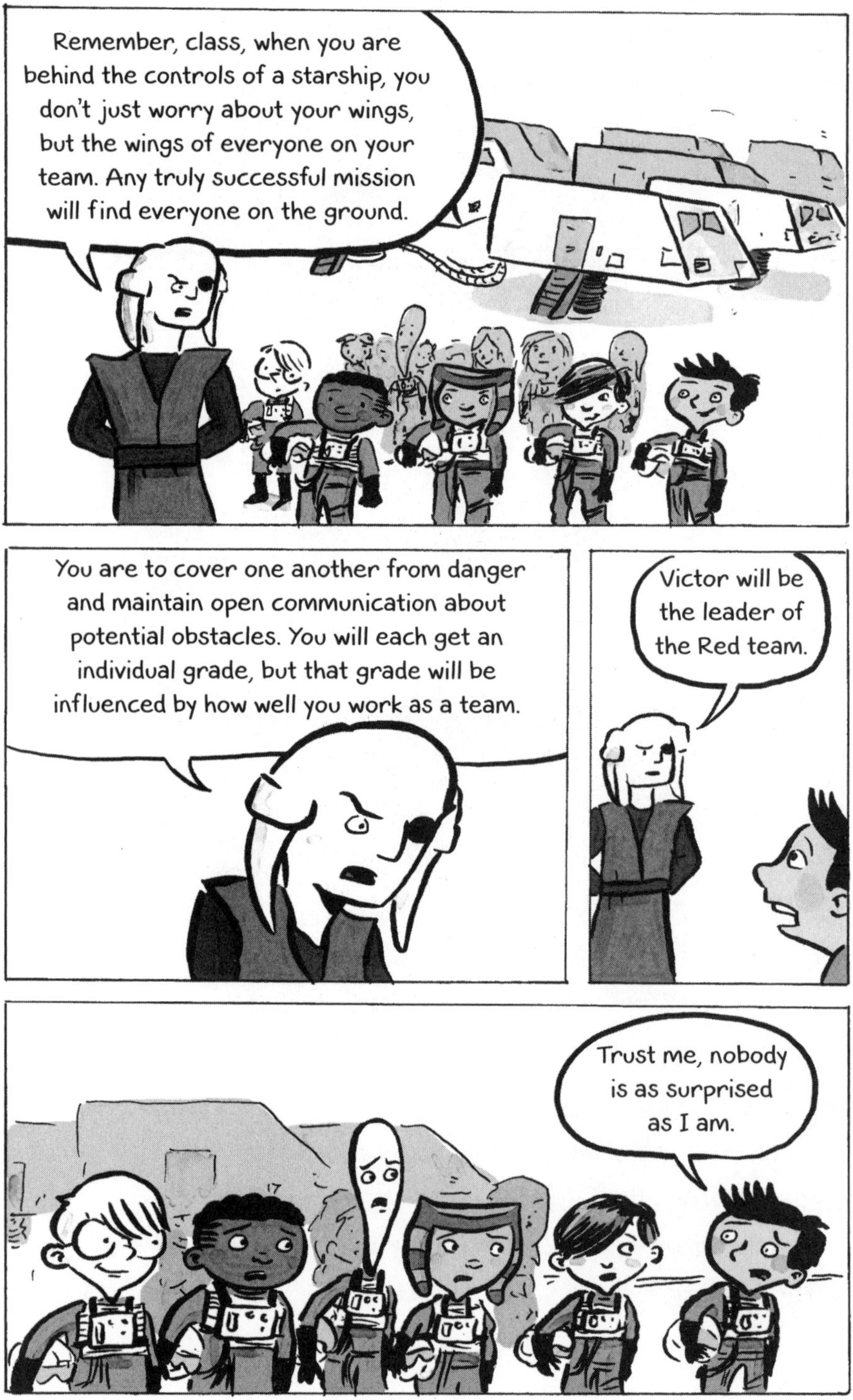
Remember, class, when you are behind the controls of a starship, you don't just worry about your wings, but the wings of everyone on your team. Any truly successful mission will find everyone on the ground.
You are to cover one another from danger and maintain open communication about potential obstacles. You will each get an individual grade, but that grade will be influenced by how well you work as a team.
Victor will be the leader of the Red team.
Trust me, nobody is as surprised as I am.

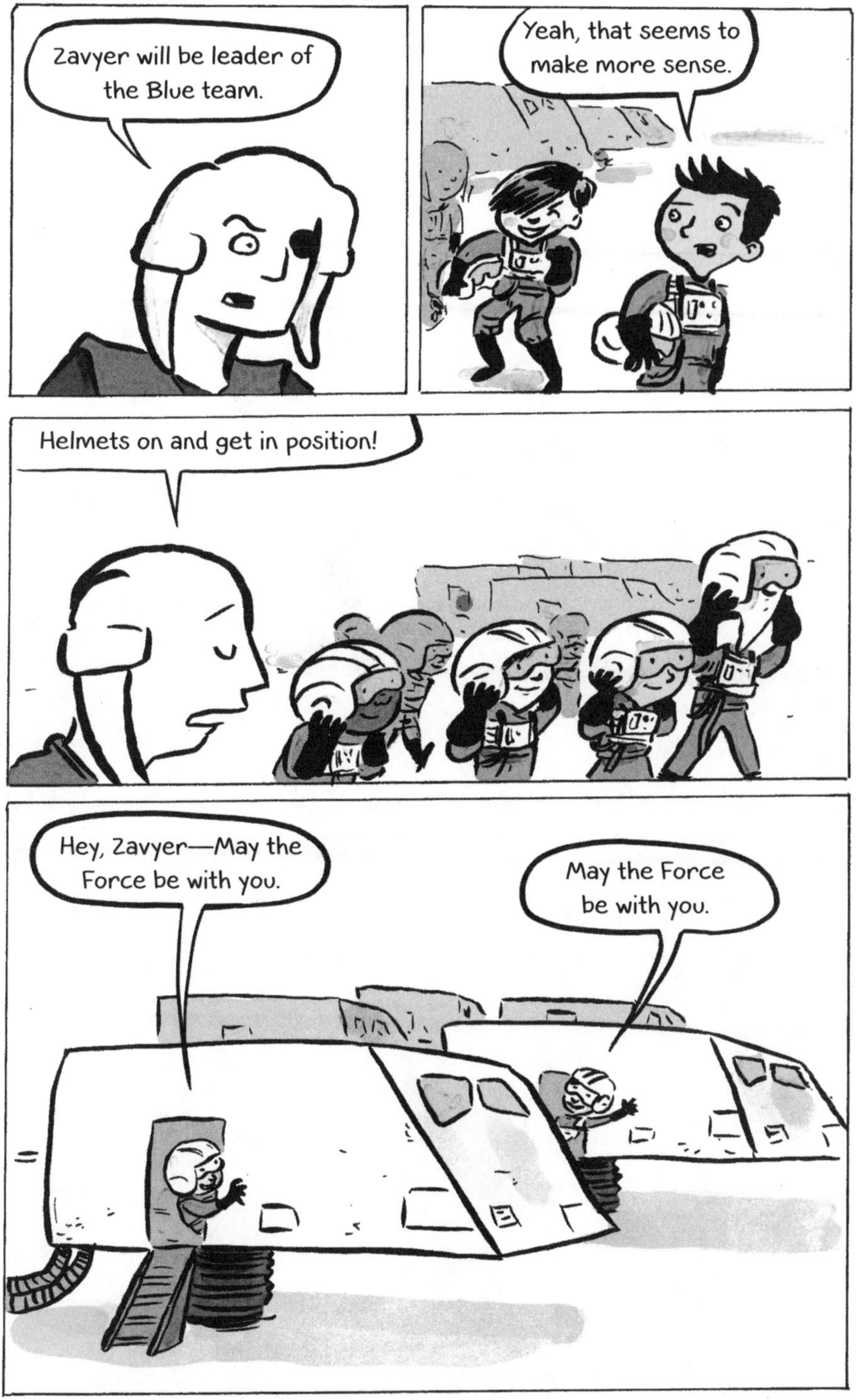
Zavyer will be leader of the Blue team.
Yeah, that seems to make more sense.
Helmets on and get in position!
Hey, Zavyer—May the Force be with you.
May the Force be with you.

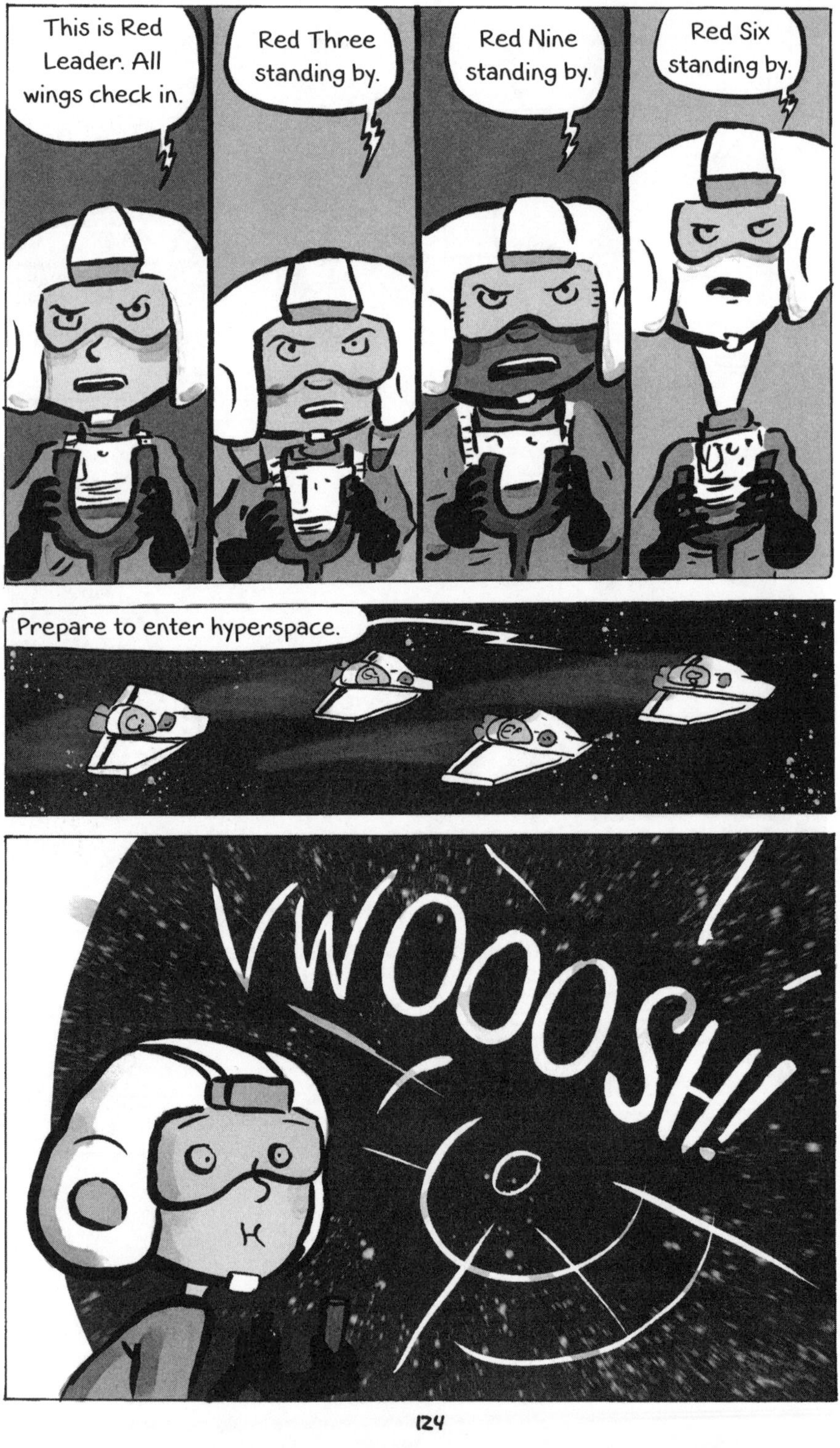
This is Red Leader. All wings check in.
Red Three standing by.
Red Nine standing by.
Red Six standing by.
Prepare to enter hyperspace.
VWOOOSH!

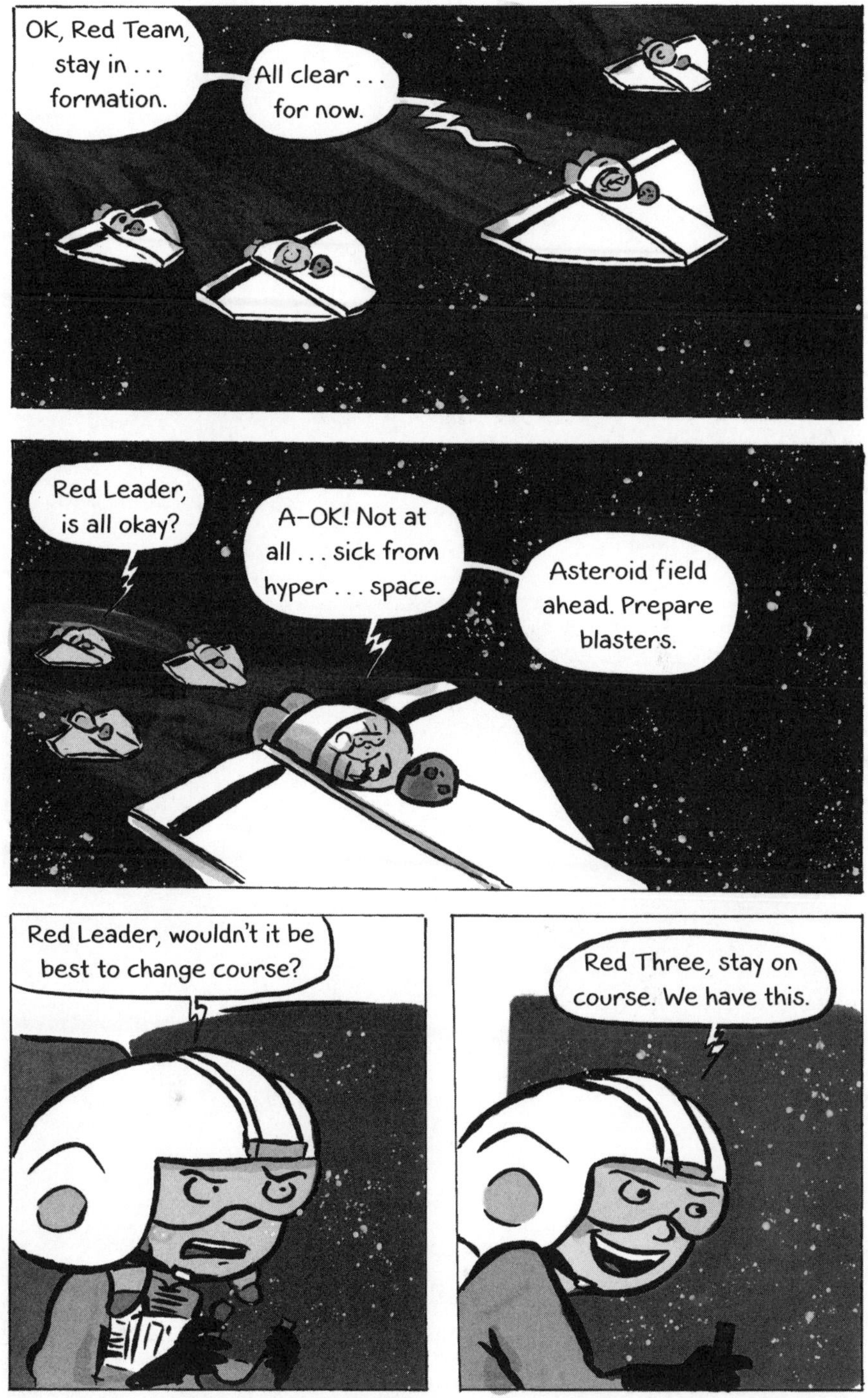
OK, Red Team, stay in . . . formation.
All clear . . . for now.
Red Leader, is all okay?
A-OK! Not at all . . . sick from hyper . . . space.
Asteroid field ahead. Prepare blasters.
Red Leader, wouldn't it be best to change course?
Red Three, stay on course. We have this.

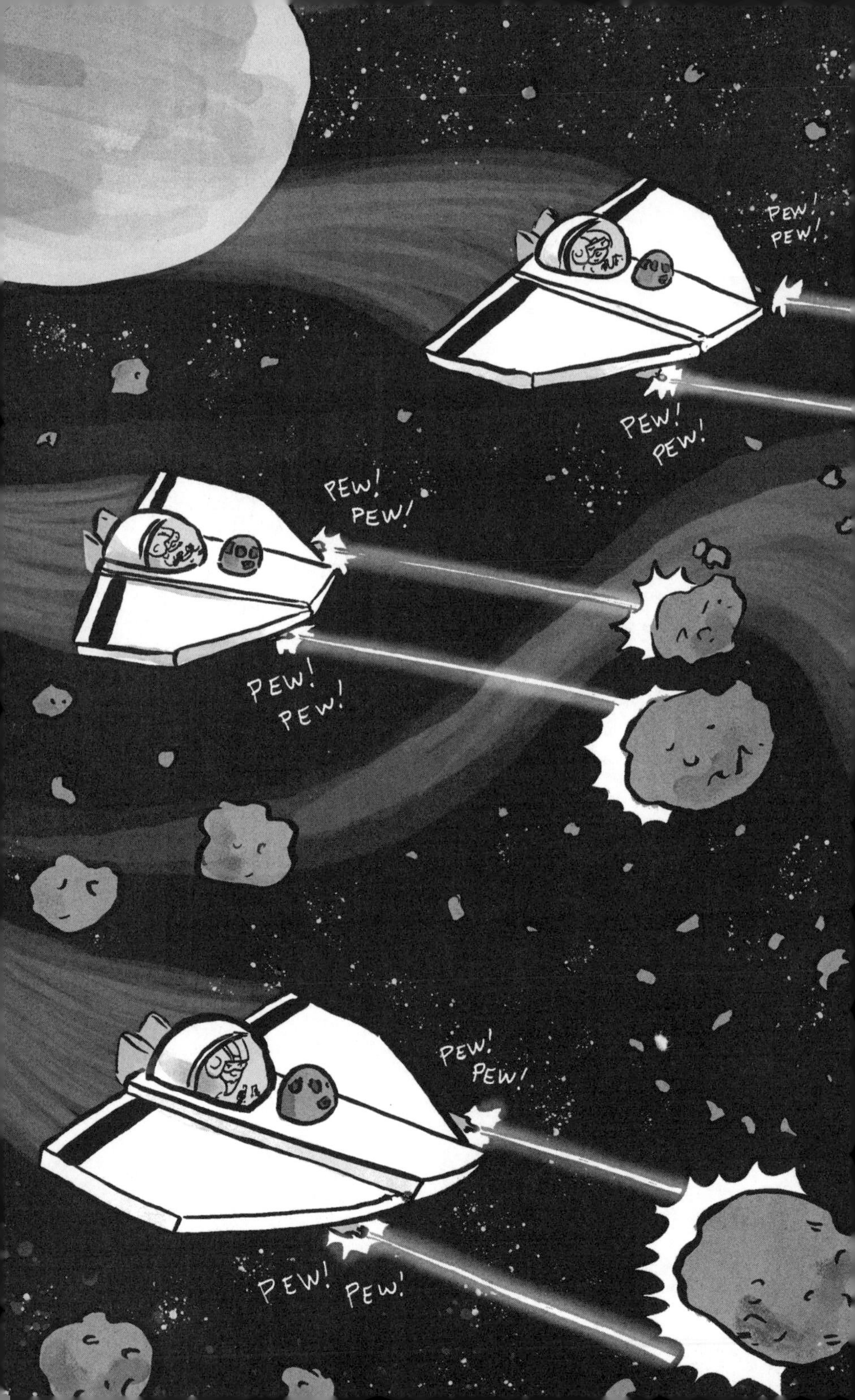
PEW! PEW!
PEW! PEW!
PEW! PEW!
PEW! PEW!
PEW! PEW!
PEW! PEW!

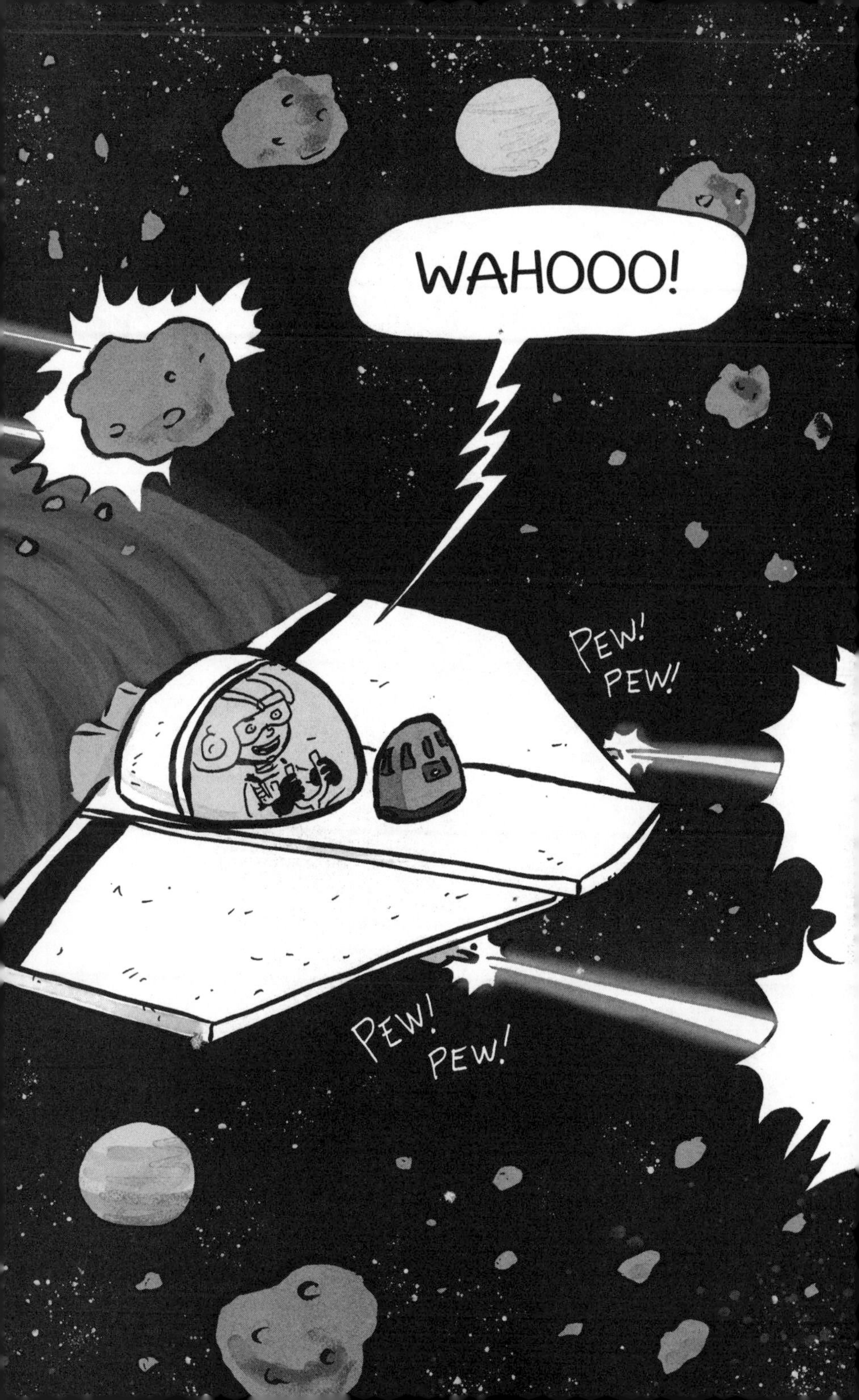
WAHOOO!
PEW! PEW!
PEW! PEW!

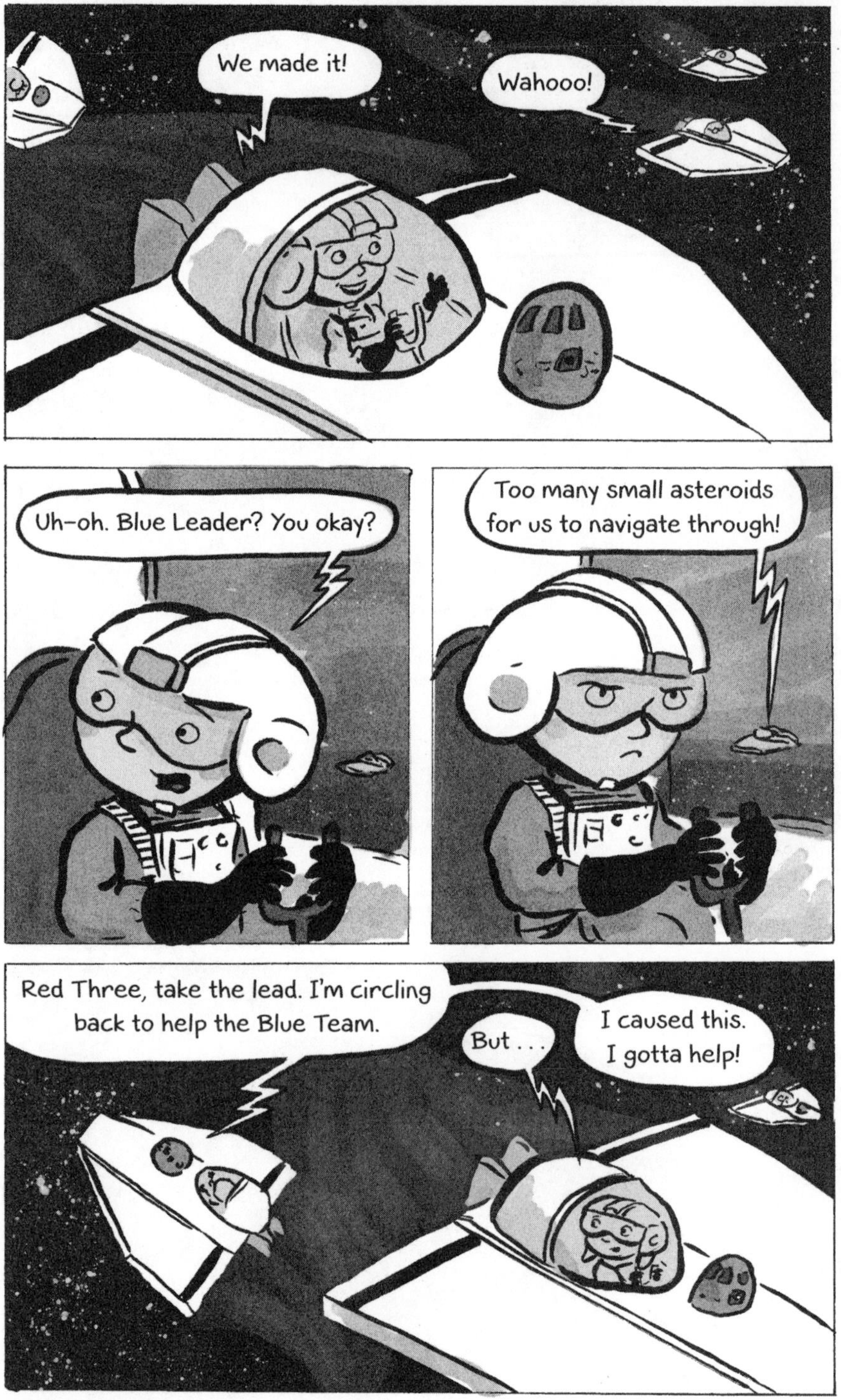
We made it!
Wahooo!
Uh-oh. Blue Leader? You okay?
Too many small asteroids for us to navigate through!
Red Three, take the lead. I'm circling back to help the Blue Team.
But . . .
I caused this. I gotta help!

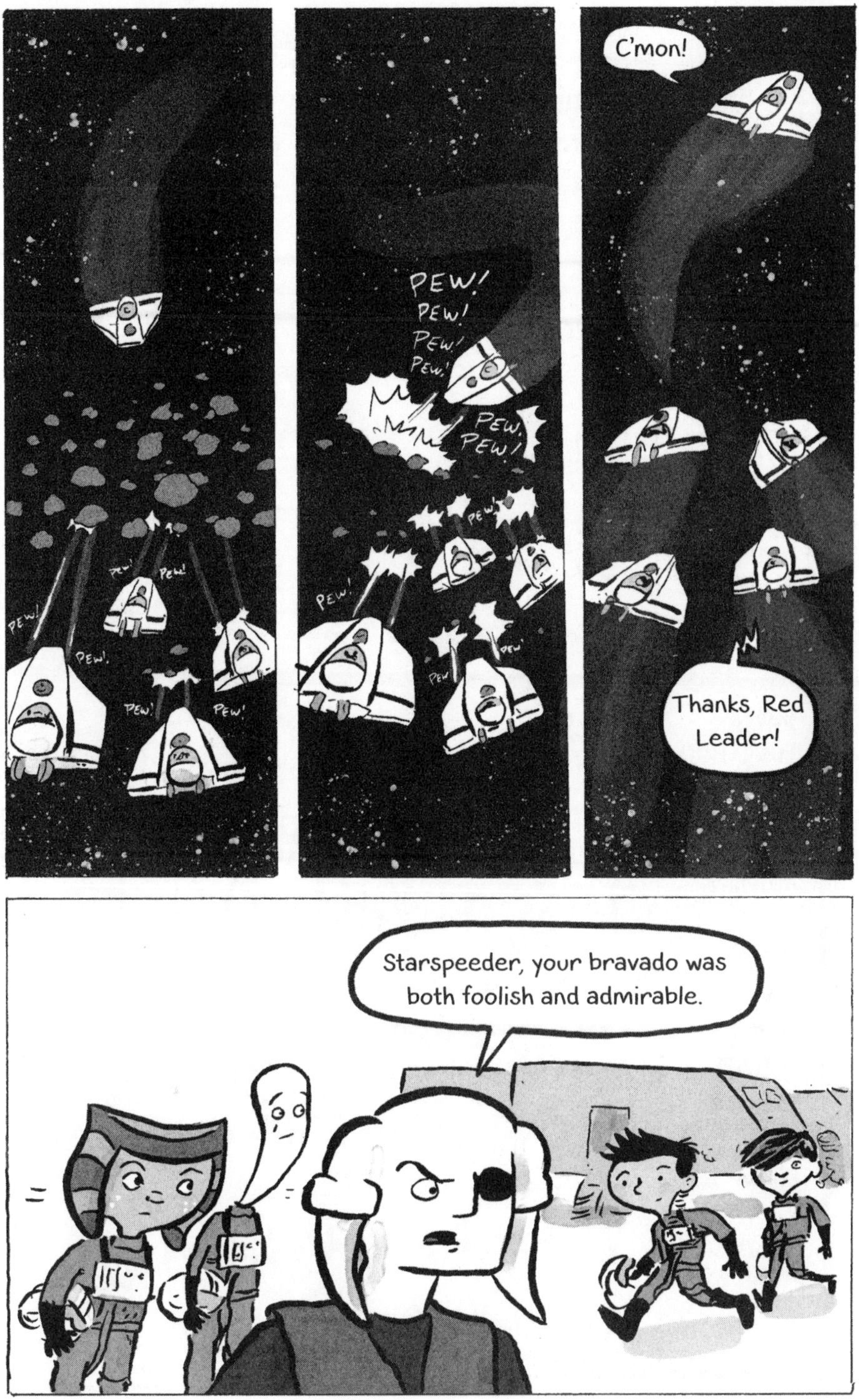
PEW!
PEW!
PEW!
PEW!
PEW!
PEW!
PEW!
PEW!
PEW!
PEW!
PEW.
PEW!
PEW!
C'mon!
Thanks, Red Leader!
Starspeeder, your bravado was both foolish and admirable.

Student Name: Victor Starspeeder
Level: Padawan
Semester: Four

JEDI ACADEMY · CORUSCANT CAMPUS ·

REPORT CARD

CLASS	NOTES	GRADES
ADVANCED FORCE	Powerful, but patience needed!	B
STARPILOT FLIGHT TRAINING	Brave, bold, and foolish!	B+
PHYSICAL EDUCATION	[illegible]	[illegible]
HYPER-ALGEBRA	I am glad this class is history	B
HISTORY OF THE JEDI ORDER	Was Victor even in my class??	C–
GALACTIC GEOGRAPHY	Clear your mind!	B
PERSUASIVE DISCOURSE	Victor has potential to arrive on time.	B–

Monoday

Well, I didn't totally flunk out of Jedi Academy, so that's good. My teachers must have taken pity on me, because I felt so unprepared for all of my final exams. But I did learn a lot in my classes this year, even if I'm not sure that they will ever really help me when I'm a Jedi. Like, when I'm off saving the galaxy, will it really matter that I know how to solve algebraic equations? And with technology, do I really need to memorize where all the planets are and what section of the galaxy they're in? I'll just ask the navicomputer, it won't steer me wrong. The big annual school dance is coming up, but it's hard to get excited for it. I don't really have happy feet these days. Elara is insisting that I go, and well, she's been so helpful to me all year. It's the least I could do. That and . . . well, Elara is pretty cool. I'm going to miss seeing her so much over break. But she said that she'd have her family stop in at Naboo on their annual vacation.

Kinda, sorta OK after all.

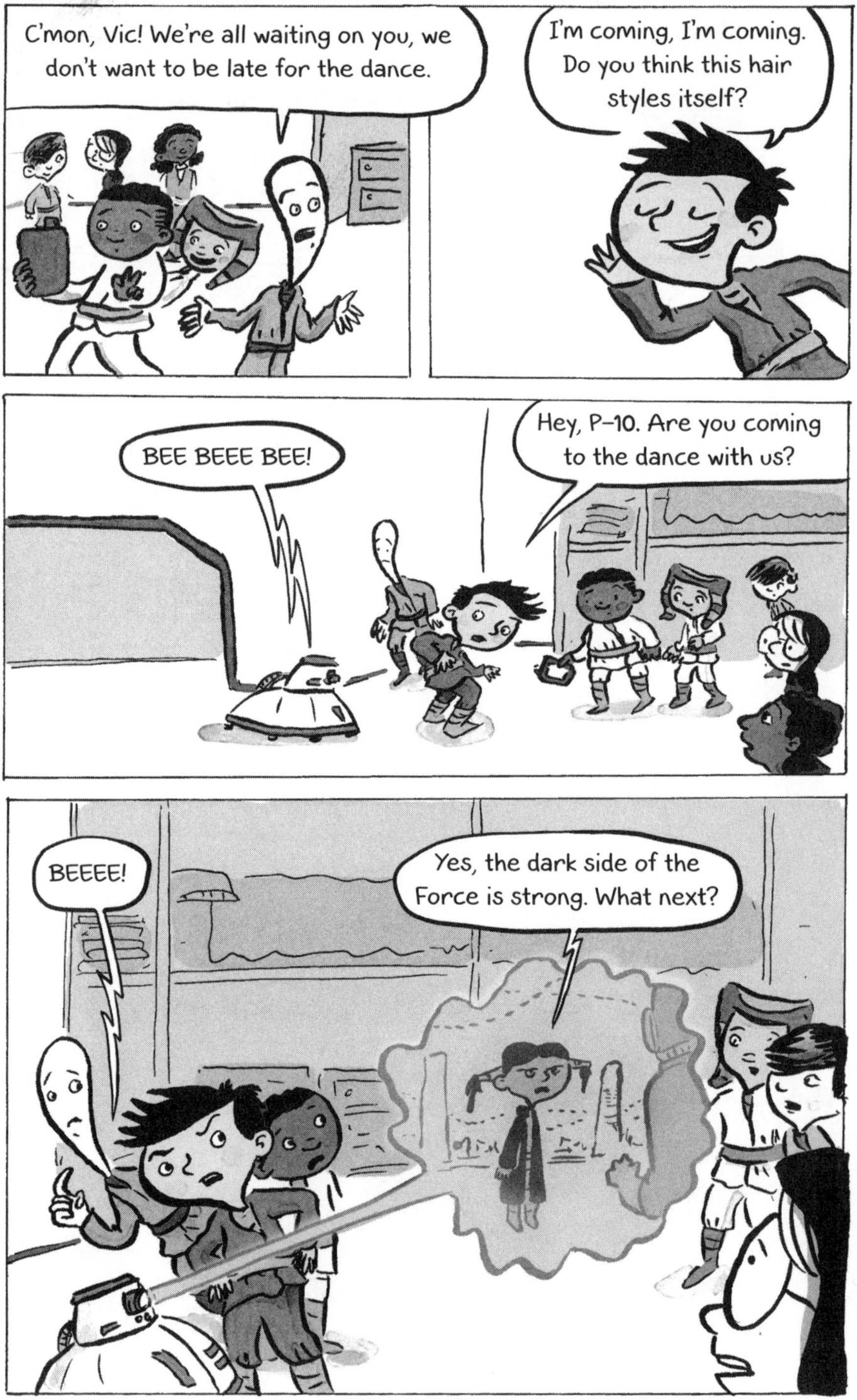
C'mon, Vic! We're all waiting on you, we don't want to be late for the dance.
I'm coming, I'm coming. Do you think this hair styles itself?
BEE BEEE BEE!
Hey, P-10. Are you coming to the dance with us?
BEEEE!
Yes, the dark side of the Force is strong. What next?

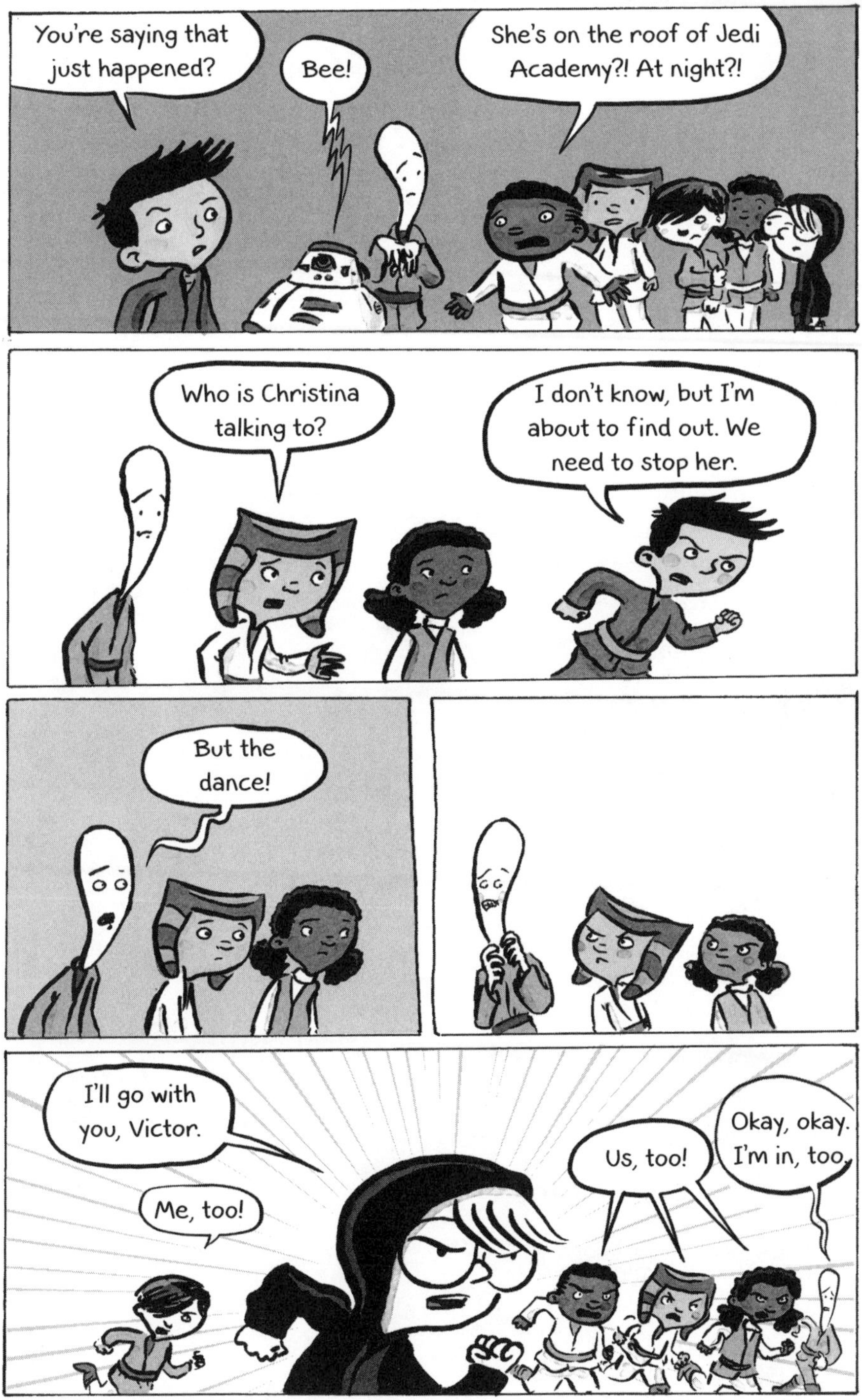
You're saying that just happened?
Bee!
She's on the roof of Jedi Academy?! At night?!
Who is Christina talking to?
I don't know, but I'm about to find out. We need to stop her.
But the dance!
I'll go with you, Victor.
Me, too!
Us, too!
Okay, okay. I'm in, too.

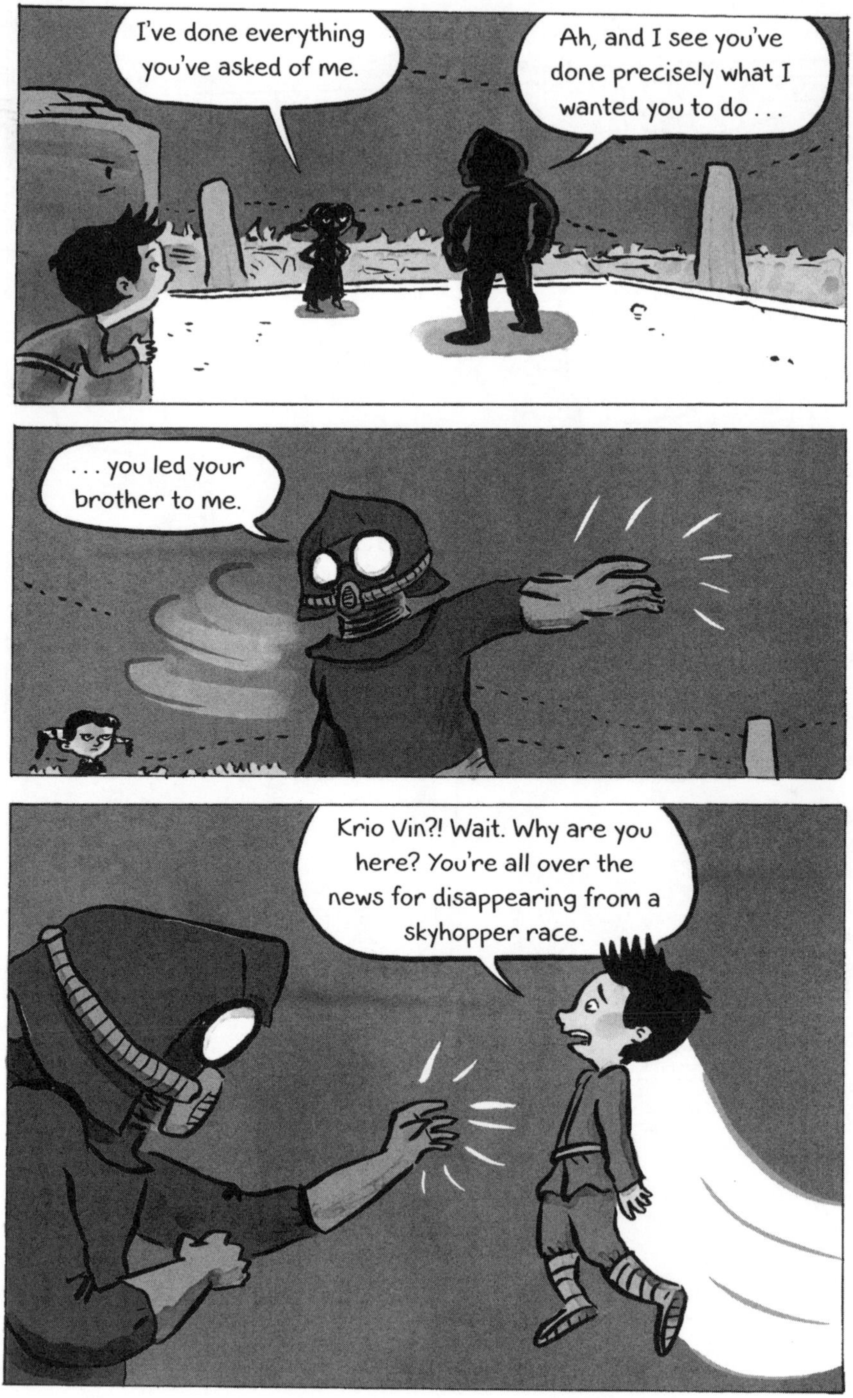
I've done everything you've asked of me.
Ah, and I see you've done precisely what I wanted you to do . . .
. . . you led your brother to me.
Krio Vin?! Wait. Why are you here? You're all over the news for disappearing from a skyhopper race.

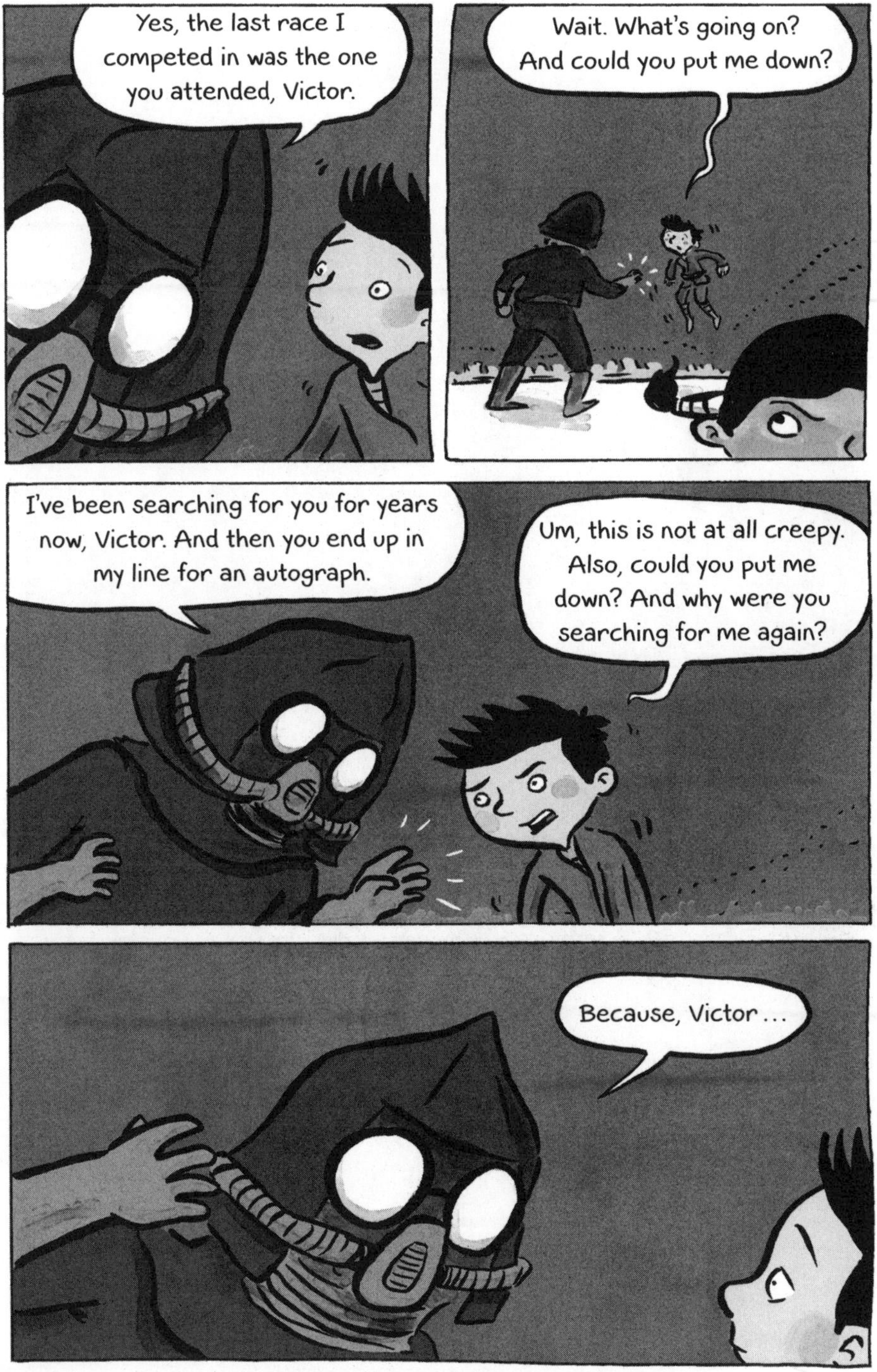
Yes, the last race I competed in was the one you attended, Victor.
Wait. What's going on? And could you put me down?
I've been searching for you for years now, Victor. And then you end up in my line for an autograph.
Um, this is not at all creepy. Also, could you put me down? And why were you searching for me again?
Because, Victor . . .

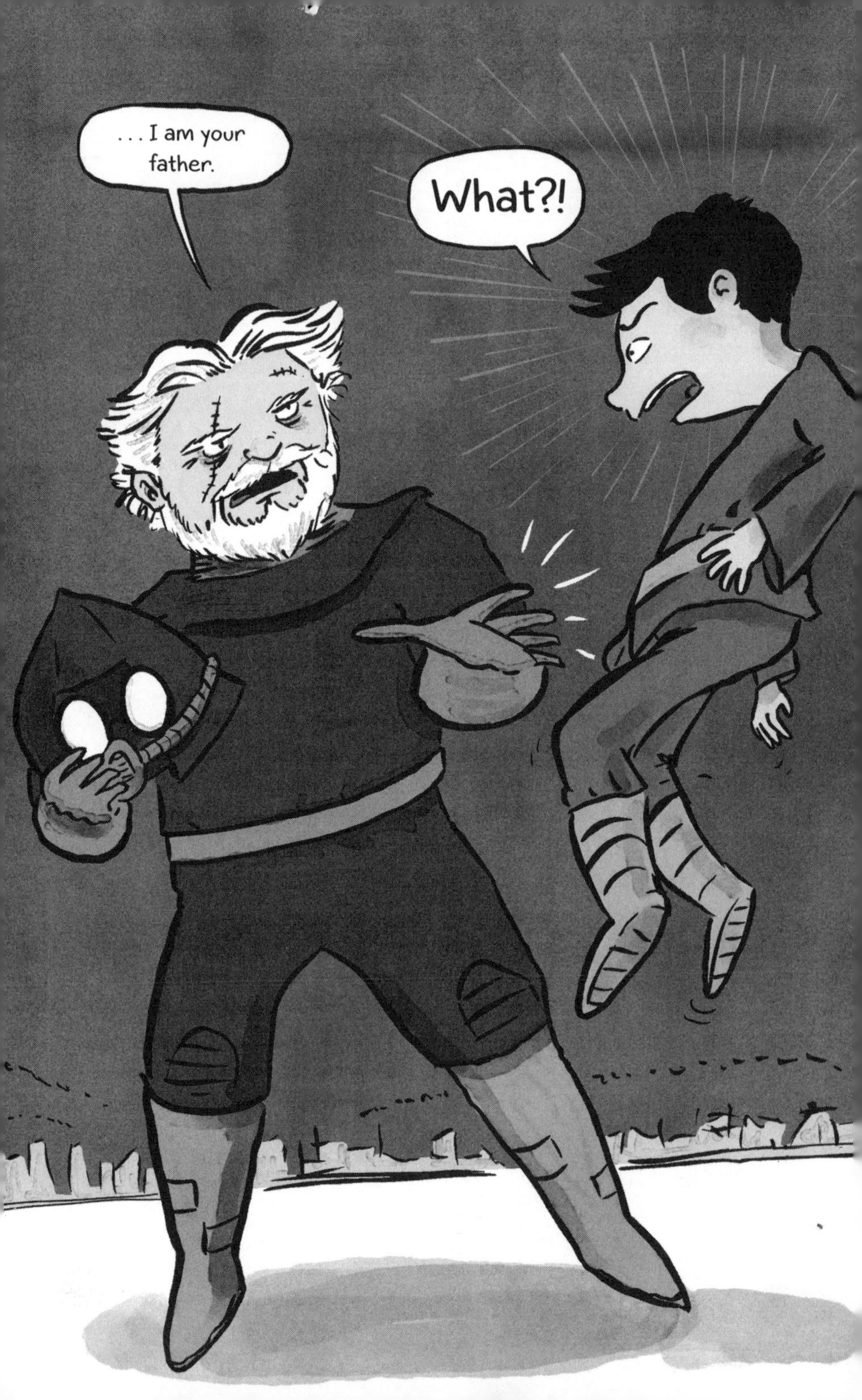
. . . I am your father.
What?!

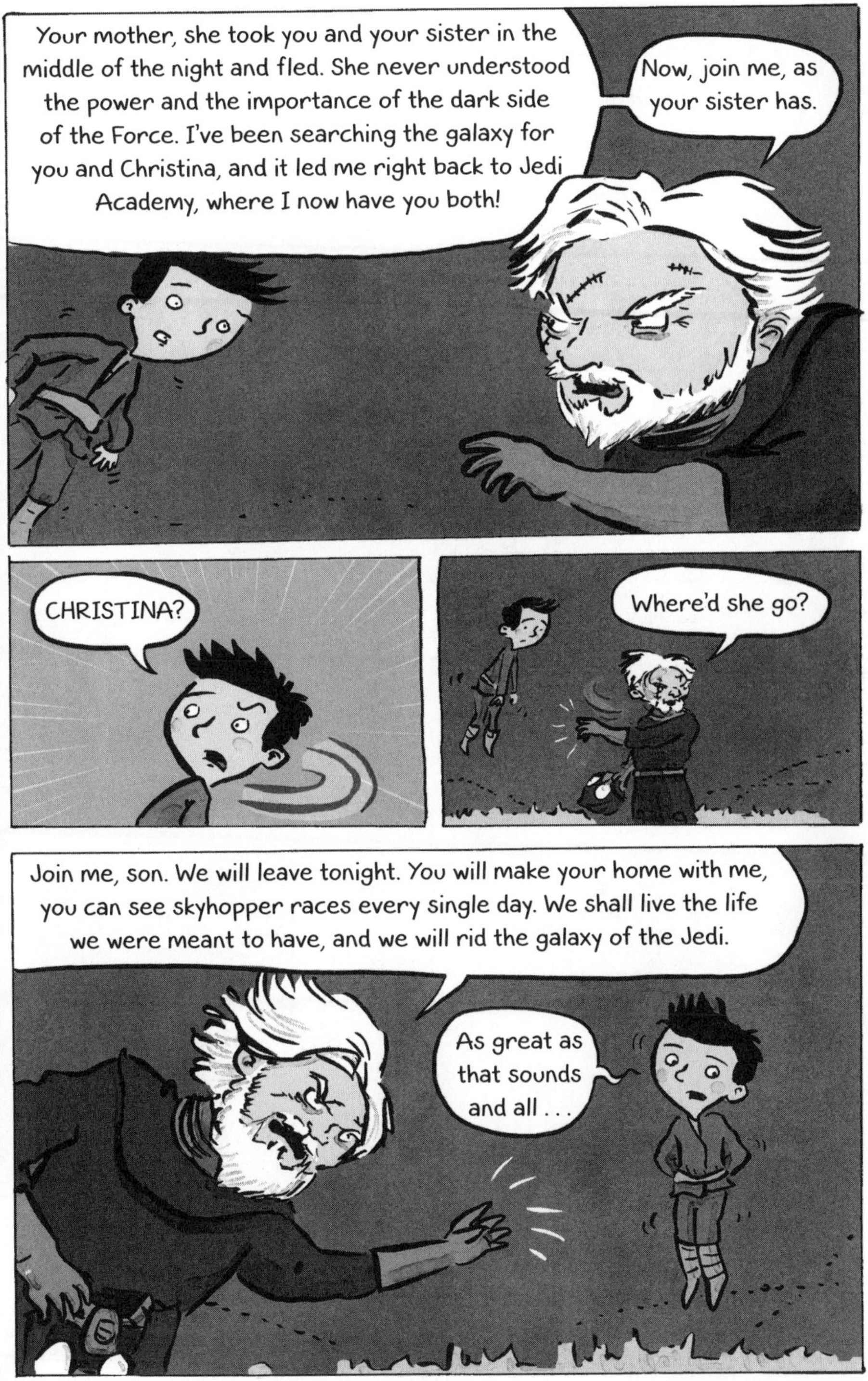
Your mother, she took you and your sister in the middle of the night and fled. She never understood the power and the importance of the dark side of the Force. I've been searching the galaxy for you and Christina, and it led me right back to Jedi Academy, where I now have you both!
Now, join me, as your sister has.
CHRISTINA?
Where'd she go?
Join me, son. We will leave tonight. You will make your home with me, you can see skyhopper races every single day. We shall live the life we were meant to have, and we will rid the galaxy of the Jedi.
As great as that sounds and all . . .

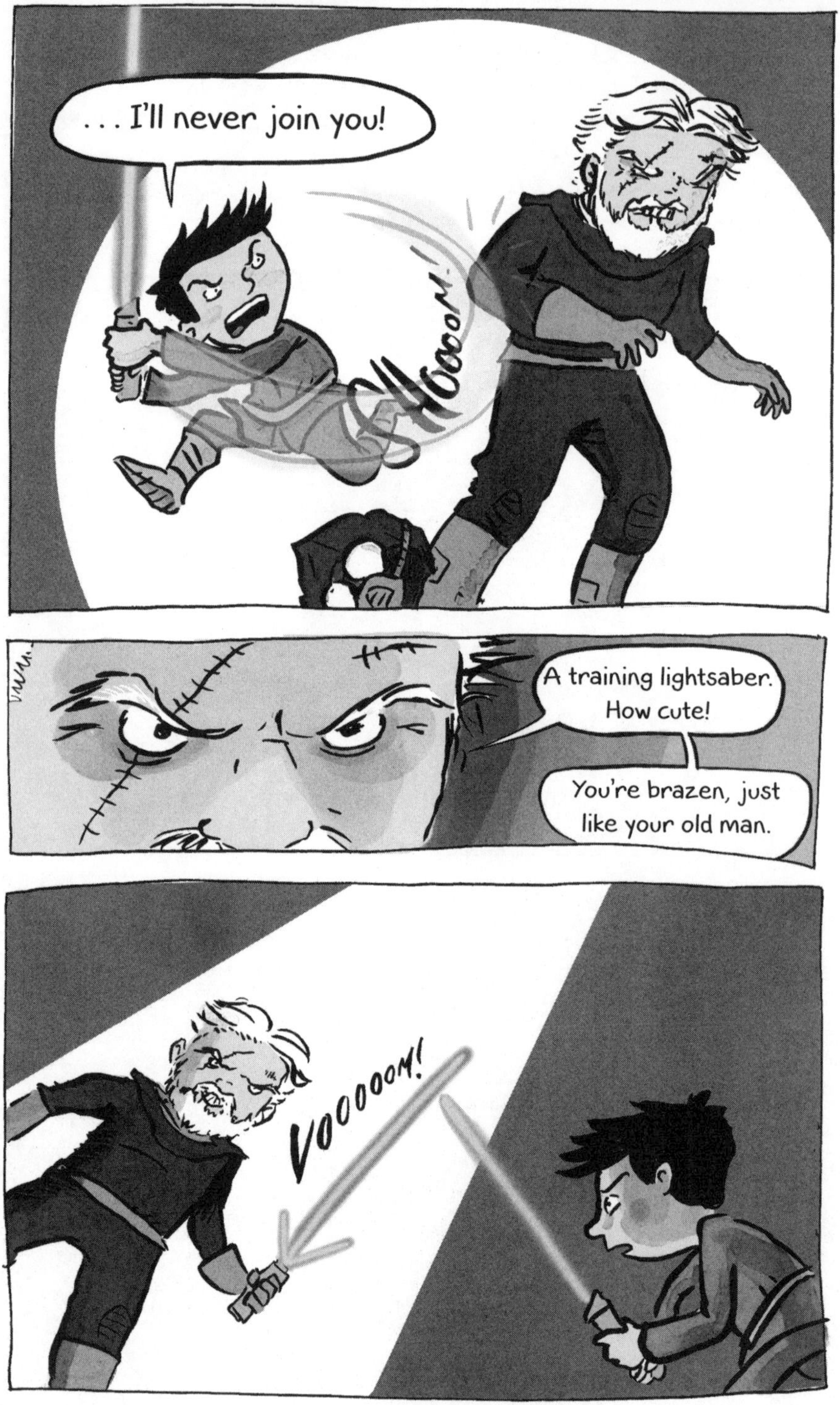
. . . I'll never join you!
A training lightsaber. How cute!
You're brazen, just like your old man.
VOOOOOM!

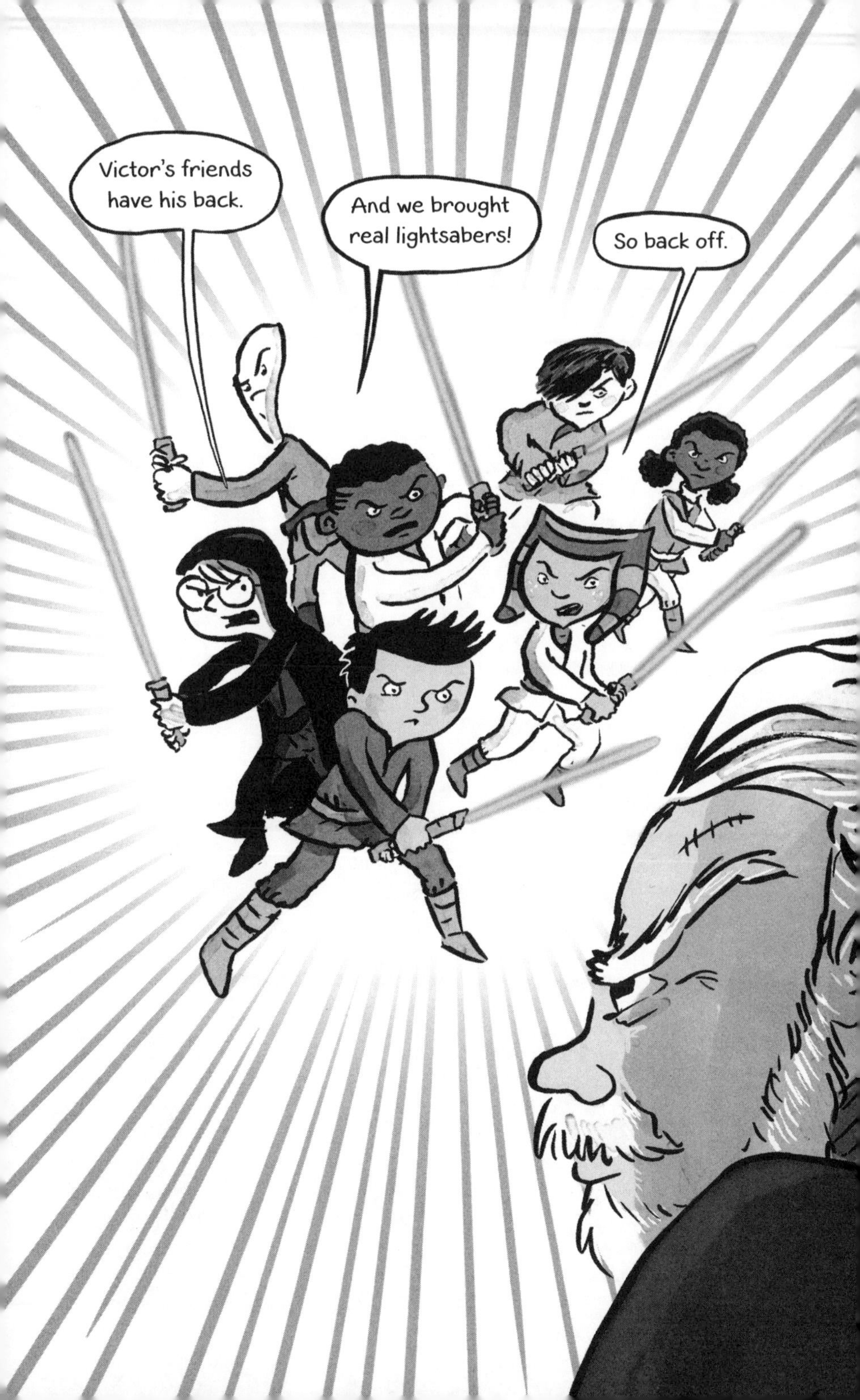
Victor's friends have his back.
And we brought real lightsabers!
So back off.

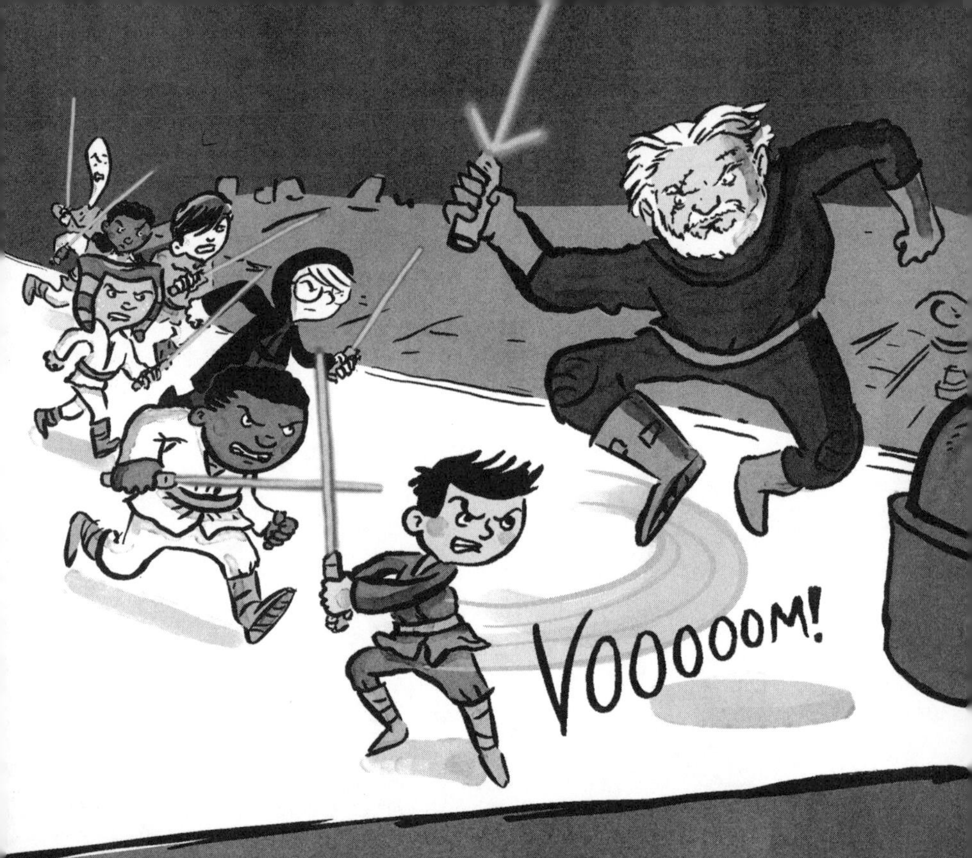
VOOOOOM!
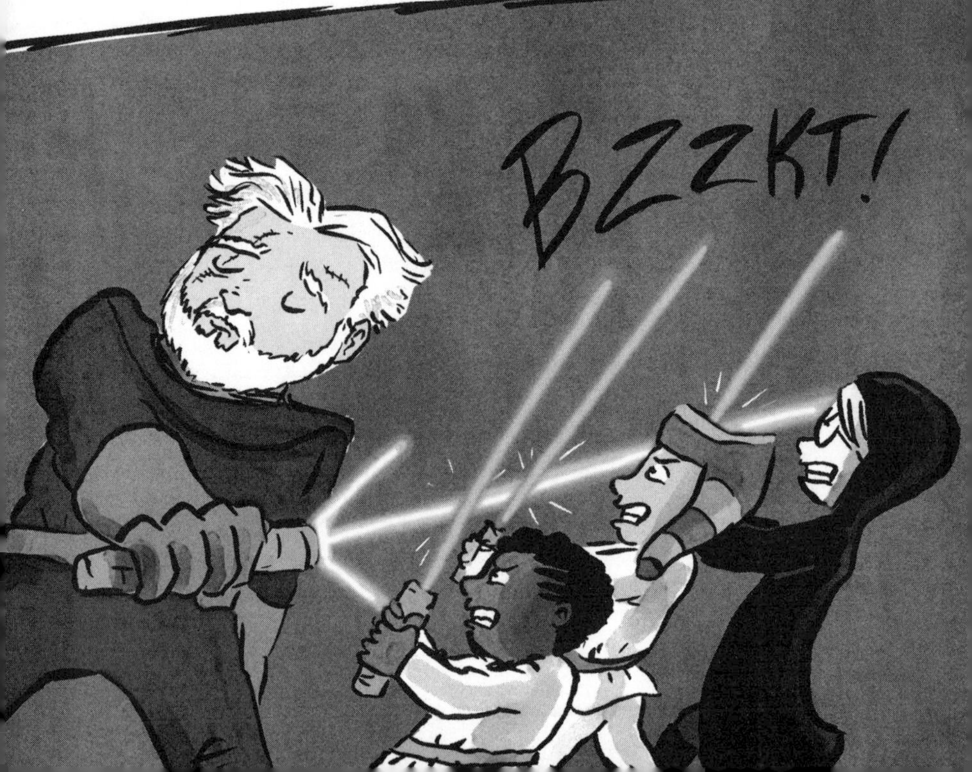
BZZKT!

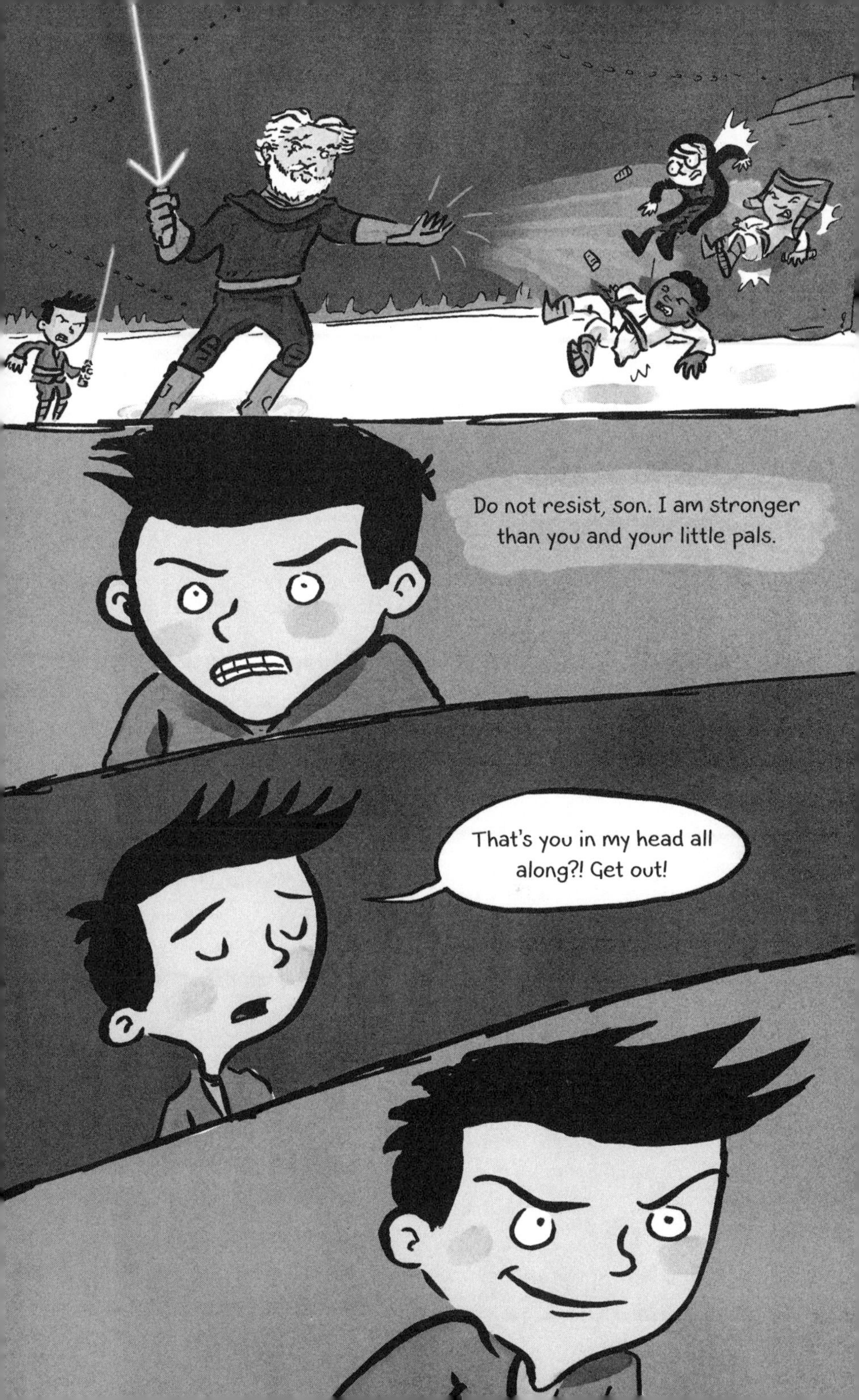
Do not resist, son. I am stronger than you and your little pals.
That's you in my head all along?! Get out!

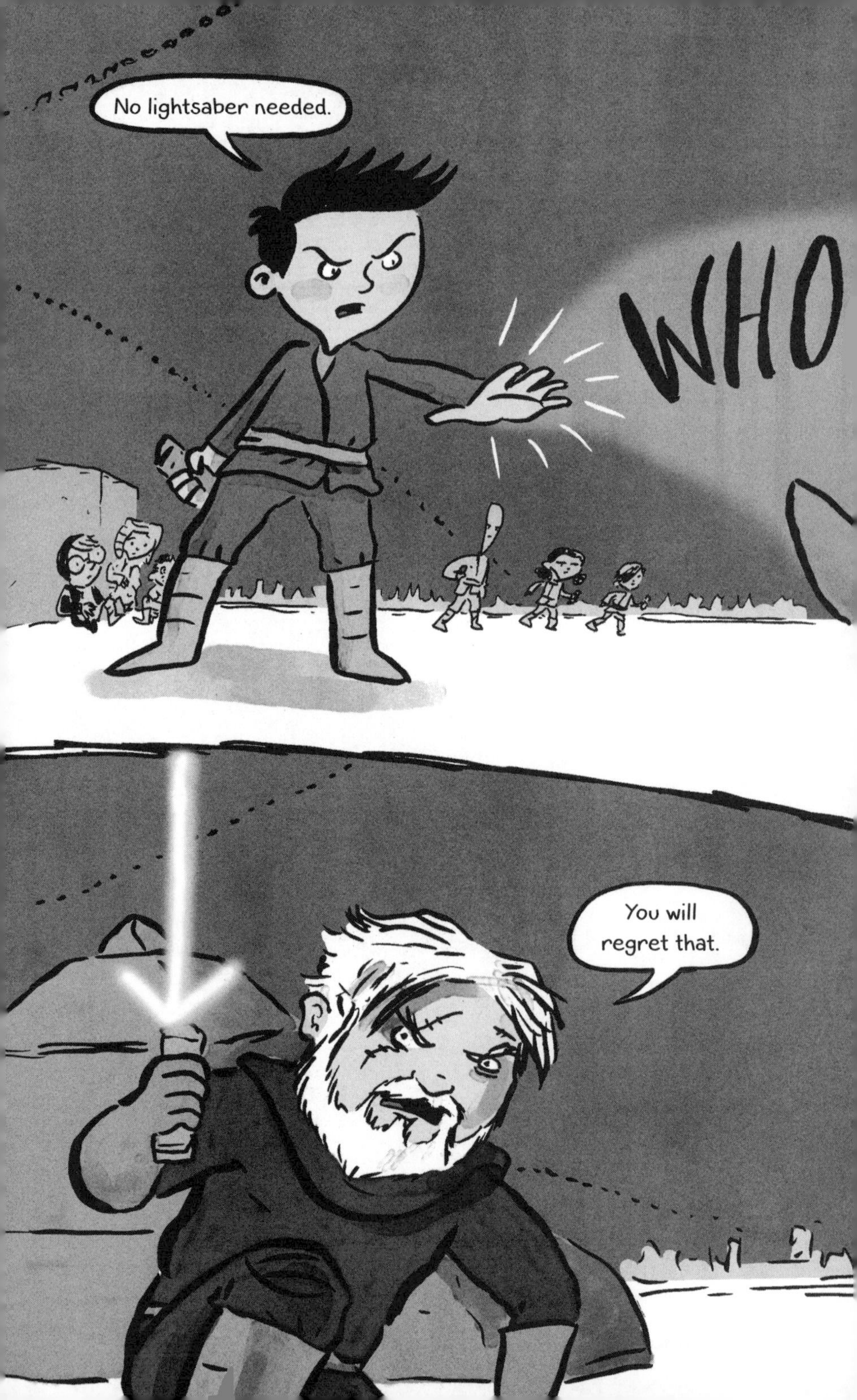
No lightsaber needed.
WHO
You will regret that.

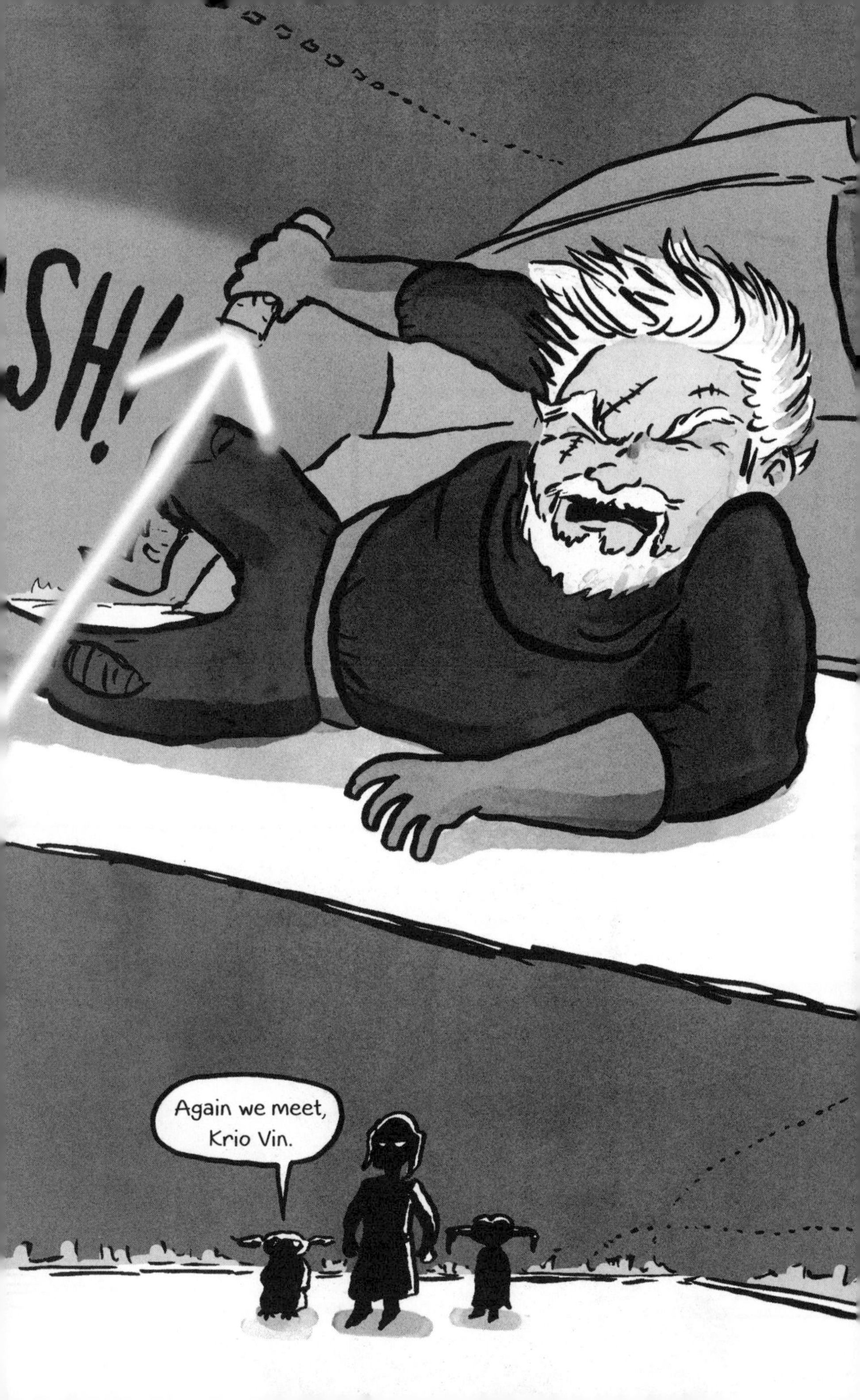
SH!
Again we meet, Krio Vin.

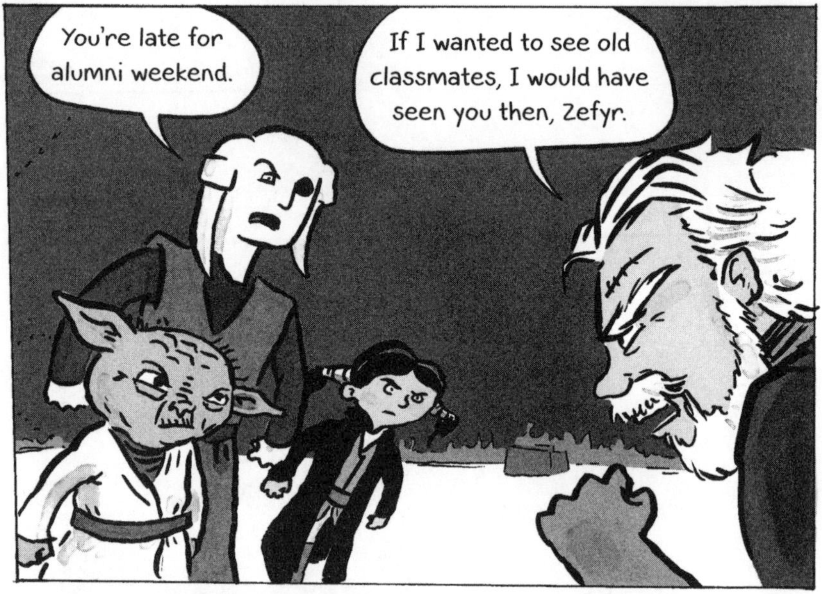
You're late for alumni weekend.
If I wanted to see old classmates, I would have seen you then, Zefyr.

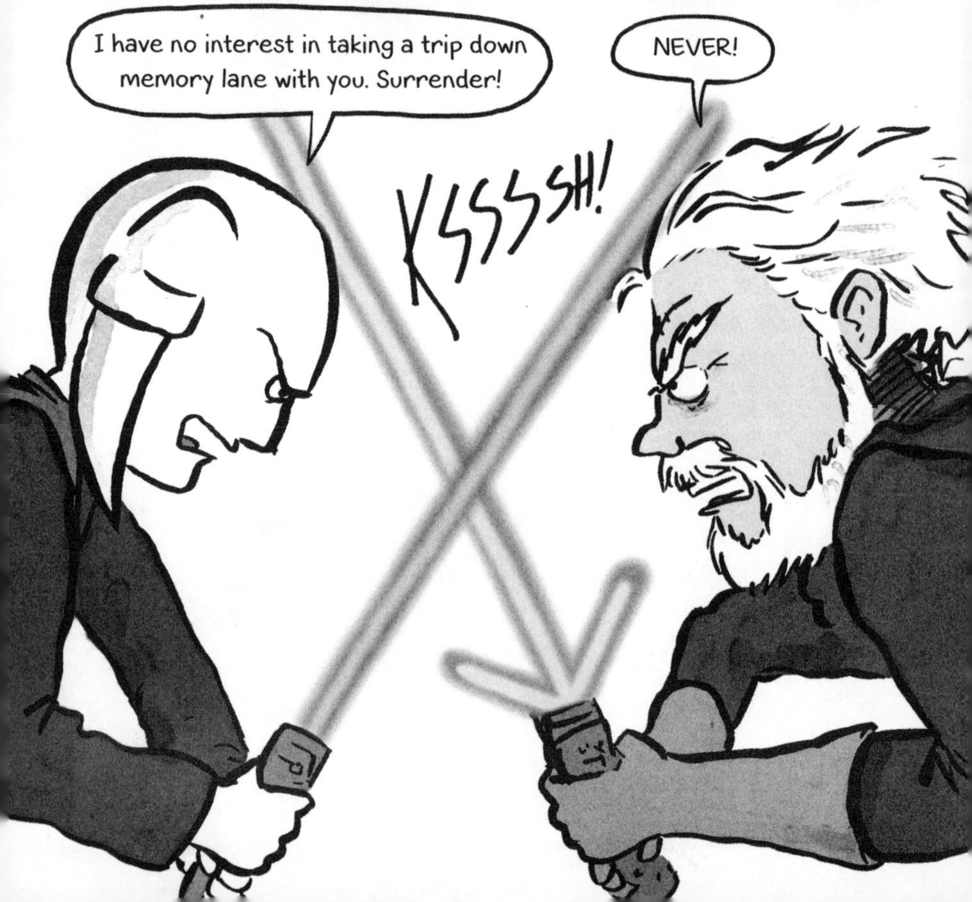
I have no interest in taking a trip down memory lane with you. Surrender!
NEVER!
KSSSSH!

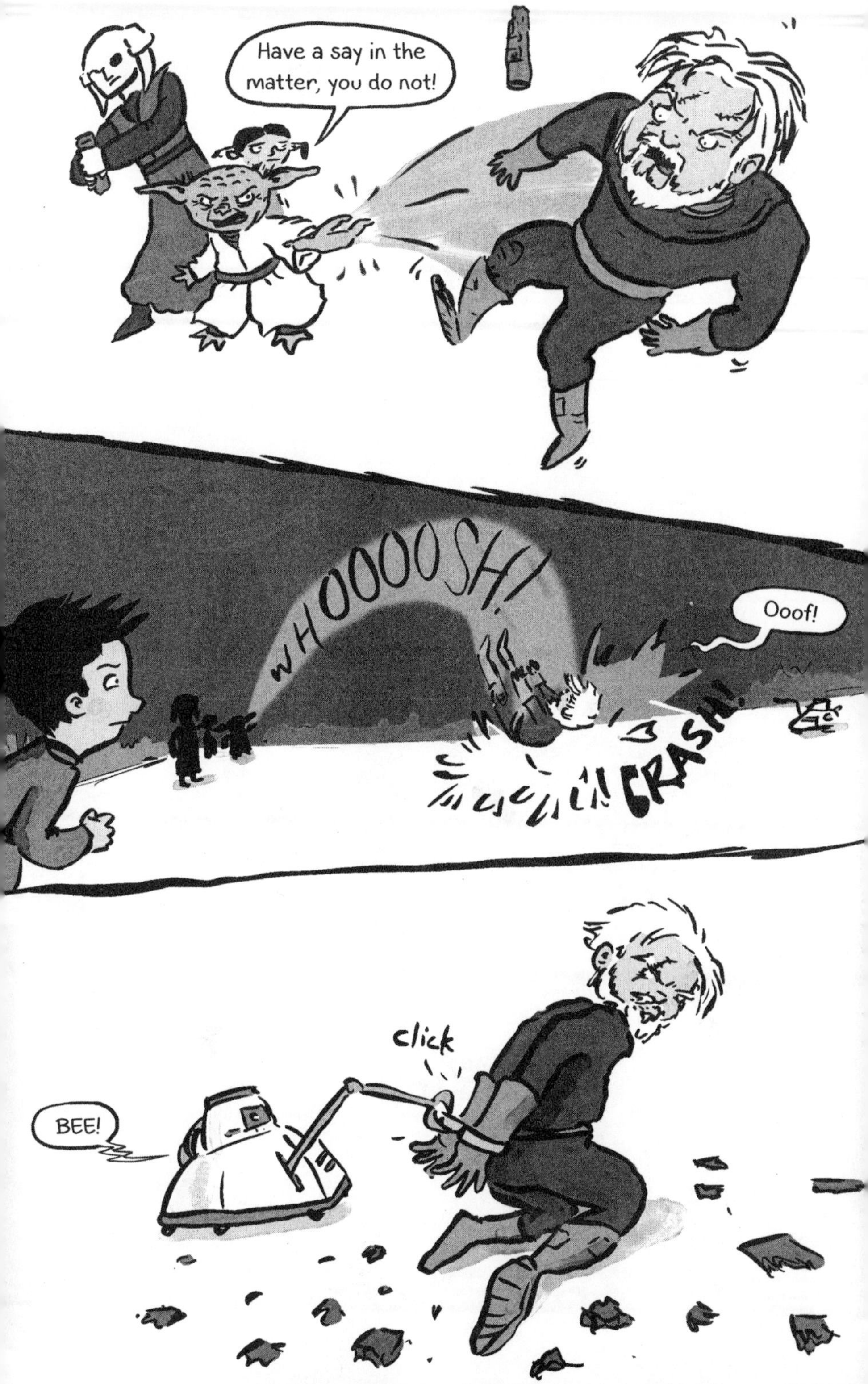

Have a say in the matter, you do not!
WHOOOOSH!
Ooof!
CRASH!
click
BEE!

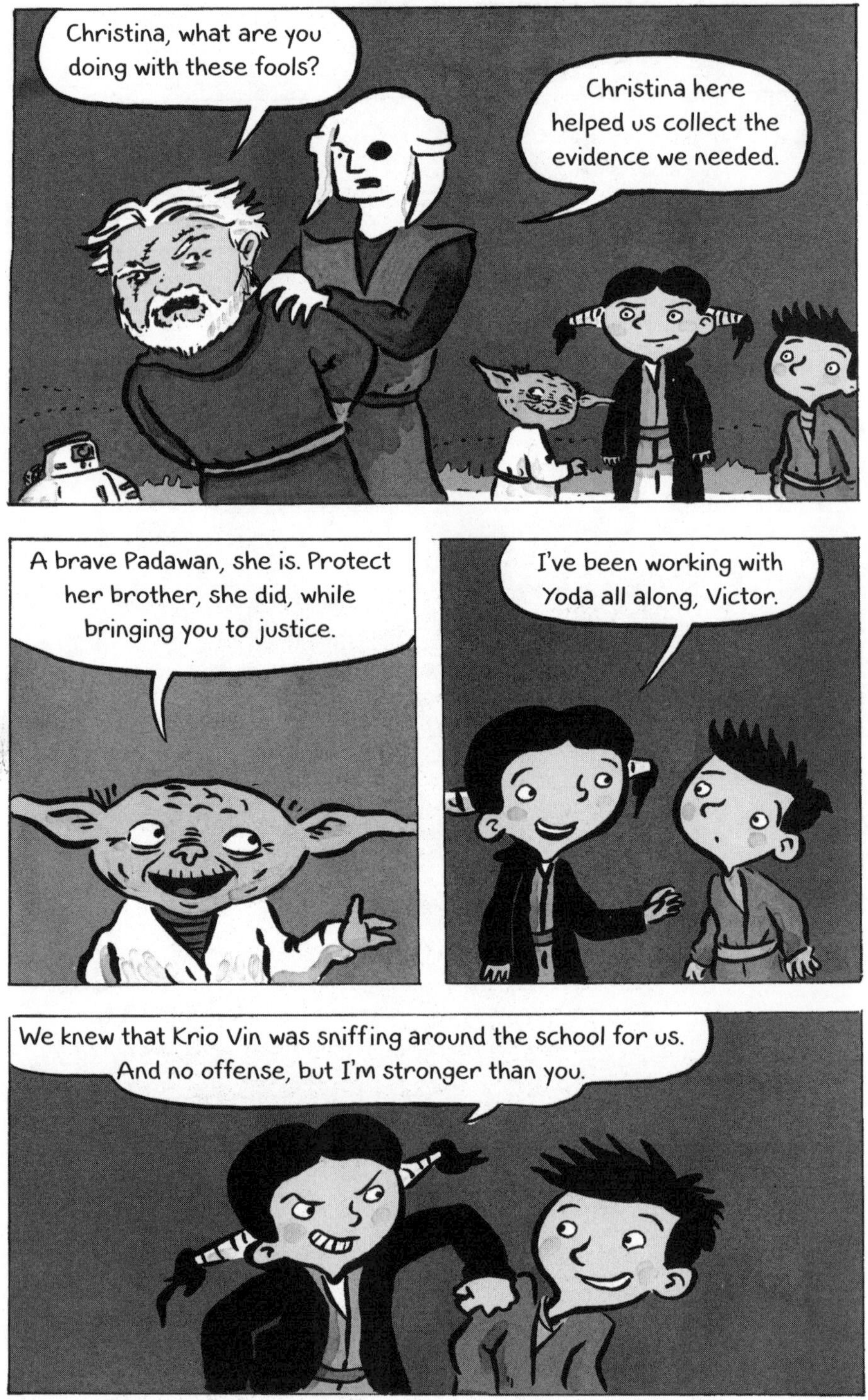
Christina, what are you doing with these fools?
Christina here helped us collect the evidence we needed.
A brave Padawan, she is. Protect her brother, she did, while bringing you to justice.
I've been working with Yoda all along, Victor.
We knew that Krio Vin was sniffing around the school for us. And no offense, but I'm stronger than you.

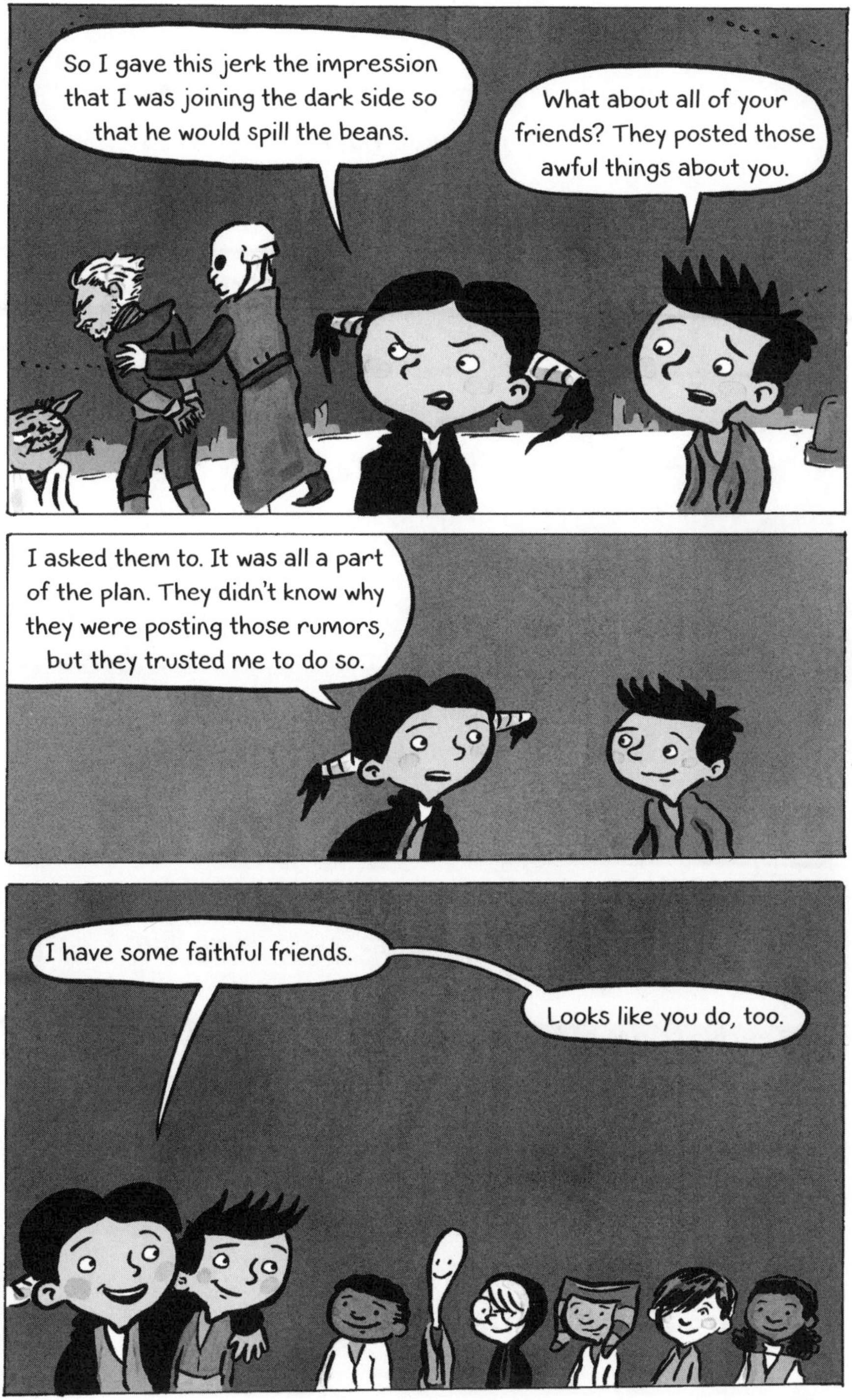
So I gave this jerk the impression that I was joining the dark side so that he would spill the beans.
What about all of your friends? They posted those awful things about you.
I asked them to. It was all a part of the plan. They didn't know why they were posting those rumors, but they trusted me to do so.
I have some faithful friends.
Looks like you do, too.

Pentaday

Well, that was an emotional ride through a meteor shower. It turns out, my dad hasn't been dead all these years, he just went to the dark side and has been working the skyhopper race circuit. Now I understand why my mom was so concerned about me getting into these races—she didn't want me reconnecting with my father. Yoda assured me that all skyhopper racers aren't this seedy, so this shouldn't let my love of the spacecraft die. I'm so relieved to know that I wasn't losing Christina to the dark side. I am amazed by her bravery. Yoda and Mr. Zefyr were right to choose her over me. I had put my dad on such a pedestal, I would have been duped into thinking he was a good guy. I also have some work to do in regards to my self-control, but I'm getting there. I am, after all, at the best school in the entire galaxy.

I'm sad that the school year is ending; it's proven that I have the best friends to exist ever. But I can't wait to see Mom and Russell at home. I have a lot to thank them for. That couldn't have been easy for them to keep up this idea that my father was dead. It was easier for me to grow up thinking that he was just gone versus him being a bad man. And as much as I always wanted to know him, I did have a dad in Russell. It isn't about who you come from, but who surrounds you. And I sure am lucky to have the best parents I could have ever asked for.

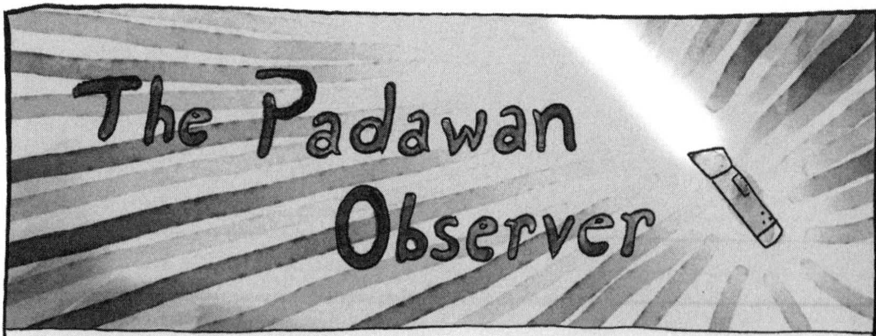
The Padawan
Observer

EDITED BY THE STUDENTS OF JEDI ACADEMY Vol. MXVI #7

GRADUATING STUDENT HAILED A HERO!

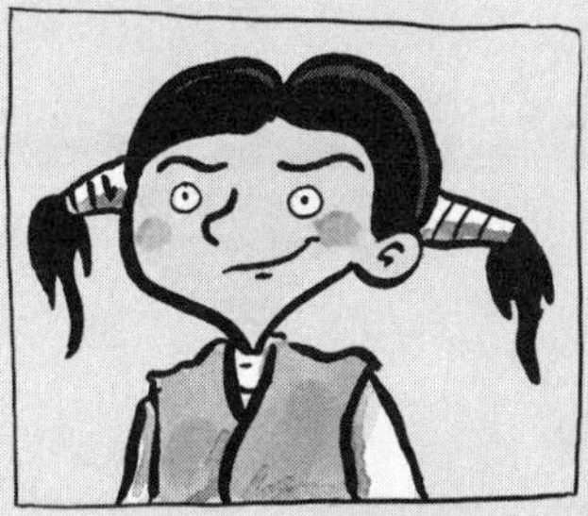

Christina Starspeeder, who is about to take her first steps beyond Jedi Academy as an alumni, is being heralded as a hero for having aided in a sting operation to vanquish a Sith. Working closely with Master Yoda and Mr. Zefyr, Ms. Starspeeder went undercover as an apprentice to one Krio Vin, pretending to be interested in the dark side of the Force. Through her diligence and the bravery of a group of second-year students, Krio Vin has been brought to justice and no longer poses a threat to the Jedi Academy community.

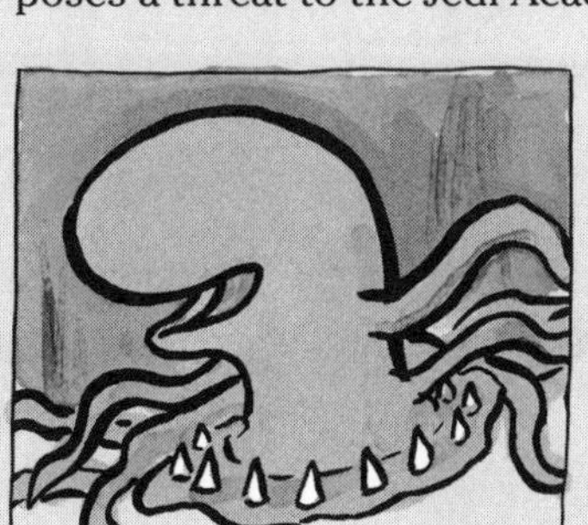

THE SHOW MUST GO ON!

The annual musical, *Little Sarlacc of Horror,* is set to be staged tonight in the Jedi Academy auditorium! There are still a few tickets left, so please send a holo to T-3PO or RW-22 in the theater office if you are interested!

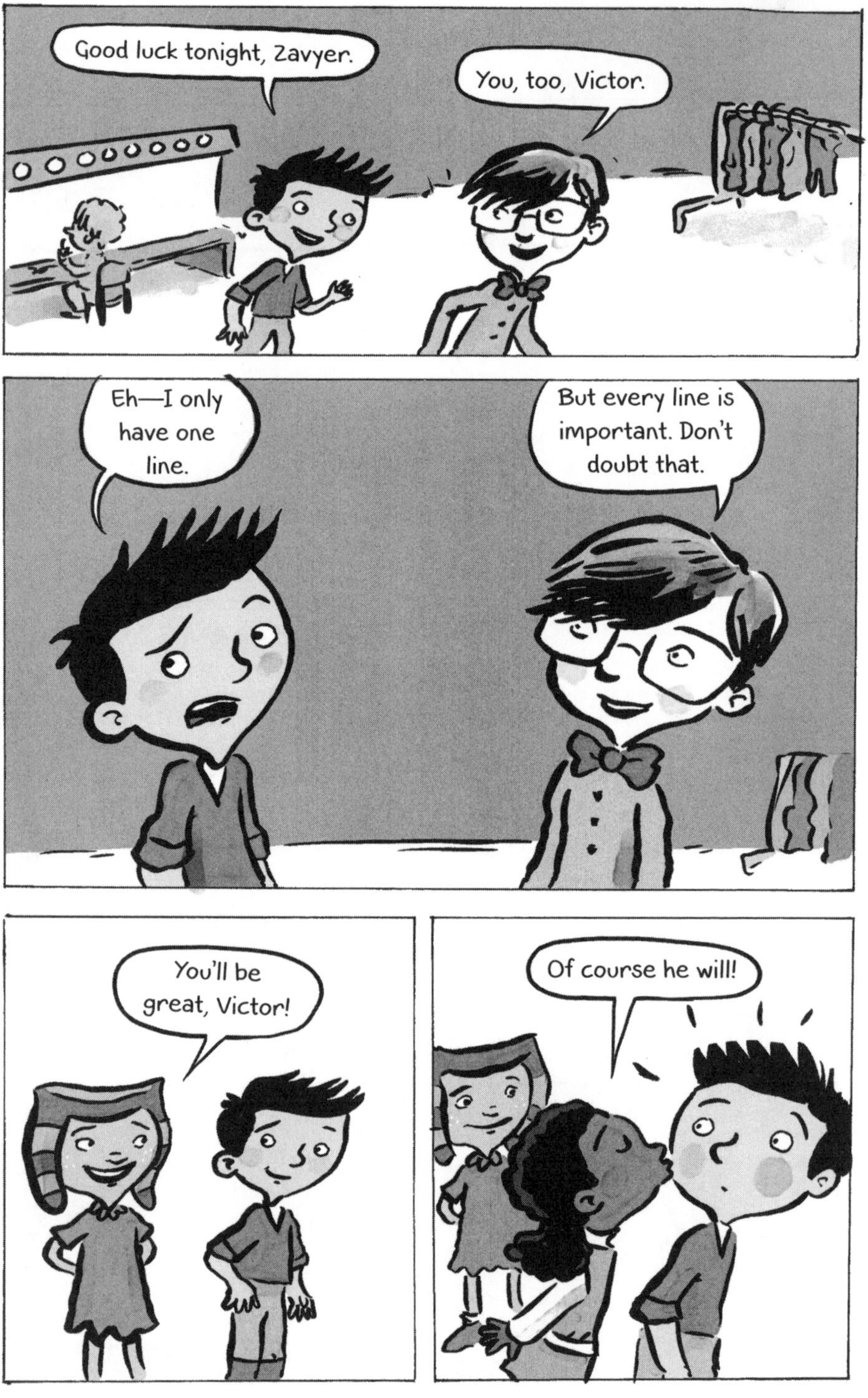
Good luck tonight, Zavyer.
You, too, Victor.
Eh—I only have one line.
But every line is important. Don't doubt that.
You'll be great, Victor!
Of course he will!

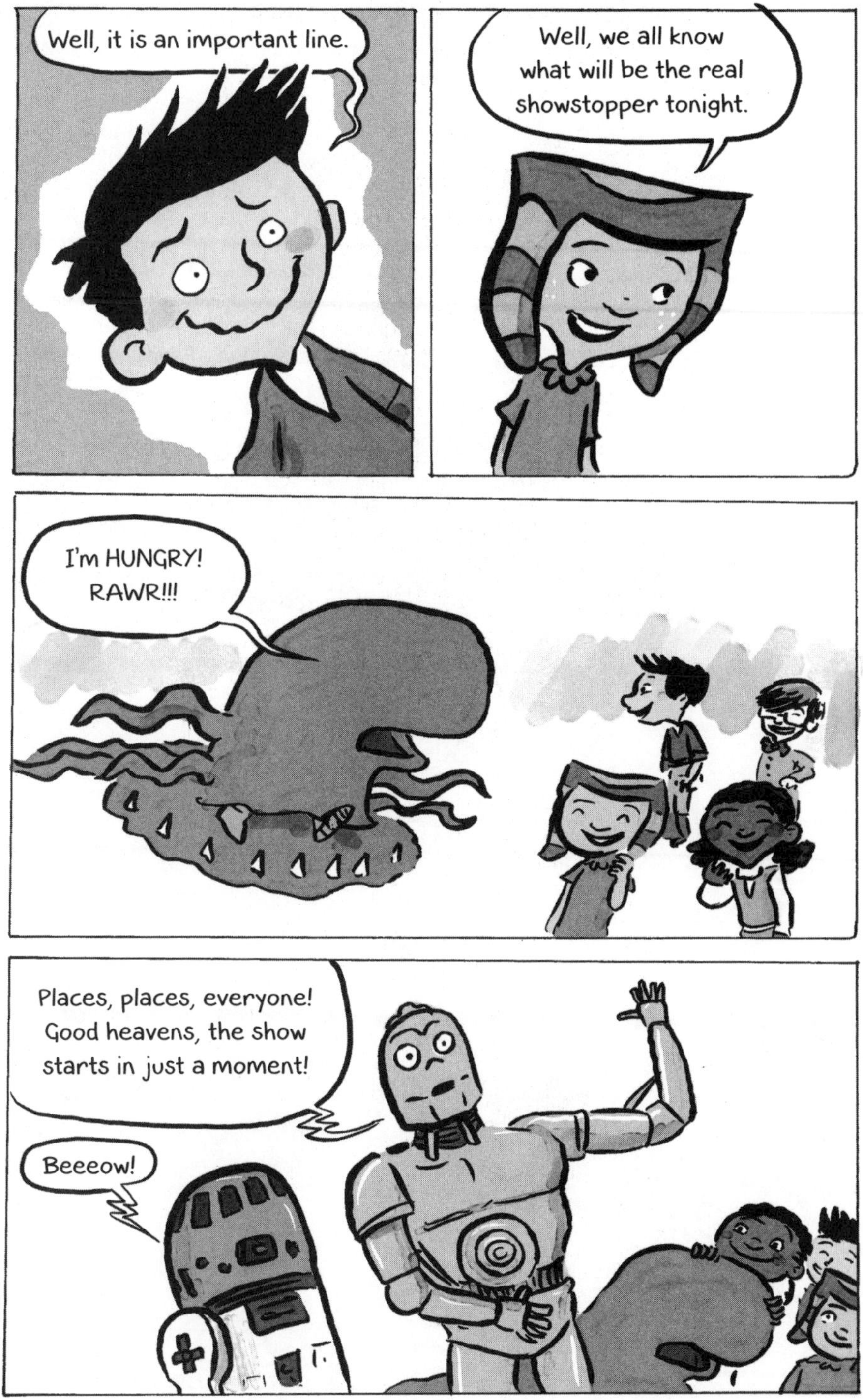
Well, it is an important line.
Well, we all know what will be the real showstopper tonight.
I'm HUNGRY! RAWR!!!
Places, places, everyone! Good heavens, the show starts in just a moment!
Beeeow!

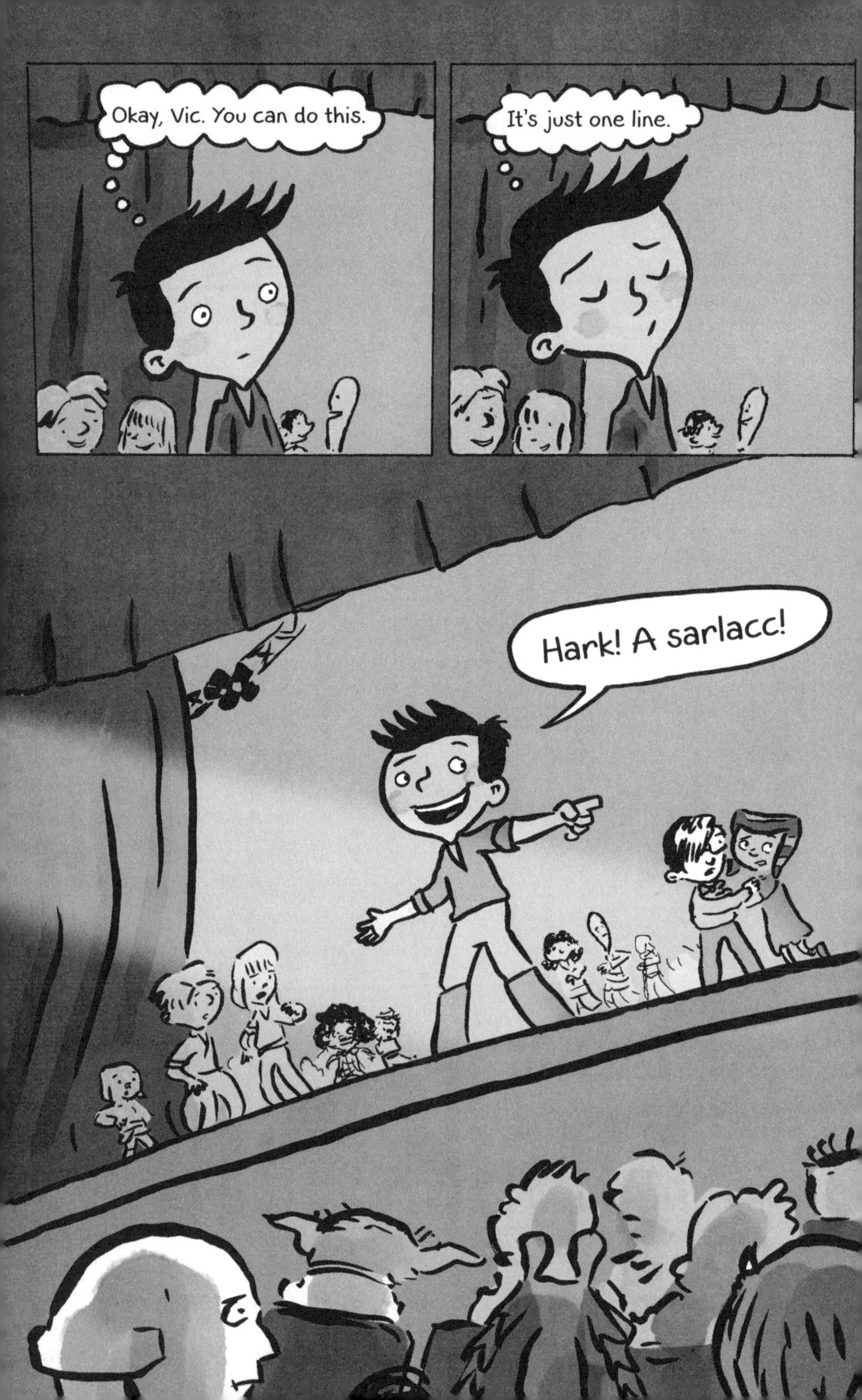
Okay, Vic. You can do this.
It's just one line.
Hark! A sarlacc!

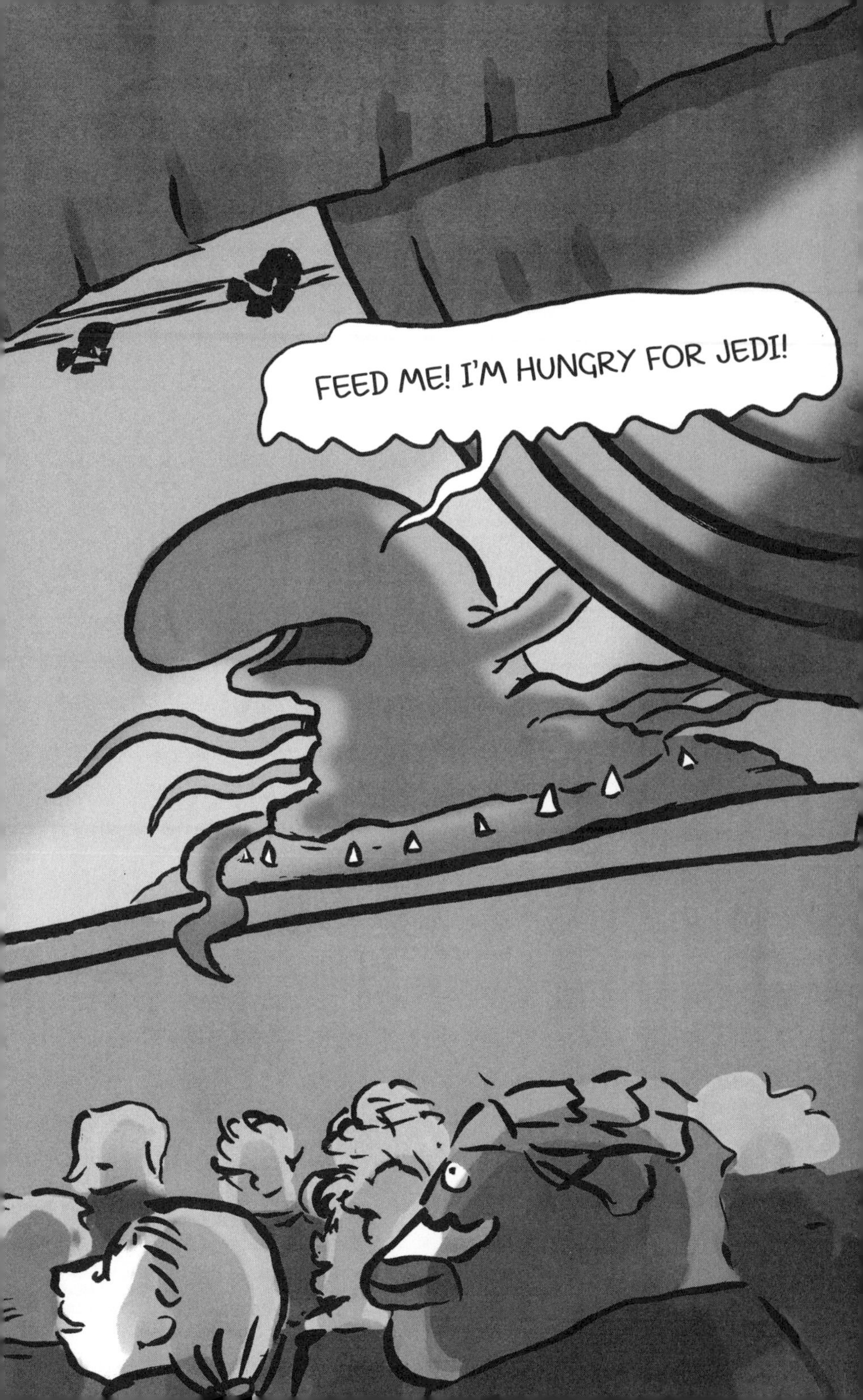
FEED ME! I'M HUNGRY FOR JEDI!

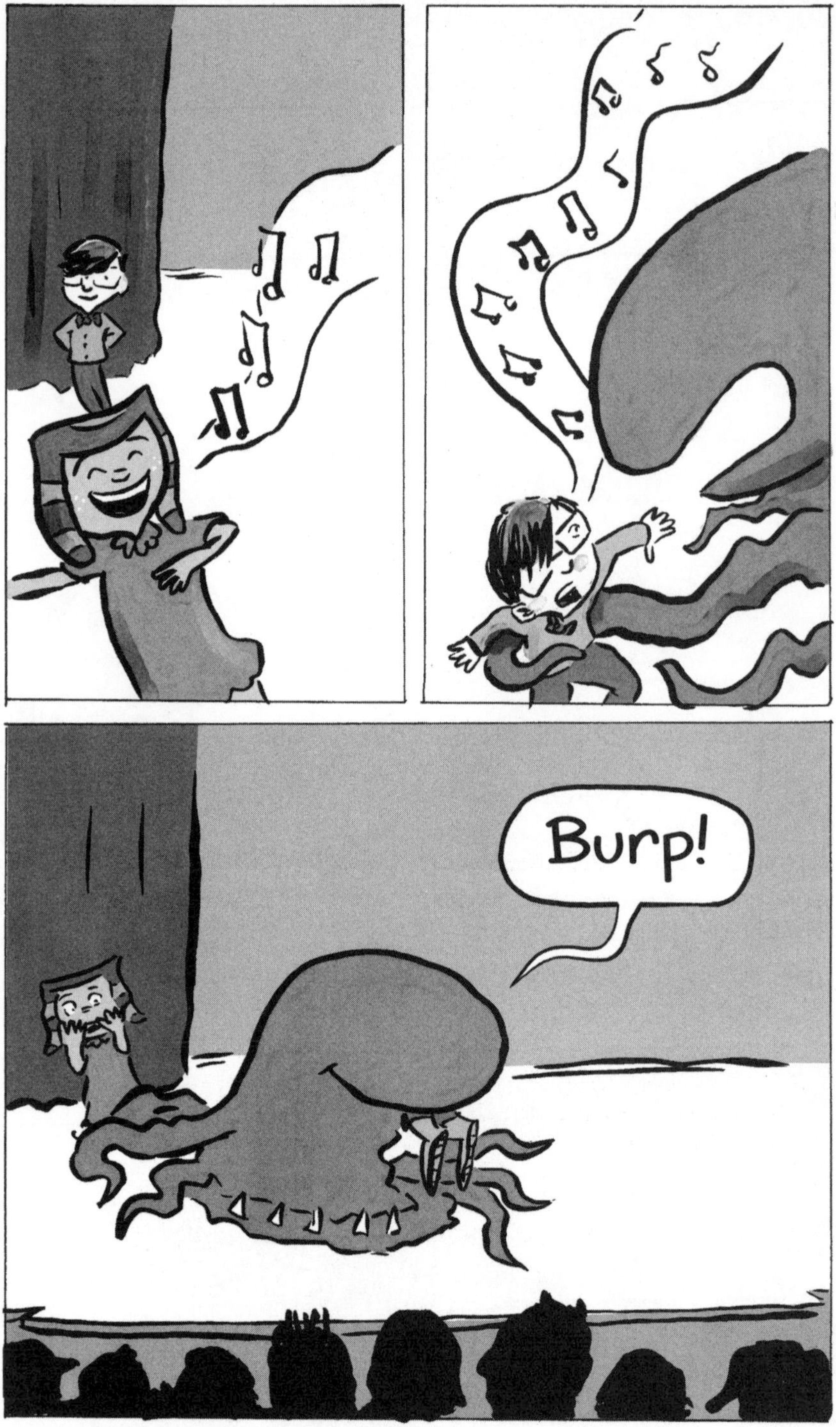
Burp!

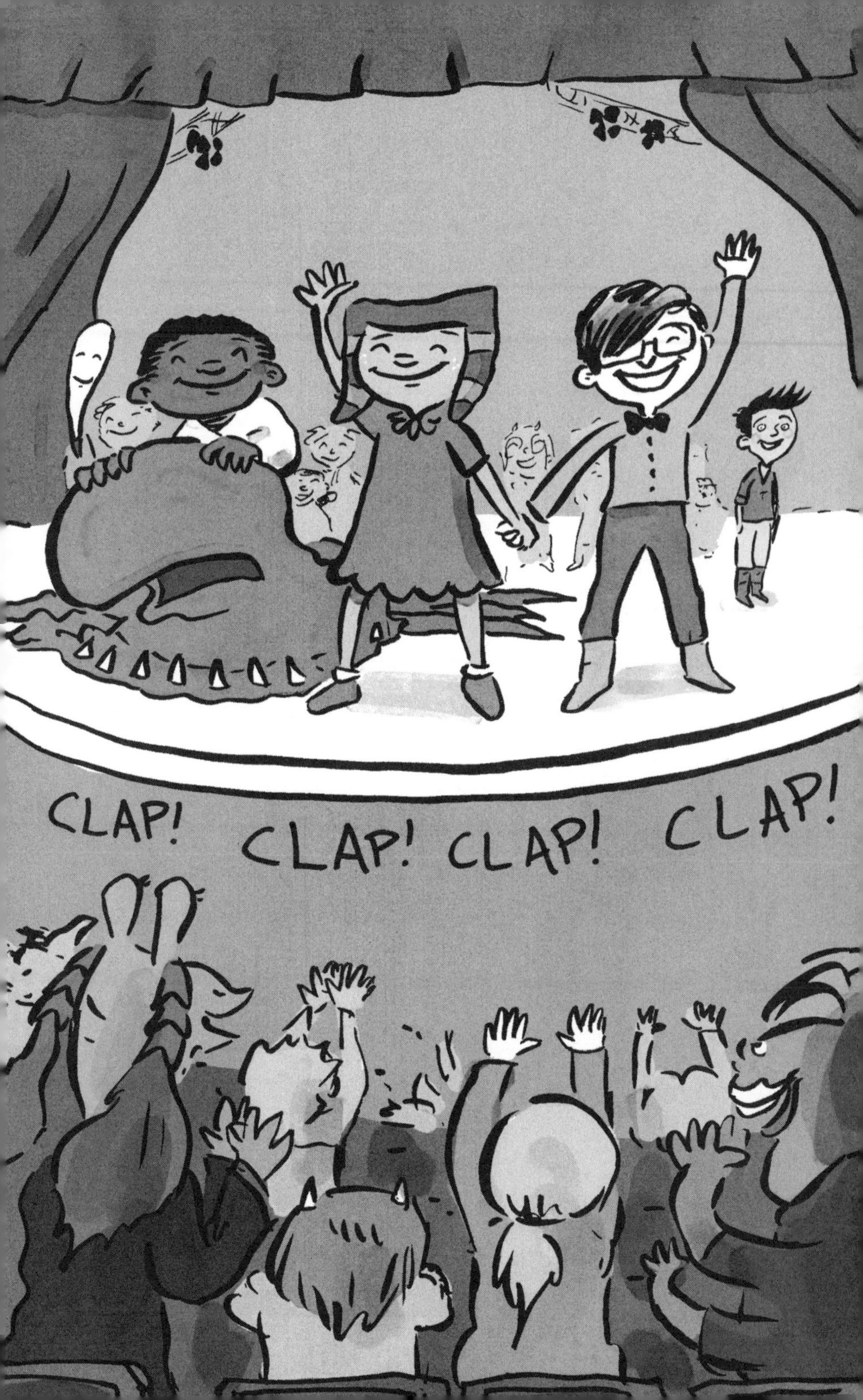
CLAP!
CLAP! CLAP!
CLAP!

Heptaday

Coleman absolutely killed it as the singing sarlacc. And I'm not just talking about what his character does on stage! (Sorry, spoiler alert!) I'm really proud of what Zavyer and I were able to do together by building that beast of a puppet. I managed to deliver my one line without falling on my face. Not as easy as one would think. My line lasted about two seconds, but the moments leading up to it felt like an eternity. I could feel my heart beat in my temples! Definitely gave me newfound respect for what Maya and Coleman do every year. How do you even memorize that many lines? On top of studying? They are mega geniuses, clearly.

Maybe I'll get a lead next year.

Mom and Russell will be arriving in the morning for Christina's graduation ceremony. It's going to be a big deal, because Christina will be getting a medal at the ceremony. Mom hasn't been on campus since Christina's first semester. When I transferred in, she wasn't able to make the trip, but she knew I had Christina to look out for me. I'm excited to show Mom my dorm and introduce her to my friends. I think that she'll really like them. (I mean, honestly, with the way she stresses about me, I think she'll be worried that I am a bad influence on them, not the other way around.)

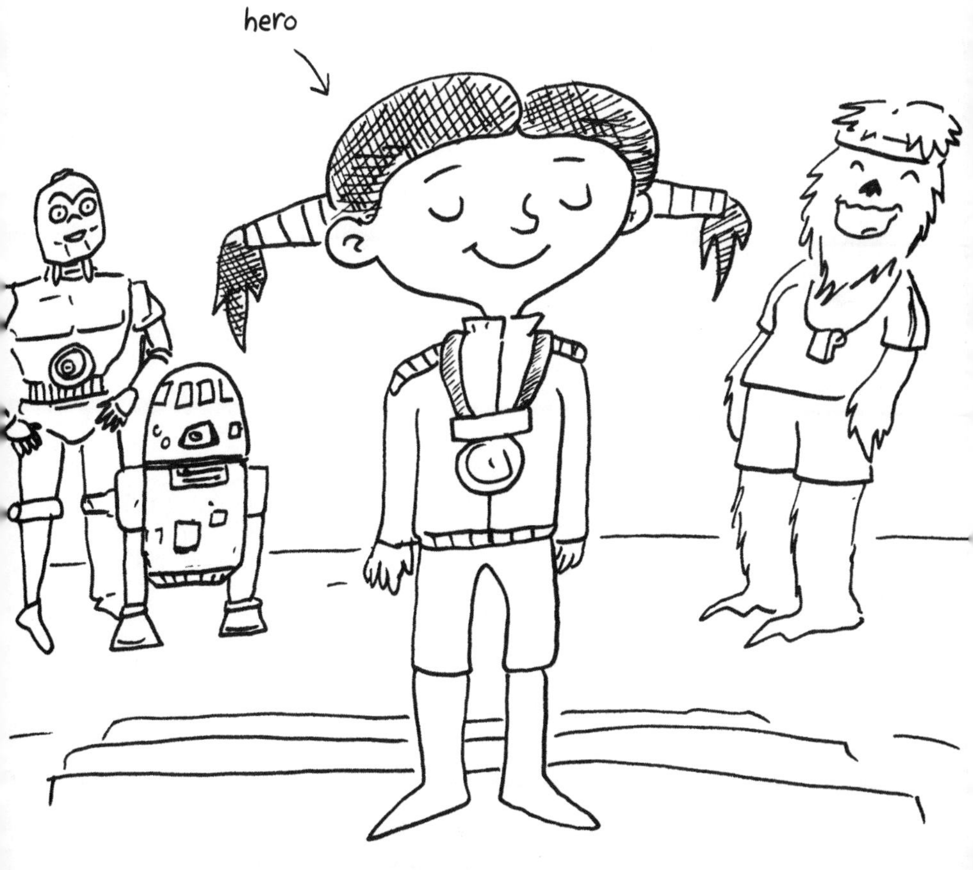
hero

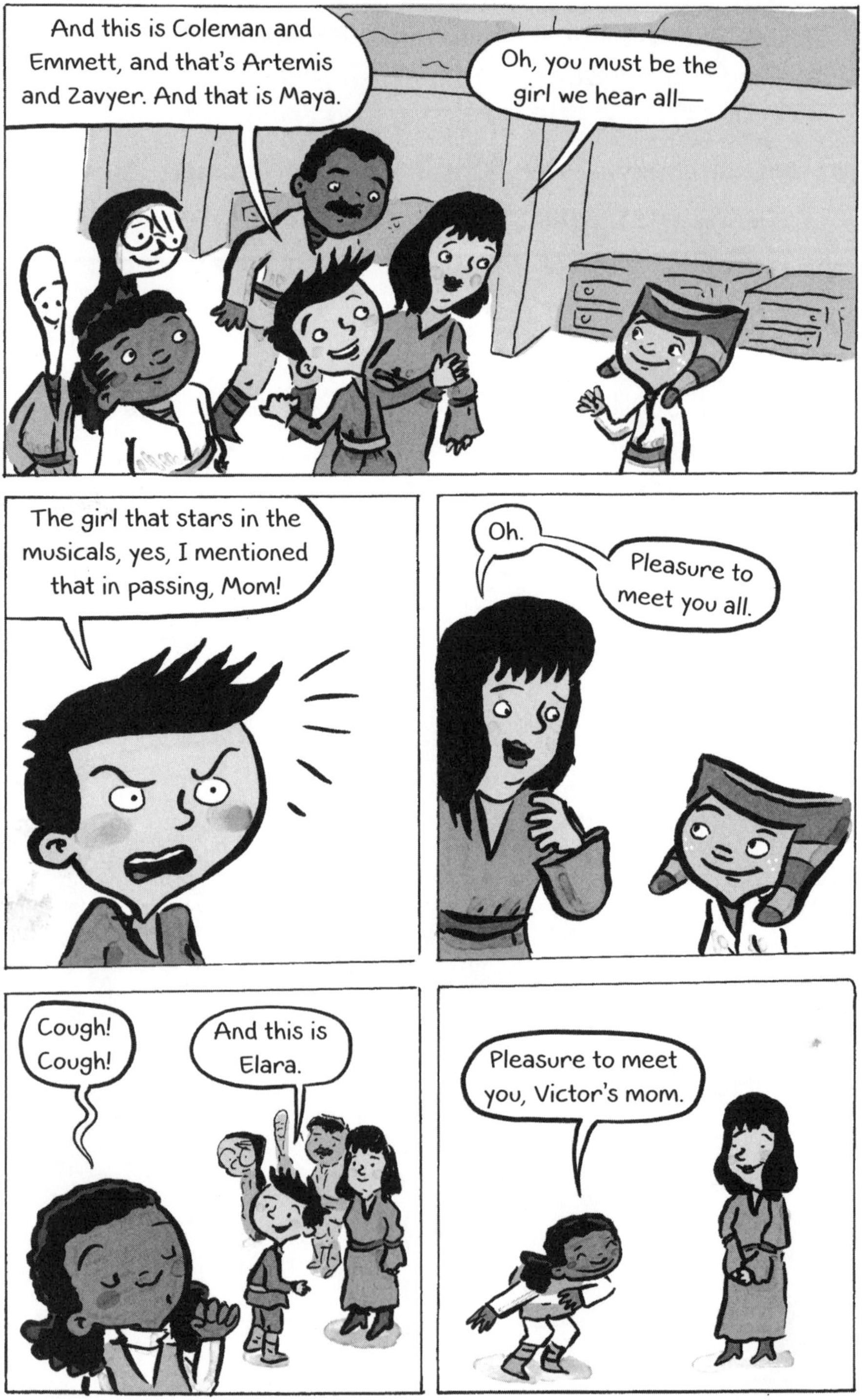
And this is Coleman and Emmett, and that's Artemis and Zavyer. And that is Maya.
Oh, you must be the girl we hear all—
The girl that stars in the musicals, yes, I mentioned that in passing, Mom!
Oh.
Pleasure to meet you all.
Cough! Cough!
And this is Elara.
Pleasure to meet you, Victor's mom.

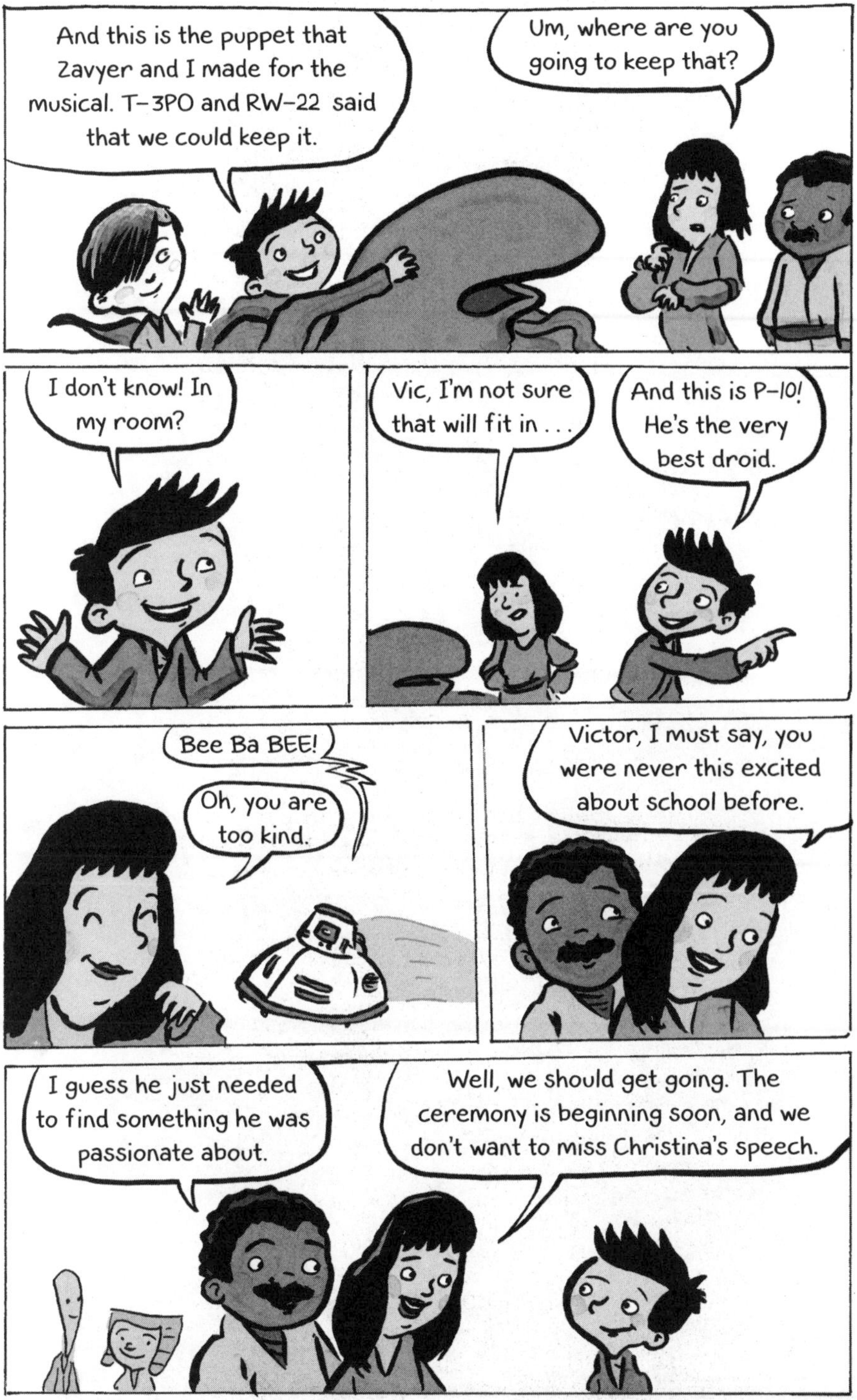
And this is the puppet that Zavyer and I made for the musical. T-3PO and RW-22 said that we could keep it.
Um, where are you going to keep that?
I don't know! In my room?
Vic, I'm not sure that will fit in . . .
And this is P-10! He's the very best droid.
Bee Ba BEE!
Oh, you are too kind.
Victor, I must say, you were never this excited about school before.
I guess he just needed to find something he was passionate about.
Well, we should get going. The ceremony is beginning soon, and we don't want to miss Christina's speech.

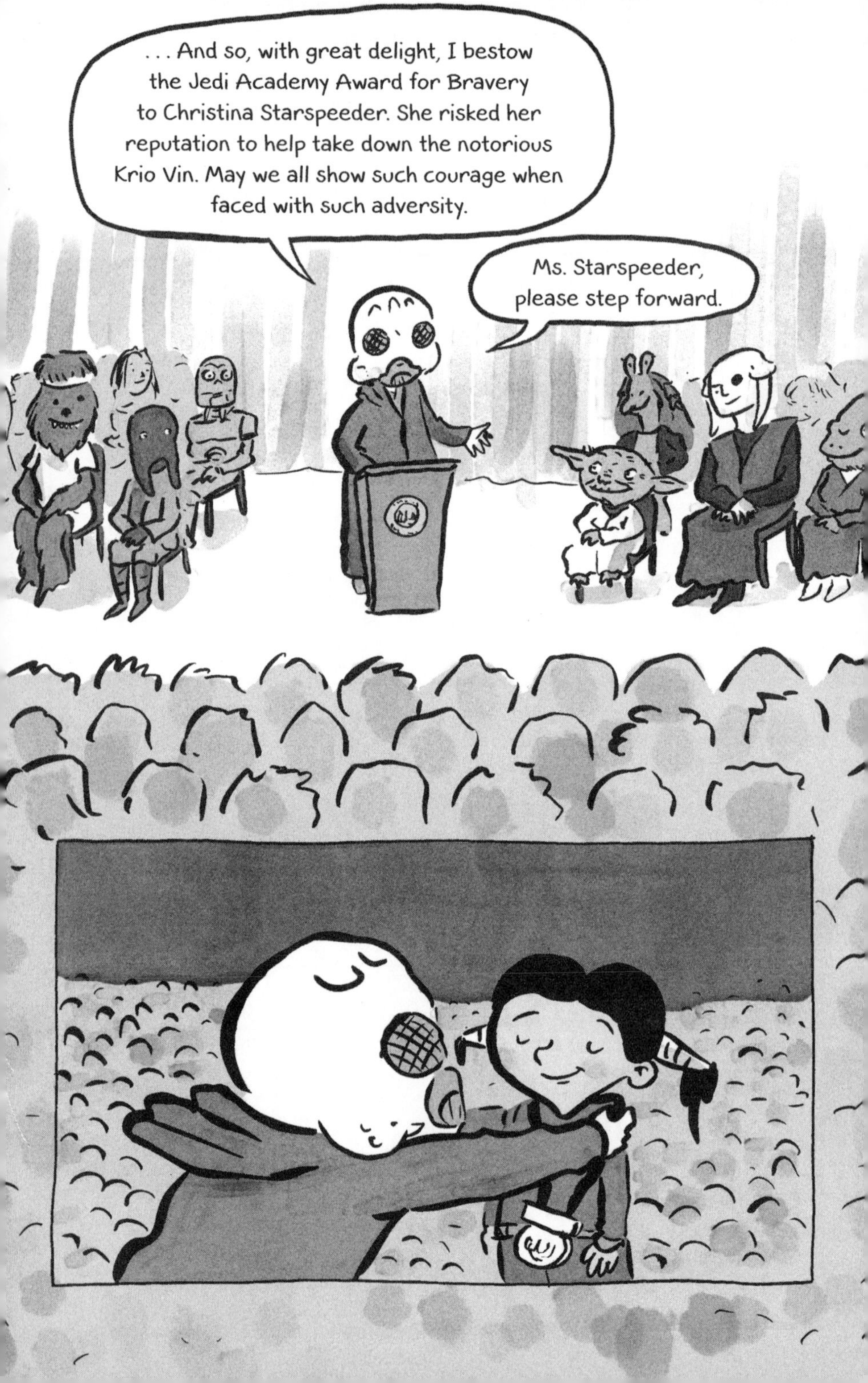
. . . And so, with great delight, I bestow the Jedi Academy Award for Bravery to Christina Starspeeder. She risked her reputation to help take down the notorious Krio Vin. May we all show such courage when faced with such adversity.
Ms. Starspeeder, please step forward.

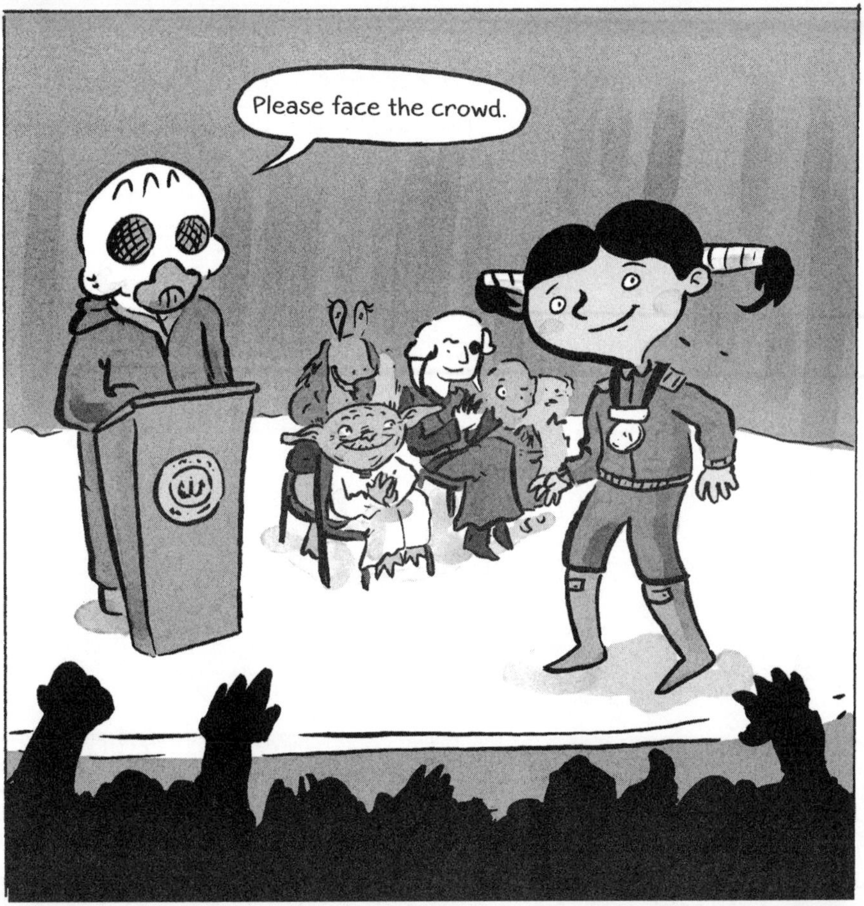
Please face the crowd.

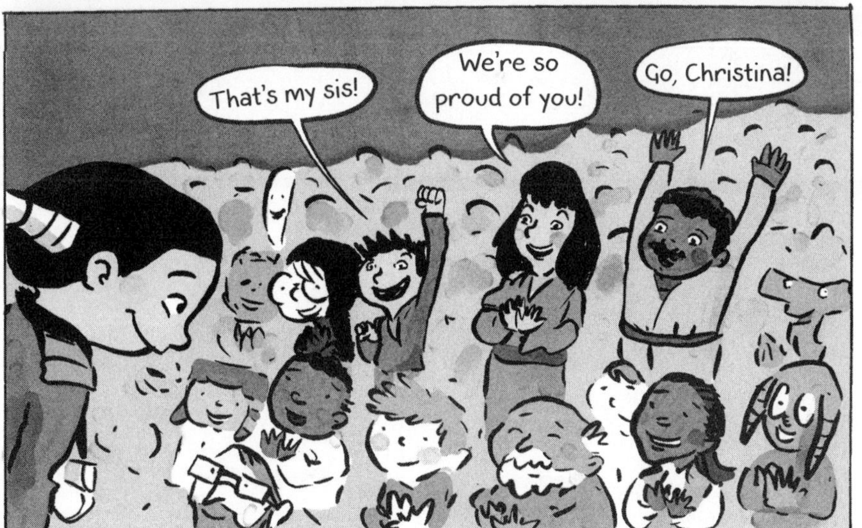
That's my sis!
We're so proud of you!
Go, Christina!

Christina gave this heartfelt speech at the awards ceremony. I think she was being complimentary of me. I asked her if I could keep her speech to post in my journal.

i have learned so much during my time here at Jedi Academy. Master Yoda, always a bright sage you were. Mr. Zefyr, your temper was only matched by your passion for education. But out of everyone who helped me, the most valuble people have been my family. Everything i ever needed to know about courage, i learned from watching my mother as she ensured a safe childhood for my brother and me. Everything i ever needed to know about compassion, i learned from my stepfather, Russell. And everything i learned about patience, i learned by dealing with my little brother, Victor.

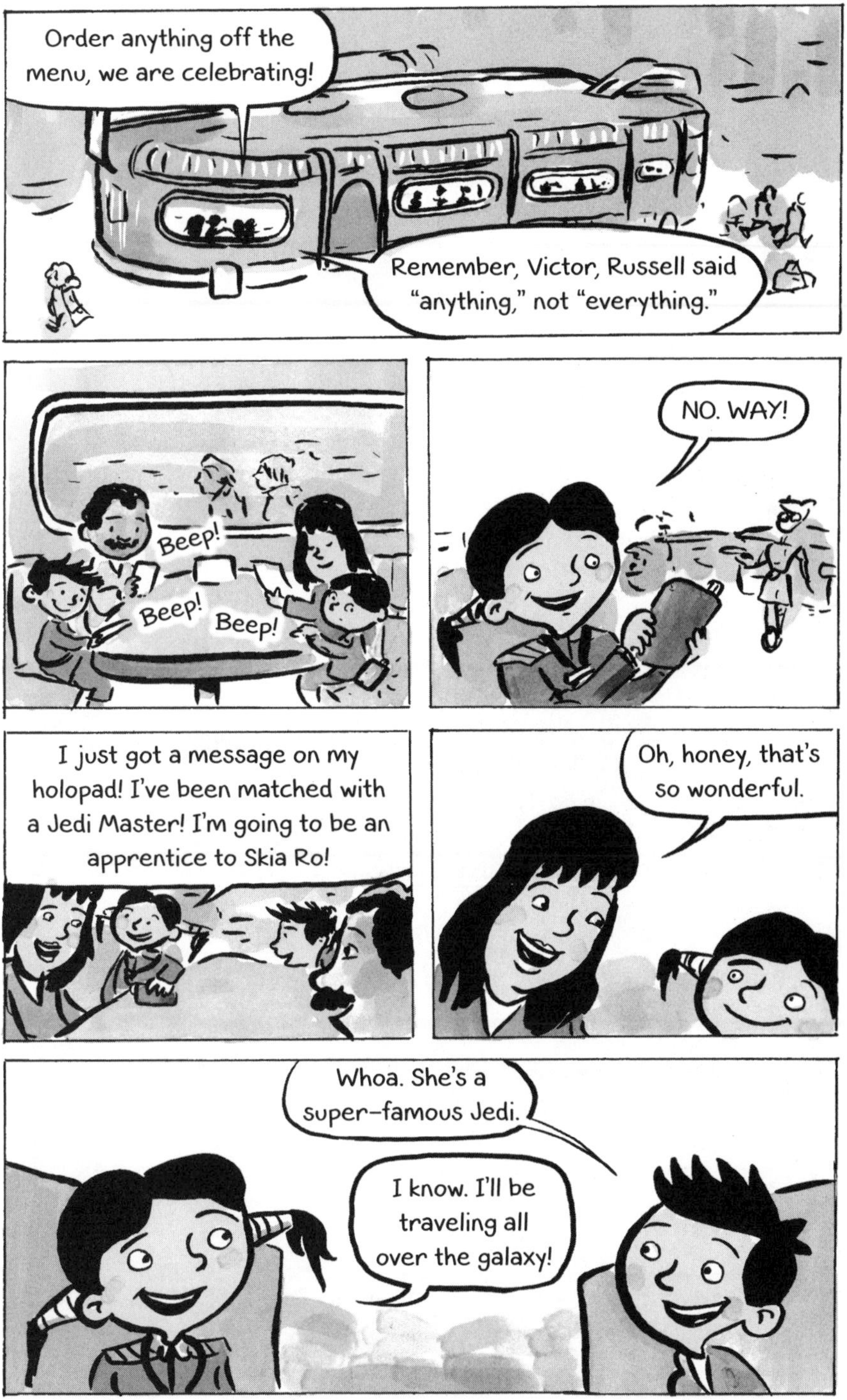
Order anything off the menu, we are celebrating!
Remember, Victor, Russell said "anything," not "everything."
Beep!
Beep!
Beep!
NO. WAY!
I just got a message on my holopad! I've been matched with a Jedi Master! I'm going to be an apprentice to Skia Ro!
Oh, honey, that's so wonderful.
Whoa. She's a super-famous Jedi.
I know. I'll be traveling all over the galaxy!

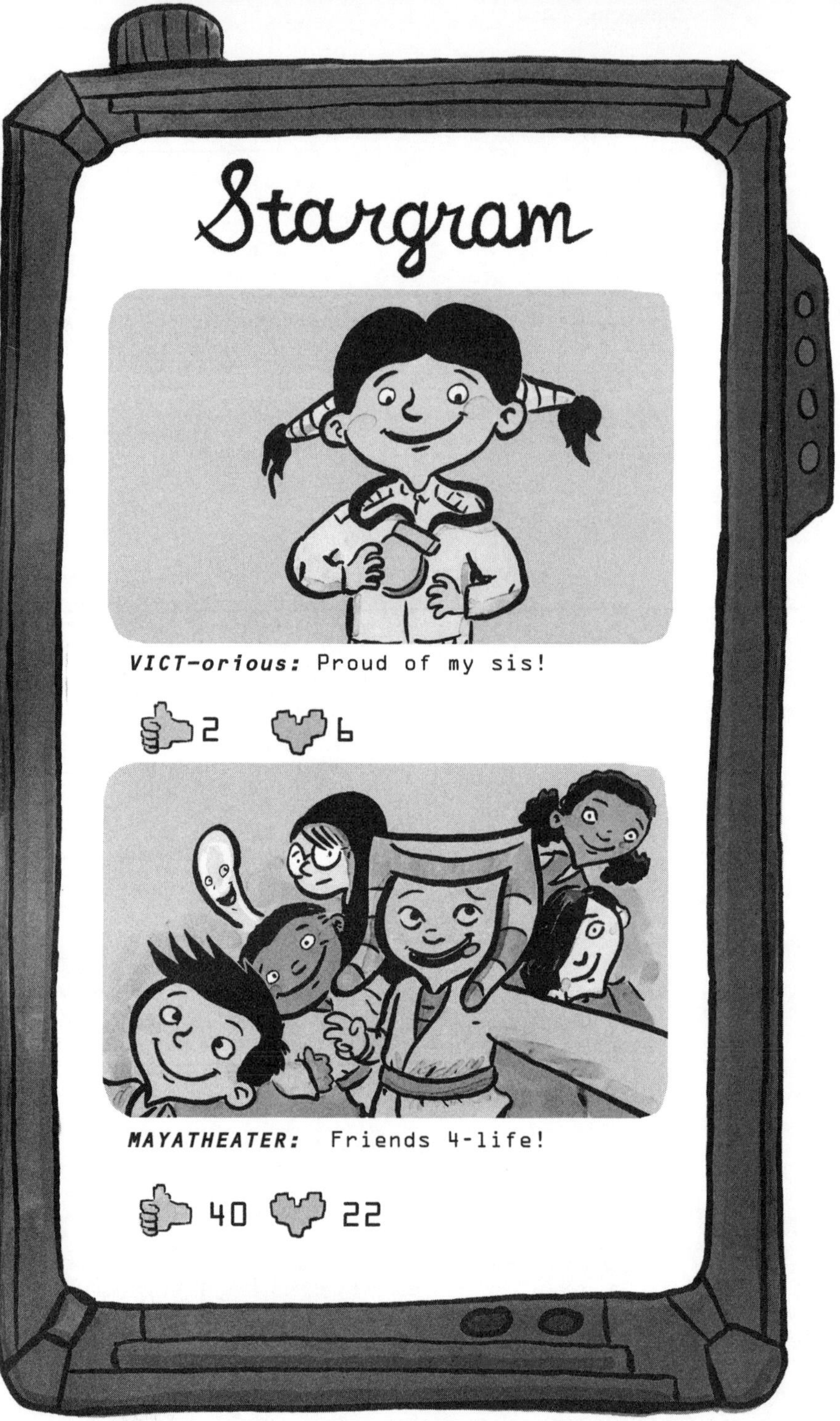
Stargram
VICT-orious: Proud of my sis!
2
6
MAYATHEATER: Friends 4-life!
40
22

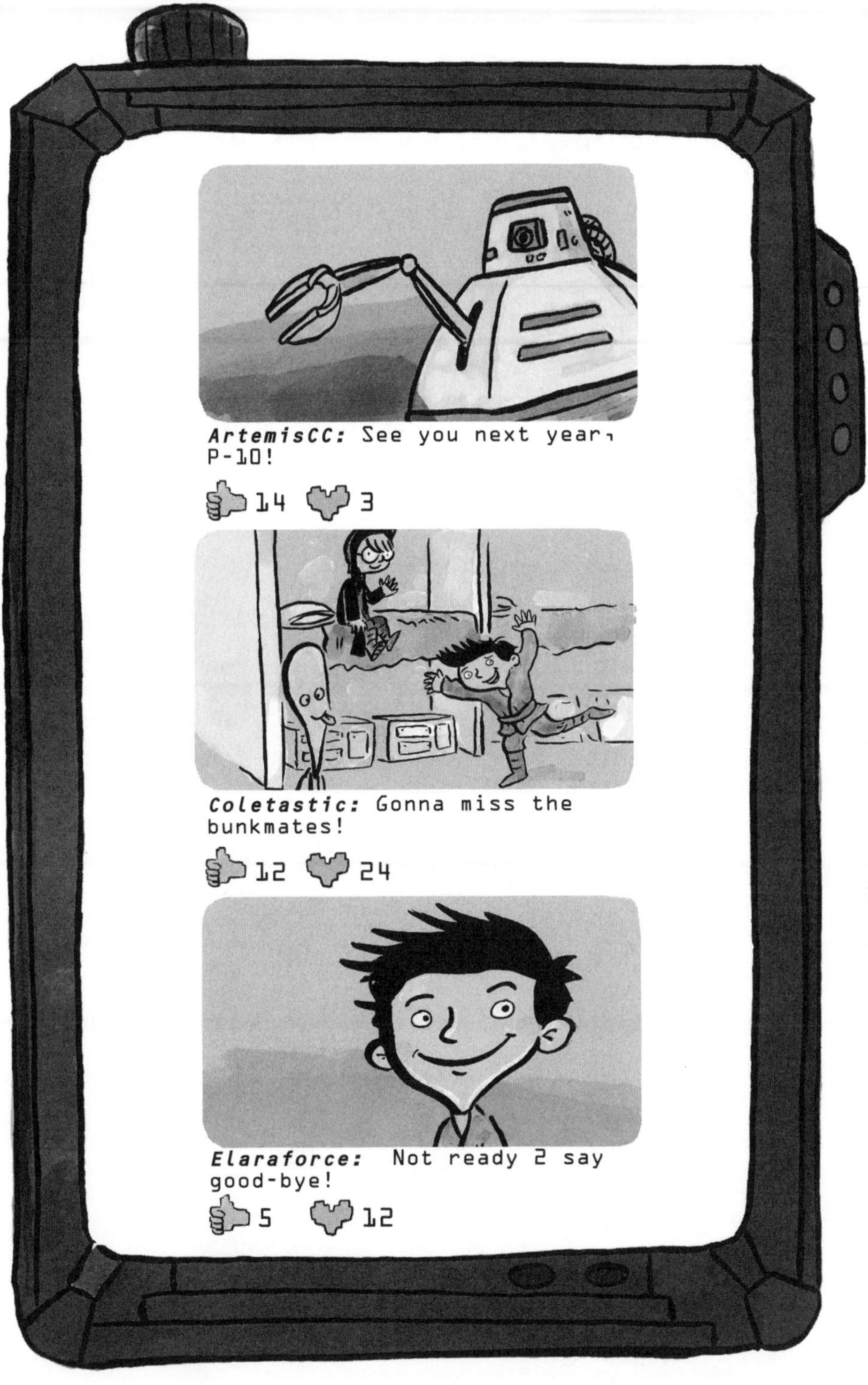
ArtemisCC: See you next year, P-10!
14 3
Coletastic: Gonna miss the bunkmates!
12 24
Elaraforce: Not ready 2 say good-bye!
5 12

Duoday

Christina got her top choice for Jedi mentor, and it hit me—I'm not going to see my sister much at all next school year. I'm going to miss having her around Jedi Academy. Sure, she gives me the cold shoulder, but everyone has their own weird way of letting their family know that they love them. I wonder what kind of mentor I'll end up with. Artemis already has a spreadsheet of possible directions for him to take. He'll have his pick of mentors, his grades are so good. Coleman and Emmett keep talking about getting mentors that work together so they won't be far from each other. I'll take whoever will have me. I'll admit it—I can be difficult to manage. But I'm fun to be around.

I thought I could fix your astromech droid! Sorry!

I just asked you to run to the market for blue milk.

Russell helped me pack my bags while Mom was in Christina's dorm helping her. I don't know how this happens, but I seem to accumulate so many things to bring home. (And I'm not just talking about that sarlacc puppet. We decided it would be best to stash that in the greenroom of the theater.) Russell was very helpful, though. He helped me stuff everything into my suitcase and sweep up my space. Even though I thought Russell could be lame at times, he is a man who turned up and helped. And he does love my mom, that is obvious. So even though he tells some super-lame jokes at times, I'm glad that he's around.

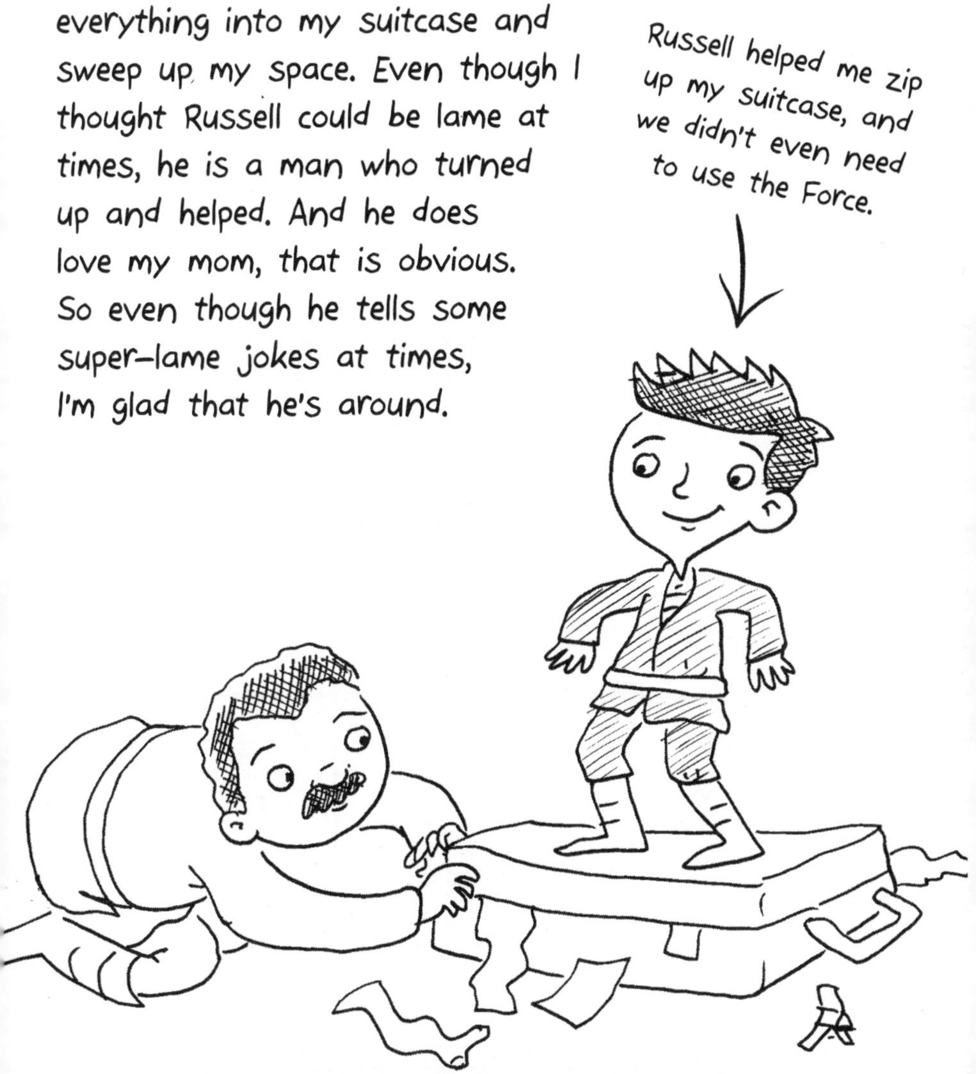

Russell helped me zip up my suitcase, and we didn't even need to use the Force.

The Padawan Observer

EDITED BY THE STUDENTS OF JEDI ACADEMY   Vol. MXVI #8

BON VOYAGE!

That is a wrap on another successful year at Jedi Academy. It is never a dull moment in these halls, and this year proved to be no exception. Whether you were training for the Lightsaber Tournament or memorizing lines for the annual musical, we hope that you feel good about your time at Jedi Academy. With the end of every year, we also must bid a bittersweet farewell to our graduating students. And what a remarkable group we have setting forth into the galaxy. You will certainly be hearing stories of the good deeds these future Jedi perform for years to come.

WHAT ARE YOU LOOKING FORWARD TO ON SEMESTER BREAK?

Artemis Oophanoe
Staying indoors and reading.

Maya Phoenix
Going to see shows.

Zavyer Kroff
Staying in touch with my new friends.

COMICS

WOOKIEE CIRCUS

SPOT THE DROIDRENCES!

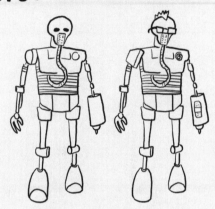

"Groawwwar? GROAWR!"

HUTTFIELD

I HATE MONODAYS.

AND HEXADAYS. AND QUADDAYS,

REALLY, JUST DAYS ENDING IN "Y."

YOUNGLINGS

ACE POD RACER TAKES THE LEAD!

IT'S GOING TO BE A HOLO FINISH!

YOU ARE SO PECULIAR.

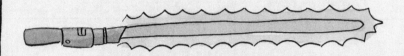

ASK MS. CATARA!

Dear Ms. Catara,

How do I handle this? I'm filled with so many conflicting emotions. I thought I liked this one girl, but she never gave me the time of day. But there is this other girl that I think might like me like me. I like her, but not necessarily like her like her. What do I do?

Signed,
Confused

Dearza Confused,

A Jedi musta clear theirs minds of such things. Love comes in all sorts of forms and shapes, like the world around us. My suggestion would be to justa make friends with everyonez. Young hearts are filled with so many confusing emotions. Just be kindz to one another and enjoy spending times with each other.

XO,
Ms. Catara

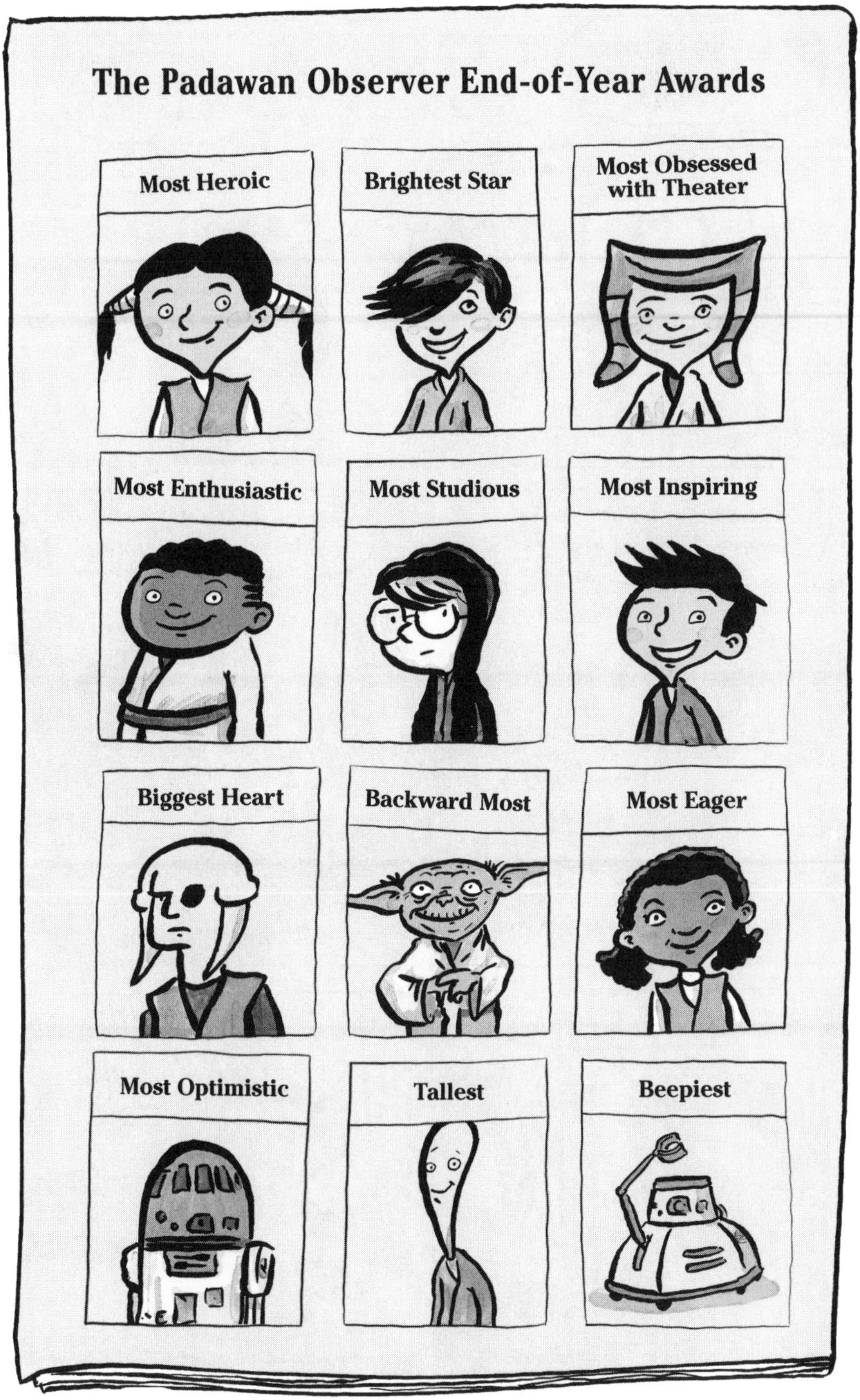
The Padawan Observer End-of-Year Awards
Most Heroic
Brightest Star
Most Obsessed with Theater
Most Enthusiastic
Most Studious
Most Inspiring
Biggest Heart
Backward Most
Most Eager
Most Optimistic
Tallest
Beepiest

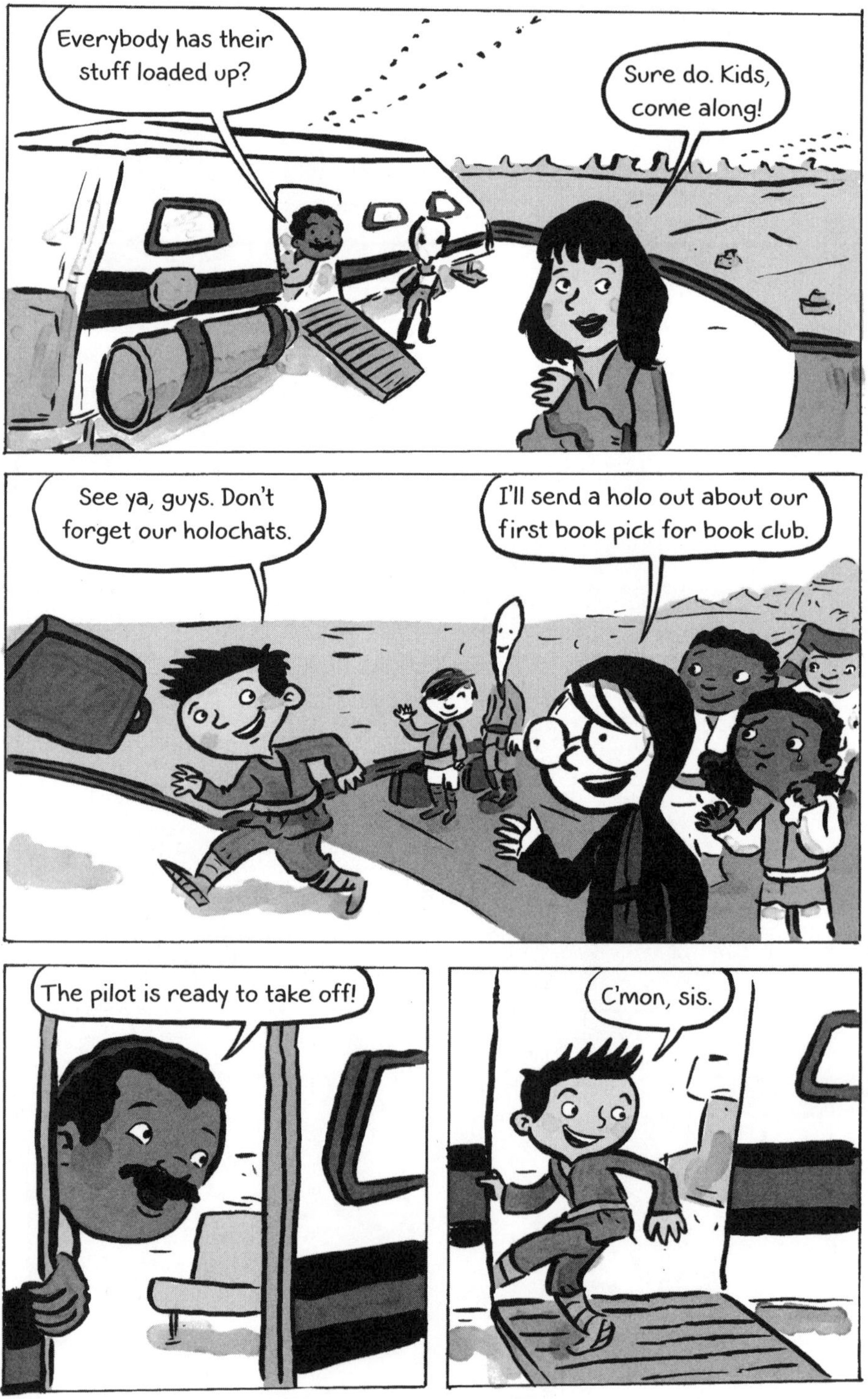
Everybody has their stuff loaded up?
Sure do. Kids, come along!
See ya, guys. Don't forget our holochats.
I'll send a holo out about our first book pick for book club.
The pilot is ready to take off!
C'mon, sis.

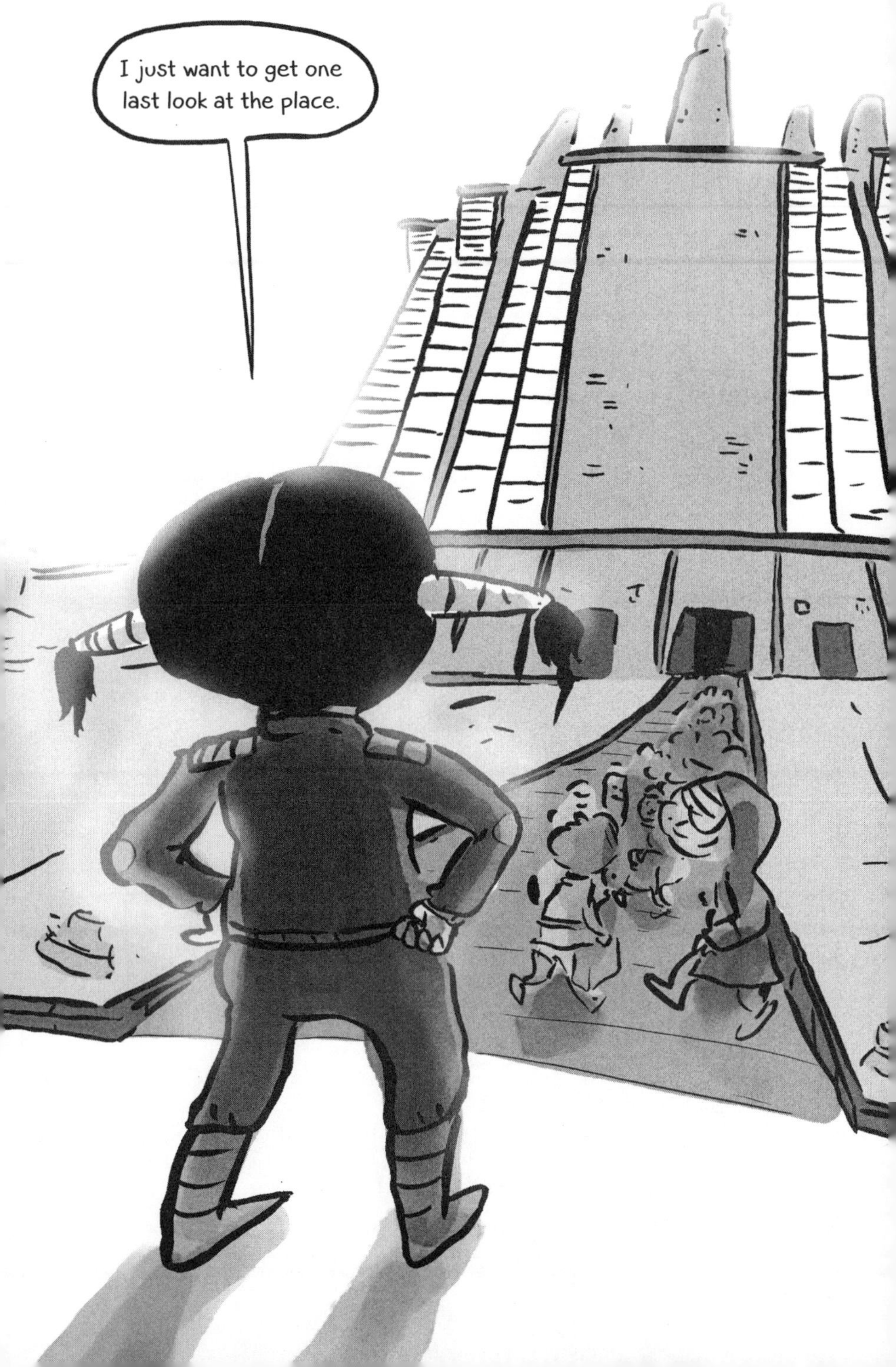
I just want to get one last look at the place.

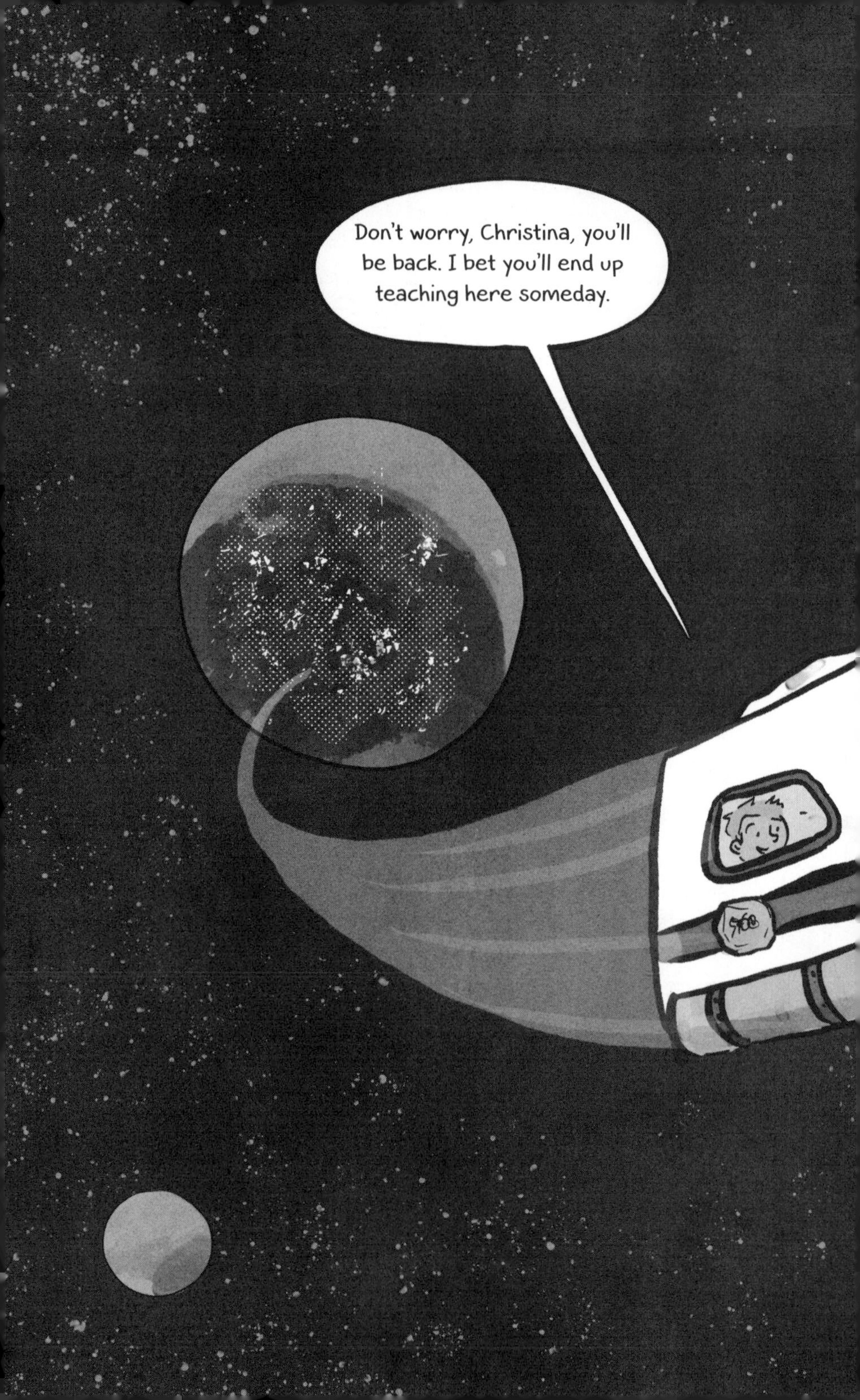
Don't worry, Christina, you'll be back. I bet you'll end up teaching here someday.

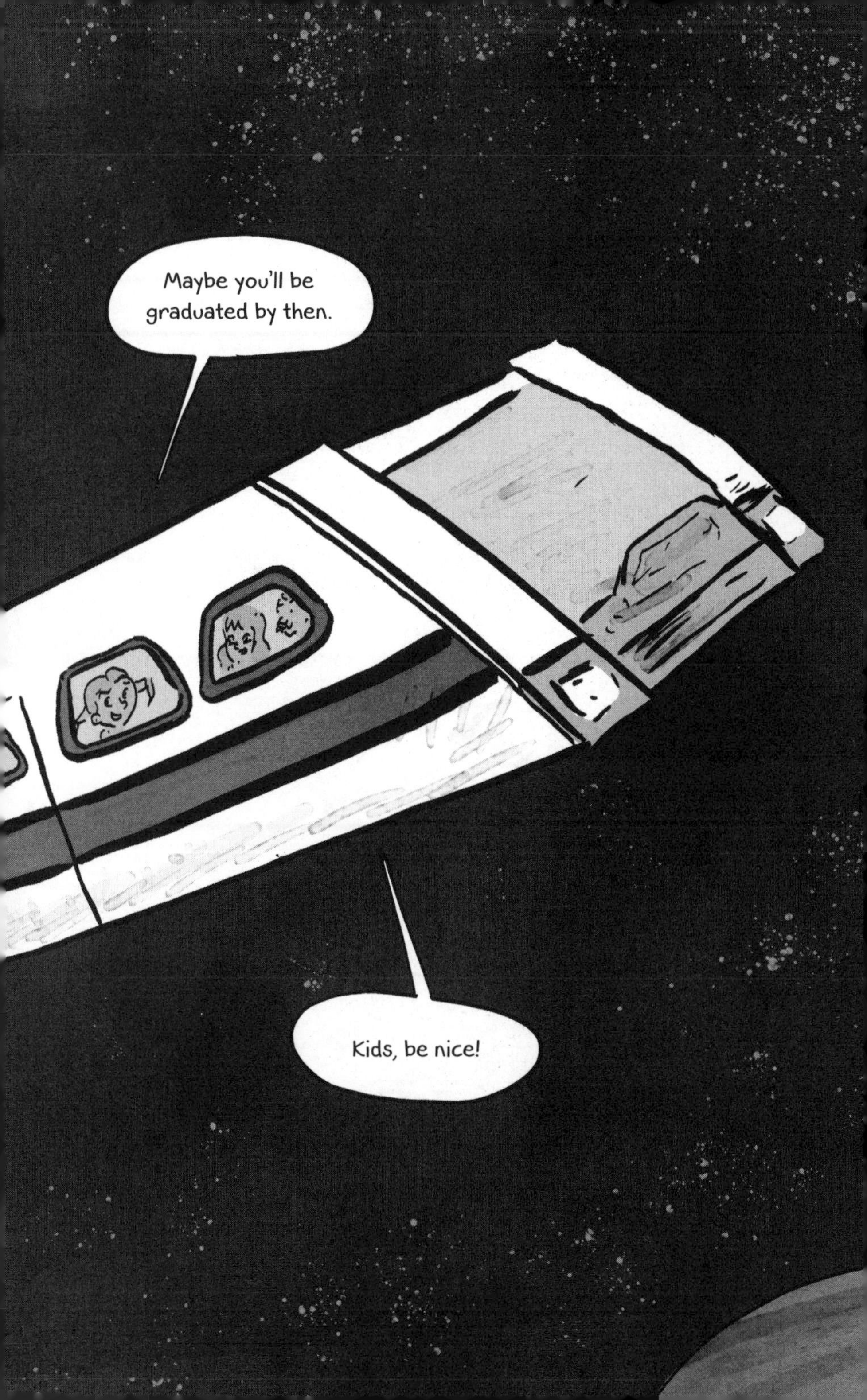
Maybe you'll be graduated by then.
Kids, be nice!

Jarrett J. Krosoczka is a *New York Times* bestselling author, a two-time winner of the Children's Choice Book Award for the Third to Fourth Grade Book of the Year, an Eisner award nominee, and is the author and/or illustrator of more than thirty books for young readers. His work includes several picture books, the Lunch Lady graphic novels, and Platypus Police Squad middle-grade novel series. Jarrett has given two TED Talks, both of which have been curated to the main page of TED.com and have collectively accrued more than two million views online. He is also the host of The Book Report with JJK on SiriusXM's Kids Place Live, a weekly segment celebrating books, authors, and reading.

Jarrett lives in Western Massachusetts with his wife and children, and their pugs, Ralph and Frank.